EVERYBODY
Wants to
RULE
WORLD
Except Me

Tserigern was a crank, but he wasn't a complete crank. He turns up within seconds of my appearance in the pool! That can't be a coincidence. *He* says he's been following some kind of prophecy, and I'm destined to save the Kingdom and blah blah, all the talk that I took very seriously a thousand years ago and now makes me want to bash his head in.

I'm not sure I believe in *destiny*. If it was *destiny* that I save the Kingdom, you'd think I would have fucking managed it one of these times instead of getting painfully murdered over and over. But what I definitely believe in is *intention*. While the loop remained exactly the same, I was prepared to accept that this was just the way things were, somehow, that I'd gotten caught in some cosmic spin cycle and it was all just the forces of the universe doing their thing. But now? I become Dark Lord, and the forces of the universe change underneath me?

No way. No *fucking* way. Tsav said it first—it feels like there's some *purpose* there. Intention. The existence of a Chosen One implies the existence of a Chooser. That *someone* out there did this to me. I don't know who that is, whether it's God or Mega-Satan or the dreams of a thousand cats, but *whoever* it is I am going to *find them* and ███████████████████████████ to their ████████████████ with a *teakettle*.

Praise for

How to Become the Dark Lord and Die Trying

"Tremendous fun"

Kirkus (starred review)

"Takes the old saying 'If you can't beat 'em, join 'em,' to the next level. A sarcastic, action-packed, intrigue-filled (mis)adventure. One of the funniest books I've read in a long time"

Matt Dinniman, author of *Dungeon Crawler Carl*

"All hail Dark Lord Davi! *How to Become the Dark Lord and Die Trying* is outrageously fun, filled with campy humor, action and unexpected warm-heartedness. I grinned from the first page to the last"   Fonda Lee, author of *Jade City*

"Funny as hell, multilayered, and affecting. Wexler's irreverent demolition of the fantasy genre doubles as a reverent exploration of where the magic comes from"

Scott Lynch, author of *The Lies of Locke Lamora*

"By turning the themes of chosen-one fantasy on their head, this sardonic romp from Wexler brings out the smiles ... Wexler balances the snarky asides with the angst of Davi's repeating existence and evolving awareness that her actions have consequences. Under the flippancy, a truly touching grimdark story lurks, complete with hilarious footnotes. Readers will be wowed"   *Publishers Weekly* (starred review)

BY DJANGO WEXLER

Dark Lord Davi

How to Become the Dark Lord and Die Trying

Everybody Wants to Rule the World Except Me

EVERYBODY
Wants to
RULE the
WORLD
Except Me

Dark Lord Davi: Book Two

DJANGO WEXLER

orbit-books.co.uk

ORBIT

First published in Great Britain in 2025 by Orbit

1 3 5 7 9 10 8 6 4 2

Copyright © 2025 by Django Wexler

Map by Tim Paul

Excerpt from *The Bone Raiders* by Jackson Ford
Copyright © 2025 by Jackson Ford

The moral right of the author has been asserted.

A CIP catalogue record for this book
is available from the British Library.

ISBN 978-0-356-51899-2

Printed and bound in Great Britain by
Clays Ltd, Elcograf, S.p.A.

Papers used by Orbit are from well-managed forests
and other responsible sources.

Orbit
An imprint of
Little, Brown Book Group
Carmelite House
50 Victoria Embankment
London, EC4Y 0DZ

The authorised representative
in the EEA is
Hachette Ireland
8 Castlecourt Centre
Dublin 15, D15 XTP3, Ireland
(email: info@hbgi.ie)

An Hachette UK Company
www.hachette.co.uk

orbit-books.co.uk

With apologies to Tears for Fears

Fangs of the Old Ones

Redtooth territory.
Full of angry orcs.

Gerald's
Hut

Pond where I begin
the nightmare
that is my life

WEST

The
KINGDOM

Vroken

Map by Tim Paul

Content Warning

Thanks to her unique, fantastic circumstances, Davi speaks casually of self-harm and suicide. In real life, however, there are no time loops and no healing spells. If you struggle with thoughts of this nature, visit blog.opencounseling.com/suicide -hotlines to find help in your area.

This book also contains depictions of violence, sexual content, and explicit language.

Previously on "The Unending Torturous Hellscape That Is My Life"

Hi! I'm **Davi**. I'm just your ordinary "girl next door who got stuck in a time loop and spent a thousand years dying in every possible agonizing fashion."[1] I finally reached my breaking point when walking ironmonger's advert **Artaxes** locked me in my own dungeon on behalf of the latest Dark Lord and let snake-lady **Sibarae** eat my fingers. After cunningly killing myself to escape, I settled on a new plan: Since my efforts to save the Kingdom from the Dark Lord had repeatedly, *repeatedly* failed, I was going to switch teams and become the Dark Lord myself. This would involve gathering a horde and crossing half the world to reach the Convocation, where they hand

---

1 A very relatable and engaging heroine for the coveted Time Loop Victim demographic.

out the pointy helmet, but I've never been one to shy away from a difficult job.[2]

Step one of this plan was intercepting **Tserigern**, the beardy mentor figure who usually tells me to save the Kingdom and then does fuck all to help, and mashing his face into paste. Step two was acquiring my first followers. I settled on a band of orcs living nearby and went about recruiting them via the brilliant strategy of having them kill me over and over again.[3]

Eventually, I gathered enough information to convince **Tsav**—the head of the band, and also a deeply sexy orc lady in a choke-me-out-with-those-biceps-and-tie-me-up mode—to let me challenge one of her people to a fight for the right to be taken seriously. I got killed a whole bunch more times, blah blah blah, and finally I killed him. Everyone seemed pretty happy about it, he was a dick apparently.

By predicting the future—which I had already experienced many times, naturally—I convinced Tsav and company that I could see my own destiny, that I was definitely going to become Dark Lord, and that they should get aboard the train early. *Choo choo!*

Next stop was the Redtooths, a larger band of orcs, fox-wilders, and stone-eaters[4] run by a nasty old chief and his daughter. I came up with another genius plan to get **Amitsugu**, chief of the fox-wilders, to help me kill his superiors in a chain of double crosses that led to me getting elected new head of the Redtooths. Though one element of this plan involved me fucking Amitsugu, which was fine in the moment[5] but perhaps not the *most* genius thing going forward.

---

2 This is a lie, I'm super lazy.

3 You may be noticing a pattern.

4 Read: rock-monsters.

5 I mean, more like *great* actually, credit where credit is due.

Anyway, now I had more of a horde! The stone-eaters, led by **Droff**, were particularly good to have around since (a) they can't lie or be corrupted and (b) they're giant rock-monsters. **Mari**, one of Amitsugu's subordinates, also joined up with the rest of the fox-wilders, though I didn't get to know her until later. I started training the wilders into a real fighting force using my centuries of experience losing battles. We ran into a big cliff marking the edge of the Firelands, a scary zone we'd have to cross to stay on schedule. To celebrate, we had a feast! And some stuff happened that we won't talk about.[6]

We built a stairway to get up the cliff. Unfortunately, an ancient beast took exception to this and attacked us, but I was able to totally slay it while quipping with a dry wit any action hero would envy. I think this is when Mari took a liking to me, since I saved her life and stuff. I did have to use magic, which I started to worry someone was going to notice.[7]

Up in the Firelands, they have rivers of lava! That was super-cool, I spent way too much time just dropping things in. They also had *pyrvir*, who are slightly dwarfish fire people with shark teeth. We met up with their Jarl, who wasn't going to let us march through until we did a side quest to defeat some bandits. I displayed lateral thinking by getting the drop on the bandits

---

6 Okay, *fine*. I make a pass at Tsav and she shoots me down. That stings and I'm super horny so I booty-call Amitsugu, and after that he starts to think we're a *thing* and it's a whole mess.

7 I can use *thaumite*, the magic rock everyone is crazy for, in two different ways. If I eat it like a wilder, eventually it gets processed and appears on my body, granting me strength or speed or extra hit points or whatever. But I can also channel power out of it like a human, so I can throw fireballs and stuff. As far as I can tell, I'm unique in this respect—wilders can't make human magic work, and humans who ingest thaumite die horribly. I assume it's because of my weird "came from Earth and got stuck in a time loop" thing.

and then recruiting them for my horde. The ex-bandits were led by **Fryndi**, a crusty old dude who takes a while to warm up to everybody. I also secure the services of **Jeffrey**, a mouse-wilder cowboy who is just *absolutely adorable*, I love his widdle ears *to death*.

Back at the pyrvir city, the Jarl agreed to let us keep going, and also gave us permission to recruit for the horde among his oppressed underclass. We got a lot of takers on our "march into the unknown and probable death" offer, which just shows *how* oppressed these people were, yeesh. Their unofficial leader was **Leifa**, who is like a nice old granny with shark teeth. Unfortunately, the Jarl's asshole son **Prince Tyrkell** took exception to our whole deal and started agitating against us. When the Jarl didn't go for it, Tyrkell got all Shakespearean and took over. He captured me by *vile treachery*, but I escaped because I am cool and awesome and also Tsav helped some.

So we marched the horde away from the city and *I* was ready to live and let live, but Tyrkell marched his own army out after us and we had to have a battle. They had a lot more guys, but I pulled some clever shit and we were generally winning until Amitsugu fucked things up before I could *unleash my masterstroke*. Tyrkell and most of his army got away. Turns out Amitsugu had been, like, pining for me, and launching a fool-hardy charge was his way of trying to get my attention.[8] Yeah. Things got weird.

Anyway, we headed up into the mountains, which was cold and horrible. There was a blizzard and we all nearly froze to death, but Tsav and I got stuck in a tent and *finally* resolved our unbearable sexual tension, so ultimately, I'm calling it a net win.

---

8 Seriously, ever heard of *flowers* or standing outside my window with a boombox playing Peter Gabriel or something?

On the other side of the mountains, we finally found the Convocation! It's held in a big ruined city, which is very weird since wilders generally don't build big cities and it's a long way from human territory. And who should be in charge of it but my old buddy Artaxes, clanking around in rusty armor and claiming to be some kind of priest of the Old Ones. Sibarae was there, too, she of the finger-eating, along with **Hufferth**, a minotaur with killer abs. The three of us were getting sworn in as candidates for Dark Lord when *Tyrkell* appeared; apparently, he'd gotten kicked out by his "allies" as soon as we left and trekked over the mountains with a few followers to try to get revenge. He joined the contest, too, which is *bullshit*.

Artaxes told us we had to complete some trials, the first of which turned out to be an *obstacle course*? Or something? Hufferth won because he's a big manly muscleman.[9] And I was all, like, what the fuck is the point of this, are we becoming Dark Lord or competing on *American Gladiators*? And then the *second* trial was, I shit you not, solving a fucking *Rubik's Cube*. Seriously. And *Sibarae* won because fuck everything.

I was feeling a bit down at that point, since I was worried this whole Dark Lord project would have been for nothing and I'd have to start over or go back to listening to Tserigern's bullshit. Tsav did her best to comfort me.[10] We were in bed in the middle of the night when some pyrvir came tunneling up from under the floor and very rudely stabbed me. I was kind of hoping to salvage things, but Tsav and Mari both got killed, too, and that took all the fun out of it. This one pyrvir asshole—she worked for Tyrkell, obviously—finished me off.

Which, you know, isn't anything that hasn't happened to me before. Frustrating, but that's my whole fucking life. Except

---

9 Slash cow.

10 (suggestive eyebrows)

except *except* instead of waking up back in the pool to wait for Tserigern, like I did after the *hundreds of other times I've died*, I woke up *only a day earlier*, not long before the second trial!

Naturally, I immediately descended into shrieking existential crisis. Because, *fuck*, I'd been proceeding under the *totally justified assumption* that everything I'd been doing was only temporary—it was all for a lark, basically, a way to keep myself from going completely crazy but not anything that *counted* in the long run. And *now* I had to face the possibility that it was permanent, that everyone I'd killed was just fucking dead with no take-backsies, and the guilt was like a kick to the guts from Artaxes's iron stompers. Not to mention that now what was going to happen the *next* time I died? I had no idea! How does everyone else live like this?!

Tsav calmed me down once I'd run out of energy for screaming. I ended up telling her everything, the time loop and my deaths and how I'd predicted the future and even that I was human-ish. I think part of me wanted her to freak out, but she didn't, and that kind of got me going again. Christ, where would we be without sexy bald orc ladies?

When I was basically functional, if still inwardly screaming a bit, the first thing I did was win the second trial by copying Sibarae's solution to the stupid cube puzzle from last time. Then we went looking for tunnels and found a whole network of them under the ruined city. I waited down there with some friends to ambush the pyrvir hit squad and finish off Miss Stabs-a-lot, but that was only half the problem.

See, the pyrvir had to know exactly where I would be, and that meant we had a traitor in our camp. It didn't take long to figure out that it was Amitsugu. He confessed and said it was all about how I'd treated him badly, which is basically like "Boo-hoo, because you wouldn't keep fucking me, I betrayed you and your girlfriend to pyrvir assassins," which has to be some kind of Nice Guy record. But because I am just a big softie at heart, I decided not to kill him immediately.

Artaxes announced the next trial, which was some kind of test-of-courage thing in the tunnels under the city. At this point, I was pretty sure I had it figured out: Sibarae poisoned Hufferth,[11] and while he didn't die, he'd had to drop out of the contest. But Artaxes didn't seem to give a shit in spite of being all "You'll be expelled if you attack the others!" like the clanking buzzkill that he is. He talked a good game with this Old One mumbo jumbo, but he didn't really believe in the sacred process of the whatever any more than I did. Telling us "Okay, go into the underground tunnels together with nobody watching" was basically him saying *You guys sort this out amongst yourselves and get back to me.*

Sibarae had apparently had some similar thoughts, because she tried to kill me and Tyrkell. Pro tip, though: If you're going to cheat, cheat for everything you're worth. I was ready for her *and* I'd brought along Tsav and a squad to handle it. Sibarae surrendered with bad grace, and I'd gotten her tied up and was moving on to Tyrkell when he ran into the tunnels, screaming like a loon.

I went after him, because I can be kind of an idiot sometimes. Turns out Artaxes had more in mind than jumping out and shouting BOO; there was a giant worm-monster down there with an anus for a mouth,[12] and in spite of my best efforts, Tyrkell got chomped. Which is like, on the one hand oh no, on the other hand fuck that guy. I hightailed it down a passage too small for the monster and tried to find my way out again, and in

---

11 This happened a couple of paragraphs ago while I was a little distracted.

12 Or maybe it eats people with its anus? That only occurred to me just now. Fuck, I don't know if that's better or worse.

the process, I stumbled into an ancient storeroom and *blew my fucking mind.*

See, there was an ancient book there. And I *happened* to glance at it, and it *happened* to be a good old King James Bible, a nice fancy one from a long time ago. I discarded the "God is real and hates me in particular" theory and the "You maniacs! You blew it up!" theory and settled on the "I'm not the first person from Earth to come to this fantasy world" theory, with the possible addendum that this big-ass ruined city was actually full of *humans* instead of wilders. Crazy, right?

Not much use contemplating if I couldn't escape, though, so I get back to it. Turns out, there was no way through without getting past the ass-face worm, so I took my bag of thaumite and made a plan. This involved decking myself out in every protective spell I could muster, letting the thing swallow me,[13] and then blasting it apart from the inside with fireballs—2/5, would not try again, I smelled like monster ass for days, but it got the job done.

And finally: the big moment! I climbed out of the tunnels, and Artaxes was waiting to announce that I'm officially the new Dark Lord. Hurrah! Except he immediately started going on about how I was going to lead the wilders to exterminate the human Kingdom, and the crowd was getting really into it and chanting "Death to the humans!" and not listening to me at all. And I might have exterminated some humans for kicks back when I thought I was just going to reset it all someday, but things have changed and I have to try my very best not to die and I don't want to exterminate *anybody*, but apparently, I'm Dark Lord of a gigantic horde screaming for blood and *what the fuck do I do now?*

So. Yeah.

---

13 Fuck, it *does* make it worse! Yuck yuck yuck.

EVERYBODY
Wants to
RULE *the*
WORLD
Except Me

Chapter One

In the far northeast of the Kingdom, a small river winds its way from north to south for the space of a few dozen miles before it turns west toward the sea. Along that stretch, the water represents the unofficial border between the domain of humanity and the endless, hostile Wilds. Human hunting parties may range beyond it, but only if they accept the risk of meeting dangerous beasts or, worse, a band of wilders looking for two-legged game. Midway along this stretch of river is an old stone bridge, crumbling but still functional. At its western foot, clinging to the muddy slope of the hill, is the human town of Shithole.

Shithole is a brown town, made of brown logs and brown bricks, peopled by peasants whose clothes, whatever color they might have been originally, are in practice perpetually daubed with the brown of the native mud. And not only mud—much of the business of the town concerns sheep and horses, who are grazed on the far side of the river and driven back at night. Their liberal contributions to the town's economy are obvious to anyone with a functioning sense of smell.

On this particular day, the slurry of dung and mud is being further churned by a pounding rain, and the setting sun is

barely a suggestion in an overcast sky. A small queue of people and animals has formed by the stockaded eastern end of
the bridge, shuffling slowly across to the west bank and safety
before night falls. In among the hunters, shepherds, carters,
and their assorted charges walk two mysterious figures in dark
cloaks, one tall and one short.

Their hoods leave their faces in shadow, but as the short
one looks up, a flash of lightning briefly illuminates a brown-
skinned face flecked with freckles. Not a classically beautiful face, certainly, but also not without its charms: a nose that
might be considered hatchet-like *but*, in the right light, could
also be described as *striking*, and eyebrows that *might* need a bit
of plucking and pampering but are basically pretty sound, and
overall, a general sort of nobility of purpose and bearing that
speaks to an intense depth of character.

RECORD SCRATCH.[1] Yup, that's me. Me, Davi! I was doing a
narrative thing so we could have kind of an establishing shot.
Hopefully it wasn't confusing.

I'm not *that* short, I just look it next to Tsav, who's tall
even for an orc and sticks out like a beanpole in this crowd of
humans. There's no convenient lightning flash to illuminate
her features, but I don't really need one, since I've familiarized
myself with every inch of them. She has a sexy bald head and
sexy green-gray skin and sexy little tusks at the corners of her
mouth that make kissing her exciting for reasons beyond the
usual.

Needless to say, those adorable orcish features would be a
death sentence anywhere in the Kingdom. Wilders are personae
non gratae, or perhaps worse: Since they have thaumite embedded in their bodies, they're more like walking treasure chests

---

1   Note for young people and other aliens: A "record scratch" is the sound of
the fourth wall being broken.

for the Guild[2] to plunder. As we get closer to the bridge, this is starting to weigh on my mind.

There are a couple of guards there, huddled under oilskin cloaks and nodding approval at the sheep as they go past. I'm not sure how many people are eager to sneak into Shithole and sample its fabled bounty, but here we are. The hunters get closer scrutiny, and since that's what Tsav and I can most plausibly claim to be, my tension rises further.

"Hey," one of the guards says as we reach the front. He holds his spitting torch a little higher. "Let's see those faces."

Shit. Probably not a good idea to start off my time in the Kingdom with murder. I pull my hood down and elbow Tsav, who slowly does likewise. The guard gives her a long look, examining her tusks and green skin with *surprising unconcern*.

"Don't know you two," he says with a glance at his companion. "First time through?"

I nod. "We went out another way."

"You paid your hunting tax? Or do I need to search those bags?"

That would be interesting, but also probably a bad idea. "We're paid up."

"Gonna have to see your chit," he says. But his tone is arch, and he raises one eyebrow.

Yup, message received, thanks. I dig a couple of silver coins out of my belt pouch and hand them over. The guard grins, and his hitherto-silent partner speaks up.

"You know, I think I remember these two," she says, as

---

2 Refresher: The Guild of Adventurers are the Kingdom's favorite murder-hoboes, a loose organization of psychotic killers who trek hundreds of miles into the Wilds and seek out the most dangerous and ferocious beasts and wilders for the sole purpose of killing them for thaumite and experience.

though narrating to an invisible audience. "I saw their chit last time."

"Oh, really?" The first guard feigns irritation. "Well, get on through, then. You're holding up the line."

Classic. They should be onstage. I put my hood back up—stealth benefits aside, it's still pouring rain—and tug Tsav onto the bridge.

"Well," I mutter, "that worked."

"You said you were sure it would work," Tsav growls back.

"*Pretty* sure. Mostly sure." I waggle a hand. "Fifty-fifty."

She rolls her eyes. "Glad I didn't near piss myself for nothing."

"Around here nobody's likely to notice." I survey the main street—well, the only street—and the services Shithole has to offer. "Come on, let's get out of the rain."

* * *

It occurs to me that I may need to back up a little.

After all, when we last left our brilliant, beautiful, charming heroine, she was standing in the midst of a massive horde of ecstatic wilders, having just been handed the title of Dark Lord along with the emphatic expectation that she lead the forces of the wild in glorious conquest-slash-genocide of the evil humans, et cetera et cetera.

And look. When I started this little venture, I might have gone for it! I mean, I'm not sure I ever really expected to get all the way to Dark Lord, it seemed impossible, but having *done* it, I'd probably have taken the chance to be the bad guy for once. It's not like I haven't seen the Kingdom levelled by Dark Lords several hundred times before, this would be a new perspective on the process. I'd just need to make sure to capture Himbo Boyfriend Johann, maybe make him wear one of those leather slave outfits for a while. Then eventually I'd get bored or possibly assassinated and go back to the beginning like always.

But things have changed. My last death inexplicably sent me back not to the usual time and place but *only a day earlier*! And I have no idea what will happen if I die again. If I can't go all the way back, everything that happened on the way to the Convocation is *permanent*, all those people are *really dead*, and if I go too far down that line of thought, I end up in a very dark place because I killed super a lot of people for not very good reasons, actually.

Not thinking about it, la la la! All I can do going forward is assume that whatever I do *now* has a chance of becoming permanent as well. Which means (a) I need to, you know, *not die* as much as possible, and (b) leading a merry orgy of death and destruction in the wreckage of the Kingdom is off the table, and not just because it might damage Johann's perfect ass. I may be a *little* twisted after a millennium of this, but not enough to wipe out a whole civilization with no reset button.

So when I take my bow and escape from the crowd, I already have a plan in mind. Well. More like a set of objectives that may become a plan in the fullness of time, even I can only scheme so fast. But clearly two things need doing:

First and most urgently, I need to prevent the horde from destroying the Kingdom. This is harder than it sounds. *But, Davi,* you might say, *you're the Dark Lord now! Surely you can order the horde to just, I don't know, start planting daisies.* Which sounds great but this is real life (kind of) and not *War-Artisan IV*, I'm an actual person and not a disembodied hand in the sky clicking on stuff. The wilders follow the Dark Lord because they think it'll get them what they want, which is apparently DEATH TO THE HUMANS; if I don't play along, maybe they'll decide that Hufferth or Sibarae has the Mandate of Heaven after all.

Secondly, let's not forget the Johnny Cash revelation(s) from under the city. If I'm reading things right, I am not the first person from Earth to come to this world. I don't know *exactly* what that means, but it has to be related to my whole deal, right? I refuse to believe that it's a coincidence that I'm stuck in a time loop *and* I got sucked here from another universe. And if this were a *human* city, way out here where supposedly no humans have ever lived, it rings some faint bells vis-à-vis the Kingdom's mythology. I never took it very seriously, but supposedly the Eight Founders brought the people to the Kingdom from some unspecified *other place*. It bears investigating.

After a break for a bath and some therapeutic screaming,[3] I dress in my Dark Lord-iest outfit and convene the new, expanded Dark Council. The roll call is:

Artaxes—high priest of the Old Ones, supposedly, and perennial assistant to Dark Lords. Badly in need of a good oiling. Who knows what he looks like under all that iron?

Sibarae—leader of the snake-wilders. Goes around topless, no boobs. Not to be trusted. Ate my fingers that one time.

Hufferth—leader of the minotaurs. Poisoned by Sibarae but got better. Also goes around topless. His pecs have pecs.

Tsav—my main squeeze and a captain of the horde. Leader of the orcs.

Mari—leader of the fox-wilders and a captain of the horde. Smol but fierce.

Droff—leader of the stone-eaters. Rock-monster. Unable to tell a lie and has trouble with flowery language.

Fryndi—pyrvir ex-bandit and a captain of the horde. Crotchety.

---

3 I was eaten by an anus-face-worm-thing, which then exploded all over me, I think I'm entitled to both.

Leifa—unofficial leader of the *sveayir*, the low-caste pyrvir who accompanied us en masse. Quiet and calm, but sharp as hardened steel when needed, like a gentle grandma who used to be a Navy SEAL.

Jeffrey—mouse-wilder with adorable ears and a John Wayne drawl. Scout and trailblazer.

Not present:

Amitsugu—former fox-wilder leader, kinda-sorta my ex, currently imprisoned for having me assassinated.

Not invited but present anyway:

Odlen—young pyrvir princess and political exile. No idea how old she's supposed to be, but mostly doesn't talk and focuses on biting things. Fortunately, still lacks teeth. Leifa usually watches her, but currently she's gnawing on Fryndi's boots.

This group is too big for our previous Dark Council tent, even if we make the eight-foot-tall Droff sit in the doorway, so instead we've appropriated a room in the city center building. It's dusty and as the setting for a Dark Council lacks a certain *je ne sais quoi*,[4] but for the present I can make do. As I'm about to inform the participants, I'm not going to be here very long.

"Welcome, everyone," I say. "So glad you could make it. Really means the world to me. Couldn't have asked for better minions."

"I am not a *minion*," Sibarae hisses. She can hiss anything, even a sentence with no sibilants. She also has no sense of humor.

"Am I a minion?" Hufferth says amiably. "What's a minion?"

---

4 French for "covered in skulls."

"It means something like 'close companion,'" Tsav supplies, which makes it hard for me to keep a straight face.

"*Anyway*," I cut in. "I'm the Dark Lord now. The Old Ones have spoken, right?"

I look at Artaxes, who makes a noise somewhere between an affirmative grunt and a creak of rusty metal. Then I switch to looking at Sibarae, who scowls but lowers her eyes. Hufferth nods and gives me a cheery smile.

"And you will lead us," Artaxes says unexpectedly, "to destroy—"

"The humans. Absolutely. We are totally going to do that. But we need to be a little careful about it. Have any of you actually been to the human Kingdom?"

I make a show of looking around, though I know they haven't. Well, none except Tsav, who used to lead a band of raiders that would sometimes burn a farm or two. But she knows her part in this and says nothing.

"Well, I have. In fact," I add, improvising, "it was traveling there that inspired me to become Dark Lord. I'm here to tell you that humans will be tougher opponents than you realize."

"I've fought against humans," Sibarae says. "So have many others in our ranks."

"You've fought against Guildblades," I tell her. "And only the very craziest of them would come out this far. There's a long way between a handful of mercenaries looking for plunder and a proper human army decked out in war magic."

This is true enough. If the various lords of the Kingdom could stop feuding and fucking one another's spouses long enough to *form* a proper army, they might actually be able to give the wilders a run for their money. I'm coming off a thousand-year run of failure that attests to the difficulty of getting them to work together, but the wilders don't need to know that.

"We've got plenty of scary fuckers on our side too," Hufferth points out. "I've never heard of a band half this big."

"Horde," I correct him. "We're a horde. And, yes, that's true. But it comes with concomitant logistical problems."

Hufferth blinks uncertainly.

"We need enough for everybody to eat," Tsav explains.

"Supplies here are ample," Artaxes says in a voice like a depressed robot.

"*Here*," I say, stabbing the table with a finger to emphasize the point. "But we've got a ways to go, don't we? Over the mountains, across the Firelands, and down through the forest to the Kingdom's border. We're not going to be able to haul everything with us."

"There are many bands between here and there," Sibarae says, waving a dismissive hand. "We will simply take what we need."

"That is not the way *this* horde operates," I shoot back. "We're destroying the humans, not other wilders."

"Then what *are* we going to do?" Hufferth says. He sounds bored already—apparently, he doesn't have a great attention span.

"Move slowly and carefully. Droff, start figuring out what it would take to get everyone over the mountains with enough reserves to make it to the Kingdom."

"Droff will begin," Droff says. His voice is deep but surprisingly mellow for a rock-monster. "The task will take considerable time."

"I know. In the meantime, we'll focus on organization and training. Fryndi, Mari, we'll talk later, but that's going to be your job."

Fryndi gives a lazy wave, as though this is his due. Mari looks uncertain but nods.

"Hufferth, Sibarae, you'll work with them to get your people on board."

Hufferth frowns, and Sibarae narrows her eyes.

"And what will *you* be doing?" she says, again managing a sibilant-free hiss.

"Scouting." I grin. "Tsav and I will be going to the Kingdom."

For a few moments, everyone starts talking at once. I hold up my hands for order and wait for them to quiet down.

"It's been years since my time there," I lie smoothly. "And charging in blindly is a recipe for disaster."

"Doesn't mean ye have t' go yerself," Jeffrey puts in. "One o' us could—"

I cut him off. "None of you have any experience with the humans. You'd be killed or captured long before you could report back."

"But Tsav is an orc," Hufferth says. "Even humans would notice that, right?"

"And it would take far too long," Sibarae says. "A journey all the way there and back . . ."

"You underestimate your Dark Lord," I snap. "I have my ways of hiding Tsav. And I won't need to journey back—Mari will be in charge while I'm away, and she'll get the horde moving when she judges the time is right."

"I will?" Mari squeaks.

Tsav, who knows the plan already, kicks her under the table until she quiets. The others go silent, too, digesting everything I've said. Sibarae glares at me and I hold her snaky gaze.[5]

"I still don't like it," she mutters eventually. "We should simply march now."

"Yeah," Hufferth says, gesturing vaguely. "Food and stuff will take care of itself, it always does."

"Then it's good for everyone that *I'm* Dark Lord and not you

---

5 I really hope she can't do the swirly-eyes hypnosis thing.

two," I say. "I don't intend to arrive at the Kingdom and face the human army with half a starving horde."

"Attention to detail is commendable." Artaxes's metallic voice startles me, since he's been silent for a while. Rusty iron grinds as he turns his head. "But you should remain with the horde. Scouting is an unnecessary risk."

This, really, is the crux of it. If anyone has the authority to derail my plan, it's Artaxes, whose vague mandate from the Old Ones carries weight with all the wilders from beyond the mountains. I try to stare him down, too, but it's impossible to see his eyes within the darkness of his helm.

Nothing for it but to double down. "I say it's necessary, so those are my orders."

"It is an unwise course," he says.

"Am I Dark Lord here?" I ask him. "Or not?"

A long, long pause. Around the table, everyone holds their breath.

"You are the Dark Lord," Artaxes grinds out. "The Old Ones have spoken."

"Good." As long as he's on board, the others won't stray. I try not to let the relief show in my face, but my insides have gone all wobbly. "Okay. Those are the basics. We'll check in later on the details." When nobody moves, I wave my hands. "Dark Council dismissed!"

* * *

"You're putting *me* in charge?" Mari says.

We're walking rapidly back to our own camp. In spite of everyone theoretically being one friendly horde now, the wilders who came with me over the mountains—orcs, fox-wilders, stone-eaters, pyrvir, and assorted volunteers, call them the Old Guard—are still keeping to themselves, as are the snake-wilders and Hufferth's minotaurs. The rest of the Convocation wilders, who by numbers make up the bulk of the horde, are scattered around the perimeter of the ruined city in smaller groups.

"Yep," I say.

"Of the horde," Mari says. "The *whole* horde."

"Yep."

"They won't listen to me."

"They will, or they'll feel the Dark Lord's wrath. You heard Artaxes."

"You won't be here!"

"You can deliver wrath in my name."

"But—" The little fox-wilder chews her lip. "There must be someone else."

I glance around. Tsav is close behind us, but the rest of them have already split up, and nobody's within earshot.

"Who?" I ask her. "Not Hufferth or Sibarae, obviously. Fryndi thinks all non-pyrvir are lazy idiots—that'd go over well. Droff is... Droff, he's not exactly suited to command. Leifa's not a fighter. And Amitsugu tried to murder me."

"So I'm the last choice?" Mari says grimly.

"No!" I could probably have phrased that better. "*You* are smart and brave and the person I trust the most after Tsav. The fox-wilders love you. Droff will help, and Leifa. You'll be fine." I think. I hope.

"I..." Mari takes a deep breath, looking back over her shoulder at Tsav. "I'll do my best. But I'm still not sure I understand everything."

"That's because I haven't told you everything. Come on."

I hurry to the small house I've been sharing with Tsav. It's partly wrecked, but we've covered over the gaps in the roof with canvas, and it's really become quite homey. Our sleeping furs are a big tangle at one end, with other gear scattered about the floor. Just over *there* is the spot where Tyrkell's assassin stabbed

Tsav, and over *there* is where she broke Mari's head against the wall—

I shake my head to dispel the memories of events that never happened. Not in *this* life, anyway. Not to anyone but me.

"Okay," I tell Mari and Tsav. "Sit."

They sit. I stand, pacing nervously. I've talked this over with Tsav, how much to take Mari into our confidence. I still don't want to tell her *everything*, the whole time loop story, but she needs to know more than the rest if this is going to work.

I take a deep breath. "So. You know I get visions of the future."

"Yeah." Mari looks uncomfortable. She's never been a true believer in the destiny side of things.

"If I lead the horde against the Kingdom, it's not going to go well." This is probably a lie; without my help, I suspect the Kingdom would get steamrolled. But I don't want *that* to happen either, obviously. "Not only would we lose but it would make them much more aggressive. Every wilder living anywhere near the border would eventually be wiped out."

Mari's eyes widen, and she looks from me to Tsav and back.

"But," she says, "you told everyone you were going to attack. If you know it won't work . . ."

"It's not that simple." I sigh heavily. "You saw what they're like. If I tell them we're not going to attack, they'll turn on me in a second. We've got to manage this more carefully."

"And that's why you're *leaving*?" Mari seems close to panic. Tsav puts a gentle hand on her shoulder, and the little fox-wilder takes a deep breath.

"The wilders hate the humans because the Guildblades hunt wilders for their thaumite and to expand human territory," I say. "If we're going to have any chance of peace, we need to get them to stop doing that. I think I have a way, but it means going there myself, and I'll need Tsav's help."

"You'll just . . . convince them to stop?" Mari says.

"Something like that." I grin. "Trust me."

"And meanwhile, *I'm* in charge here." She seems to be coming to grips with the idea. "Doing what?"

"Everything I said: training, organizing, moving toward the Kingdom, but *slowly*. I'll need time to get there and get things moving. If it all works out, by the time they hear there's an army of wilders approaching the border, they'll be ready to make peace. And then..." I falter briefly, because I haven't really thought about *and then*. Not getting everyone killed seems like a solid start, though.

Mari, fortunately, is lost in thought. Tsav catches my eye; she looks worried. We're asking a lot of Mari, but I'm convinced she's up to it. She's a lot tougher than she looks.

"I can...try," she says eventually. "But..."

I brace myself internally. Here's where it gets a little tricky.

"I have something that will help," I tell her. "But I need you to trust me."

Her brow wrinkles. "Of course I trust you."

"Wear this."

I take a necklace from my pocket. It's a simple leather thong tied around a polished purple crystal about the size of a grape. Thaumite, of course. Purple is one of the trickiest varieties, dealing with matters of the mind and perception. This particular stone is already imbued with a spell I cast the night before. It's larger than it really needs to be, both to make up for not being cut into an ideal shape and to act as a power reserve to make it last longer. If I've done this right, it should function for half a year or so before it runs down.

What makes this the tricky part is that using thaumite this way is human-style magic. A wilder could eat this stone and, once it was processed and appeared on their body, derive power from it. But no wilder can do what *I'm* about to do, which is why I don't do it where anybody can see. On the other hand, most wilders aren't really familiar with magic and its effects, especially anything more subtle than a fireball. And Mari trusts me, which means I *hope* we can get through this without her freaking out. Tsav, of course, knows the whole story.

"W-*wear* it?" Mari says. "Why?"

"Just try it," Tsav says gently.

Hesitantly, she slips the necklace over her head. I put my hand in my pocket, where a second chunk of purple thaumite sits, and mutter words of power under my breath. The spell comes to life, and I focus my thoughts.

[As long as you wear it, I can speak to you like this.] My voice is projected directly into Mari's mind. She startles, her tail fluffing out and her ears standing straight up.[6] [Think hard, and I can hear you.]

[You can hear me *thinking*?] she sends back.

[Only if you want me to.] I grin. [I'm not going to be spying on your naughty daydreams.]

Her face flushes a little and she looks down at the stone. "I've never heard of anything like this."

"It's not common knowledge," I say. "In fact, I suggest you keep the stone hidden from everyone. Don't let them know we communicate. But this way, you can keep me up to date and I'll help however I can, no matter how far away I am."

This is, if not a lie, then an oversimplification. I can actually do the telepathy trick within a relatively wide radius whether the target is wearing a beacon stone or not: many miles for people I know well, considerably shorter for strangers. The problem is always picking out a mind from background noise, and the greater the distance, the harder that gets. The thing I've given Mari, what I call a beacon stone, is a very simple—and thus long-lasting—spell that provides a signal for my mind to

---

6 I shouldn't be thinking how adorable it is, but *of course I am*.

latch on to. I haven't tested it on a *planetary* scale, obviously, but it ought to be good over hundreds of miles, enough to cover the distance from here to the Kingdom.

It's not *just* to help Mari cope either. My plan, to the extent that I have one, is going to require me to tell the horde what to do once they get closer. As much as anything else, that's why I want Mari in charge. I don't think any of the others would be comfortable with this.

[If I think like this,] she sends, [you hear it?]

"Exactly," I say aloud. "You've got it."

There's a long pause. Mari seems to be gathering herself. When she finally speaks, her expression has hardened.

"Okay." She blows out a breath. "What exactly do you need me to do?"

* * *

So that part went okay! Better than expected, even. I brief the rest of the commanders on their new duties, and then Tsav and I sneak out of the camp like thieves in the night, so everyone wakes up in the morning with Mari in charge.

We have to climb back up into the mountains and brave the pass again, but it's considerably easier this time. We've got good gear, plenty of food, and most importantly, I'm now free to use magic to help. I've gone without it for the past few months, at first from necessity since I didn't have any thaumite anyway, and later because I didn't want to risk giving the game away to the wilders. Tsav knows all my secrets, though, and my satchel is full of the stones I liberated from the anus-mouth worm, which was *quite* a haul. There are enough large crystals in various colors for me to use anything in my arsenal. A little fire channeled through a red stone is enough to keep us warm and toasty, even at altitude.

Once we're through the pass, we're back in the Firelands. We give the lands of the Jarl a wide berth rather than retrace our steps, since I have no idea how things played out there after Tyrkell got himself exiled. It's a lot easier to make our way as a pair of travelers than it was as an army, especially with enough thaumite in my pack to barbecue a mammoth. Anything that troubles us does so only very briefly.

When we're not walking, we spend our time on a variety of useful pursuits:

a) Gem cutting, at which I'm fairly proficient. You use the heat from red thaumite concentrated down to a tiny beam to shape the gems and enhance their magic. A cut gem will still be usable for general-purpose applications, but will be much stronger and more useful for whatever task it's designed for. That's the basics, anyway, though there's a lot of arcane theory that's 90 percent bullshit.

b) Educating Tsav. If she's going to help me in the Kingdom, she needs to know a lot more about humans, and in particular she needs to speak good Common. That's a lot to cram into the time we have, but fortunately, purple thaumite comes through again. You can use it to sort of spoon big dollops of information into a willing target's mind, then practice to get everything locked and settled before it fades. It still takes a while, but it's a lot faster than doing it the old-fashioned way.[7]

c) Fucking like bunnies, which should be self-explanatory.

---

7 It doesn't feel *great*, though. Like stirring cold dollops of sour cream into the warm bowl of chili that is your mind. If Tsav didn't already have the Best Partner Award for, you know, everything, she'd win it here by bearing up with no complaints. Also, *man*, I could go for some chili.

I also explain everything that happened to me in the tunnels in a bit more detail, including my discovery of the probably-from-Earth Bible and my theories about what it means. This entails a lot more explanations of things I barely remember[8] and sound kind of weird when you say them out loud.

"So the sky-father," Tsav says slowly, "that's Zeus. With the lightning bolt."

"Yeah," I say with more confidence than I feel.

"He sends his son Neo to Earth to die."

"Right."

"To make peace with the machines."

"I *think* so."

"Who are looking for John Connor."

"Yeah."

"Who is . . . who exactly?"

I scratch the back of my head. "I'm a little fuzzy on that bit. I think he's friends with Thor."

"What do the machines want with him?"

"Search me. I never paid much attention in church."[9]

"And everyone on Earth believed this?"

"Oh, no. There were lots of different versions. They used to fight all the time. Protestants versus Catholics, Marvel versus DC, Nintendo versus Sega, that sort of thing."

"What's a Sega?"

"Also, not sure." I rack my brain. "Something about . . . hedgehogs?"

"Earth," Tsav pronounces, "must be a very strange place."

Honestly, tasks (a) and (c) are going much better than (b).

---

8 After a thousand years, my memories of everything Earth-related are pretty bad, except when it comes to song lyrics.

9 Although I now have the distinct impression that if there *is* a Hell, I'm probably going there.

* * *

And so, in a vaguely honeymoon atmosphere, we make our way down from the Firelands, through the forests beyond, and arrive at the border of the Kingdom. The closer we get, the more certain I am of the geography, and I aim away from the Red-tooths' old territory, where someone might recognize a wandering Dark Lord and her minion. Instead, we aim for Shithole, a town on the border that probably has an actual name but fuck if I'm going to bother remembering it.

That's about where we came in, right? Okay. End of flash-back.

* * *

Shithole sucks. Fucking shocker, I know.

At least there's an inn, because this is a border town. It's a ramshackle two-story thing with a big common room on the ground floor and rooms for rent up top, run by an older woman with wild red hair and enormous tits. I think I've been here once in a previous life, but apart from the innkeep's bazongas, it didn't make much of an impression.

Now, though, I find myself automatically seeing it through Tsav's eyes, and everything is strange and new. With a few rare exceptions like the pyrvir, wilders don't have cities and towns, and they *definitely* don't have inns.[10] The bar, the hearth with its inevitable pot of bubbling stew, and most of all, the tables with their groups of relative strangers are all foreign to her. She stares around, trying not to be obvious about it, while I get us

---

10 Or really much in the way of commerce. They understand the idea of trade, but explaining *currency* and what you can do with it took up a chunk of the All About Humans curriculum.

beers and a promise of food.[11] We sit at an open table and take off our sodden cloaks to bask in the warm, stuffy heat.

After a while, Tsav says, "You don't even introduce yourself?"

"To whom?" I answer very grammatically.

"Anyone?" She waves a hand at the other patrons.

"Depends." I shrug. "If it were a village watering hole, you might know people. But this is a traveler's inn, everyone's just passing through."

"Are all humans that unfriendly?"

"Kinda. We can be real assholes."

I see her point, though. In a wilder camp, a visitor might be invited to eat with the band, but they'd certainly be expected to socialize. So by their standards, everyone here *is* being an asshole. Culture clash is a trip.

"How's the beer?" I ask.

Tsav sips it, getting foam on her tusks. "Odd."[12]

In truth, it's only middling, but I still relish a long pull. It's been a while. "You'll get used to it."

She gives me a weak smile. "Do I have to?"

I'm trying to take it easy on Tsav. Coming here with me is an almost mind-blowingly brave thing for her to do, all the more so given that she doesn't actually have any *proof* that all the shit I've been saying is true. (Except, of course, my occasional ability to predict the near-term future.) I fretted a lot about bringing her along, thought about doing the whole Spider-Man "I must leave you to protect you" nonsense, but fuck that shit. Tsav's a grown woman and can make her own choices.

---

11 Fortunately, the Redtooth treasury contained quite a bit of loot from human lands, so in addition to the absolute king's ransom in thaumite in my pack, there's also a small fortune in Kingdom coins.

12 They don't have beer out in the Wilds; it's an agricultural thing. What the Bottle Fairy brings the wilders is closer to vodka.

And God knows recent events have shown that I need her around to maintain my tentative grip on sanity. She's the only person in the world who even *kind* of understands what's happening to me.

The door opens during these contemplations and a new party comes in. And *party* is right, since that's the traditional descriptor for the small combined-arms teams in which the Guildblades prosecute their business.

This one is typical: One knight in shining armor, though the bulky plate is currently packed away out of the rain. One lithe sneaky type for skulking and stabbing. One wizard, identifiable by the silver chain set with cut thaumite around her neck. The last is a young man in loose clothes whom I guess, by process of elimination, to be a healing specialist, though he isn't flashing his green thaumite around.

They bustle in like they own the place and shout across the room for drinks instead of walking to the bar like ordinary mortals. I realize with mounting horror that the only open table is next to ours, and stare down into my beer as they clomp over in mud-caked boots and drop their equipment with a clatter.

It's fine. It's probably fine.

See, Tsav is wearing a big purple gem under her clothes. I carved it on our trip over and cast the actual spell just before we walked into Shithole. It's a subtle mental effect that makes anyone looking at her ignore her orcish features; not invisibility, just a gentle suggestion that this is a *perfectly ordinary human*. Green skin? Tusks? What are you talking about? Maybe you should go lie down.

That it works is obvious from the fact that we're standing here without having to slaughter the guards at the bridge. The nice thing about keeping the effect small is that it's relatively hard to detect; another wizard searching with purple thaumite would have to be looking right at it to notice, and even then, they might not know what they were seeing. Skill with purple stones, apart from a few standard protective spells, is one of the rarest. Not everyone has had two hundred lifetimes to explore every obscure corner of the magic system, right?

Still, if anyone is going to cause trouble, it's Guildblades. These are guys who raise professional paranoia to an art form, and they have access to a *lot* more thaumite than your average villagers. I try to convey to Tsav with my eyebrows not to look too closely. Nothing to see here, murder-hoboes . . .

Fortunately for us, they're a bit distracted.

"Well, *that* was a fucking mess," says the knight. She's a big broad-shouldered woman, hair cropped short to fit under a helmet.

"It worked, didn't it?" the wizard says defensively. She's smaller, pale-skinned, and wide-eyed with a furtive look.

"*You* didn't have to stick Rupert's arm back on," says the healer, who has a truly unfortunate goatee.

The skulker, presumably Rupert, works one shoulder and winces. The innkeeper boobs her way over and serves beer and stew, attracting admiring gazes. She drops food off at our table as well, and I have to direct Tsav's attention to it to keep her from staring at the Guildblades. I can't help listening with half an ear.

"We got there in the end, though," the wizard says.

"Most of us," Rupert mumbles through a mug of beer.

"That rattail was a mean bitch, but she went down fast enough," the knight says. "Remember when we tracked the little one to the end of the burrow? And she had her hair standing on end, trying to make herself look big, with two even smaller fuckers hiding behind her."

"Right!" The wizard barks an unpleasant laugh. "I was like, your mom chopped Rupert's arm off, where do you think *you're* going?" She lifts her necklace, fingering a red stone. "Three fried rats coming up."

"Little 'uns never have much color[13] in 'em," Rupert says. "Waste of breath."

"It's the principle of the thing," the wizard says, looking to the knight for support.

"Right." She drains her mug and gives a mighty belch. "Mess with the Guild, you get the blade. That's the rule."

I notice, too late, that Tsav's knuckles are white on the table.

"Hey." I have to keep my voice low. "Hey. Tsav. Look at me." When she doesn't respond, I switch to Wilder, hoping the Guildblades are loud enough nobody will overhear. "Tsav, *look at me.*"

Very slowly, she turns. Her eyes are white all around.

"We're going upstairs." I flag the innkeep from across the room, gesture upward. She nods approvingly and I grab the bowls of stew. "Come on. Nice and slow."

There's a dangerous moment as Tsav pushes her chair back and it scrapes loudly on the floorboards. Rupert glances in our direction, frowning, but the laughter of the knight and wizard pulls his attention back. I extract us from the corner and guide the glowering Tsav up the stairs. The little rooms up above are mostly empty, so I pick one at random.

"I know," I say in Wilder as soon as the door is closed.

"They were *laughing.*" There are tears at the corners of Tsav's eyes.

"I *know.*"

"The mother fought," Tsav grinds out. "And when she was dead, her daughter fought. And they—"

There's a lot of things I could say. Like *Look, it's a constant, nothing new here, worse things happen at sea.* Like *The wilders along the border raid human farms all the time, it's not like there haven't been plenty of human kids facing down a wolf-wilder*

---

13 Slang for thaumite.

with bloody teeth. Like *Have you seen what the wilders do to each other? Remember what Gevalkin and the Redtooths did to anybody who talked back?*

But logic isn't what she needs at the moment. If she explodes, I'm going to have to burn down the inn and possibly the whole town, and that's not a fucking great note to start on. And if we're *really* being honest, I'm not sure Tsav is wrong and burning down the town would be such a bad idea.

Wilders raid us for food, loot, that sort of thing. But humans hunt *them* like prey for the thaumite in their bodies. You can't put atrocities up on a whiteboard and game out that *this* one is worth 937 War Crimes Points versus only 478 over here, but somehow the difference feels pretty fucking important.

No wonder the crowd back at the Convocation is all *Death to the Humans.* They're a long way from the Kingdom, but that might make it even worse; stories grow in the telling. The pyrvir told me that humans are ten feet tall and have atomic breath.

"We would boast, when we came back from raids." Tsav, evidently, has been thinking along the same lines. "But we never *laughed.*"

"I know," I repeat. "That's because you're not a bunch of complete psychos."

"And humans are?"

"I mean, #NotAllHumans. But the Guild are ... Well, look. When you have an organization whose stated purpose is to go out and murder strangers for no real reason, you tend to get a *certain type of recruit.*"

There *are* good Guildblades, I guess, who worry more about protecting humanity than collecting loot.[14] But when the met-

---

14 This makes me think of Kelda for a minute, who is—was—gentle and kind and fun to kiss and is now dead dead really *for real* dead because of me—*nope* nope nope not thinking about it.

ric for success is "thaumite accumulated," the nasty shit tends
to rise to the top of the stew.

"What are we going to do?"

"Do?"

"About *them*." Tsav bares her teeth.

"The ones downstairs? Nothing." The hurt in her face makes
me wince. But we have a plan, and I'm out of continues. I can't
take unnecessary risks. "But this is what we're here to put a
stop to, right? Convince the humans that they're *really* better
off living in peace rather than getting flattened by the horde."

"To save the humans."

"To save *everybody*." I blink back tears. "Please, Tsav. That's
the whole point."

If Tsav turns away from me, I don't know what I'll do. I'm
holding on to hope by a thread here.

But with a great shuddering breath, she lets her shoulders
slump. I take a tentative step closer, and when she doesn't pull
away, I wrap her in my arms. She hugs me back, heavy and warm.

"I'm sorry," I tell her. "I'm sorry I brought you here. I knew
it would be hard, but..."

"I knew it too," she says, mildly rebuking. "I didn't realize...
how strongly I felt."

Once we get past the border, this sort of thing will be less
obvious. But that doesn't mean it's not still happening, out
where the farms meet the Wilds.

As far as peace is concerned, the Guild is *definitely* going to
be a problem.

* * *

Before we leave Shithole, I replace our wilder-made tent and
packs with (markedly inferior) human gear that won't look
obviously foreign. By unspoken agreement, we spend the next

few nights by the side of the road rather than stopping over in the villages we pass. We're not likely to run into more Guild-blades, but I'd rather not take the chance.

We're getting into fall now, and the landscape is turning golden with swaying fields of wheat or barley or whatever the shit I'm not a farmer, okay? It's different, is what I'm saying, from the wilderness I've been tromping through for the last few months. No rivers of lava, for one thing, and a lot fewer trees.

Tsav stares a bit, but I think that's less about the landscape than the *people*. Farmers work the field, carters pass us regularly on the roads, riders trot by, children play, and generally the whole fucking panorama of bucolic plenitude plays out before our very eyes.

"There are so many of them. Of you." Tsav shakes her head. "They always said humans breed like rats, but . . ."

She looks at me, worried I might be offended, but I grin back at her.

"That sounds about right. As long as there's food, you'll get more humans. We're kind of insidious." I wave a hand. "And this is nothing. Wait until you see Vroken." That's the capital of the Kingdom, a big place by current standards, though nowhere near the size of the ruined city that hosted the Convocation.

"I'm not sure I want to," Tsav says. "I already feel . . . pressed."

She shudders, and I put a sympathetic hand on her shoulder. We continue down the road until the sun is getting low in the sky and I finally spot the tree I've been looking for, a huge old oak rising like a sentinel from the crest of a hill some distance off. We have to hike down a mess of confusing country lanes to get there, and by the time we're climbing the winding path up the hillside, the light has turned golden and syrupy.

Close up, you can see that the tree rises out of a two-story wooden building, so ramshackle and poorly built that it looks like it's leaning on the trunk for support. Other plants grow around and through it, some incorporated into its structure and others gradually tearing that structure to pieces. The roof and rafters are spattered with birdshit, the woodshed is home to a multigenerational family of raccoons, and haphazard beds of wildflowers line the front. These are now being choked out by weeds since nobody's tended them for a while. I feel a sudden flash of guilt.

Fuck me. Guilt for *Tserigern*? That lying old geezer? What have I become?

This is, of course, his house. It reeks of his style, half "charmingly eccentric wizard" and half "actually just living in filth." I've been here before, but only with the old man in tow, puttering around making tea and rambling about prophecies and destiny. Since Tserigern is currently otherwise occupied, moldering into a skeleton by the side of a pond—*guilt*—the house is empty.

Fuck. There were rabbits in the house. Were those pets? If I open the door and find a bunch of pet rabbits starved to death when he didn't come home, I might lose it.

"Tsav, can you open the door for me?"

She frowns, puzzled, but pulls the badly made door open on its rope hinges. I have my eyes closed.

"Are there a bunch of dead rabbits lying around?"

"No," Tsav says slowly, in her *humor Davi when she acts crazy* voice. "No dead rabbits."

I cautiously open one eye. The ground floor is much as I remember it, with the trunk of the tree sticking up through the center of the roof, surrounded by benches and low tables. A circle of stones against one wall makes a crude hearth, long cold. Miscellaneous sacks and earthenware jars are scattered about. No dead rabbits, or live ones either, though hard pellets all over the dirt floor provide copious evidence of their existence.

Probably the rabbits wandered out to lead happy rabbit lives. They're better off, even. Be free, rabbits! Glad we got that sorted. There *is* what looks like a mouse skeleton in one corner, but I'm pretty sure it was always there.

Tsav surveys the house with the expert eye of someone used to living rough. She snorts.

"What a dump."

"Right?" I say. "Fucking Tserigern."

"Remind me why we're here?"

"To look for clues."

"What kind of clues?"

"Just clues generally." I frown at the mess. "I want to know where the old coot got his ideas."

Because here's the thing: Tserigern was a crank, but he wasn't a *complete* crank. He turns up within seconds of my appearance in the pool! That can't be a coincidence. *He* says he's been following some kind of prophecy, and I'm destined to save the Kingdom and blah blah, all the talk that I took very seriously a thousand years ago and now makes me want to bash his head in.

I'm not sure I believe in *destiny*. If it was *destiny* that I save the Kingdom, you'd think I would have fucking managed it one of these times instead of getting painfully murdered over and over. But what I definitely believe in is *intention*. While the loop remained exactly the same, I was prepared to accept that this was just the way things were, somehow, that I'd gotten caught in some cosmic spin cycle and it was all just the forces of the universe doing their thing. But now? I become Dark Lord, and the forces of the universe change underneath me?

No way. No *fucking* way. Tsav said it first—it feels like there's some *purpose* there. Intention. The existence of a Chosen One implies the existence of a Chooser. That *someone* out there did this to me. I don't know who that is, whether it's God or Mega-Satan or the dreams of a thousand cats, but *whoever* it is I am going to *find them* and ███████████████████████ to their ██████████████ with a *teakettle*.

Sorry. Getting a little ahead of myself. The point is, if it really is a person we're looking for rather than the Will of the Universe or whatever, it raises the question of where exactly Tserigern got his information. Where did this surprisingly accurate prophecy come from? I don't believe the old codger was the architect of the whole thing, that'd be way too easy, but he was clearly *involved*. Thus: toss his place looking for clues.

Unfortunately, clues are in somewhat short supply, or at least hard to recognize in the literal rat's nest Tserigern called home. Tsav and I putter about the ground floor for a while, but there's nothing but rotten food and rodent turds. The second story is accessed via a rickety ladder in the back. I trust it with my weight only reluctantly. It creaks but holds, and Tsav follows me up to the loft.

This looks a little more promising. There's Tserigern's sleeping furs, which I lack the appropriate ten-foot pole to investigate, but also a desk made from a slice of tree trunk. It's covered with scraps of paper and pots of unidentifiable substances. There's also what looks kind of like a book, albeit a book constructed by a four-year-old from bits of construction paper she found in the woods. I flip it open, wishing for a pair of latex gloves. Tsav looks over my shoulder. Dense chicken-scratch writing spiders across the page, and I have to peer close to read.

"...from yesterday. Attempted to move my bowels without result. The first boil appears to have shrunk a fraction, but the second grows larger and encroaches on my genitals. Mushrooms have fermented sufficiently to allow..."

"Oh, fuck me." I sink down and lay my head on the table. Tsav, reading along, pats me sympathetically on the shoulder.

This may take a while.

* * *

We reluctantly stay the night, laying out our bedrolls in the cleanest part of the loft and taking turns reading Tserigern's diary-slash-horrifying-medical-chart. The vast majority of it is taken up with detailed descriptions of his various ailments and his passion for gathering what he describes as the "bounty of the forest," which seems to consist of various nuts, berries, barks, and mushrooms that will not *quite* kill you.

Mentions of actual *magic* are few and far between. Tserigern, you are the worst wizard ever. I'm rapidly losing my guilt and starting to wish he was still around so I could bash his head in again.

"Who's Cyrus?" Tsav says.

"Hmm?"

She's taking her turn with the book while I cook our dinner directly with red thaumite—I'm not going to risk a fire in this place, all the dried dung would go up like dead grass. Tsav sits cross-legged, expression grave, one finger slowly tracking across the page.[15]

"Cyrus," she repeats. "Is it a common name? Tserigern... talks to him. Or possibly dreams about him? I'm not clear. He mentions 'founders.'"

I snap my fingers. "*Founder* Cyrus. That's right."

"Who is he?"

"From the Kingdom's creation myth." When she cocks her head, I ask, "Do wilders have an explanation for where they came from? Or who created the world?"

Her brow wrinkles. "Nobody created the world. It's always been here, and wilders have always lived in it."

That tracks with what I know of the wilders' quasi-religion. They swear by the Old Ones, but they're not referring to *gods* in the conventional sense, just beings like themselves who've

---

15   It's adorable, she needs a pair of half-moon librarian glasses.

managed to live enormously long lives by consuming huge amounts of thaumite and thus become incredibly powerful. Since this is demonstrably possible and beings matching that description actually exist, it's not so much mythology as fact. Though I've never seen any evidence that these Old Ones guide mortal affairs in the way that Artaxes describes. The wilders don't seem to require any just-so stories to accept the world as it is.

"In the Kingdom," I explain, "they have a story that humans used to live somewhere else, somewhere better. But something bad happened and they had to flee. A group of eight people called the Founders led them to where the Kingdom is now and hung around for a while to write laws." I pause. "And, um, slaughter the wilders, I guess. There's a lot of stories about that. The Founders were supposed to be very powerful, with magic we don't know how to do anymore."

"And Cyrus was one of them?"

"Yeah." I frown. "I don't remember much of the story about him, though. I never paid all that much attention to the Founder stuff."

"Why not?"

"I figured it was all a myth." She looks confused again and I try to explain. "A made-up story, something you tell kids when they ask annoying questions. Humans love that shit, trust me. There's all *kinds* of stories that definitely never happened."

"But with what you found at the Convocation—"

"Yeah." I crawl around to look at the book, pressing my shoulder against hers. "What does it say about Cyrus?"

"It's just passing references." She points. "Here. 'Cyrus spoke again while I slept.' Or here, 'While I sought tiger-mold to salve my pus, the Founder instructed me.'"

"The Founders are all dead," I say. "The stories are very clear about that. Humans don't live forever, no matter how much magic we use."

"Tserigern definitely thought he was talking to someone." She turns the makeshift pages, back toward the beginning of the diary. "Here. He says Cyrus *visits* him, in person."

" 'He showed me again his visions of the world to come,' " I read aloud. " 'And when I asked what they meant, he grew angry and said he had already explained too often.' " I snort. "Apparently, even Cyrus gets frustrated with Tserigern."

"After that, it's just more stuff about glandular swelling," Tsav says, scanning forward. "The first time Cyrus visited must be before he started writing this."

"But this still tells us a lot." My mind is buzzing. "Someone *was* feeding info to Tserigern, and it turned out to be dead-on. At least as far as finding me was concerned. Whoever this Cyrus really is has to be involved."

"We don't know anything about him, though," Tsav says. "There's no details here."

"We have a name," I say. "That's something. When we get to the palace, we can look for more on Cyrus in the library."

"The palace," Tsav says. She seems nervous. "Where the human leader resides."

"We call her the Queen." I throw an arm around her shoulders and squeeze. "It'll be fine, trust me."

It will! Probably.

Next step: pay a visit to Himbo Boyfriend Johann.

Chapter Two

Like most cities, Vroken can be smelled long before you can see it. The inimitable odor of too many humans in too small a space—not to mention the livestock—wafts for miles on a good wind, providing a little foretaste of what's to come. It gives the nose a bit of time to acclimate, or more accurately shut down before it gets overwhelmed.

I notice Tsav sniffing unhappily as we get closer. I sympathize. For me, the smell carries a complex bouquet of emotions; this is *civilization*, or at least civilization's by-products. I've had a lot of good times here. But also a lot of the worst days of many lives have been spent in Vroken, often while it's in the process of burning down.

There's no formal boundary of the city, whose walls were long ago torn down for their masonry. The fields by the side of the road gradually become vegetable gardens, then holding pens for sheep, cattle, and pigs, each with their own flavorful additions to the general atmosphere. The buildings grow larger and more numerous, with brick and stone replacing wood and plaster. And then, at some point, you're walking down a street that's more building than open space, and somebody elbows you in the kidneys and shouts "Make way!" and your urban adventure has begun.

Needless to say, this is all a bit of a shock for poor Tsav. I've done my best over the past few days to describe it, but you can't really appreciate a city of humans in all our claustrophobic awfulness until you see it. Virgard, though an order of magnitude larger than most wilder camps, isn't a patch on the chaos of this place. Tsav stumbles like a drunk, staring around, and I have to thread my arm through hers to keep her from getting run over by carts.

Fortunately, she's not alone in this attitude. Most of the population of the Kingdom has never seen Vroken, and there's always a few fresh arrivals gawping at the sights. I pull us out of the main flow of the crowd and into a line for a food stall. A few minutes later, munching on one of the great works of civilization—fried dough on a stick[1]—we lean against the brick wall of a corn depository and try to take it all in.

Up the street, flanking the big square, are statues of the Founders: Atlian, Grithka, Satorel, and the rest. Cyrus is halfway along, a pinch-faced man who looks more like an accountant than a famous wizard. I give him a suspicious look as I tear off a mouthful of dumpling.

"It's . . . big," Tsav manages.

"Mmph," I agree, my mouth full of oily goodness.

Tsav bites into her dumpling and chews thoughtfully.

"The thing I don't understand," she says after a moment, "is how the humans can *lose*."

"Sorry?"

"In your past lives, you said the Dark Lord brings an army here and burns the city every time, right?"

---

1 A staple of Vroken street food they just call "dumplings"—it's a bit like a cross between Japanese *dango* and a corn dog.

I nod.

"But there are *so many humans*. Look at this place!" She waves her dumpling vaguely. "There are probably more people on this street than in the whole horde!"

Maybe not *that* many, but she has a point. "They can't fight, though."

"Humans can fight."

"*Some* of them can. It's hard to explain."

This is another one of those cultural differences. Thanks to thaumite, obviously, the average wilder is stronger and tougher than the average human, but it's more than that. In a wilder band, when there's fighting to be done, *everybody* fights except children. It's just an expected part of every adult's responsibilities, and everyone spends a certain amount of time training for it. Whereas with humans...

"Look at that guy, for example." I point to a young man in a floppy hat riding with a cartload of bundled straw. "He's a farmer. He'll spend his whole life farming. He'll get pretty good at it, know exactly when to plant things and harvest them and so on. But spending all that time farming means he's *not* learning to fight, and he doesn't have spare time or money to get armor and weapons anyway."

"So, what does he do if someone attacks him?"

"He has a lord who fights for him. In exchange, he pays the lord taxes or does work for him."

"And the lords can't fight the wilders?"

"They can *try*. But there aren't enough of them."

More importantly, the main problem the Kingdom's military has faced in my previous lives is an overconcentration of thaumite. A fighter augmented and supported with magic can be devastatingly effective in a direct confrontation, and the nobility has spent the last century or so in a kind of arms race, acquiring larger and larger hoards of the stuff to overpower their rivals. Unfortunately, fielding a few thousand souped-up men-at-arms is less than effective against hordes of tens of thousands of wilders who ignore all the conventional rules of war and refuse to face off on nice open battlefields.

Getting the lords to give up their arsenals to equip a much larger number of fighters has always been an insurmountable political problem. Even when I make some headway, there's never enough time to train more fighters before the Dark Lord arrives and flattens us.

Tsav is wearing a thoughtful expression as she watches the farmer turn the corner.

"In that case," she says, "who protects the people from the lords?"

"Good fucking question." I rip the last of my dumpling from the stick and bolt it down. "Come on, let's hit the palace."

* * *

The palace—like the Kingdom, it doesn't have a name, because there's only one of it—isn't so much a castle as vaguely castle-esque. Like a pug or Pomeranian, with wolves *somewhere* in their ancestry but clearly something terrible has happened in the meantime, the palace is descended from actual fortifications but tamed, scaled down, and made convenient. There's no curtain wall, just iron fences concealed by artfully planted hedgerows. Inside, beyond vast gardens maintained by thaumite in a permanent state of perfection, stone towers are topped with faux crenellations, connected by long, low wings lit by rainbow strings of lanterns.

Everything about it screams power, but not in the brutal, obvious language of stone and steel. Instead, the extravagant decoration says that the masters of this place have magic to burn, so much thaumite that they can afford to waste it on pretty gardens and colored lights. It's a neat bit of theater, which I currently appreciate for an entirely different reason: An actual fortress would be a lot harder to sneak into.

Admittedly, you'd need quite a fortress to keep *me* out, especially here. I've spent a *lot* of time in the palace, and I know it nearly as well as the region around my spawning pool. After literally centuries, I know where the loose bricks are, which hallways no one uses, all the unused rooms where you can sneak in a quickie while you're supposed to be working. I even know a lot of the staff, no small feat given how many people it takes to keep this place running.

It's no great trick, therefore, to get inside. We go to a side gate used only infrequently by the gardeners, and I give the lock a little lift-and-twist that pops it right open. It leads into a sunken lane, which offers convenient cover as we stroll along to a toolshed tucked neatly out of sight behind some flowering vines.

The thing about beautiful palaces is that *somebody* has to do the actual work. But the people who pay for the beauty don't want to see a bunch of grubby peasants scrabbling about making things grow, it smacks of *effort*. As much as possible, they build things so the workers can stay out of sight, and when that fails, the owners just ignore the help as part of the landscape. Thus, helping myself to a stained brown coat and a wheelbarrow from the shed is as good as donning an invisibility cloak. Tsav and I are able to stroll right around back of the main building without attracting so much as a curious glance.

This is a good thing, because Tsav is staring around like a tourist. I'm not sure the palace is having its intended effect, since she doesn't really appreciate how expensive everything is, but it has to be a little overwhelming even so. It's almost a relief when we pass from the gardens into the more utilitarian areas in the rear. Servants in brown and white uniforms bustle about, fetching and carrying and cleaning and generally keeping the world on its axis.

Gardeners aren't supposed to go inside, so I wait to ditch the wheelbarrow until there aren't any eyes on us, and slip into a servants' corridor. These are woven all throughout the palace like really mundane secret passages, with the doors concealed in moldings or behind hangings. Again, the goal is that everything should just *happen*, invisibly, as though by magic.[2] It makes it really easy to sneak around, but hey, if you want everything to look neat, you have to risk a few assassinations, right?

Anyway, we make it to the big audience room without anybody hassling us. I've timed this pretty carefully. Johann hates doing audiences, but tradition requires he sit on the throne for a couple of hours every afternoon while various ministers argue with exalted guests, and that's when he'll be easiest to get to. The hidden door has a peephole—wouldn't do to open it too fast and flatten some drunken baron—and through it I can see that court is indeed in session. Well attended, too, so my view is entirely a bunch of exquisitely tailored backsides. But reconnaissance is unnecessary, since this is a scene I know like the back of my hand.

I consider doffing the grody brown coat, but decide to keep it, it fits with the vibe I'm going to try to project. Tsav looks nervous and I waggle my eyebrows at her.

"Relax. This is the easy part."

"Hmm." She touches the purple thaumite at her throat, and I know she's worrying about the disguise. "Let's hope."

"Just stay quiet until we're in private and I can introduce you."

She gives a dark laugh. "I wouldn't know what to say."

I would. That's the whole point. I've hung out with Prince Johann for more than a century, measured by my personal fucked-up solipsistic time line; he won't remember me, obviously,

---

2   But not like *literally* by magic, that's different.

but I know everything about *him*, and especially what will pique his interest. Still, I find myself taking a deep breath before I push the door open. Not that I'm not confident, it's just—no do-overs, right? Don't fuck this up, Davi.

The murmur of conversation is a dull roar. Court is as much a place to hobnob with your fellow good-and-greats as it is to actually do business with the throne, which is why there's a phalanx of trumpeters to blow *Shut the fuck up* before the Prince says anything. We emerge from the wall in our dirty coats and make our way through the crowd. I watch people notice us, then *un*-notice us as they realize we are, quite obviously, beneath their notice. We progress in a bubble of pointed-lack-of-stares.

Being noticed is obviously the currency of choice around here. It's a sea of colorful, expensive fabric; the buttery gleam of gold and the glittering moonlight of silver chasing; furs and lace and, above all, thaumite. Tiny bits of color that glow from within, set into rings and bracelets and necklaces nestled deep in artful décolletage.[3]

It's beauty as military threat, even if the wearers don't think of it as such. "If I can waste this many stones on *decoration*," every outfit says, "think how many more must be locked in a vault under my castle, ready for a fight. Don't fuck with me."

The audience chamber itself, of course, is designed to achieve a similar effect on everyone present. It's heavy on polished marble inset with intricate gold tracery and thick velvet curtains to muffle the echoes. There's a long red carpet leading to a dais at the front, where the throne sits, with several steps providing space for an entourage of guards and minders. In front of this, lower down but still at the center of attention, are chairs for the ministers who actually get things done.

When we finally push free of the crowd, I'm prepared to see

---

3 Titties.

these worthies engaged in earnest dickering with some count or other while Johann lounges bonelessly on the throne. However, the voices I hear don't sound like the usual ministers, who tend toward the beardy-old-dude-slash-wizened-crone end of the spectrum.

No matter. I slip around a portly countess and break through onto the empty carpet. At the same time, I put a hand in my pocket and touch my thaumite to generate special effects. Lightning flashes indoors, and there's a roll of thunder loud enough to startle everyone. All eyes are abruptly on me.

But something's wrong. There are no ministers, just a couple of cringing barons on their knees in front of the throne, and the man sitting in the big chair is *definitely* not Himbo Boyfriend Johann. He's short but powerfully built, with wings of gray in his dark hair and a pointed little goatee that just *screams* Traitorous Grand Vizier.

Duke Aster. Pallas fucking Aster, Grand Slayer of the fucking Guild of Adventurers, is sitting on the throne like he belongs there, and he doesn't look happy to see me.

* * *

Okay, pause. Time-out. Because there's some context here that you probably don't appreciate.

History lesson![4] Back in the mythic past when the Kingdom was set up, one of the Founders—a dude named Atlian—fathered the first king. And a *whole* bunch of other people, it turned out. Atlian got *around*. All the current nobility of the Kingdom claims to be descended from him to

---

4 I *promise* this isn't going to turn into "In the beginning, Hezekiah begat Jacobson, and he reigned for twenty-two summers and died from eating eel pie." Stay with me.

varying degrees,[5] with tons of complex bullshit determining precedence and rank. There are several prominent branches of this extended family tree. One of them gives us the current set of royals, but the others are dukes and powerful in their own right.

Currently the Kingdom is nominally ruled by Johann's grandmother, Queen Hesta. But she is getting on in years and while not completely batty has more or less stepped out of the spotlight to give Johann a shot at learning the ropes.[6] Johann is pretty bored by the whole concept of kinging, and his inattention has led to the formation of a party that thinks he should be quietly shuffled off to a pleasure garden while someone more vigorous takes over. Duke Aster is the favored candidate, most of all by himself, on the grounds that he's Atlian's great-great-nth-grand-nephew or something plus he has a big castle and lots of soldiers.

He's *also* a major supporter of the Guild and has spent much of his career riding around sticking his sword / lance / other phallic symbol into any wilder he can get his hands on. They have rewarded him with the title of Grand Slayer, which is what you get when you're *really* good at murder-hoboing.

This is all tiresomely familiar to me because it's one of the first problems I have to resolve when I get here in a normal[7] life. The feud between Johann's supporters and Aster's cripples the Kingdom's response to the wilders, so it's got to be dealt with. My sympathies are obviously with Johann, but I've played out

---

5 Although given the penchant of the powerful for following in great-grand-daddy's philandering footsteps, it's pretty much certain that *everyone* in the Kingdom is descended from Atlian by now.

6 Johann's father perished some decades earlier in a bizarre incident involving an exploding manure pit.

7 To the extent that anything about my life is normal.

every possible variation in the name of science. I even married Aster once.[8]

What *hasn't* happened, though, is Aster taking the throne without my help. Not after only four or five months; left to themselves, the nobles will squabble about this for *years*. I haven't been anywhere near the Kingdom to change anything, so what the *fuck* is he doing here?

* * *

Having gotten everyone's attention, I have to say *something*. Unfortunately, my lines were carefully tailored to intrigue Prince Johann. The Duke is an entirely different proposition, but I can do only so much rewriting on the fly.

"*Beware!*" I intone.[9] It's a good first line, gets everyone interested. "The prophecy has been fulfilled!"

Prophecy is the best. Anytime you want somebody to do something and can't be bothered to think of a good reason, just throw in a fucking prophecy.

The assembled nobility, now that their surprise is wearing off, is not enthused. There's some dark mutterings, some titters of forced laughter. But Duke Aster is willing to play along, at least to a point. He gives his trademark expression, a sort of weary smirk that says "I *guess* I'll deign to notice you, but you should be grateful for the privilege," and waves down the guards who'd taken a threatening step forward.

"Who," he says, "might you be?"

"I am the successor to the mighty Tserigern," I say, somehow keeping a straight face. "Once his apprentice, and now

---

8 But only once. Dude fucks like he's jousting with his prick. Which for the record isn't much of a lance.

9 *Nailed* the intone this time.

assuming his mantle. You may call me Davi, and I bring urgent news. A terrible fate will befall the Kingdom unless we move swiftly."

"Tserigern." Aster scratches his chin. "Dirty fellow, leaves in his beard? Lives in the woods?"

Not *in*accurate. Johann always had a soft spot for Tserigern and found his talk of prophecy and destiny appealing. Aster is evidently less sympathetic.

"He was a wizard of great . . . wizardness," I say stiffly. "And he knew many things."[10]

"Was?" Aster's eyebrows rise. "Has something happened to him?"

"Tserigern is dead," I say. "He fell nobly in battle." That ought to appeal to Duke Stabs-a-lot. "And with his last breath, he bade me bring you warning."

"I see." A nasty smile threatens to overwhelm his stern expression. "Well, by all means, deliver your warning."

More tittering laughter from the nobles, who are now catching the Duke's drift. I grit my teeth. Clearly, I am humping the wrong leg here.

"I was directed to bring my words to Prince Johann. Please tell him I beg an audience. He," I add pointedly, "always valued my master's counsel."

This is a risky move, but I'm not sure where else to go with it. This whole attempt is in imitation of something Tserigern usually did when introducing *me*, but in retrospect, he probably knew he'd have a sympathetic audience. I'm sort of hoping Duke Aster goes the "Great, let's fob this lunatic off on my rival the Prince" route rather than the "How *dare* you mention my rival the Prince?!" route, but I can see from the way his face goes hard that I lost that particular coin flip.

---

10 Like the precise details of twenty years' worth of bowel movements.

"The *Prince*," he grates, "has many demands on his time. I will see to it that he receives word that you want to speak with him. If he wishes to grant you an audience, he will send for you. In the meantime, I think it best if you and your companion return to the city to wait."

Tsav has emerged from the crowd by now, just in time to be thrown out of the party. Guards are closing in on us from both sides. I feel my anger rising.

"It's really quite important," I manage. "If I could see him for just a few minutes—"

Duke Aster, however, has already moved on, summoning the next pair of petitioners to approach the throne. The guards don't exactly take hold of us, but they loom as though doing so would be the next logical step. Tsav gives me a *What now?* look, but short of whipping out my thaumite and laying waste to the throne room, I haven't got much to suggest.

"You want the truth?" I tell the guards. "You can't *handle* the truth."

They ignore me. Nobody appreciates the classics anymore.

* * *

"It should have worked," I mutter into my beer.

"You said it's been four months," Tsav says. "Since you— what do you call it?"

"Spawned."

"That makes it sound like you squirted eggs all over the place." Tsav makes a face. "Anyway. We're four months past your usual starting point. Things could have changed."

"Not *this* much," I say. "I've tried leaving them alone to see if they work it out, and they never do."

"If this Duke wants to be chief, he should challenge the Prince and be done with it."

"Not how it works here." Although, in some ways, that would be a lot more convenient. "Instead, they fight each other with, like...cutting repartee."

"What's repartee?"

"Pretending to be nice while being a dick, basically." I shake my head. "It's a good thing we didn't bring Droff. Everybody lies all the time, hanging around this place might overheat his brain."

"Also, he's an eight-foot-tall rock." Tsav fiddles with the purple thaumite around her neck. "I doubt even this would get people to overlook him."

"Probably not."

We're both carefully avoiding the real question, which is, again, *Now what?* After I got tossed out of the palace on my ass, we repaired to a nearby inn with as much dignity as we could muster. The inns on the streets close to the palace are, naturally, the snobbiest in the city, but any reluctance they had to host two rather grubby-looking strangers was overcome with a hefty dose of clinking cash. It's not completely unheard of for Guildblades to hang around in high circles, after all, and they're often hard to tell apart from your average filthy bandit.

Now we're sitting in a cozy nook at the edge of the common room, drinking rather good beer and moping. Uniformed waiters bustle around serving dinner and the better-dressed patrons give us curious looks, but nobody comments.

The silence stretches longer than intended. I stare down into my beer, then finish it off and try to marshal my flagging spirits. Tsav gives an awkward cough.

"Hmm?" I say.

"I was just going to ask how you plan to proceed," Tsav says. "I don't imagine you're planning to give up on getting to Johann."

"I don't think we have another choice. We need someone

with power on our side to convince the humans to negotiate with the horde, and he's the only going candidate. Duke Aster certainly isn't likely to listen to me. He's spent his whole life hunting wilders for sport." I shake my head. "If I can get to Johann, I'm sure I can convince him."

"The question is how much power he still has."

"Usually, he just needs to have his spine stiffened a little." Or a swift kick to his perfect ass. "He's a good person, deep down, he just has a lot of hang-ups to get over."

Tsav gives a noncommittal grunt. I close my eyes for a moment and think.

"I'm going to have to go directly to Johann. As long as I can talk to him, everything will be fine."

"Duke Aster didn't seem inclined to allow that."

"That's why I'm not going to ask him this time. I know how to get in and out of Johann's bedroom without being seen, I've done it often enough."

Tsav's eyebrow twitches. "Are you sure that's a good idea?"

"No, but I don't have another one. Do you?"

She gives a defeated sigh. "I wouldn't know where to start."

"The route I'm thinking of will be easier if I'm alone. You can stay here tonight, and once I'm in, I'll have him send for you."

"You're doing this *tonight*?"

"I don't think we can afford to waste time, do you?"

Tsav purses her lips. "I'm worried about Mari."

It had been a while since I'd thought about her. One part of the plan that *hadn't* worked was the little communicator I'd given Mari so we could keep in touch. I'd tested it a few times after we crossed the mountains and gotten her mental responses, but soon after we reached the Firelands, I'd no longer been able to lock on to the beacon and find her. We'd briefly debated turning back, but ultimately, I didn't think we could afford to wait that long. I'd trusted Mari—and Droff and Leifa and the rest—for a reason, and I'd have to hope she was equal to it.

Tsav fretted more than I did, probably because she wasn't familiar with human magic and its unreliability. Crafting spells that last a long time or work over vast distances is a delicate art, and the odds were strong that I'd simply fucked this one up. Mari is going to kill me when I get back, but I'll deal with that when I come to it.

Either way, though, it raises the urgency. If we *knew* everything was okay back at the horde, we might be able to take our time a little, but as it is, we have to proceed as though we're on the clock.

"Me too," I agree. "All the more reason to get this done quickly."

She gives a tight nod. I grab her hand across the table, then pull back, fingers drumming worriedly.

"There's another thing."

"Oh?" Her voice is tense. I wonder if she's worked this out already.

"If I'm going to get Johann ónside"—deep breath—"I might have to seduce him."

Tsav looks at me levelly. "Seduce him."

"It's the most effective method I've found!"

"I'm sure," she deadpans.

"And you and I haven't really talked about our parameters."

"Our 'parameters'?"

"Our fucking parameters. The parameters of our fucking. Like, in the context of our fucking, am I allowed to bang hot princes if it's the only way to further our *super important mission* of achieving world peace?"

"You want my permission to sleep with Johann."

"Um. Kinda."

"Your ex-boyfriend."

"He's not exactly my ex-boyfriend," I protest. "As far as *he* knows, we've never met. And on my personal time line, every Johann I had a relationship with has died horribly, so he's more like my *late* boyfriend. Only not really, because then this would be necrophilia and I'm not into that. Temporally speaking, it's complicated—"

"Davi."

I trail off. She stares at me, and there's something odd in her eyes. Sadness, but not boo-hoo sadness. More like quiet resignation.

"You'll do what you have to do," Tsav says. "Like you always do."

"I—" I shake my head. "What? Tsav, what do you mean—"

She's already gotten up from the table.

* * *

You'll do what you have to do. Uh, obviously? But does that mean I'm supposed to fuck Johann or not?

Over the centuries, I have developed certain skills—archery, magic, oral sex—to the absolute peak of perfection. But it's possible that certain others have somewhat atrophied from lack of use, and one of them may be the practice of actually being *in* a relationship. It's not something you get a lot of time to work on when your life is all preparing for the wilder invasion and then getting slaughtered in said invasion. I'm not saying I didn't spend a lot of time around certain people while also regularly fucking them, but I have a vague recollection that there's more to it than that.

And it's not as if Himbo Boyfriend Johann ever made a fuss about me finding other partners, unless it was over not bringing them home to share with the class. His general attitude of

"I'm a Prince and social convention doesn't apply to me" was a good match for my "I've been in this time loop too long to give a shit." One of many reasons we're so compatible.

Maybe that's what worries Tsav. Maybe I should have talked to her about it before we got here.

Maybe. Fuck.

These are the thoughts that go through my mind as I equip myself for my late-night rendezvous. My travel-stained clothes plus a gardener's cloak aren't going to cut it here, not if I want to make the right first impression. The outfit I assemble, after a visit to several big outfitters and a few more discreet shops in the alley behind the square, has a vibe I would describe as "slutty ninja."

The secret entrance is in the basement of a run-down tavern around the side of the palace, a surprising distance from the grounds. It gives me a heavy shot of nostalgia as I go in— the peeling plaster, the cracked dartboards, the tables sticky with yesterday's unmentionable fluids. I even recognize the girl behind the bar, a tired-looking blonde with a "Why do I put up with this shit?" attitude. Though the answer is pretty clear, in this case—Johann pays everyone in the establishment for their discretion.

It's like going back to that bar where everybody knows your name.[11] Except nobody here knows my name, because all the good times I've spent here in Johann's company have been rudely erased from existence by my intervening demise(s). My whole life is filled with people I know intimately who don't remember me; is it any wonder this time loop stuff can drive you crazy?

"Hi," I tell the bartender. "I was hoping you had a bottle of the Janus '31."

---

11 You're singing it now, aren't you.

Her eyebrows go up, and she looks around the room before nodding. "There might be one left in the basement. Would you like to come check?"

"Sounds delightful."

She pulls open a trapdoor in one corner and I follow her down a dusty staircase. The basement is indeed full of kegs and bottles, but we walk past all of them to a makeshift door set into the ancient stonework of one wall.

"You know where you're going?" the tired girl says.

"Oh yes." I grin at her. "Not my first rodeo."

She shrugs and opens the door. There's only darkness beyond, but I step confidently through. The air on the other side is colder and smells of damp. Once the girl closes the door behind me, I touch my red thaumite and conjure a tiny light.

The Prince didn't build the tunnels, obviously. I think they used to bring water from the river, back in the days when there was an actual fortress on this site. The Prince found this one when he accidentally demolished the floor in his chamber[12] and quickly realized it was an excellent way of sneaking off from his minders. It's a twisty path to get to his tower, but there are arrows[13] carved into the walls to navigate by.

Eventually I climb a ladder, open another door, and find myself in a servants' stair. This is a narrow, plain thing wrapped around the outer perimeter of the tower where the Prince has his chambers, imaginatively named the Prince's Tower. It's a squat, wide affair rather than one of the fairy-tale spires, so I only have to climb three floors to reach the bedroom. The door there has a convenient peephole, to prevent some servant

---

12 Don't ask. He was a teenager.

13 I mean. I *say* arrows, but they're mostly giant penises pointing the way in showers of jizz. Again, teenager.

bringing a nightcap from walking in on the Prince in flagrante delicto[14] to everyone's mutual embarrassment.[15]

The bedroom is gaudy and over-furnished, dominated by a huge four-poster with silk sheets and a mound of embroidered pillows. Johann isn't here, which is a bit of luck. I slip out of the hidden door and jump on the bed; the little creak it gives fills me with nostalgia and, not to put too fine a point on it, horniness. I've had a lot of good times on this bed. I briefly consider rubbing one out while I wait—if Johann walked in on me, it would *definitely* capture his attention—but that brings Tsav to mind, and the expression on her face as she walked away, and suddenly I'm not feeling it anymore.

Which, fuck. *Fuck.* Come on, Davi, get your head and other relevant bits in the *game*. There's work to do here.

Someone is moving around in the suite outside. I try arranging myself in a seductive position, although honestly, it's been a while since I really engaged in *seduction* beyond the *Nice shoes, wanna fuck?* level, I may have forgotten some of my moves. The ninja outfit isn't helping, it won't drape right and keeps slipping down to loudly shout what I'm trying to slyly suggest. And then, when it slips *particularly* low, I realize I have a bigger problem.

Yes, reader, you may have figured this one out before I did. Congratulations. The thaumite doesn't really feel like anything, so you stop thinking about it, but there's no avoiding the fact that there's a bunch of gems embedded in my flesh just below my collarbone. Even for Johann, this is going to require some explanation, and I'd been hoping to save the complicated questions until *after* I'd wrapped him around my little finger.

---

14 Fucking.

15 Unnecessary for *this* prince. As far as I can tell, Johann is incapable of embarrassment, or even really understanding the concept.

Double fuck. I'm in the midst of sitting up and stuffing my boobs back into the flimsy excuse for a shirt when the door opens and there's a little scream.

Which is odd. Johann wouldn't scream at the sight of a suggestively dressed girl in his bed, whether he'd been expecting her or not. I get myself recombobulated and look up, and then *I* nearly scream, because the person standing in the doorway is *not* Johann. He's shorter and skinnier, maybe twenty years old, with a mop of mousy brown hair and wide-lensed nerd glasses that take up most of his face. He's wearing a nightgown and carrying a thick book under one arm, which he's dropped in his astonishment.

"Who are *you*?" I blurt out before I can think better of it.

"I—who—what—" the strange young man sputters. He looks over his shoulder and then back to me. "Who are *you*? This is my bedroom!"

Fuck me. Has Johann changed his sleeping arrangements? He's never done that before, and all his stuff is still here.

"I'm, um, Tserigern's apprentice," I manage. "Davi. You know Tserigern, the wizard? I'm here to. Uh. Deliver a prophecy?"

"Deliver a *prophecy*? In our bedroom?"

"Sounds like Tserigern," says a blessedly familiar voice from the other room, getting closer. "That dude is always doing weird shit."

Johann appears at last, standing behind the stranger. He's the same as ever, a floppy coif of dark hair and a bright-eyed, careless smile in a face that could have launched *way* more than a thousand ships.

"Should I call the guards?" the young man says.

"Nah." Thank you, Himbo Boyfriend. "Tserigern's a weirdo, but he's a good dude. He knows things. He once helped me figure out why my mushroom salad kept making people puke." Johann waggles his eyebrows. "Turns out it was the mushrooms."

"But—"

Johann pats the stranger's arm. "Davi, you said? What's up? Prophecy?"

"Yeah." I force myself to relax. "My master wanted me to tell you as soon as possible."

"Cool. I'm Johann. You probably already knew that." He grins wider and pats the young man's arm again. "This is my husband, Matthias. Good to meet you."

Chapter Three

You could have knocked me over with a feather.

Not because Johann married a man—he's always been enthusiastically omnisexual—but because Johann got *married*. In 287 lifetimes, I hadn't seen him express any interest in a permanent partnership. He'd married *me* a few times, for political reasons, but that hadn't exactly been an exclusive arrangement.

What's more, the bespectacled Matthias wasn't anyone I knew. Since there certainly hadn't been anyone in the running *before* my origin point—all those other lives proved that—Matthias and the Prince must have met, courted, and consummated in the last four months. Even for Johann, that's fast work.

"Do you know her?" Matthias says.

"Nope," Johann says cheerfully. He leads his doubtful husband into the room and flops onto an upholstered love seat. Matthias sits carefully beside him, clutching his bathrobe as though worried I have designs on his virtue. "Tserigern never mentioned an apprentice."

"I've been...working in secret," I say, thinking as fast as I can. I shift to face them, trying to subtly rearrange my ninja outfit to be a bit less revealing. "In the shadows, you might say."

"In the shadows." Johann grins. "Badass."

"You said something about a prophecy," Matthias says, adjusting his glasses.

"Tserigern told me all about it," Johann says. "There's a bad guy who wants to destroy the whole Kingdom, and there's a totally awesome girl who's going to turn up and save everybody. He always told me I was fated to be her protector or something."

"You never told me about this," Matthias says.

Johann's grin turns sheepish. "It didn't seem that important."

"The Kingdom being destroyed sounds pretty important!"

"Yeah, but . . . it gets saved, right?" He looks to me for confirmation. "It's all taken care of. Or something."

Briefly, I consider switching my story and claiming to be the savior of the Kingdom after all. Johann's obviously primed for it. But "savior that defeats the Dark Lord" is exactly who I *don't* want to be; if the humans get the idea that they should be *fighting* the wilders, then everybody's fucked.

"Besides," Johann goes on before I can say anything, "that all happened already, I think. Tserigern told me the prophecy was going to be fulfilled in a few days when I last saw him, and that was, like, months ago. Before we met." His grin goes sunny again. "I bet he took care of everything himself."

"Evidently not," Matthias says, "since now his apprentice is here."

Johann might not be the sharpest tack in the drawer, but Matthias is giving irritating signs of being one of the smart ones. I clear my throat.

"Things have not gone according to plan, I'm afraid. Tserigern is dead."

"Whoa," Johann says, eyes widening. "I didn't even know he was sick!"

"He was killed," I say patiently. "By the Dark Lord.[1] It falls to me to carry on his work."

"Meaning what, exactly?" Matthias says.

"I have been . . . reinterpreting the prophecy, in light of recent events," I tell them. "I feel confident in my conclusions. No mysterious savior is coming to help us. Johann, *you* are the savior of the Kingdom."

"*Whoa*," the Prince says again. Then, for good measure, "Whoa."

"There's a great deal to prepare before the Dark Lord arrives," I say, hoping to skate over a wide variety of unanswerable questions. "We must speak to the nobles. Defenses need to be arranged—"

Johann holds up a hand and shakes his head. "It's not me you want for that stuff. You need to talk to Pally."

Matthias digs an elbow into the Prince's ribs. "You know he doesn't like it when you call him that."

After a blank moment, I get it. Pally, Pallas, meaning— "Duke Aster?"

"Yeah. In the morning, I can show you the way to his office." Johann frowns. "Well, I can ask someone to show us the way. He'll take care of defending the nobles and things."

"Duke Aster is part of the problem. You need to get rid of him and take your rightful place on the throne, Johann."

The pair of them look at each other. Matthias's big eyes are worried, but Johann only laughs.

"He might be a little hard to get rid of," the Prince says, pulling his husband close, "since I married his cousin!"

* * *

---

1   This isn't actually a lie, just a little temporally confused.

This revelation answers a number of questions but leaves me with a bunch of new ones. *Somehow* Duke Aster has contrived to get Johann to marry one of his family—this Matthias can't be very important, since I'd never heard of him in any previous lives—and in doing so, Johann has put himself under the Duke's thumb, hence Aster lording it up in the throne room.

But why? How? Obviously, whatever he's done is going to have to be *un*done to get things going the way I need them to go. Is Matthias an active part of the Duke's plan, or is he a victim here? Does Aster have some kind of hold on Johann? His thick skull and complete lack of shame make him more or less impervious to blackmail, but—

I spend a little too long contemplating. Matthias coughs.

"I think," he says, "that I would like to go to bed."

"Yeah," Johann says. "This has been fun, Davi, but you'd better go back to your room. We can talk later, you can tell me more about the whole 'prophecy of doom' thing."

Maybe I can salvage *something* from this fucking mess. (Because there's no going back and trying again, not this time, it's *real*—okay, stop, focus.)

"I don't exactly have a room," I say. "I snuck in, remember?"

"Oh." Johann frowns. "Then—"

"But I *would* like to talk to you later."

The Prince's face clears. "Take a room, then. We've got lots."

"Thank you." At least *that* part of the Prince's personality hasn't changed: an instinctive generosity compounded by a complete lack of guile. "If you could send for someone—"

He's already yanking a cord by the bed. There's the distant sound of a bell, and after an interval that seems too short, Jeeves materializes in the bedroom doorway without so much as a footfall.

Ah, Jeeves. Obviously, *I* call him Jeeves. That's not his real name, but he *looks* like a Jeeves. He's sort of a distinguished older gentleman in a dark suit who has been the Prince's major-domo since Johann was a kid. And let me tell you, anyone who has been with Johann during his teenage years has seen some *shit*, so Jeeves is just completely unflappable. He wouldn't lift an eyebrow if all three of us were naked and superimposed, or indeed if we were sacrificing baby goats to Cthulhu.[2]

"Yes, sir?" he says, registering no surprise at my unexpected presence.

"This is Davi," Johann says. "She needs a room. Set her up, will you?"

"Certainly, sir." Jeeves gives a slight bow. "If madam would follow me?"

So that's a win, at least. If I'm the Prince's guest, that gives me the run of the palace whether Duke Aster likes it or not. Although in this new configuration, the Duke might be able to overrule the Prince, so let's just stay out of his way on general principle. Jeeves leads me down from the Prince's Tower and into the adjacent wing, toward one of the palace's apparently endless supply of guest suites.

"I wonder if I could ask," I murmur as we reach the door, "for a messenger to be sent to my companion? She's still in the city, but I'd very much like her to join me."

"Certainly, madam," Jeeves says.

The palace is a lot like a members-only resort in that respect—once you've got a membership card, it's all bowing and scraping and let me shine your shoes, sir. One reason they're careful about handing out the invitations, I guess. Thank God for himbo boyfriends. The suite is clean and cheery, with a bowl of fruit on the table just on the off chance somebody might stop in. I munch a pear—I missed dinner today—and pace anxiously for an hour or so until Tsav arrives.

---

2 "May I bring you a towel, sir?"

"Oh," she says at the sight of me. She's carrying both our packs, and she drops them on the rug with a clatter.

"Oh?" I repeat. "What were you expecting?"

"I had no idea. A man in shiny armor woke me up and told me I had to go to the palace. I figured you'd either succeeded or I was going to get my head chopped off."

"Well, it's neither." I throw myself dramatically into a chair. Tsav seems unimpressed. There's something hard around her eyes. "We have problems."

"Can we have problems tomorrow?"

"I guess?"

"Then I'm going back to bed." She shucks off her cloak and lets it fall to the floor beside the packs. "Good night."

"I didn't fuck him," I blurt out.

"Good for you."

"He's married now. I don't know—"

"Tomorrow, Davi," Tsav says. She shuffles into one of the suite's bedrooms and closes the door firmly behind her.

Well. Fuck.

* * *

It takes me a long time to get to sleep. I keep replaying my conversation with the Prince, wondering what I'm going to do about him. And then when I finally manage to shut that down, I'm replaying my conversations with Tsav and wondering what I'm going to do about *her*.

God damn it. Have I fucked this up already? I didn't think far enough ahead and now I'm *stuck* and I can't *go back*—

Then I think about Matthias, with his big glasses and his tousled just-shagged hair, and it takes me a while to realize that I'm *jealous*. Johann is *my* himbo boyfriend! Grr, hiss, invasion of territory, bark bark bark. Maybe I should piss on him to make it clear. It's been a minute since I've reacted like this, but the novelty quickly wears thin.

Emotions, man. Who fucking asked for them?

Needless to say, when morning rolls around, I am not exactly well rested. I stagger into the dining room to find Tsav poking suspiciously at the breakfast that has materialized while we slept.

"What *are* these?" she says, poking something yellow and wobbly.

"Eggs."

"They don't look like eggs."

"Welcome to high cuisine. Nothing looks like what it actually is." I grab one of the little rolled-up omelets, a bit like *tamagoyaki* but drizzled with honey. When I pop it into my mouth, I literally almost fall over, my knees go so wobbly.

Fuck. Food. I forgot that food could be . . . food. Good. Food good.

It takes a few seconds for higher brain function to return. It has been a while, let's say, since I was in the presence of masters of the culinary arts. For the last few months, my diet has varied from "half a hardtack cracker and muddy water" to "meat hopefully cooked all the way through," depending on our circumstances. Hunger may make the best sauce, but goddamn if cinnamon honey butter doesn't give it a run for its money.

Tsav, watching me, picks up one of the omelets and gives it a little sniff, then throws it in her mouth. I watch the expression on her face change over several seconds until she takes a shaky breath.

"It's *pretty* good," she allows. "Could use more meat."

I snort, but put further conversation on hold because there's more. A *lot* more, the palace kitchens don't stint the guests. There's airy bread and sharp cheese and pastries so delicate they crumble if you glance sidelong at them, revealing centers drippling with fruit jam. There's meat enough to please even

Tsav in the form of various fried bits of pig. There are things cut up small and stuffed inside other things.

You'd think after a thousand years, I'd be blasé about this sort of thing. But just as bodies can never be convinced not to freak out about having pieces chopped off, so, too, will they always throw excited parades when you shovel in sugar and starch garnished with salty fat. I've had a lot of bad times in this palace, but living in the lap of luxury definitely has its attractions too. If I'm honest, I hadn't reckoned with how much I missed it.

Eventually, having reached the limits of gastric capacity, Tsav and I sag in opposite chairs and look at each other over the remains. She carefully cleans the engravings on her tusks with a napkin, and I try to figure out what to say.

So, are we still fucking or what? lacks a certain something, right?

"Do you want to talk—" I manage to begin.

"Not really." She puts the napkin down. "Where do we stand with the Prince?"

I explain what happened last night, with particular emphasis on everyone remaining fully clothed at all times. Tsav frowns when I get to the part about the Duke using Matthias to entrap Johann.

"Just because they're related, you think they're plotting together?"

"That's how it works here," I explain. Among wilders, chosen families and bands can be more important than literal blood ties. "It's all lines of descent and who married who three generations back. What family you're born into determines what team you play for."

"But you said you didn't know anything about Matthias from your past lives."

"There's a lot of nobility. Even I can't keep track of them

all, especially the ones who don't come to the palace. That just means Matthias wasn't anyone important before now."

"So, how did he end up married to the Prince?"

"That's what we're going to discover." I pause. "Or at least that's what I'm going to discover. No offense, but this may be out of your league."

Her eyes are hooded. "Really."

"Really. The palace runs on gossip. I know how to tap into it and get a picture of what people are saying." At her expression, I add, "It's a tricky business! You can't be *obviously* nosy."

"And what do you want me to do while you're listening at keyholes?"

"Look through the library and see what you can find on Cyrus and the other Founders. There's a lot of myth, but we want the best guess as to what actually happened."

"Hmm." Tsav rubs one tusk thoughtfully. "That could take a while, if the library is as big as you say."

"I know. We need to get through this and get back to the horde." Guilt gnaws at me. "I tried to contact Mari again last night and didn't get anywhere. She knows how long we were going to take getting here, so I'm sure she's still keeping a lid on things, but—"

"Yeah." Tsav pushes back from the table. "I'd better get started, then."

I guess we're just leaving whatever-this-is hanging between us to fester another day, then. Why the fuck not? I show her how to use one of the discreet bellpulls to summon a servant who can guide her to the library. If the man is uncertain who exactly we are, he doesn't show it.[3]

For my own part, it's time for another costume change, since

---

3   In fairness, we're hardly the oddest guests the Prince has installed without telling anybody.

neither travel-stained explorer nor ninja prostitute is ideal for roaming the halls of the palace in relative obscurity. Fortunately, the servants will help you take care of that, too, and before long I'm picking out an acceptable suit and jacket in the current fashion. While it's being altered to fit, I go into the bathroom to get cleaned off, and—

Fuck. Bath. Warm. Bath good. Davi melting.

Whew. Okay. It's not even so much *having* a bath—that can be arranged even out in the Wilds—it's being able to turn the tap above the gold-chased clawfoot tub and have hot water come spilling out in a beautiful unending torrent. And there's little mother-of-pearl boxes with salts and fragrant oils and little cakes of soap shaped like seashells.

This bath is big enough for Tsav to climb in here with me, if we squeeze a little. I can sit in her lap with her arms around me, leaning my head back against her—

Fuck. *Fuck.*

Enough of this. Head in the game, Davi. Thousands of probably-definitely-real lives are riding on you, worry about a spat with your girlfriend later. I dress and brush my hair and straighten my jacket and shoot my cuffs and generally feel like a proper human again for the first time in a while.

Time to find out what the *fuck* is going on.

* * *

There is a knack, or rather an art, to gossip.

The trick is to be both an insider and an outsider. Part of the club, but also not—the kind of person you'd be happy to share juicy stories with, but who probably wouldn't already know them. You can't *ask*, but you can share a story of your own and wait for reciprocity to kick in.

The servants always have the most accurate information, so

I pose as one of them. The outfit I selected is appropriate for a senior manservant of visiting nobility; palace servants hold themselves as superior to anyone from the sticks, and they're eager to show off. The news that strange new friends of the Prince have arrived is spreading fast, and everybody saw Tsav come in late last night, so naturally I claim to be attached to this new curiosity. Stories about the mysterious woman, with her shabby clothes and impressive build, are excellent currency belowstairs.

"She's from the far south," I tell a chambermaid while she folds linens. "A border noble. A real warrior."

"The stories they tell about her," I inform an underbutler checking barrels of wine, "are hard to believe, but the household swears they're true. I heard that she brought down a wilder the size of a barn with her bare hands."

"Just jumped up on its back, wrapped her arms around its neck, and squeezed," I assure a fascinated group of potboys who should be scouring. "Brought it down, then walked right off and ordered a whole stoneboar for dinner, calm as you please."

"And, of course, she's a notorious beauty," I whisper to a scandalized kitchen girl elbow-deep in stuffing a pig. "Left a trail of broken hearts across half the frontier, that one."

In return for this vital data, I get the goings-on of the palace, the things everyone knows but nobody says out loud. Some of it is just as accurate as my own offerings, of course, but with enough samples one can cross-collate and arrive at an approximation of the truth.

Thus—the Queen is ill and mostly retired, just as I recall. Some people in the court were trying to get the Prince to step up and take on more responsibility, while others thought the Duke would make a better leader. Check, check, all good so far. Then the Duke came to town with a retinue of family in tow, and—

"They fell in love at first sight," says the chambermaid with an envious sigh, twirling a ringlet of brown hair around one finger. "Their eyes met across a crowded room, and Prince Johann just knew that Matthias was the one."

"The Prince finally met his match, right?" the kitchen girl tells me in low tones. "You know how he is, bringing in new boys and girls every day of the week. But the Duke picked this Matthias because he's the best lover in Sarton, and he fucked our Johann so good that now he's got him wrapped around his little finger."

"It was an alliance," the underbutler pronounces. "Very practical. Everyone knows the Duke would be better on the throne, but this way, the Prince can be king and just let the Duke handle everything."

"Matthias is a big crybaby," one of the potboys informs me solemnly. "He came out to play kickrock with us once and had to go inside after just one round. Tommard didn't even kick him that hard."

This last may or may not be useful.

In any event, having married the young cousin of Duke Aster, the Prince has happily agreed to let his new uncle take over his public functions. *That* sounds like Johann, frankly, who was always happy to pass off what he called "boring shit" to someone else.[4] Since then, the Duke has been more or less in charge, and the Queen has retired to a private retreat to get on with dying.

What I'm still missing is the *why*. Something has knocked events off their usual path; if I let this dynamic play out, what normally happens is that eventually Johann reluctantly takes the throne and makes a bit of a hash of things. On the other hand, maybe the why isn't actually that important—it's been

---

4 A useful trait when that someone is *me*.

four months, which is plenty of time for the proverbial butterfly to cause the proverbial hurricane. It rained for five more minutes, so somebody didn't step in dogshit and yadda yadda yadda the world ends in fire.

I'm used to thinking in terms of what I could change for next time, but obviously that's not useful anymore. This is really real and everything I do counts, every day that passes is one more day gone and never to be recovered and, *fuck*, how do you people *live* with the *constant existential crisis?*

Anyway.

When I return to our room after a long day of whispers and innuendo, a servant is waiting to inquire if madam would like dinner brought up. Madam *most certainly* would, please and thank you. The page bows and hands over a creamy envelope sealed with blue wax, then shimmers out. I recognize the seal on the note, a stag beetle rampant—Aster.

I'm sitting at the table and contemplating the note when Tsav arrives, looking a little haggard and clutching a thick sheaf of paper. I feel a brief pang of sympathy.

"Food's coming," I tell her.

"Thank the Old Ones," she says, collapsing into a chair. "I couldn't figure out how to get lunch."

"Ask a servant. That's the answer to everything."

"They all seem so . . . busy." The palace attitude of effortless condescension toward the staff doesn't come naturally to Tsav, which probably speaks well of her.

"Did you have any problems finding what we need?"

"One of the librarians was *very* snooty at me," Tsav says. "But, no. Honestly, there's too much." She pats her stack of notes. "This is just the start. Fortunately, not everyone was unhelpful."

Once again, I'm impressed by this woman's sheer . . . *persistence*. When I met her, she was the head of a raider band eking out a living on the edge of the Kingdom, always one step ahead of murderous Guildblades. Then *I* turned up in her life and blew it the fuck apart, and pretty soon she's a general officer in a rapidly growing horde, with paperwork and strength reports and drills. And she just sort of rolls with it, puts her head down and works and does a fucking great job.

And *then* I unload my whole insane life story of time loops and other worlds and "Oh yeah, you just *died*," and she handles that like a champ! Now here we are in a completely foreign place and I ask her to do research on some weird mythological figure and she just *does* it. I feel like I would be on the floor in a sobbing ball by now. Hell, I *was* on the floor in a sobbing ball and *she* got me out of it!

And in every other life I've lived, this brave, beautiful hero was hacked to pieces with a dozen other wilders, and I didn't even *notice*. One more dead orc with a pathetic little bit of thaumite, barely worth looting. How many other stories like hers are there? How many will get cut off, for really real this time, if I can't stop the horde from trashing the Kingdom or vice versa?

These thoughts, unbidden, land on my good mood like a falling boulder and send jellied bits in all directions. I spend a moment just breathing.

"Davi?" Tsav leans closer. "Are you all right?"

No. "Yes. Sorry. What did you find?"

"It'll take a couple more days, I think," Tsav says, looking down at her notes. "I'm trying to compare the different sources like you said, but I've got to go through them all first."

"Good." I breathe out. "That's good."

"What about you? Get anything useful?"

"A little bit." I explain the gist. "I still don't know *why* the Prince got married, but everyone agrees that it was the key to the Duke taking over. That's something. And then there's this." I tap the now-open envelope.

"What is it?"

"A love note from the Duke. He wants to have a chat." I make a face.

"That's progress, right?" Tsav says. "Yesterday he wouldn't even talk to you."

"I doubt it'll be any more productive."

Tsav gives a quiet shrug. "Maybe you should keep an open mind. I know you thought Johann was the only one who might listen, but if he's not interested, isn't it possible the Duke is?"

"Only if he sees something in it for himself. I know Aster."

"You knew the Prince too."

A touch, for certain. I open my mouth to reply, hesitate, and then two servants arrive with steaming platters, and the smell of them obliterates all thought. Food *good* om nom nom.

Chapter Four

In the morning, the news is everywhere: There's been a wilder raid in the north, a big one, more than the local defenders can handle. Duke Aster, ever eager to slaughter a few wilders, has called for a hunt—he intends to ride out personally along with whatever nobles and Guildblades want to get in on the fun. Providing the supplies, equipment, mounts, and so on for this expedition on such short notice is a strain on the palace's logistics, and everyone is running back and forth in a tizzy.

Amid this air of chaos, Tsav has gone back to the library while I wait to be summoned. Around midday, a servant wearing Aster's stag beetle badge and a bad attitude arrives and deigns to inform me that the great man is prepared to suffer my presence. I follow her to another wing of the palace, where she ushers me into a private dining room elaborately decorated with a fresco depicting the Eight Founders. A big table has been laid for two, and Duke Aster is at one end of it, cutting up something rare and bloody with a silver knife.

"Davi," he says, "apprentice of the great Tserigern. Sit, please."

I spare a moment to glance around. The servant has shut the door behind me, and there are no others in the room; whatever we're going to discuss, the Duke would like it to be very private indeed. I briefly contemplate just fucking killing him, which would solve a lot of problems. But there are several large pieces of thaumite embedded in his jewelry, and he's plenty experienced in personal combat. I could probably take him with the gems in my pouch, but I couldn't keep it quiet, and that would be worse than useless.

Putting these thoughts of murder aside, I plaster a bland smile on my face and take the chair opposite him. The food looks appetizing, but I refrain for now. Duke Aster continues to slash his steak into bloody shreds and savor each bite.

"I wanted to apologize," he says, patting juice from his chin with an embroidered napkin. "Your appearance in the throne room was unexpected, and I may have reacted hastily. Tserigern, as you say, has always been a friend to the throne." He pauses. "Is he likely to join us?"

"No," I say. "Not likely."

"Pity." Aster licks his lips and reaches for his wineglass.

"I can speak for him," I say. "If you're willing to listen."

"My understanding," the Duke says, "is that Tserigern insisted he was following a prophecy, revealed specifically to him, about a new Dark Lord who would arise to threaten the Kingdom. A savior would be sent to us—I was never quite clear on how—and only if we went along with them could we escape destruction. Is that about right?"

"That is . . . one interpretation," I say carefully. Could he actually be willing to listen? "There have been additional revelations, shall we say, that have changed our understanding of what's to come. That's why I'm here."

"Interesting. I assume these revelations aren't along the lines of 'The Dark Lord is not a threat after all'?" At the look on my face, he laughs. "They never are. What would a prophet of doom be without his doom?"

"There *is* a new Dark Lord," I say flatly. "She has already been chosen at the wilders' Convocation. Her horde will come to the borders of the Kingdom, sooner rather than later."

"How exactly do you know this?"

"What would a prophet of doom be without a few secrets?"

Duke Aster snorts. "Fine. So, as Tserigern would have it, we ought to be looking for his 'savior.' If I recall correctly, he was very specific about the time and place this person would appear."

"That is where we have had to reinterpret prophecy in light of recent events."

"Lovely. That's the best thing about prophecy, really." He smiles, and there's something lizard-like about it. "And it's what I wanted to speak to you about. If we're *reinterpreting*, then that might provide us with an opportunity for . . . mutual benefit."

The Duke sets his wineglass down and steeples his hands.

"For example," he goes on, "perhaps the notion that the savior would *arrive* is wrong. Perhaps the savior is *already here*. Someone we all know. It was"—he waves his hand vaguely—"a metaphor, an allegory, one of those things the poets are so fond of. What it *really* means is that somebody will step up to the challenge and we should all do what he says."

"I don't think—" I begin.

"Let me be blunt," the Duke interrupts. "I don't believe in prophecy. Maybe there is a new Dark Lord, maybe not. If there is, the forces of the Kingdom will meet her in battle and destroy her as they have many times before. Tserigern was a doddering old fool, but his starry-eyed nonsense had a certain following, and right now the Kingdom needs unity. If you, the old man's apprentice, were to proclaim that *I* was the savior that we all must follow, well . . ."

"It's not about who's the savior," I say, but my heart is already sinking. "There are steps that must be taken."

"And I promise to take them," the Duke says, waving his hand again. "Defending the Kingdom against the Dark Lord is obviously in my interest, is it not? Of course I would be happy to take any appropriate precautions. And *you* can remain at court as official royal prognosticator, with your own rooms and a nice salary instead of whatever hovel the old man has you sleeping in. A reasonable bargain, I would say?"

I stare across the table at him. He gives me that lizard smile and cuts another bite off his steak.

What I want to say is: "I know you, Pallas Aster. I've lived with you. I've *fucked* you, for my sins. You're a small-minded, incurious time-server who accepts the subservience of the world as his due for having squirted from the right vagina, and all you've ever accomplished in your miserable life is using the magical prowess your station affords to slaughter a bunch of people for the crime of living on land somebody wants. You've climbed to the top of this little fishbowl and you think it makes you king shit. But the horrible truth is that if it wasn't you, it'd be someone else, because there are a hundred more right behind you and just as bad."

I didn't realize until just now how much I hate this guy.

If I were still in the business of trying to save the Kingdom by leading a heroic defense against the wilders, I might consider his offer. Because he's right, in some sense—getting the lords of the Kingdom to work *together* is the hardest part of the whole business. I never actually tried murdering Tserigern and taking his place before, it's an interesting approach I might have been inclined to experiment with.

Might have, once. But there's no room for experiments now, and anyway I don't want the humans to *beat* the wilders, I want to defuse this whole Dark Lord thing without everyone winding up dead so I have time to figure out the time loop business and maybe finally live long enough to worry about gray hairs and back pain. If I tell the Duke that the prophecy demands he *stop* fighting the wilders, he'll have me out of here on my ass so fast I'll leave skid marks. If he doesn't just toss me in the dungeon.

"I will have to consider the prophecy," I say after a long moment. "And consult some secret wisdom and shit."

"I see." The Duke's smile fades away. "I imagine that secret wisdom takes a great deal of deciphering."

"You wouldn't believe."

"Well. Keep me informed." His chair screeches on the polished floor as he stands abruptly. "I have business to attend to. The hunt approaches, you know."

"So I hear."

Halfway to the door, he pauses as though a thought has just occurred to him. "In fact, perhaps it would be best if you accompanied me. I would hate for there to be some question arising from your secret wisdom that I might be able to answer. Time is of the essence, I'm sure."

I stare at him. He may still be speaking in euphemisms, but the mask is off now and his expression is cold. His face says that this is not a request.

"I'm here as a guest of the Prince," I venture.

"That settles it, then," he says without even a fake smile. "The Prince and his husband are joining us."

"I see." I raise my eyebrows. "In that case, of course I'll come along as well."

"Splendid. We depart in the morning."

"I'll be ready." I pick up a knife and fork and point to the rest of his steak. "Mind if I eat this?"

* * *

I don't actually eat it, don't be gross. I don't want Duke-cooties.[1]

Say what you like about Pallas Aster, but he's not *entirely* stupid. At first, he thought I was just some crazy weirdo[2] and tried to blow me off completely. Now, though, he's worried that I am who I claim to be—that is, a representative of Tserigern—which means that I might be able to at least irritate him. As he said, there are some people in the court who take the old wizard seriously. What he absolutely does not want is for me to declare someone *else* the savior—like, say, the Prince—while he's off gallivanting in the woods slaughtering everything that moves.

Accordingly, I get invited to come along so he can keep an eye on me, which doubles as a not-particularly-subtle threat. Out on the hunt, surrounded by Guildblades, I'll be comfortably in his power. (Or *would* be in his power, I should say, if I were actually some half-crazed hedge-wizard and not the fucking Dark Lord.) I can't refuse, so if I don't want to go, Tsav and I would have to flee the palace, and that wouldn't help our standing.

So, a-hunting we will go. But I need to talk it through with Tsav, so after pacing and muttering to myself for a while, I go to find her.

The library is in one of the oldest parts of the palace, a grand vaulted stone hall that was once the primary audience chamber. Subsequent additions have moved most activity into newer, more fashionable buildings, and some past monarch had the bright idea to convert the gloomy place into a library. From the outside, it looks more like a cathedral than anything else, set among its own gardens and surrounded by dilapidated outbuildings.

---

1 But there's an untouched dish of those fried potato-mushroom cakes swimming in butter, and fuck if I'm letting *that* go to waste.

2 Which, fair.

When I push through the heavy double door, the smell of the place is an instant trigger for hundreds of years of memories. Dust and books and old stone, with the hushed quality that makes visitors feel like ants trespassing in some vast emptiness. Bookshelves tall enough to need their own rolling ladders[3] form several aisles down the length of the old reception hall.

At the raised end of the room, where the throne used to be, there are huge scarred tables for the use of visiting scholars. I've spent many hours here across many lifetimes, reading everything the Kingdom has to offer on whatever subjects seemed relevant. Even that wasn't enough to fully plumb the depths of the library, though. The rate of book accumulation has varied with each passing monarch, but the sum total has gone far past the critical threshold where anyone can keep track of it all. Its coverage tends to be deep but spotty, with well-stocked sections reflecting some dead king's interest in, say, lace making or butterflies.

No scholars seem to be in residence at present, so it's easy to spot Tsav bent over her notes at a table stacked high with books. I start to hurry over, then pause, because she's not alone. There's a young man with her, light gleaming off the broad lenses of his glasses.

There's no reason why *he* should be here. And yet here he indisputably is. I finish my approach at a more measured pace, watching the two of them; they sit across the table from each other, reading and periodically making notes. As I watch,

---

3 If you try to do the Belle thing, what happens is that just as you reach the crescendo—"provincial *liiiiiife!*"—the ladder hits the end of its track and whips you off, you slam into the opposite bookshelf, break your neck when you hit the marble floor, and then about ten tons of books topple over and bury you. Ask me how I know.

Matthias tears a strip of paper to make a bookmark, then hands the volume he's reading across to Tsav.

They're so absorbed that neither one of them looks up, in spite of my sharp footsteps on the stone floor. Eventually I clear my throat pointedly.

"Davi!" Tsav glances at Matthias, and I swear there's a hint of guilt on her face. "I wasn't expecting to see you until dinner." She gives an awkward cough. "This is Matthias, he's been helping me. Matthias, this is—"

"We've met," Matthias says stiffly, inclining his head the slightest fraction.

Apparently, Matthias hasn't shared certain pertinent facts, like the name of his husband. Well. There's nothing actually *wrong* with his helping Tsav, it's not like our research into Cyrus is relevant to the whole Johann–Duke Aster problem. But I still haven't figured out if Matthias is an innocent victim in whatever scheme the Duke is running, or if he's been in on it from the beginning. And clearly, he's not particularly happy with *me*, which is perhaps understandable. Sooooo, this should be interesting.

"Matthias is a scholar," Tsav says, "and his specialty is the Founding era. He's been very helpful."

"Oh, you're overselling me." Matthias reddens, his guardedness vanishing for a moment under habitual self-deprecation. "I'm an amateur with a lot of time on my hands for reading, at best."

"That's about ninety percent of the way to a scholar," I say, dropping onto a chair beside Tsav, "and the rest is having *really* strong opinions about minor points of academic etiquette. Thank you for taking the time to help."

"Yes, well." He adjusts his glasses. "I wasn't actually aware that Tsav was your companion. But she seemed lost, and it happens that I have *some* familiarity with the area she's interested in."

"We've about gone through the main sources," Tsav says, gesturing at the piles of books. "I was just putting everything together, but since you're here, Matthias might as well fill you in on the basics. He still knows them better than me."

"I—" Matthias straightens up, taken aback. "I suppose I could. If Davi is interested."

I try to catch Tsav's eye, but she's buried her nose in the book again. I guess it can't *hurt* to get to know Matthias a little. Disentangling him from Johann still seems like my best play, but doing it is going to require delving into what kind of scheme got them together in the first place. And I *am* curious about Cyrus.

"Fascinated," I tell him, and do my best to look disarming.

"Well." He clears his throat. "Where should I begin?"

"I know some of the mythology," I say. "But I'm interested in what about Cyrus is actually *real*."

"That's the key question, obviously." Matthias adjusts his glasses again. He still looks suspicious, but as he talks his voice becomes more animated. His enthusiasm for the material is obviously not feigned. "We have good evidence that the basics of the myth are true. Our people came here from somewhere to the east, led by the eight heroes we know as the Founders."

"The east" includes the ruined city but doesn't actually narrow it down that much—all that's west is ocean. "Were the Founders human? In the myths, they sound more like demigods."

"They certainly called themselves human," Matthias says, warming to his subject. "But some of their verifiable feats are beyond the abilities of any wizard today. There are limits to the amount of power that can be channeled through a human body, no matter how much thaumite you wield. Somehow the Founders were able to surpass them. They used their power in the initial battles with wilders that carved out the Kingdom, though four of the eight died in the process. The first king, Artem, was a child of Founder Atlian, and the Founders continued to advise several generations of his descendants."

"*Several* generations?" I frown. "How long did they live?"

"Evidence is...thin," Matthias says. "But otherwise reliable chronicles mention the Founders for several centuries after the Kingdom was established. It's another of the central mysteries of their existence. Magister Rowl claims that the name was assumed by apprentices, but Magister Frank's analysis suggests..."

I stop paying attention for a bit. Something is tickling the back of my mind, some idea, but I can't quite put a finger on it.

"Okay," I say once the academic debate has wound down. "What about Cyrus?"

"He's often described as the most enigmatic of the Founders," Matthias says, excited. "He survived the Founding itself, obviously, but once the Kingdom was established, he appears in the sources only rarely, and always in the company of one of the others. There's remarkably little about his personality or goals, as compared to someone like Atlian. He was apparently a great wizard and held himself somewhat aloof from ordinary affairs."

"And what happened to him?"

"He and Founder Satorel were the last of the eight. They went together to fight an Old One, a dragon that had wreaked untold havoc on the Kingdom's eastern border." I perk up at the mention of a dragon, the one entry in the fantasy bestiary that has been conspicuous by its absence from my adventures. "The creature was destroyed, but both Founders died of their wounds, and the site of the battle was lost in the devastation. For a long time, Guild treasure-hunters searched for it, hoping to plunder the thaumite, but it was never found."

Well, *that's* not suspicious at all. "So, how certain are we that Cyrus actually died there?"

"Not certain at all!" Matthias says. When he grins, dimples appear in his cheeks, and for a moment, I understand what Johann sees in him. He's kind of adorkable. "There are no confirmed mentions of Cyrus after that, but Magister Ventoss argues..."

I tune out again for a bit, the Duke problem briefly driven from my mind. So these Founders have special powers and are maybe-kinda immortal. Cyrus comes here from the lost city and hangs around for a while, then disappears under mysterious circumstances. Then, however many centuries later, he's chatting up Tserigern and telling him about a "prophecy" of a savior, which leads directly to me.

There's a lot of assumptions in there—for starters, that the Cyrus who talked to Tserigern really is the Founder—but it *kind* of hangs together. Cyrus is a grumpy old dude who's all, "I *guess* I'll save the Kingdom, grumble grumble," and after a while he nopes out and goes off to hide under a rock somewhere. But then he gets word that a new Dark Lord is going to destroy the Kingdom, so he's like *fine* and turns up again to—

To *what*? That's where it falls apart. If he's interested in saving the Kingdom, where the *fuck* has he been for these past 287 lives? Why send Tserigern to *me* rather than turning up and doing it himself? He's a *Founder*, there'd be no better way to get the Kingdom to fall in line than just announcing himself. For that matter, he's the one going around slaying dragons and so on, why not just get himself to the Convocation and zap the Dark Lord before he gets started?

But instead, there's me. Ordinary girl from Earth, no special powers other than a can-do attitude and a high tolerance for pain. Did *Cyrus* do that? Did he somehow summon me across worlds and stick me in a time loop, then fuck off back to Club Med for Wizards? "Don't worry about the whole Dark

Lord thing, Davi'll figure it out eventually, I'm sure." What the *fuck?*

And *then* there's the change in the loop at the Convocation, the cause of all my current angst. Tsav said it can't have been coincidence, and I'm inclined to agree. Maybe Cyrus just sort of liked what he was seeing and hit the Save Game button? The thought that some ancient wizard is *watching* me struggle along, like a kid looking on as all the ants in his colony die, is simultaneously creepy and *utterly rage inducing.* I swear to every fucking god, if I find out that's what's going on, I'm going to kill him *so hard* his fucking *ancestors* will die. That makes no goddamn sense but I'm going to do it anyway.

It still feels wrong, though. Like there's something I'm missing. If Cyrus wants me to save the Kingdom, why would he just leave me alone with only *Tserigern* for help? A few pointers could have saved me literally centuries of hard work—

I become aware that Matthias has stopped talking.

"Okay," I say. "Thank you. That's very helpful." I glance at Tsav, and she raises her eyebrows. "I think my companion and I are needed for dinner, but I hope we'll be able to talk again soon? I'm sure I'll have more questions."

Matthias deflates a little, fiddling with his glasses. "It may be a while. Johann insists on going with the Duke on his ridiculous hunt. But when we return, certainly."

Tsav's eyes widen a bit at the Prince's name, but she doesn't speak up until I've made our excuses and we've retreated from the library.

"He knows Johann?" she asks me as we walk back to our room.

"He's *married* to Johann. That's the husband. The one who's Duke Aster's cousin. It didn't come up?"

"We didn't talk about much except research." Tsav rubs her bald head with one hand. "He's . . . very enthusiastic."

"Not only did Duke Aster make Johann get married, he made him marry a *nerd*. The situation is worse than I thought." I shake my head. "And speaking of Duke Aster..."

* * *

"I could walk faster than this," Tsav complains, crossing her legs uncomfortably.

I sigh. "Probably."

The landscape slowly unrolls around us, fields and pastures and tame woodlands. At least the rain has stopped.

"I could carry all our *stuff* and walk faster than this," Tsav says.

"*You* could," I point out, "but some pasty little nobleman who's never lifted anything heavier than his father's disapproval couldn't. Especially considering he probably has a lot more stuff."

"Then we should leave him behind," she grumbles. "I thought this was a hunt."

"It's *kind* of a hunt." I give her a sidelong look. "You know who we're hunting, right?"

Tsav snorts, but I can sense her unease. Some of that comes from our position on the box of a slow-moving cart; draft animals are foreign to most wilders, and she eyes the elderly mare in the traces with deep suspicion. The royal stables had offered us riding horses, but that was obviously a nonstarter for Tsav, so I'd talked them into lending us a cart.

The vehicle they'd come up with was more suited to hauling animal feed than going on a grand hunt, but it's right at home amid the tail of the column. Up ahead, the Duke, the Prince, and Aster's closest cronies lead the way, brilliant as peacocks in colorful silks atop their gleaming white mounts; back here are the wagons full of tents, gear, food, and drink. *Especially* drink. Some of the carts are just giant tuns on wheels.

For the moment, it's still a relatively small party as these things go, the Duke and a dozen retainers plus ten times that many servants and porters. But Aster has put the word out. In theory, the Queen—and thus in her absence, the Duke—has the right to call on the feudal service obligations of the nobles of the Kingdom and muster them for battle; in practice, this opens up such a complicated legal can of worms that nobody does it short of outright civil war. Given his position as a Grand Slayer of the Guild of Adventurers, the Duke has a much easier alternative: Just announce a time and place and let the murder-hobo whisper network bring together a horde of heavily armed lunatics ready for action. The rendezvous is near the northern border, a few days' ride on a fast horse or a bit longer if you're hauling enough wine to drown a small village.

Some of the servants, I'm sure, are keeping surreptitious tabs on Tsav and me, making sure we aren't sneaking off or trying to get in touch with the Prince. I would actually deeply like to talk to Johann and see how willingly he's along for this ride, but the Duke is keeping him and Matthias close. So I bide my time.

When we camp, it's just me and Tsav in our slightly leaky human-style tent. Me and Tsav in decidedly separate bedrolls, or in her case just a pile of furs she burrows into like a nest. It's a very comfortable nest, especially with her in it all warm and soft and breathing gently on the back of your neck, but she's made it clear that these delights are not for me at the present.

I keep trying to talk to her about it, about *us*, and she keeps evading. She doesn't seem *angry*, exactly, and she's not sulking. We're just . . . not fucking anymore? I guess.

It seriously sucks, if we're being honest.

Is this really because I asked if I could fuck Johann? I didn't even *get* to, that seems very unfair. And I may not be the *best* romantic companion, okay, I can be a little weird and I've forgotten a lot about how to human and I've killed, like, a *lot* of people, but on the plus side, I'm funny and cute and I can do that thing with my tongue.

And if I've fucked this up somehow, then this is *it* and I don't get another chance, God *damn* it—

Fuck.

And so we wend our way north, in a cloud of horse excrement and sexual frustration.

* * *

When we reach the rendezvous, a stretch of pastureland beside a placid lake, it's already thick with tents. The Duke has called and the Guildblades have come, hundreds of them, an impromptu convention of magically augmented psychos with dubious origin stories.[4] They line the road to greet the royal procession, cheering and waving swords in the air, enthusiastic for the Duke and the Prince but ecstatic at the sight of all the wine. We make camp even though it's barely midday, and the stewards begin preparing the feast.

The young woman who turns up outside our tent has clearly been preparing, too, and has somehow managed to keep her page's uniform pristine, the Duke's beetle emblem proudly embroidered at the collar. Even her boots are still shiny. She looks me up and down dubiously and clears her throat.

"His Grace does you the honor of inviting you to his table for dinner tonight," she says with a superior sniff. "You will be expected at sundown."

---

4 Seriously, try talking to them sometime, it's always the same. "My family were all slaughtered by wilders, so I dedicated myself to a life of revenge." Oh, really, funny coincidence, that's what the last guy said! Come on, dude, you ran away from your dad's farm because your older brothers made fun of you, and the neighbor girl wouldn't put out. And your name is Chadwick, not Revensgore the Umber Dread.

"Is there a vegan option?" I ask her. "I bet there isn't. There's never a vegan option at these things."

The page blinks and narrows her eyes, eventually deciding, correctly, that I'm making fun of her. She pulls herself up so straight that she's in danger of leaving the ground, turns on her heel, and stalks off.

"What's a vegan?" Tsav asks from inside the tent. "Is it tasty?"

"You know what, I'm going with yes. All-natural and free-range. Good marbling."

She bends over to lace up her boots, and I take the opportunity to admire the curve of ass thus presented. "I take it we're going to attend," she says.

"Doesn't sound like we have much choice. I'm going to try to get Johann alone later in the evening. We need to figure out what the Duke has over him, and he's likely to be more forthcoming once he's drunk."

Tsav straightens up. "Anything *I* should do?"

I purse my lips. "You and Matthias are friends now, try drinking him under the table and see what happens."

"I wouldn't say we're *friends*."

"You'd be surprised. I don't think he has many." That was something that had come up in my gossipmongering— the Prince's husband didn't get out much. Small wonder he thought the chance to lecture me on Cyrus was exciting. "Get him wasted and see if he admits to any evil schemes."

"He didn't seem like a scheming sort of person," Tsav says. "I like him, actually."

I make a face. I'm prejudiced against Johann's husband for being inconvenient, but on balance I have to admit Tsav is right. Unless he's a fantastic actor, the vibes he gives off are more bewildered naïf than nefarious mastermind. That pointed in the direction of him being an innocent victim of his cousin's plans, since someone like Aster probably couldn't get out of *bed* without scheming along the way.

"Do what you can," I tell Tsav. I hesitate a moment, then add, "And . . . be careful."

She shrugs into her leather coat and fiddles with the collar. "Careful of what?"

"These are Guildblades. They're not likely to show up to dinner loaded with protective magic, but they're not *un*likely to do that either, right? If anything is going to be a problem for that"—I indicate the purple thaumite glowing on Tsav's chest—"it's going to be a collection of paranoid lunatics like these guys. And if they *do* find you . . ."

I trail off, unwilling to even think about the consequences. It would be difficult to think of a crowd more inclined to hack first and ask questions later.

Tsav taps the gem with one finger. "You're the expert, not me. Should I hide out in the tent?"

"No. The Duke would notice. And it'll probably be fine. If they're not actually suspicious of you, then nothing defensive should fire. Just don't . . . get into any fights, that sort of thing." I tense up again, thinking of the inn in Shithole. "There may be more of the sort of talk we overheard that first night."

Tsav snorts. "I'll make sure to keep my temper in check."

"Good." I let out a breath. "We can always make our excuses if it gets too rowdy. You ready?"

She grunts and turns around. Her outfit, with the rumpled jacket over some nicer things we hurriedly bought before leaving, is actually rather fetching. It has a sort of Indiana Jones vibe, especially when she gives me a half smile around her tusks. She'd look good in the hat too. And if she had the whip, she could tie me—

Focus, Davi. Focus.

"Lead the way, Dark Lord," she says, which does *not* make it easier.

"Quiet."

She snickers. "Hail Dark Lord Davi!"

"We're *not* doing hail!"

That had been Euria the deer-wilder's thing. It's been a few days since I've thought about her, or Mari and the rest of the horde. My attempts at using the communicator still aren't getting through. I hope she's still holding everything together.

"Okay," I say, tugging my coat straight. "Let's do it."

* * *

My own costume is leaning into the role of wizard's apprentice, though I'm going for more of a "cool and dangerous" look as opposed to Tserigern's trademark "wallowing in filth." Nicely cut coat in dark burgundy, black on black underneath with silver accents. Feels like I just stepped out of a spy thriller. It definitely sets me apart from the other guests, who are in a mix of ordinary field clothes (for the poorer Guildblades) and particolored explosions of expensive fabric (for the wealthier ones hoping to impress the Duke). Most importantly, of course, there's a lot of thaumite in evidence, not just the ordinary jewelry and show-off-your-fat-bankroll kind but also functioning, dangerous gemstones cut for war. Sword hilts, bracers, and rings glitter in every color of the rainbow.

The feast is just getting started when Tsav and I arrive, but the drinking is well underway. The Guildblades sit at long wooden tables around a central fire, while the Duke and other VIPs dine on a white tablecloth rapidly being ruined by mud and spills. Aster is in the center, of course, surrounded by a few favored Guildblades, while Johann drinks and laughs down toward one end. The Prince is always at his best in a feast context, but Matthias looks miserable.

We have seats at the high table, and a page directs us to the far end beside a minor Aster cousin. More servants are bringing the food, which is heavy on meats, hearty but not exactly subtle. Tsav and I are immediately faced with the daunting prospect of mashed yams piled high with raisins and swimming in melted butter. Tsav dives in with admirable vigor, but I restrain myself to a small portion. It's going to be a long night.

After doing honorable battle with the first courses, we get a breather. A fiddler starts up and people begin to circulate, so I give Tsav a meaningful glance and get up to try to work my way toward Johann. There's a knot of well-wishers and sycophants around the Duke. I give them a wide berth and head out into the crowd.

Guildblades are everywhere, laughing, talking, slapping one another on the back. I've probably fought beside most of the people at the tables in one life or another, but few faces stick out in my memory. Even before I switched sides, I was never fond of the Guild, who are more of a hindrance than a help when the Dark Lord comes knocking. They can fight, sure, but they're not used to working in large groups and they *hate* taking orders. Now, though, I keep overhearing snatches of conversation that set my teeth on edge:

"—set the webbing ablaze, and all the spiders run about burning—"

"—tricky to get the thaumite out, you need a really good boning knife—"

"—fuckers should have known better, we've been clearing them out of those woods for months—"

Fucking hell. Was it always like this? Was *I* like this?

I resist the urge to look back at Tsav. I have to trust her to keep her cool.

The sight of a familiar face, or more accurately a familiar head and shoulders rising above the rest, perks me up a little. Gena and Micah are here, then. Those two are all right. The

Guild attracts mostly the sort of people for whom "murder strangers and take their shit" sounds like an attractive profession, but every so often you get a few who are genuinely interested in protecting the vulnerable and defending the defenseless. Raiders may not be a threat to the Kingdom as a whole, but that's not much consolation to the peasant whose barn is burning down.

Gena is one of these, a wizard equally versed in healing and destruction who devotes a lot of her time to the boring, unglamorous tasks of putting destroyed lives back together. Her husband, Micah, serves as her meat shield, considerably aided by the fact that he's about seven feet tall and as broad as an ox. He's at the fringe of a larger group, and I spot Gena farther in, a small woman with mousy brown hair telling a story with lots of animated hand gestures.[5] I debate going over to say hello, but of course, they don't know me in this lifetime, and coming up with an explanation would be too awkward.

Instead, I continue to the end of the table where Johann is sitting. There's not as many people around him as you'd normally expect, since the Duke has made it very clear who's the star of this show. But the Prince is in party mode anyway, mugging and grinning, offering toasts to anyone who passes. A ruddy glow in his cheeks tells me that even Johann's legendary capacity for drink is being tested.

In fact, as I watch him, there's something a little bit *forced* about it. Yes, Himbo Boyfriend was always the life of the party, but usually it was *his* party and he had something to do besides just laughing and swilling wine. The Guildblades pass by him, nodding or hoisting a glass on their way to pay court to the Duke, but more out of politeness than excitement. Johann pays

---

5   Okay, elephant in the room (so to speak): What's the sex like? She has to be on top, right? Dude would crush you like an egg. I mean . . . hmm. *Hmm.*

no heed at all to Matthias, who's hunched in on himself, looking like he'd much rather be back in the library.

As I suspected, something's badly wrong. I insert myself into the line of people wandering past and after a few minutes come face-to-face with the well-sloshed Prince, who raises a cup and spills most of it.

"Davi!" he says, a note of genuine excitement in his voice. "Pally told me he'd asked you to come along. A little fun to go with all the prosphesing. Porphesying. Prophophing." He belches. "Seeing the future, I mean. How's it going?"

"Wanted to talk to you about that. Important prophecy business."

"*Prophecy* business!" He gives a sloppy grin. "Dude. I'm all ears."

"*Secret* prophecy business." I glance around the noisy campsite. "Can we step away for a minute?"

"Sure." He belches again. "Need a piss anyway. This stuff goes right through me."

He staggers to his feet and lurches away. I glance at Matthias, but he's got a good sulk going and isn't paying attention. Hopefully Tsav will take the opportunity to give him a shoulder to cry on.

The Prince leads me uncertainly back from the campfire and out into the empty camp. He seems to be searching for something, and I consider providing guidance toward the latrine pits. Before I can, he lets out an excited cry.

"That's Roddy's tent." Another belch as he points to a fine red structure of expensive-looking cloth. "Pally loooooves Roddy, takes him wherever he goes. I used to steal his underwear so he'd go crying to his mom, you know that? Now the dude acts like he's on top of the world."

I avert my eyes as Johann fumbles his trousers down and unleashes a stream of piss against the red tent with a groan of satisfaction. It goes on far too long, with him sighing and moaning and me standing there waiting awkwardly, wondering how much one man's bladder can hold and if Tserigern ever had to deal with this sort of shit. I can tell you that *I*, as a subject of prophecy, was considerably more respectful.[6]

Eventually the Prince's mighty torrent runs dry, and he heaves a breath as though he's just accomplished something heroic. He turns to me with a big goofy grin.

"Needed that. So what's up in prophecy-land?"

"Prophecy says to put your dick away."

"Whoa." Johann blinks and looks down. "Prophets, man. How do they *know*?"

"Mysterious." I glance back at the campfire. "Your husband doesn't seem to be enjoying himself."

"Matty?" Johann makes a face, but I can see real pain in his eyes. "He didn't want to come. He'll get over it."

"Did *you* want to come?"

"Course!" He spreads his arms. "What's not to love?"

"You didn't used to be a big fan of hunts. I think you once said they have all the drawbacks of an outdoor orgy with none of the redeeming features."

Someone else might have wondered under what context I'd overheard that line, but drunken Johann is an even easier audience than regular Johann. He snorts a laugh.

"It's true, right? This one time, these two girls told me to meet them—"

"Johann," I interrupt.

"Never did find the damn acorn," he mutters. "So, okay, it's not the *best* party. But there's wine and roasted things and wine and . . . uh . . . all Pally's friends, I guess." He perks up. "You see that one dude? He was *huge!*"

---

6 I mean. Apart from that one time.

"I know."

"You ever think what it'd be like—"

"Yes." God bless Himbo Boyfriend. "But these aren't exactly your people and there's wine back at the palace. If Matthias wanted to stay behind, why couldn't you?"

"I mean . . ." He sighs. "Pally wanted me to come. Come and have fun, he said. And, you know, I married into his family and all. I owe him."

"Owe him?" I say quickly. "Owe him for what?"

Johann makes a face. "They weren't going to let Matty and me get married. Pally straightened it all out."

I search his broad, flushed features. Johann is a fundamentally honest person—well, no, he *isn't*, but he's so bad at lying it amounts to the same thing. I don't think he's lying here. But . . . it doesn't make *sense*. How did the Duke get the two of them together in the first place, much less provide sufficient incentive that Johann would be willing to go to these lengths?

Unless it really is true love. But having partied with Johann through several hundred lifetimes, that strikes me as exceedingly unlikely.

Johann stares, mouth working as a thought percolates through his sodden brain.

"Is that important?" he says. "For the prophecy. You said it was about *me*, right?"

"Yeah. I need you to save the Kingdom." Though I'm starting to question that part of the plan.

"So, like . . . Tserigern saw all this? He knew what was going to happen?"

"More or less."

"So, he was watching me pissing just now?" Johann shakes his head and cups his hands around his mouth. "Hey, old man, how about a little privacy!"

"He—" I start to correct him, then just shrug.

"What a weirdo, right?" Johann frowns. "So, what does the prophecy say about me and Matty?"

The opportunity is so unexpected that I stumble, like leaning against a door that's abruptly opened.

"It's, um, complicated." I'm thinking fast. Can I come out and tell Johann prophecy requires him to ditch his husband? Will that be enough to get him to break up with the Duke? Or will he just give up on me altogether? "It says—"

"There you are," a man's voice interrupts. I'm almost grateful. "My Prince. His Grace requests your presence."

Our interlocutor is a Guildblade, not a servant. I recognize him as one of those who were sitting at the high table with the Duke. Johann goggles at him.

"Does he?" the Prince says. "Whatever for?"

"The toasts," the Guildblade says patiently. "We discussed this."

"Oh yes. The toasts." He turns to me. "The toasts! Duty calls, apparently."

I follow the two of them on a more direct route back to the fire. When we arrive, Duke Aster is at the tail end of a not-very-good speech about how the assembled psychopaths represent the Best Traditions of the Kingdom[7] and the Thin Line of Steel separating humanity from the Fury of the Wild. Whoever wrote the remarks for him didn't take into account the Duke's reedy voice, so when he hits the peroration, he sounds like a teenage boy whose voice just broke gamely trying for high C regardless.

Still, the well-lubricated Guildblades are happy to applaud. The Duke sits back down looking pleased with himself. Another man stands in front of the table, apparently serving as master of ceremonies, and he raises his hands for silence. He looks familiar, but it takes me a few moments to recognize him.

---

7 I'd rather have rum, sodomy, and the lash any day.

Roddy, *of course*. Sir Roderick Spatha, possibly the worst of a bad lot. Tall, broad shouldered, white-blonde Malfoy hair, generally looks like he should be shoving nerdy kids into lockers. If Gena is the rare Guildblade who actually wants to help the helpless, Sir Roderick is the opposite, interested mainly in tormenting anybody weaker than he is. Which, since he's always been a favorite of Duke Aster's thanks to shameless sycophancy, I imagine now includes just about everyone. If Johann has to make nice with him, it's no wonder he's drinking heavily. The two of them never got along; if Roddy is the uptight preppy captain of the football team, Johann is the Fonz.

Sure enough, there's an ugly grin on the Guildblade's face as he prepares to rub it in. "Prince Johann!"

The Prince, back in his place beside Matthias, sits up as though he'd nodded off. "Yes! What?"

"Would you like," Roddy says, "to say a few words? To mark our impending victory?"

"We're marking it now?" Johann blinks owlishly. "Sure, why not? Saves time, having the celebration before the battle. Plus, anybody who gets killed still gets to have a good time. Seems unfair, the other way."

"I doubt we will suffer casualties tomorrow," Duke Aster puts in. "The foe are scattered and ill prepared, and our cause is just!"

"Absolutely." Johann manages to get to his feet. "Blades of the Guild! I, your Prince, hereby give you my, you know, princely advice." He beams around, eyes a bit mad. "Try not to get stabbed! I hear it really sucks." He grabs a mug from the table and holds it high. "To not getting stabbed!"

There's a roar of laughter from the Guildblades and a few shouts of "To not getting stabbed!" I see Sir Roderick glance at the Duke, who thinks for a moment and then gives an approving nod. All of a sudden, I see what's going on here. It's not just

Aster lording his authority over Johann, it's a show for public consumption. Here's the brave, martial Duke and the drunken, foolish Prince, aren't you glad we've got the right one heading for the throne? Even Himbo Boyfriend seems to have intuited his natural part in the farce.

I'm still in the shadows beyond the fire, watching from the crowd's perspective. Roddy starts casting about, but it's only once his eyes fix on me, I realize that *I* have a designated part in the night's entertainment.

"Davi!" he shouts, pointing me out for the uninitiated. "Apprentice to the great wizard Tserigern, bringer of prophecy. We are honored to have you with us!"

"I, uh." I feel like I've been abruptly picked out of the crowd by a spotlight. "Great to be here. Have a fun night. Tip your waitress!"

The Guildblades are staring.

"I wondered," Roddy says, "if you would favor us with a display of your skills. Tserigern is said to be one of the most subtle wizards in the Kingdom, but he rarely offered any kind of demonstration of his power. Perhaps his apprentice will be more forthcoming?"

A glance from Sir Roderick to the Duke tells me all I need to know about who's wondering what, and my role becomes clear. This is a crowd of hardened Guildblades, not a bunch of slack-jawed yokels. They're not likely to be impressed by anything *I* could conjure up. So either I refuse and the message is "Hey, this Davi seems like a fraud," or I play along and it's "She's not all that impressive." Either way, it helps disarm me and the threat I might offer wielding Tserigern's reputation.

But I'm abruptly done playing along. The Duke has no idea who he's fucking with, and it's time he learned.

"You want to see a little magic?" I raise my eyebrows and turn to the crowd. "Is that it?"

Shouts of "Yes!" and "Give us a trick!" Duke Aster leans forward, chin in his hands. Tsav, who knows me well, is leaning back in her seat and shaking her head.

Most of my thaumite is safely hidden away, but I keep a few pieces around for emergencies. I put one hand in my pouch and mutter Words under my breath, my fingers contorting in arcane gestures a little showier than strictly necessary. I draw it out.

The ground begins to rumble.

By far, the most common field of study for Kingdom mages is red thaumite, for its obvious utility in blowing shit up. Green and brown offer healing and enhancement, but there's little interest in what they can do beyond that. Purple, aside from basic defensive measures, is the province of a few specialists. But over two hundred lifetimes, I've had the opportunity to explore a bit further and polish up areas of my skills that are off the beaten track.

A green shoot pokes up from the ground in front of the bon-fire. It thickens and expands, edges crisping in the heat but driven by the unstoppable force of green thaumite, a canopy of spreading branches rapidly expanding. Burning logs lift into the air as the trunk shoots upward, spraying glowing embers in all directions. Adding a twist of red thaumite—two spells at once, tricky—makes the flames dance along the edges of the unfolding leaves, limning the new tree in numinous fire. In seconds, it towers over Roddy and the Duke, still rising, shedding sparks like snow.

The face that forms within the flames is stark and imperious, and the voice that booms forth is wrought from the crackle and snap of fire.

"*Roderick Spatha!*" it says. "*Do not meddle in the affairs of wizards, for they are subtle and quick to anger. I'm sure I read that somewhere.*"

Sir Roderick has taken a step back, gone white in the flickering glow. I twitch my fingers again, and the face in the flames leaps forward abruptly, turning its gaze to Duke Aster. To my everlasting delight, he starts from his chair, hand dropping to a sword that isn't there.

"*As for you, Pallas Aster,*" the voice booms. "*You would do well to pay more heed to the wisdom of any sexy lady wizards in the vicinity. Not naming names. But just a totally unbiased thought off the top of my head.*"

Then the flames die, and the tree, its animating energy suddenly removed, crumbles into dust and bark. The rain of sparks has started numerous small fires, which I quell with another muttered Word.

"I hope," I tell the glaring Duke and his sycophant Guildblade, "that was sufficient?"

Then I turn on my heel, making my coat swirl like a supercool badass as I stalk off into the night.[8]

---

8   Though I realize about halfway that I'm stalking in the wrong direction and end up circling the camp to get back to my tent. You can't let little details like that mess up a good exit.

Chapter Five

The village, by a staggering coincidence, is also called Shithole.[1]

It's a border settlement, smaller than the last Shithole and without the protection of a convenient river. Instead, the small cluster of homes is huddled behind a log stockade, not much of a fortification but enough to beat back a wandering band of orcs.

Only in this case, it wasn't. From what I gather, a larger-than-usual raider band of wilders emerged from the forest and broke down the gate with axes. Most of the citizens fled south to seek the protection of the local lord, who sent his soldiers to restore the situation. Uncharacteristically, the raiders were holed up in the town and mounted a vigorous defense, seeing off the troops with heavy losses. Word got back to Vroken, and here we are.

"They're on the walls," Sir Roderick says with some surprise. "I see bows."

"Bloody animals must have stolen them," another Guild-blade mutters. "Been raiding awhile."

---

1 At least by me.

I wish abruptly that I could take this lot and whisk them to Virgard to see what wilders can build when left to themselves. *Bows* aren't the half of it. Beside me, Tsav is gloomy and silent, but I can sense her tension.

Frankly, I wish she wasn't there at all. The Duke insists that I accompany him—and in any event, I want to keep an eye on Johann and make sure there aren't any convenient friendly fire incidents—but he didn't say anything about Tsav. But she insisted on coming along, though her eyes have grown darker and darker as we watch the preparations and listen to the jokes and bragging of the Guildblades.

"Ten gold I get more than you."

"You're on, slowpoke!"

"Keep an eye out for a bit of red, would you? I'm running short."

"Try not to roast them so hard this time, it makes finding the thaumite such a pain . . ."

Now we stand a few hundred yards from the town, just ahead of where the servants are gathering the horses and preparing for the celebratory victory picnic. The Guildblades are in full kit, warriors well armored, swords oiled and bows strung, wizards dripping with war-cut thaumite. Duke Aster wears a spectacular suit of full plate so highly polished that the midday sun sends shimmering reflections across the fields. Even Johann, not known as a fighter, has his own royal war gear.

The sight of him armoring up, queasy and hungover, is so familiar that it takes my breath away. This whole affair is giving me PTSD flashbacks, frankly—how often have I been with human armies, large and small, as they confidently charge out to engage the Dark Lord's horde and get slaughtered? For obvious reasons, that *shouldn't* be a problem today, but I still have an itchy feeling of wrongness. Something here is not as it seems.

I can't see the wilders in the town very well, just a few heads poking over the top of the palisade. If they're expecting another attack by a handful of ill-prepared soldiers, they're going to get a nasty surprise.

Perspective flips. Those are my old ways of thinking. The wilders are people and they're about to be massacred. I should be *helping* them. But Aster already finds me suspicious; if I try to help his prey escape, he'll have me tossed in the dungeon. And right now, there's enough magical might on the battlefield to give even me pause.

I can't look at Tsav.

Duke Aster draws himself up, and for a horrible second, I think he's going to give another speech. But he's not in the mood today, apparently, so he only makes a chopping gesture and shouts, "Augment!"

Three dozen wizards start casting at once, the static charge of residual magic making the hair on my arms stand up and crackle. The casters move around their more heavily armored companions, gesturing and muttering, building the layers of spells from the inside out: green for vitality and rapid healing, brown for sturdiness and protection, red for strength, purple for mental defense. It's similar to what I did under the ruined city, buffing myself so I could survive my plunge into the mouth/anus of the tunnel worm and the subsequent explosion that ripped it apart. But that was an ad hoc, spur-of-the-moment thing, while this is a carefully planned routine, customized for each Guildblade. This, far more than fireballs, is what makes human magic so formidable.

It takes a few minutes before the chanting trails off. The front line of Guildblades is now absolutely humming with magical power, layers of augmentation and protection visible around them like a shimmering heat haze in the air. Duke Aster, most formidable of all, is just a shuddering mass of bright reflections. The rest of the Guildblades—the archers, wizards, and healers—fall back into the second rank. Everyone watches the Duke, who in turn looks to Gena.

My friend-from-a-past-life is standing beside her giant husband. He's encased in steel and spells like the other tanks, but Gena has only a faint shimmer around her. She's frowning at Aster and saying something, but it's lost in the buzz and crackle of magic. He snaps an order at her, and she frowns harder and turns toward Shithole, a brooch bearing a large brown thaumite stone in one hand. Her free hand moves quickly and efficiently through a complex set of gestures.

There's the classic comedy beat, that moment of "Wait, nothing happened!" and then the ground starts shaking. The earth at the foot of the palisade ripples like kneaded dough. The wooden walls buckle in seconds, logs splitting off and falling in several directions, spilling the tiny figures standing atop the wall-walk. Farther into the town, several buildings begin to sway.

"Attack!" the Duke yells, struggling to be heard above the rumbling. "For the Kingdom!"

"For the Kingdom!"

The Guildblades reply in a rough chorus and break into a trot. The formation quickly becomes ragged, augmented tanks outdistancing the rest with huge, tireless strides. The Duke and Sir Roderick are among them, powerful leaps covering ground like they were bounding along on the moon, while Tsav and I stay with the rear line.

Whatever defense the wilders were prepared to offer has been completely disrupted by Gena's spell. Figures are picking themselves up out of the rubble, but only a few arrows come our way, and none come close to their targets. Only as the Guildblades cover the final few yards do the wilders manage to form up again, presenting a line of fighters stretching across the gap in the palisade. Behind them, several houses are slowly collapsing, fatally wounded by the shaking of the earth.

Duke Aster hits the wilder line like a high-velocity tank shell. He swings his sword as he gets close, but his impact is what does the damage, tossing bodies away from him like an NFL linebacker plowing into a crowd of third graders. Roddy slams in just beside him and adds to the carnage, with the rest of the line of tanks close behind. Few of the wilders get a chance to use their weapons, and those who do, find their attacks bouncing away from hardened steel and the augmented flesh beneath. A few more arrows loop down at us from the eaves of the buildings; Guildblade wizards gesture and point, sending bolts of flame streaking back that erupt in rains of burning roof tiles.

The battle, such as it is, is over in seconds. The wilders still on their feet break and flee, and any cohesion the Guildblades have dissolves as they pursue. With augmented strength and speed, they easily overtake one opponent after another, cutting them down from behind. Some of the Guildblades immediately start searching their victims, ripping their clothes away to find their clusters of thaumite, while others leave this vital task to the other members of their party.

By the time Tsav and I pick our way through the broken palisade, the hunt is well and truly on. Some wilders try to flee the town, but there's no cover in the fields outside and they're quickly mowed down with arrows or spells. Others have barricaded themselves in the houses, and the Guildblades set to searching them out. The air is full of the crackle of flames—several houses are burning now—punctuated by screams and the crash of axes on wood.

I finally risk looking at Tsav, and the blank-eyed shock on her face is more worrisome than a snarl of rage. She's been at my side for a dozen fights large and small, and commanded a third of my horde in our field battle against the pyrvir army, but the speed and ferocity of the Guildblades' charge are astonishing. They may be murder-hoboes, but they're *good* at the murder part.

I'm tempted to take her hand, but I feel like she might stab me reflexively.

"Davi," she hisses. "Over there."

She points to one of the collapsed houses where there's a flicker of movement, a waving hand. Someone's trapped under the rubble, trying to pull themselves free. For the moment, no Guildblades are nearby.

"You can't—" I hiss, but she's already moving. I swear and hurry after her.

The remains of the house aren't on fire yet, but it won't be long. The roof has come down, scattering beams and tiles. A wilder woman lies half-covered, legs pinned by timber, one of them obviously broken. She's still conscious, though, white-faced with pain but desperately clawing at the earth in an attempt to free herself.

Tsav looks back at me, and her expression brooks no argument. She kneels by the wilder while I go to the beam and work my fingers underneath. I'm not as strong as these buffed-up meatheads, but there's still a chunk of red thaumite on my chest, and when I heave, the wood shifts upward. Tsav takes the wilder by the shoulders and pulls her forward onto clear ground, the woman's scream thankfully lost in the general cacophony.

I let the beam settle and hurry to them, reaching for the green thaumite in my pocket. Mending a broken leg takes time, but I can kill pain immediately. The wilder woman shudders with relief, large furry ears twitching. She's a fox-wilder, but not quite like Mari and the others in the horde—her fur is red instead of white, and her face is more vulpine, narrow and angular. She looks up at us with wide bright-yellow eyes.

"It's all right," Tsav says in the Wilder tongue. "We won't hurt you."

Her eyes widen further, shocked to hear her own language. I kneel on the other side of her.

"What happened here?" I ask. "This wasn't a raid."

Tsav shoots me a dark look, but we need information. Raiders steal and run if they want to survive. They don't occupy towns and stand up to Kingdom soldiery. And the band here seems too large for a simple raiding force.

"We had no choice," she gabbles, still terrified. "They moved in on our hunting grounds, raided our village. We had to leave, and there was nowhere else to go. Some of the others headed west, but Rentrick said if we could take a town by surprise, we could defend it—"

She moans, and I repeat the painkiller spell. Tsav takes her shoulders and tries to shift her, but it only brings fresh whimpers of agony.

"*Who* moved in on you?" I ask her urgently.

"Davi!" Tsav snaps in Common. "What are you doing?"

"What are *you* doing?" I respond in the same language.

"Helping!"

"If the Guildblades spot us—"

"They'll *kill* her. We have to get her away, not ask questions!"

She's dead already, I want to say. Where could we possibly take her? We're in the middle of open fields with Guildblades all around. Weaving another disguise like Tsav's would take hours. Any minute, someone is going to see us, and we'll have some tricky explanations to make—

"Canceri," the woman moans. "The Canceri. They're coming."

"They're launching a raid?" I say "Or—"

There's a crunch behind me, and a horribly familiar voice.

"You speak their gabble?" Duke Aster says. "How unusual."

I turn, my mind awhirl. He looms over us in his brilliant armor, spells spinning and shimmering around him.

"Tserigern taught me to search for knowledge," I say, trying to sound arch and mostly failing. "Regardless of the source. You can learn a great deal if you know how to listen."

He snorts. "I've never found the rambling of vermin particularly enlightening."

"This wasn't a raid, she says. They'd been driven out of their lands and had come to stay—"

"What does it matter?" he interrupts. "They defied the Kingdom and paid the price. That's the end of it. Are you claiming this one?"

"Yes," Tsav blurts out. "She's our prisoner."

"For further interrogation," I supply. "There might be more of them out there, and we could find out where."

"We don't take wilder *prisoners*," the Duke says with a sharp laugh. "Prisoners are for when you're fighting someone with a sense of honor. You can be sure they wouldn't make prisoners of *us* if the situation were reversed. They didn't take prisoners from the people who lived here."

"Your Grace—"

He's not listening. "Besides, you can only make a claim if you fought, and I don't recall you raising your blade. You lurked in the rear, just like that coward Prince. I'll take this one for myself, though I doubt she's worth much."

Aster leans down over the fox-wilder, who just stares up at him, frozen in terror. Not seeing her thaumite, he grabs her collar and rips downward, tearing her shirt away and exposing her small breasts. Two little gems gleam between them, one brown and one green.

"Pathetic," the Duke says, and reaches down.

Tsav's knife starts to slide out of its sheath. Her face is a brutal snarl, the tusks only I can see jutting. I feel an echo of her rage, but it's shot through with terror—here and now, without time to prepare, we're no match for Aster. If she attacks him, he'll kill her without a second thought.

My hand shoots out and grabs her wrist, forcing her dagger back into its sheath. She struggles, but she's taken only small chips of red thaumite, and my grip is stronger.

Aster takes the wilder woman's green thaumite between thumb and forefinger and pulls. She screams, a throat-rending sound, and her hands scratch at his armored gauntlet. Detaching thaumite isn't easy, but augmented as he is, the Duke could pull rocks apart with his bare hands; the gem comes free with a sucking, tearing sound. Instantly, the wilder's shriek cuts off and her eyes go dead, head lolling back and hands falling to her sides with a few final twitches.

Tsav's jaw is locked shut with the effort of not screaming.

Aster frees the brown thaumite with a wet crunch and tosses the two tiny slivers into his hand. He regards them with a disappointed air.

"Hardly worth the effort," he says, and turns away.

* * *

The Guildblades take their time with the looting and murder, and no one stops me and Tsav from slipping back to camp. Johann, I notice, has already done the same. On the brief ride, I clear my throat a few times but can't find anything to say. Tsav wears the fixedly neutral expression of a woman making polite conversation with the cop at a traffic stop while desperately hoping the corpses in her trunk haven't started to smell.

Sharing a tent has never been so awkward. Tsav retreats to her nest of furs, focusing ferociously on a book she brought from the library and responding to my hesitant entreaties in monotone grunts. I want to make my excuses—there was nothing we could have done, I couldn't have talked Aster out of it, we're waiting for our moment—but she's clearly not interested. The dark aura emanating from her corner eventually forces me out entirely, and I spend the rest of the day wandering through the camp. I put on my best wizardly scowl to keep anyone from trying to make conversation.

When the Guildblades return, I have to retreat even farther, lest the triumphal atmosphere turn my stomach. Drinking has started already, and I can tell that yesterday's feast will be tame by comparison with tonight's. I'm certainly no stranger to the appeal of an after-battle pint and/or fuck, but what happened today was hardly a battle.

"More of a massacre," someone says nearby, as though in response to my thoughts.

I start, but the words aren't directed at me. Just ahead, a few people sit around a small folding table, some distance from the bonfire and celebrations. I recognize the massive form of Micah, with Gena nestled against his side like a chick against a hen.

"Nobody was hurt?" says another woman. She's dressed as a servant, but her outfit has a fine cut, so a superior one.

"A few arrows," Gena says. "Nothing that couldn't be dealt with in the field."

"So, Aster has his victory," Micah says. A man his size seems like he ought to be a dummy, but his deep voice is surprisingly erudite. "Now what?"

"We go home, I suppose," says the servant woman.

"With no idea of what these poor idiots were *doing* here," Gena says. "No raiders would hang around just to get flattened."

I step forward with a cough, and the three of them look around at me. Gena's eyes widen.

"You're Davi," she says. "Tserigern's apprentice, right?"

"The one who had the Duke and Sir Roderick practically pissing themselves," Micah rumbles approvingly.

"I am," I tell them, trying to look wizardly.[2] "And you're Gena and Micah, Guildblades of some repute."

Gena snorts. "At least the wizard has heard of us."

It's an awkward feeling, introducing yourself to someone you've spent several lifetimes talking to, fighting beside, having idle sex fantasies about, et cetera, who now doesn't know *you* from a hole in the ground. Fortunately, this *particular* awkwardness is *excruciatingly* familiar to me and I've gotten good at gliding over it.[3]

"This is our steward, Andrea," Gena says, indicating the other woman. From the knowing look that passes between them, I get the strong impression that "steward" is understating her duties. I nod politely.

"I couldn't help but overhear," I say, "that you're also concerned about what our . . . opponents were doing here."

"Makes no sense," Micah says. "They had to know we were coming."

I raise an eyebrow mysteriously. "If they weren't raiders but a band living farther from the border, they might not have understood how effective our response would be." For many wilders, the Kingdom is half legend. I think of the pyrvir, solemnly insisting that humans are ten feet tall and breathe fire.

"Makes sense," Gena says. "But if they aren't regular raiders, that still leaves us with the question of what they're doing here."

"Does the name Canceri mean anything to any of you?" I venture.

They all shake their heads. I knew that was a long shot. Even

---

2 I need a big gnarly staff. With a knob on the end.

3 Being a mysterious wizard is a pretty good move, actually—you're practically expected to know more than you should. I don't know why I never tried it before!

among Guildblades who aren't homicidal maniacs, very few bother to go as far as communicating with wilders.

"I believe our problems may not be over," I tell them. "Remain alert if you can."

Which is just the sort of vague prognostication that gives wizards a bad name. But they nod sagely, as though I've said something of great import.[4] I'm not sure *exactly* what I expect to happen, but there's an edge to the air as I reluctantly return to our tent, a feeling of expectation I can't shake. Tsav is burrowed into her furs, apparently asleep. Tempting odors waft in, but fuck if I'm going out to watch these bastards gloat and celebrate; I nibble some of my stale travel rations and try to ignore my traitorous stomach's rumbling.

When I finally fall asleep, my dreams are dark and full of blood. No surprise there, honestly, my dreams are always dark and full of blood, but this time the blood isn't my own but that of the countless wilders who have ended up on the business side of my sword. In some of these lives, I've been as gleeful a serial killer as Duke Aster.

I guess you could argue I always got my comeuppance, right? Is *that* what the changes to the time loop have been about? Someone is *It's a Wonderful Life*-ing me into realizing that wilders are people, too, the Ghost of Massacres Past coming over to get me to change my evil ways? If so, they could have been a little more fucking direct with the lesson. And why *me*? Why is nobody haunting Duke Aster?

I wake up to a sound it takes me a second to recognize, because I've never heard it before. Tsav is crying. I roll over as quietly as I can and see her hunched among her furs, head hanging and shoulders shaking with each tiny sob.

---

4 I need a pipe to puff on while I'm deep in thought. And a hat.*

  * Okay, this is just turning into Ian McKellen cosplay.

POP QUIZ, DAVI. Do you (a) go and wrap your arms around her in a tender embrace, or (b) roll over and stay quiet so she can pretend no one saw her moment of weakness? Up until fairly recently, I would have said *obviously* (a), but given the "It's complicated" between us right now, I hesitate for a few seconds. When I do finally decide to go for it, I'm too loud getting out of my bedroll and she straightens up before I'm halfway across the tent, a stiff shadow in the semidarkness. Something in her posture tells me the tender embrace is right out, so I sit down opposite her instead. We spend a few seconds staring, to the extent that we can actually see.

"Hey," I say eventually.

"Hey?" Tsav sniffs and wipes her eyes. "That's it?"

"Feel like I missed my window to say something clever," I say. "And it was getting awkward."

She gives a bubbly snort of a laugh and shakes her head. "Fuck. Davi—"

"We need to talk."

"Yeah." Tsav pulls in on herself a little. "I just don't know if I can."

"Today was rough, I know—"

"*Rough?*" Her voice is a little raw. "Nearly freezing to death in the mountains was *rough*. This was . . ."

She trails off, and I stay quiet.

"Everyone knows the humans kill wilders," Tsav says. "We kill humans when we raid too. But not like *that*." She swallowed. "She was helpless, and he ripped her thaumite out with his *bare hands*."[5]

Another silence.

---

5 It's possible that the full horror of this doesn't register for me, since I haven't grown up with a wilder's sensibilities. An approximation might be a villain wrenching the still-beating heart from a screaming victim.

"Every step of the way, I thought I was doing the right thing." Her voice is very quiet. "I threw my band in with you because it seemed like the best shot we had. I stuck with you, and you kept winning. And now . . ."

"Hey." I lean closer. "We're going to get through this."

Tsav gives another snort. "You still don't get it."

"Of course I don't!" The words explode out of me, somewhat louder than I intended. "You won't *tell* me. I'm sorry, should I pull out my purple thaumite and search your mind? Tsav—"

I stop, because her hand has gone to the purple gem at her throat. A nervous gesture, and even in the dark, I can read her look. My breath catches.

"You're scared of me."

She swallows. It's loud in the silence.

"I can't help it." Her voice is a whisper.

"I would never hurt you, Tsav. Never never never, I *swear*—"

"You wouldn't have to do anything. You'd just have to turn this thing off." She clutches the disguise stone. "We're in a camp full of *Guildblades*. It wouldn't take half a minute for me to end up like all the rest of the wilders."

"But I *wouldn't*!" There are tears in my eyes now too.

"What if it was the only way to get what you wanted?"

"I would *find another way*, for fuck's sake! How long have you known me?"

"Less than six fucking months, Davi!" Her voice is rising as well. "I thought you were doing better after the Convocation, once you finally told me everything. I thought I understood, but once we got here, you started doing it again."

"Doing *what*?"

"Treating people like *things*," she blurts out. "Like objects. Stepping-stones on the path to whatever you want."

I sputter with indignation. "That's— I don't—"

Then I trail off because, uh, yeah, *obviously* that is kind of my *whole thing*. After so many lifetimes, can you really blame me? I guess you can! Or at least Tsav can!

Tsav speaks into the silence. "When you first... offered, I turned you down."

"I remember," I whisper. Spurred by the rejection, I'd unwisely fucked Amitsugu instead, setting off a whole chain of jealousy and badness that ended in him betraying and murdering me several months later. What I've never really thought about is how Tsav felt about it.

"I knew there was something between us," she says. "But at that point, our relationship was purely for mutual benefit, and I thought it would be better to keep it that way. People who got in your way—Gevalkin and his daughter, Amitsugu—they got pushed aside or run over. After Virgard, though, I thought you were changing. It seemed like you *cared*."

"I did," I say. "I do."

"Do you? Or had we just gotten far enough along that you couldn't just start over?" She wipes her hand across her eyes again. "How many times did you reset me in the beginning because things didn't go the way you wanted?"

"I didn't—I mean—" Enough sputtering. I take a breath. "I didn't go back unless one of your people killed me. Except that *one* time with Gerald, but that was just a fuck break, you can't blame me—"

"I don't blame you, Davi. I can only barely imagine what you've been through. I don't think anyone can, it's a miracle you're still halfway sane. But after you told me everything, I let myself think that things were going to be different."

"They *are* different! I *can't* reset now—"

"But you *haven't changed*." She leans closer. "When you told me you were going to seduce Johann, did you think I was *jealous*?"

"Um. Yes?"

Tsav closes her eyes for a moment. "I can't pretend I would be *happy* to share your affection. But if you had told me you truly cared for Johann, I could have accepted it. Talking about him seemed like one of the few bright spots in your past lives. But instead, you casually announced you were going to *use* him to get what you wanted."

"But..." It takes me a second to rally. "You don't know Johann. You think I would, what, break his heart? That's not how he works."

"Are you sure?"

"I *have* known him for *centuries*, Tsav."

"All I have to go on is what I've seen in this life," Tsav says. "Because it's the only one I get."

That hangs there between us for a bit. In the silence that follows, I try to think of something to say, but my mind is unaccountably blank.

I mean, I do what I have to do, right? For the Kingdom, for the horde, for *her*. I just have to explain that. Shouldn't be hard. Going to start riiiiight *now*.

Any minute now.

The sudden chorus of screams from outside is a profound relief.

* * *

The sound of mayhem is followed by blowing horns, fast and frantic, calling the camp to arms. I hear shouts, confusion, the clanking of weapons and armor. In between, there's a strange clicking and calls in deep, inhuman voices. I can't make out the words, but I can tell they're speaking Wilder.

"They're attacking the camp." I try not to sound too relieved. Is it bad that I'd rather face a horde of screaming monsters than Emotions?

"Who is?" Tsav is already grabbing her gear.

"Wilders. Maybe friends of the ones in town."

Tsav shakes her head. "It'll be another massacre."

I'm not so sure, or at least not certain who'll be getting massacred. While being at the business end of a party of fully buffed Guildblades is a terrifying prospect, they tend to be a bit fragile—come at them from the wrong direction at the wrong time, and they run around with their panties around their ankles. That was how Tsav's little band had wiped out Sir Otto and his party back when all of this was just getting started. It was possible the Duke had been assiduous in laying out pickets and defenses, but given the volume of revelry, I thought it more likely that everyone was just getting wasted.

This theory is given a boost when a large green claw pushes through the flap, grabs hold of the central pole of our tent, and squeezes it so hard the wood splinters. The roof flutters as the tent twists and collapses, burying us in mounds of fabric. For a moment, all I can see is falling canvas.

Not a bad way to get the drop on someone, and a real shitty way to die. I'm not going to stand for it, however. I have my bag of thaumite, the really good stuff we collected from the corpse of the Old One under the ruined city, and one of those gems is a red stone the size of my *fist*. Here in the Kingdom, where I don't have to hide my ability to use human magic, that means I can *fuck* shit *up*.

I spit a Word, and fire blazes straight up all around me, shredding the ruined tent and blasting the scraps outward. I get to my feet like an avenging angel wreathed in rising sparks, ready to wreak terrible revenge on sinners and devils. I can almost hear the soundtrack blasting.[6]

---

6 Maybe that Nolan *bwaaam* sound. BWAAAM. You'll have to imagine it.[*]

   [*] Unless this is the audiobook, then the poor narrator has to do it.

The claw belongs to a giant crab. Crab-wilder, I guess, but they're at the "dangerously furry" end of the anthropomorphic-animal spectrum.[7] The thing has four stilt-like legs, an armored body, and two sets of arms—one thick and ending in crab claws the size of my head, the other thinner and sporting four pincerlike manipulators forming a kind of hand. Its face is about halfway between the nightmare that is an actual crab's facial features[8] and some approximation of human, with bulging eyes and a complicated multipart mouth. It screeches and clicks at the same time.

Fireball time? Definitely fireball time. I dial it down a bit to reduce collateral damage. A column of brilliant flames punches out of the ground beneath the wilder, engulfing it completely in white-hot plasma. There's a high-pitched shriek—which I am *assured* is just air escaping under pressure—and, distressingly, a delicious smell. I close my hand, and the fire vanishes, leaving a blackened, flaking shell.

I'm not the only one cutting loose. Random explosions and bursts of light are blooming all over camp, rendering it a flickering hellscape of twisting shadows. Several tents are already burning. Amid this visual chaos, it's hard to make out more than shadows, but I can see people running in every direction and the hulking shapes of more crab-wilders everywhere. No coherent defense seems to be emerging.

Tsav frees herself from the remains of the tent with a shout and takes in the boiled crab.

"Ever heard of these guys?" I ask her.

She shakes her head. "There are stories of crab-wilder bands in the northeast, but—"

---

7 Is it a furry thing if they're crabs? Chitins? Shellies? Whatever, I'm sure it's somebody's fetish.

8 Seriously, Google it. Or better yet, don't.

"Fill me in later. We have to find Johann."

Tsav looks around at the chaos and gives a grim nod. I start jogging toward the Prince. Tents are down everywhere, some with people still inside, and the camp has become an obstacle course. Corpses start to add an exciting new element, too, some wilder but mostly human, Guildblades and servants mixed together wherever the crabs' claws found them.

Smoke fills the air, making things even more confusing. Through the murk I can hear shouting, a voice that sounds like Duke Aster's. Pity, I'd been hoping some crab made things easy for me while he was sleeping, but it sounds like he's rallying a defense. Tsav hears it, too, and gives me a questioning look.

"The Prince," I tell her, and we keep running. Aster certainly isn't going to stick his neck out for Johann, which means it's up to us.

More and more crabs are reaching the encampment, squads of them scuttling behind leaders carrying spears in their manipulator-hands. We dodge them for the most part, but when one gets too close, I'm forced to roast it. That draws more unwanted attention, and I hunt frantically through my bag for a chip of brown thaumite—I really ought to put those things on a bandolier—

"Johann!"

He's up ahead, standing in the ruins of his tent with sword drawn. A crab looms over him, steel clanging on chitin as it probes curiously at his defense. Behind him, Matthias is half-naked, holding his glasses on with one hand while he scrabbles for one of the tentpoles with the other.

Too close for fireballs.[9] I've got the brown gem now, and I do a delicate little spell with brown and red both, scraping a

---

9 Stupid friendly fire escort quests grumble grumble.

handful of dirt from the ground and shaping it into a blade infused with blazing flames. With the gems in my free hand, I hit the crab at a run, sword crunching into its midsection with a sizzling hiss. It shrieks and staggers away, legs collapsing underneath it.

"Davi?" Johann says, staring around. "Hey, the camp's under attack!"

Sweet Himbo Johann. "Brilliant deduction. Come on!"

"Matthias—"

"I'm okay," Matthias gasps, climbing to his feet with the pole in hand like a makeshift spear.

"Now!" There's a whole squad of crabs coming after us. I let the flaming sword go and lob a fireball their way, and they scatter in all directions. "We're getting out of here!"

"Shouldn't we help the others?" Johann searches the gloom, brow wrinkling. Bless him, but I'm losing patience. I grab him around the midsection and lift him easily off the ground with red-thaumite strength.

"Tsav, get Matthias!" I yell over my shoulder.

We break for the woods, a small copse of tame trees at the edge of camp. It's not very thick, but it's the only cover on offer. Hopefully, the crabs will have other things to worry about. The flash and strobe of more serious magic is visible through the smoke toward the center of camp. It sounds like the Duke and the Guildblades are giving a good account of themselves.

"You're stronger than you look," Johann says amiably as we cross the tree line and brush whips at my thighs.

"I work out," I mumble, face pressed against the small of his back.

In the middle of the woodland is a little gully with a stream running down the center. We pile into it and plant ourselves against the bank, more or less concealed from the campsite. I let Johann down, and he immediately hurries to Matthias's side.

"You okay?" I ask Tsav.

She nods, then makes a face. "Left my spear behind."

Apart from Johann's sword, we are notably light in the weapons department, though the bag of thaumite goes a long way toward evening the odds. I peek over the edge of the bank and see fires raging in the camp but no sign of crabs coming after us.

"What the hell happened?" Matthias says.

"Wilders," I say, "obviously. The Canceri, if I had to guess. They must have tracked us from the town and waited for night to storm the camp."

"Can they *do* that?" Johann says.

"Apparently, my cousin didn't take precautions," Matthias says bitterly. "I told you—"

"Don't say it," Johann groans. "I know. You were right."

"Right about what?" Tsav says.

"He warned me this would be dangerous." Johann gives his husband's shoulder a cheerful buffet. "He's always right, I don't know why I bother."

"Not the time for I told you so," I say, scanning the brush. "We're not out of this yet. Some of them were on our trail—"

Tsav grabs my shoulder and yanks me round in time to see four crabs entering the gully farther downstream. The leader spots us, raising its spear, and it gives a series of warbling clicks. I lob a fireball at them and they scatter, the leader coming our way while the followers leap into the woods. One doesn't make it up the bank and gets roasted with a high-pitched screech.

I plant myself in the incoming wilder's path, summoning the earth-and-fire sword again. Supernatural strength or not, the crab-wilder outweighs me ten to one, so meeting it head-on is a losing proposition. Instead, I charge to meet it, slipping sideways out of the direct path and slashing at its legs. I connect, but the chitinous armor holds, and the thing slews around and reaches for me with a massive claw.

Tsav comes up behind it, wielding the tentpole Matthias dragged along. It *thocks* into the crab, not punching through the armor but doing a wonderful job of throwing it off-balance. Tsav doesn't have as much red as I do, but she has more weight to work with. The crab stumbles, legs working, and I duck its claw and get in close to thrust my blade into that nightmare mouth. It ducks, losing an eye instead. I can see a collection of thaumite gleaming along its back-ridge—no wonder the damn thing's so tough, it's the crab equivalent of Tyrkell's pet assassin.

There's another screech, and I risk a glance over my shoulder. A second crab has come down over the bank of the stream toward Johann, who is once again fending it off with his sword.

"Help him!" I shout to Tsav. I surround the tip of her tentpole with a variant of the spell I use for my sword, giving it a fiery aura. Keeping all of this going is starting to become a strain even for me, so we need to finish this before I fuck something up. As Tsav spins away to engage Johann's opponent, I lay into the leader crab, wild slashes leaving brilliant curtains of fire in the air. It takes the blows on its pincers, crisscrossing black scorch marks painting its armor.

Finally, the thing runs out of room, back legs coming up against the bank of the gully, and it shifts to a desperate attack. I duck the swipes of its claws, but the spear in its manipulator-hand scrapes my side, drawing a long, shallow cut. But now I'm inside its guard, and I lunge up to plant the sword right in the center of its interlocking mouthparts.[10] It sags, twitching like a dying bug. I flick my blade to shed the blood like a triumphant samurai—unnecessary since my blade is made of fire, but it looks cool—and turn—

---

10 Thus striking its weak point for *massive damage*.

Just in time to see the final crab emerge from the brush on the *other* side of the gully, rushing toward Johann from behind.

The Prince and Tsav have their opponent on the back foot, but their attention is entirely absorbed. My fight with the leader has taken me some distance away, and the world moves in slow motion as I start to run. I let the sword go and grab for my thaumite, beginning to shout a warning—

"Johann!"

The voice isn't mine but Matthias's. Johann's husband surges up from a defensive crouch, armed with nothing better than his bare hands, and throws himself in the path of the onrushing mountain of seafood. The crab thrusts with its pincer, and Matthias takes the blow meant for Johann in the stomach, sharpened chitin sliding easily into unprotected flesh. His back bumps against Johann, who half turns at the sound of his name, his eyes going very wide. He ducks the crab's other pincer, reaching for Matthias, but the wilder shakes the young man off and sends him flopping into the stream trailing gore.

My lagging fingers finally reach the end of the spell. Johann's too close for comfort, so I try to direct the blast upward, a blaze of fire rising from the ground and cooking the crab where it stands. The wave of heat frizzles the Prince's eyebrows and blackens his face with soot. Behind him, Tsav has finally cracked her opponent open with her flaming spear, driving it to the earth leaking blood and steam.

For a moment, the world seems to pause.

* * *

Johann drops to his knees beside his husband, rolling him onto his back and cradling his head in his arms. Matthias's stomach is a mess, shreds of ropy intestine visible through the massive rent, his whole body slick with blood and wet from the stream.

His eyes are open and he's trying to speak, but only a soft gurgle emerges.

"You're okay," Johann says against all available evidence. "You'll be okay. There are healers in the camp—we'll find a healer—" He looks around desperately and latches on to me. "Davi! He needs a healer, *please*—" Matthias gurgles, and Johann looks back down at him, patting his cheek. "It's *fine*, Matthias, *please*."

The sense of déjà vu that washes over me is intense. I've been here before, in a hundred lifetimes, but it always hurts. The moment when tragedy punctures Johann's armor of blithe insouciance, the layabout Prince forced to confront the real world in all its horror. He's lost someone on a hundred battlefields—a friend, a lover, *me*. I know the look on his face as intimately as the contours of his body.

Even so, there's something new here, a desperate terror that contorts those affable features into a rictus of despair. I've had lives where that face is my last memory, begging me not to die as my vision goes black, but I don't think it's ever looked quite like that.

Matthias is going to die. Even if a Guildblade healer were standing right here, they wouldn't be enough, not for a wound like that. To mend that in time, you'd need a *massive* chunk of green thaumite, wielded by someone with experience in the healing arts beyond what most people could achieve in a lifetime.

Which . . . well.

Seeing the look on Johann's face, I finally understand. Matthias *is* the hold Duke Aster has over him. There's no devious plot, no hidden blackmail to keep them together. My himbo Prince has just fallen in love, utterly and completely, with someone who loves him just as deeply in return. That this soulmate happens to be a member of Duke Aster's family, thus placing Johann in the Duke's power, is just a spectacular piece of bad luck.[11]

If Matthias dies, that hold is broken. It would be easy enough to turn the Prince's grief and anger against the Duke—it was Aster, after all, who led him here, who let this happen. I can see what I'd have to say and do laid out before me like a map, channeling Johann into crushing his rival and then giving me all the authority I need. Johann's kind soul means he always blames himself most of all, and that self-loathing would make things easy.

These thoughts occur to me in an instant, unbidden. A way forward, placing the game pieces just so, and all I have to do is nothing. Johann won't know I could have changed things. Even Tsav won't suspect—she doesn't know the limits of human magic.

Treating people like *things*.

Because the alternative is terrifying.

I flop to my knees in the stream beside Johann, digging through my bag of thaumite for the biggest chunk of green.

"Move," I tell the Prince.

"But—"

"And shut up, I need to concentrate." I lay a hand on Matthias's shuddering form and close my eyes.

Imagine one of those really big Lego sets, like a working full-sized R2-D2 made out of plastic bricks. You build it carefully from labeled bags, following the instructions, and just when you've got it going *bleep-bloop* at you, some asshole rushes in and takes a sledgehammer to it. Tiny pieces everywhere! So now you've got to fix it and the instructions are no help, *plus* you'll never find all the pieces, there's seriously one stuck in the *ceiling*, so you've got to make some shit up on the fly.

---

11 I *knew* Aster wasn't smart enough to pull something like this off. I've been giving him too much credit.

Most healing is just encouraging the body to do its thing, but here that means "die screaming," so we need another approach. I stitch and tuck and improvise. It's not pretty, and when I'm done, it feels like I've just sprinted a marathon. But Matthias is still breathing and not spurting any untoward fluids, so I count it as a win.

Johann is staring at me, wiping his eyes. "Is . . . is he . . ."

"He'll sleep for a while, but he'll live." I let out a long sigh, weariness landing on me like a ton of rocks. "Side effects may include dry mouth, nausea, and difficulty perceiving dog farts. If you experience an erection lasting for longer than four hours, give your doctor a high five—"

Johann wraps me in a hug so tight I nearly pass out. So that's all right.

* * *

"Davi," Tsav says.

The Prince releases me and carefully picks up his husband. I want to collapse into the stream and let the freezing water run over me until I turn into an ice pop, but I heroically stand up and give Tsav my attention.

"Over here." She's pointing to the crab she skewered. The thing is still alive, pincers waving feebly, and it's saying something in Wilder. I stumble over to it and try to prod my brain back to operation.

". . . feast on your steaming guts," the crab is gurgling. "Your Kingdom will fall at last, and your monstrous Guild will not haunt the nightmares of our spawn. This is the *end* of humans."

"Yeah, yeah. It'd be more convincing if we hadn't just turned you into a kebab," I tell the creature. I can see surprise on its inhuman face at the sound of its own language. "You guys are the Canceri, right?"

"Yes. The mightiest band—"

"Shut up. What are you doing here? Are you really planning on destroying the Kingdom by yourselves? Because you may not have thought that brilliant plan all the way through."

"By ourselves?" The wilder gives a wet bubble of a laugh. To my surprise, it switches to broken but intelligible Common, and Johann jerks his head up behind me. "We are only the *first*. The Dark Lord is *coming*, humans, with fury and fire. When the horde arrives, all of you . . . will beg . . . for death . . ."

This tirade having apparently exhausted its strength, the crab gives a final gurgle and expires. I look at Tsav and find her expression a mirror of my own.

Well, *fuck*.

Chapter Six

No one suggests leaving the gully before morning. I conjure some warmth from red thaumite and we huddle together for the rest of the night. I even catch an hour or two of sleep pressed close against Tsav, lulled by the steady beat of her heart.

In the morning, I poke my head up like Punxsutawney Phil looking for an excuse to sleep in, but the forest is quiet. I leave Tsav to watch Johann and head back a ways toward the camp. It's still smoking somewhat, but the fires seem to be out and a few human-shaped people are moving around at an unhurried pace. I retrieve the others and we cautiously approach, Tsav hefting the still-unconscious Matthias.

There are a lot fewer Guildblades around than there used to be. Many of the tents have been burned, torn, or trampled into the muck, but someone has been busy establishing a kind of order. The supply carts have been circled around the central bonfire to create a defensible perimeter, and as we approach, a number of bows are aimed in our direction. Fortunately, we're clearly not giant crab-monsters, so they hold their fire until I'm close enough to shout a hoarse greeting.

"Who the fuck's that?" someone shouts back, and I'm relieved to recognize Gena's voice.

"Davi!" I offer, then elbow Johann in the ribs. He blinks and clears his throat.

"And, um, Prince Johann!"

Murmurs of conversation from within. One of the carts is pushed out far enough to make an opening. Micah, looking even bigger than usual in full armor, beckons us inside. Within the impromptu holdfast, a couple of dozen people are still on their feet, with quite a few more laid out on bedrolls in various states of disassembly. Gena seems to be in charge, yelling expletive-laced orders at all and sundry. I wait for a break in the shouting while Johann and Tsav hurry to make Matthias comfortable.

"What happened to the Duke?" I ask when Gena subsides for a moment. Please be dead, please be dead, please be dead.

"He and his cronies fucked off," Gena says, and I stifle a really *choice* string of curses. "Heading northwest, last I saw. Probably keep running until he gets to his own shithole castle. Fucking crabs decided they'd had enough not long after, haven't seen 'em since." She narrows her eyes at me. "Where were you hiding the Prince?"

"A bunch of them chased us into the woods, but we managed to take care of them."

"That glasses kid going to live?"

I nod. "He was badly wounded, but I healed him."

"If you've got anything left, we've got some people here who would really fucking appreciate it." Gena gestures at the lines of wounded.

I want to talk strategy, but I bite my lip; as far as she's concerned, I'm just the apprentice of some hedge-wizard. Instead, I give another nod and head for the makeshift hospital. A few Guildblade healers are at work and I join in, keeping my thaumite in its bag so as not to advertise the size of my hoard. I work my way over to the Prince and Tsav, leaving sighs of relief in my wake.

Johann is kneeling beside Matthias. The way he stares makes it clear he hasn't noticed anything else. I crouch beside him and gently touch his shoulder.

"Davi?" He blinks as if coming out of a trance. "He...he still hasn't woken up."

"It may be a few days. His body needs to recover."

"You're sure?" There's a childlike need for reassurance in his voice. "He won't..."

"I promise you." I try to infuse the words with wizardly gravitas. "Matthias will be fine. He just needs to rest."

"I..." He swallows and nods. "Thank you."

"But I need something from you, Johann."

"From me?" He looks around, brow furrowing as he starts to take in his surroundings. "What can I do?"

"I need you to take charge. Someone has to give orders."

"But..." His frown deepens. "Where's Duke Aster?"

"Fled. We need to get back to Vroken as soon as we can. Those wilders might return."

Which is true, I guess. Though from the number of steaming crab corpses around, they'd get quite a kicking. But they *might*. More importantly, if we get back to the palace while Duke Aster is still hiding with his tail tucked between his legs, we might be able to start unpicking this knot.

Fuck. Am I doing it again?

Johann straightens up, visibly pulling himself together. That's my (now I guess ex-) himbo boyfriend; when it really counts, he gives it his best.

"I understand." He looks around again. "Is there a Guildblade in command?"

"Talk to Gena." I point. "We'll take care of Matthias."

He nods and gets to his feet, looking more princely by the moment.

* * *

It's not hard to convince the Guildblades that retreat is in order. By midday we've packed the wounded onto the remaining carts and started south, gathering stray horses as we go. Stray humans as well—many of the servants fled during the attack and took shelter in the surrounding fields. Putting some distance between ourselves and the site of the battle is reassuring, and that evening, Gena blisters the air arranging sentries and a defensive plan and all the other things Duke Aster didn't bother with.

Tsav and I have a new tent—there were plenty to spare—and even managed to retrieve most of our things from the wreckage. She retires early, but I find myself lingering at dinner. It's been a long day and I'm ready to collapse, but there's one more thing I need to do. And...*fuck*. It feels like there's a sharp chunk of ice lodged in my chest.

Eventually I woman up and head back to our tent. Tsav is nestled in her furs and reading by lamplight. I sit down on my own bedroll and pull off my boots as slowly as possible, prolonging the awkward silence.

"We need to talk," I say for probably the second time in a thousand years. I am *not* usually the one who starts the relationship conversations.

"If you're ready," Tsav says. There's gentle concern in her gaze as she looks up at me. "I know you're exhausted."

"Yeah, but if I put this off, I might chicken out. What you were saying, before we were, uh, rudely interrupted..."

She winces, rubbing her tusks with one finger. "I didn't

mean to get so . . . heated. You are who you are, Davi. I can't ask you to change."

"That's the thing." I shuffle forward on hands and knees. "You can. You *should*. You're right. I . . ."

I take a deep breath, and she regards me silently.

"After I died and came back in the ruined city, you . . . saved me. It was a . . . moment of clarity. I knew what I needed to do, how I needed to move forward. To act like this life is a *real* life, my one-and-only, and pay attention to . . . to *people*. I *knew* all that, but . . ."

"It's easy to fall back into bad habits," Tsav says quietly.

"*No.*" I'm surprised by my own forcefulness. "Well, I mean. Yes. That too. I've been doing this a long time. But it's not *just* that. Doing things the right way, *thinking* the right way, is . . ." I swallow. "Fucking *terrifying*."

Tsav blinks, taken aback.

"Everything I do is *real*." My voice falls away to a whisper. "I hurt people and they stay hurt. I make choices and I can't take them back. If I think about it too long it feels like my head is going to explode, like I'll start screaming and never stop. I'm so afraid, all the time, about what might happen and what *could* happen and I can't *do* anything about any of it. I . . ."

I pause to brush unshed tears from eyes. My throat is thick and tight.

"Thinking the old way lets me forget about it for a minute. Everything's just pieces to be moved around. I know I can't reset the board and try again, but it's so much easier to pretend I can. I try not to, but it just *comes* to me. I was looking down at Matthias, and I thought . . ."

"That it would be easier if he died?" Tsav says.

"Yes." I mime flicking a piece off an invisible board. "All taken care of."

"But you healed him."

"Only because you said what you said. And I realized you were right."

"Davi..."

"I can't make you my conscience, that's not fair to you. But..." I swallow again. "I will never, ever look at *you* and see a piece to be moved or sacrificed, I swear it. If you think I'm doing something fucked up, please, just let me hear it. I will try to do better, but I'll probably need a few swift kicks in the ass."

The corner of her mouth turns into a faint smile around her tusk, and the ice inside me melts a little.

"I can probably provide those," she says.

Pause to breathe. Push forward.

"You know what scared me the most, this past week? The thought that I'd fucked *this* up." I wave my hands to indicate her, me, and whatever it is that's between us. "For real. No going back and trying again or picking a different romance for this playthrough. Fuck. I just..."

My words run out, but thank *God* she's still smiling.

"Well." She puts on a thoughtful expression. "You haven't *entirely* fucked it up. Yet."

I shuffle a little closer. "Permission to hug, Captain?"

"Permission granted."

Her big arms encircle me, and for a while all's right with the world.

* * *

For once, hugging doesn't turn into sweaty *extreme* hugging. I fall asleep burrowed into the nest of furs beside her, and wake in the morning little-spooned against her snoring, slightly smelly bulk, happy as a cat with an electric blanket. I want to clutch this moment to me and make it last for years, and I feel a pang of regret as the noise of the waking camp penetrates the tent and sexy bald orc lady starts to stir.[1]

The return journey to the palace is a lot faster than our trip out, since our party is both smaller and considerably more motivated. At my suggestion, Johann encourages Gena and the remaining Guildblades to stick with us instead of disbanding. I have a feeling we're going to want them handy. Tsav brings up the elephant in the room while we sit on the box of our cart, out of earshot of the rest of the column.

"That Canceri," she says.

My face is stony. "Yeah."

"It said that the Dark Lord is coming."

"Yeah."

"The horde should still be on the other side of the mountains."

"It could just be rumor," I say. "I'm sure we've had some deserters, and word must have gotten around that the Convocation picked somebody. Maybe the Canceri just got excited."

"Maybe." Tsav's lip twists. "It's a lot to risk on a rumor."

"Yeah."

"Have you tried to reach Mari?"

I nod wearily. I'd spent an hour with my purple thaumite, groping blindly among disparate minds for a familiar one.

"I can't sense the beacon I gave her. Without it, my range doesn't extend much past the borders of the Kingdom. Either the spell failed, she lost it—"

"Or she's dead," Tsav says grimly.

"If someone *else* was wearing the beacon, I'd still be able to find it," I point out.

---

[1] Though she's not quite bald right now, grooming being a low priority recently. I love running my fingers through the peach fuzz on her scalp.

"It's a big chunk of purple," Tsav says. "Somebody probably ate it."

We ride in silence for a moment, contemplating that cheery scenario.

"*Probably* I just fucked up the spell," I announce. "Probably everything is fine."

"You don't believe that."

"Shut up, I'm manifesting."

We get an example of the speed of rumor when we return to Vroken. Word has obviously preceded us, and the Guildblades have to clear a path through nervous crowds to the palace gates. At my prompting, Johann stands up and waves, letting everyone get a good look at him and the fact that he's not dead. Rumors like *that* can get started all too easily, especially when it's so obvious that the expedition didn't exactly go as planned.

Back behind the spiky iron fences of the palace grounds, things are so normal you might think the past week hadn't happened. But nervous chatter fills the halls immediately. Everyone knows the Duke hasn't returned. Servants walk quietly, as though afraid to break the silence, and everyone seems to be waiting for the other shoe to drop.

Johann retreats to his chambers with Matthias and a palace healer, and I spend another nervous hour or so pacing. When we finally get a summons to attend him, I have to restrain myself from sprinting down the halls. When we arrive, Jeeves gives us a bow of sincere respect before opening the door. I guess saving the Prince and his husband got me in the major-domo's good books.

Matthias is up and about at last. Or he's *awake*, at least; he's sitting in an armchair swaddled in every available blanket. His features are still a bit pale, but his eyes are alert behind a fresh pair of spectacles. Johann walks back and forth behind him, occasionally asking if he needs another blanket or cup of tea.

"I've already *got* a cup of tea, love," Matthias says. "What would I do with a second one?"

"It might've gone cold," Johann says. "Cold tea isn't healthy, I'm sure I read that somewhere."

Matthias looks down at the steaming mug in his hands and wisely doesn't comment. I clear my throat politely, and they both look up.

"Davi," the Prince says. He rushes over and takes my hand. "He's okay. You said he would be and he is."

"I try to keep my promises." I give him a grin and lean to one side to speak to Matthias. "You're feeling all right? The palace healer didn't find any problems? I didn't have time to do the most thorough job."

"Considering the last thing I remember is my guts sliding through my fingers, I feel wonderful," Matthias says.

"Can you *not* talk like that?" Johann says.

"Look, when *you* get stabbed, you can talk about it any way you like." Matthias clears his throat and meets my eyes. "Obviously I . . . um. Well. Thank you, for starters. I may have been . . . a little unkind, before, and I apologize."

"Don't worry about it," I say breezily. "*I* wouldn't trust me under the same circumstances. And you were willing to help with Tsav's research anyway."

"You have *my* thanks as well," Johann says. "More than that. Whatever you want. Do you want a castle? We have some lovely castles."

"We *could* use a castle," Tsav says thoughtfully.

"No castle needed," I tell them. "All I want to do is help you and the Kingdom. Hear me out and that'll be enough."

Johann nods emphatically. "Certainly. Here, sit. Tea? Tea? I'll get tea."

A little while later, when we've all been provided with tea and snacks, I get to the point.

"You remember what I told you when I first arrived?"

"Of course," Johann says. He glances at Matthias, who raises an eyebrow skeptically. "Just, ah, refresh my memory."

"She said that you're the savior from the prophecy," Matthias says. "That you have to protect the Kingdom from the Dark Lord."

"Right, that's right." Johann takes a deep breath. "I mean. You're *sure* about this? Because I don't really feel like much of a savior. You were at the battle, I wasn't exactly smiting foes left and right."

"It's not about smiting foes," I tell him. "I can't emphasize that enough. You're not going to fight the Dark Lord."

"That's reassuring," Matthias says. He still looks skeptical.

"The Dark Lord *is* coming, though? With a great and terrible horde and all that?" The Prince's brow furrows. "I'm pretty sure that crab said something about it."

I'd sort of hoped he hadn't picked up on that, but I roll with it. "The Dark Lord is coming. I don't know exactly when"—still no contact with Mari, though I've been trying every evening— "but it probably won't be much longer."

"We should tell Pally," Johann says.

I snort. "Assuming he ever stopped running."

"We've had word from Duke Aster," Matthias says. "He's back at our family seat, raising forces to scour the border."

That's news to me, and it brings me some relief. If the Duke was worried about a threat from the Prince, he'd have hurried back to the heart of power. Now we'll have at least a little more time.

"The Duke is part of the problem," I say. I've thought long and hard about this part, and settled on a mostly true version of events that leaves out certain inconvenient facts, like the fact that I *am* the Dark Lord in question. "This new Dark Lord is different from those that have risen in the past. She doesn't want to destroy the Kingdom, only live and let live in peace."

"Live beside wilders in peace?" Matthias makes a face. "I grew up on the border, and they never seemed interested in peace before."

"Neither have we," I say. "The Guild is always pushing the edges of human territory outward. What the Dark Lord wants is for us to rein them in, and in return she'll put a stop to the raiders."

"Seems fair, seems fair," Johann says. "It's a deal!"

"No, it isn't," Matthias says.

"No, it isn't, apparently," Johann amends. "Why not?"

"Because the Guild will never agree," Matthias says. "My cousin least of all."

"Exactly," I say. "That's why the Duke is part of the problem."

"He'd say the wilders can't be trusted," Matthias goes on. "And—no offense to you or your master, Davi—I'd be inclined to agree with him. How can you possibly know all this?"

I take a deep breath. I'd thought this might be the tricky part.

"Because I have spent time among the wilders," I tell him. "Quite a lot of time, actually."

Matthias scoffs. "No human could survive long on their side of the border. They'd kill you as soon as look at you."

Johann looks uncomfortable at contradicting me, but he nods along. "I've never met a wilder who was keen on conversation rather than slaughter."

Nothing for it. I glance at Tsav, and she gives a halting nod. "You have."

"I have?" Johann blinks. "When?"

"Now. Please don't scream."

I hold out my hand, and Tsav pulls the purple gem from

around her neck and hands it to me. From my point of view, nothing changes. But for these two, her features will shift and blur, reshaping themselves from an ordinary human woman into my beloved sexy bald orc lady, tusks and green skin and all.

Tsav puts on a smile like someone determined to be cheery in the face of a firing squad, and I can see the hints of panic in her eyes. I've got one hand on my thaumite—in the absolute worst case, I figure I can knock these two out and get her out of the palace before they come to.

Nobody screams for the guards, so that's a win. Johann starts out of his chair, while Matthias merely widens his eyes beneath his glasses, his mug of tea shaking a little in his hand.

"My name is Tsav," Tsav says, like we practiced. "I am, as you can see, a wilder. An orc, Davi calls me. I was chief of a band of raiders on the northern border, and Davi begged to join us. Not . . . long afterward, I became one of the principal lieutenants to the new Dark Lord."

She's not a natural liar, but I have to say I'm impressed. I wouldn't have seen the slight hesitation if I wasn't looking for it.

"You're a wilder," Johann says, goggling openly. "Really?"

"Really," Tsav says gravely.

"And you've come here to speak for the Dark Lord?"

Tsav's eyes briefly flick in my direction. "I have."

"At great personal risk, I might add." I put a protective hand on Tsav's shoulder. "You understand what would happen to her if she was discovered?"

"I . . ." Matthias shudders a little. "Yes. I can imagine."

"*Really* a wilder?" Johann says, not keeping up with events.

"She and I have come to broker a peace," I say. "A lasting peace, not just a temporary truce. The Dark Lord is prepared to accept the border where it currently stands and to control the raiders if the Kingdom can control the Guild." Both would be a tall order, obviously, but if we can agree *in principle*, then that's a good starting place. "We have been in the Wilds for most of the past year. I had hoped to make my case to the Prince, who had always been a friend to my master—"

"But you got here and found my cousin running things instead," Matthias says. This kid is *sharp*. So far, though, he seems to be following me where I want him to go.

"The Duke was . . . less receptive."

There's a pause. Matthias appears lost in contemplation. Johann is still staring at Tsav, who isn't sure what to do with the attention.

Matthias clears his throat. "I think—"

"Can I feel your tusks?" Johann blurts out.

"My—" Tsav's hand goes up to her mouth. "Why?"

"They're so *freaky*. Do you have to brush them?"

"Um," Tsav says.

"Do they get in the way when you're making out?"[2]

"No," I say, sotto voce.

"Johann," Matthias snaps. "She's an ambassador, not a circus animal."

"Just for a second," Johann says. "Please?"

"I . . . guess?" Tsav looks at me, and all I can do is shrug.

"Wild." Johann gets out of his chair and approaches Tsav, who stares like a deer faced with an oncoming eighteen-wheeler. I'm trying very hard not to laugh.

"*Anyway*," Matthias says, studiously ignoring the scene. "I was going to ask what any of this has to do with Cyrus. The two of you seemed to want to know everything about him, and I don't think it was a purely academic interest."

Very sharp. I speak carefully. "It's possible Cyrus is . . . involved. Someone using that name communicated with my

---

2 In some ways, Johann and I have very similar minds.

master, and he knew things that were hard to explain. The
Dark Lord also found hints that point to the Founders, and she
wishes to know more. We were looking for any evidence that
Cyrus was connected with Dark Lords in the past, or that he
was active after his supposed death."

("They're so smooth. Do you polish them?"

" 'O."

"Sorry, does this hurt?"

" 'O. 'Eels 'eird.")

"Fascinating," Matthias says, his scholarly curiosity resur-
facing. "I've never heard of any confirmed accounts of Cyrus
still being alive, though there are always rumors about all the
Founders."

("You can feel my teeth, if you like."

" 'O 'ank 'oo.")

"Do you think we might find anything else in the library?"

Matthias shakes his head. "Just the standard scholarship.
There are a few people I might consult, but I doubt—"

"Have you looked in the secret archive?" Johann says.

We both turn to look at him, as though on swivels. He's
kneeling in front of Tsav, who has her mouth obligingly open as
though suffering through a dentist's inspection.

"The secret archive," Matthias says flatly.

"Yeah. There's lots of stuff from the Founders in there."

"I can't imagine why we didn't think to check the *secret
archive*," I say. Johann stares guilelessly back at me for a long
moment before the light bulb turns on.

"Ooooooh," he says. "Because it's a *secret*."

Two hundred lives, and he never told *me* about the secret
archive. Himbo Ex-boyfriend has hidden depths, or at least
hidden shallows.

"Perhaps," Matthias says with admirable restraint, "you
should show us."

* * *

There's a brief argument when Matthias insists on coming over Johann's objections. Matthias prevails, but agrees to wear three fluffy bedrobes against the chill. We make our way through the palace with him looking like an overstuffed pillow. Tsav, walking quietly behind me, keeps rubbing her tusks.

We end up in the oldest part of the palace, even older than the library. Several squat, round towers crouch at the top of a gentle hill. They look like they might actually have provided some military value, and were probably once encircled by a wooden wall. In the present day, they're used as storage by the gardeners, a fact that becomes obvious from the smell of manure that enfolds us.

"Grandma showed me this when I was a teenager," Johann says. "Secrets of the royal line and all that. There's a hidden door in the wine cellar too!"

"What's in there?" I can't help but ask.

"More wine. But, like, older."

Great bins of manure line the empty interior of the tower Johann leads us to, along with crates of tools and racks of seedlings. A stone staircase winds around the wall, leading up past floors that no longer exist to the roof. Johann heads for it, but instead of venturing upward, he goes around the back, where the rising steps define a cramped triangular space.

"One, two, three, four," he mutters to himself, poking at the stones. "There you'll find the hidden door." Sensing our questioning gazes, he adds, "Grandma made me memorize it. I had to study for *days*."

"Amazing! I've got the same combination on my luggage," I whisper to no one in particular.

The fourth stone, when pressed, sinks back with a *click*. One of the big flagstones rises a fraction, revealing itself to be a thin layer of stone over a wooden frame, easily levered aside to expose a narrow stairway extending down in the dark. Johann beams like the cat who got the canary.

"Fascinating," Matthias says. It seems to be his favorite word.

"Come on," Johann says. "It's a bit tight, but there's no death traps or anything like that. Always disappointed me a little when I was kid."

"Right?" I say. "At least some poison darts or a big rolling ball. Shows a little effort!"

"Exactly!"

Matthias and Tsav exchange long-suffering looks.

I conjure some light with red thaumite as we descend in a tight spiral. There are, indeed, no death traps, and the walls and floor are ancient but boringly mundane stone. It feels more like a basement everybody forgot about than a secret archive, although I suppose it amounts to the same thing. At the bottom of the stairs is a stout door, closed but unlocked. Beyond—

Now, *this* is much more satisfying secret-archive territory. It's a *mess*, first of all, books piled haphazardly on shelves and tables, some of which have collapsed over the years and spilled their contents across the floor. There are other objects mixed in, loose papers, weapons, crystal goblets, and pouches of who-knows-what. A layer of dust and cobwebs covers everything, with only a few sets of fading footprints. It feels like the grandma's neglected attic of an entire kingdom.

"Did the Queen tell you what any of this stuff *is*?" Matthias says. He pokes a stack of books and sneezes in the resulting plume of dust.

"Sure," Johann says. "That's Founder Atlian's sword over there!"

The indicated weapon is unimpressive, rusty metal showing through ragged gaps in the scabbard.

"Atlian's sword is in the treasury," Matthias said. "I saw it last Founders' Day. It's covered in gold and gems."

"That's what I told Grandma," Johann says. "She says this is his *real* sword."

"Makes sense," I comment. "Too much gold and gems can really throw off a sword's balance."

In that vein, we're invited to survey Founder Grithka's saddlebags (moldy), Founder Brennia's undergarments (moth-eaten), and Founder Zebelard's miraculous jug of holy water (dried up). The royals of the Kingdom have always had a strong sense of showmanship, and I get the sense that this place is a dumping ground for relics no longer useful for *performing* kingship. The books, on the other hand, appear to be mostly journals, diaries, and other primary sources, only occasionally labeled.

"And *this* shelf," Johann says, "holds the invisible helm of Founder Ulema!" He feels around the apparently empty space and frowns. "It used to, anyway."

"Nobody trip over it," I say. "Okay. We're looking for anything about Cyrus. Especially anything *by* Cyrus. I'll start over there"—I point to the darkest corner with the densest layer of cobwebs—"and work my way around. You guys split up the rest?"

Matthias and, surprisingly, Tsav both look excited to dive in, while Johann stares at the books unenthusiastically. I leave them to it and start gently blowing away the dust while trying to keep the cobwebs out of my hair. In addition to information on Cyrus, I have a sneaking suspicion that I want to confirm.

While there are a lot of books, they're fairly easy to sort through. Royal journals from long after the time we're interested in compose most of the pile, along with compendiums of moldy secrets by spymasters long dead. In spite of the dust, the *truly* ancient books are few and far between.

There are a couple, though. My hands shake a little as I find what I'm looking for. It's clearly a copy of a much older book, written in an awkward, inexpert hand. But . . .

"Look at this," I tell Tsav quietly.

She frowns at it. "I can't read it. What letters are those?"

"We call them the Roman alphabet, back on Earth." I trace the uncertain writing. "*A, B, C.*"

"Can you read it?"

I shake my head. "We have lots of languages and I only understand one. I think this is German." Maybe? There's a scattering of ümläuts. The closest I get is high school French, and that was like a thousand years ago.[3]

"So, you don't know if it says anything useful."

"I'm sure it doesn't. But that's not the point." I grip the fading pages a little tighter, a tangible link with a nearly forgotten life. "This confirms our theory. That people from Earth came here before and traveled from the ruined city to the Kingdom."

Johann wanders over and I show him the book. He gives an uninterested shrug.

"Oh yeah. Grandma said those are really old but nobody knows how to read them anymore."

"Do you know if they're related to the Founders?"

Another shrug. "She didn't say."

I'd be tempted to try to interview Grandma, but the times I've met with the old woman, I've found her not particularly compos mentis. If I were still resetting, I'd take a few lives to carefully extract everything I could from her, but right now I don't have that kind of time to waste. Still, frustration nags at me as I put the book back on the shelf. There has to be *something* here related—

---

3 Though I still remember how to say "I am a library," for some reason.

"I think I've got something." Matthias sounds excited. "Take a look at this."

We gather round, dusty and web shrouded. He's paging through a leather-bound journal of considerable antiquity, flaking at the edges but still quite legible.

"This is the journal of a man named Laeritt," Matthias said. "He lived during the last years of the Founders, when Cyrus was one of the only ones left. Apparently, Cyrus was working with the Crown during this period, and Laeritt was assisting him. But he was also writing everything down." He frowns. "Reading between the lines, I think he was a bit of a spy. The Queen at the time didn't trust Cyrus."

Tsav frowns. "I thought humans revered the Founders."

"In theory," I say. "But royalty is always jealous of anyone else with power."

"Exactly," Matthias said. "Anyway, most of it is pretty dull. Whom Cyrus talked to, where he went in the palace. Politics. But there's this." He puts a finger on the page. "He accompanied Cyrus outside the city. At one point, he was supposed to wait in their camp, but he followed Cyrus instead and watched him open a door into the side of a hill. Laeritt says that what he could see inside looked like some kind of workshop."

My heart rate speeds up. "Please tell me he gives directions."

"He does." Matthias smiles and turns the page. "He even drew a little map."

"In all this time, nobody has found the place?" Tsav says.

"It's plausible." I'm staring at the sketched lines and comparing them to the map in my head. "That area's all hills and forest. Some hunters wandering around, probably, but they're not likely to stumble upon a secret door into a cave."

"So, you think it's still there?" Matthias says.

I grin at him. "Only one way to find out."

Chapter Seven

Eager as I am to find out more about Cyrus and maybe unearth what the *fuck* has been going on for the last thousand years, there's work to be done first. I have a plan for this, which I tinkered with all through the trip to the Kingdom and have since been adapting to our unexpected circumstances.

If Johann is going to take power for himself and convince the Guild to cool it, he's going to need support among the movers and shakers of the Kingdom. Fortunately for him, I've done this before, since a standard element of a *typical* lifetime is convincing those same powers that be to take the threat of the Dark Lord seriously. I've done it so often I can speedrun the whole thing. Threaten Count Whatsit, bribe Duke Whoever, blackmail Minister Someotherguy by mentioning that little incident he *thought* he'd concealed so carefully. Johann plays his part willingly and really seems to enjoy himself once he gets the hang of it; he doesn't ask how I know all of this, chalking it all up to wizardly wiles.

Not every lead is going to pan out, but that's okay. We make a solid start with the notables who are actually in the palace, and my letters over Johann's signature are soon winging their way out into the Kingdom more generally. I also consult with Gena, who—between tirades about the incompetence of Duke Aster—is happy to sound out her colleagues on the Prince's behalf. I don't read her in on the Dark Lord stuff, but in the aftermath of the battle, it's plausible enough that Johann wants to refocus the Guild on the defense of the Kingdom rather than ranging across the border.

In sum, a lot of boring political bullshit, but it goes pretty well. In further promising news, I intimate to Tsav that my bedroom in our suite has really nice linens, super-high-thread-count sheets, *very* comfortable, and she allows that it seems a shame to make the maids clean *two* rooms when the beds are actually quite large, and then *mmm mmm* slobber squelch oh fuck *oh God* don't stop et cetera. In case you were, you know, worried about me.[1]

Best of all,[2] we get word that Duke Aster has gone in pursuit of the remaining Canceri, determined to avenge the stain on his honor and prestige. So we're rid of him for a while longer. He sends back instructions, but I arrange for them to come directly to Johann, who passes them along or not at my discretion. If Duke Aster were a savvy would-be ruler, he'd have his own people here to warn him something was up, but as I noted previously, he's not very good at the parts of the job that don't involve hitting things.

After about a week of this, matters are sufficiently under control that we can afford to take time for more private pursuits. The royal stores equip us with horses and supplies, and it's only a day's bracing ride through the country to the edge of the woods. The following morning, we leave the horses and tromp onward, following the map of the long-dead spy.

---

1 Forget the political stuff, I know what you're *really* here for.
2 This is a lie, the previous bit was definitely the best part.

"We should have brought backup," Matthias frets. "We have no idea what we're going to find in there."

"Bring anyone else along and we'd never keep it quiet," I say. "Besides, the place has probably been dead for centuries."

"There could be traps." Johann seems excited at the prospect. "Or monsters! One of those dungeon crawls the Guild is always talking about."

"Even monsters need to eat." I pat my reassuringly full sack of thaumite. "And I can handle a few traps."

Tsav looks a bit nervous as well, but she says nothing. She's wearing the purple thaumite again, to keep up the habit and because her tusks keep distracting Johann.

The air is getting a bit chill, but otherwise the walk is quite pleasant, and Laeritt, God bless him, drew with an accurate hand. A few landmarks have changed, but we find the rocky ridge he camped on easily enough. Across a gentle valley, a broad hill juts up from the forest like a wart, trees finding little purchase on its rocky slopes.

The spy's notes lead us to the southeastern face, but here the trail goes cold. He places the door in reference to a couple of carefully described rock spires, but nothing like that is visible. From the look of the scree, rockfalls are a regular occurrence here, and the shape of the hill has probably changed quite a bit since Laeritt's time. Based only on the notes, there's no way to tell exactly where his door might be.

Fortunately, there's magic for that. Johann and Matthias go bug-eyed as I pull out a piece of brown thaumite as big as an apple; here in the Kingdom, anything close to that size is locked up in some noble's treasury like the nuclear codes waiting for Judgment Day. I speak Words and contort my fingers, causing waves of power to flow out from me and into the surrounding earth and rock. They bounce back to me, revealing the contours and crystals deep below the surface, carrying the echoes of hidden chambers and underground streams. The smooth-walled artificiality of human construction sticks out like a thumbtack in Play-Doh.

The door has been buried by recent rockslides, but that's not a problem either. I concentrate and the scree crumbles further, reduced to the consistency of loose soil. What's left behind is a massive slab of metal, apparently featureless, which resembles a door in the same sense that caution tape and tire spikes are welcoming decor. *Fuck off*, it tells the casual visitor, in no uncertain terms.

Looks, however, can be deceiving. The same fugue of echoes that revealed the door's location also shows me the catch, a bit of metal deep inside it that could only ever be tripped by magic of this sort. I twist it and the slab splits apart with a clank, both halves swinging inward on silent hinges to reveal a corridor cut from the rock.

"Melon," I tell the door for good measure. "Preferably cantaloupe."

"Bones of the bloody Old Ones," Tsav swears in Wilder. Johann and Matthias don't understand, of course, but they nod as though they can appreciate the sentiment.

I'm practically vibrating with excitement. This *has* to be something Cyrus left behind. No ordinary human wizard would be able to unlock it the way I just did; whoever came in and out this way had centuries of experience and lots of thaumite, just like me.

"Are we just . . . going inside?" Matthias says.

"We should have flaming torches," Johann says. "In stories, they always have flaming torches."

"Torches just get smoke in your eyes. Magic is better." I put the brown thaumite away and conjure some light with a bit of red. "Come on."

"Careful, Davi," Tsav murmurs.

"Come along *carefully*," I amend. The feeling of finally getting somewhere may have me a bit too far on the bubbly optimistic side, it's true. But nothing moves as I step over the threshold, my light showing the way to a darkened doorway at the other end of the passage. Passing through that, my boot clangs unexpectedly on a metal grating. The corridor ends at a railing, and I get the sense of vast space beyond. I feel a spell activate with a flicker of magic, and glowing spheres snap into life at regular intervals, bathing the whole scene in soft while light.

Picture a wedding cake. One of those multitiered monsters with a dozen different levels, each of diminishing size, until at the tippy top there's a tiny one with the little plastic bride and groom. Doesn't matter what flavor, chocolate is fine. There can be little strawberries if you like.

Take the cake and flip it over. Forget about gravity for a second, this is Imagination Time. Teeny layer on the bottom, biggest layer on the top. Still with me? Now invert that image, so the *cake* part is empty space and everything around it is solid rock. *That* is, very roughly, the shape of Cyrus's laboratory. Imagination is fun!

The top layer, where we're standing, has to be a hundred yards across. A catwalk stretches around it in a complete circle, with several bridges cutting cords through empty space. Tight spiral stairs descend through holes in the grating. Below is another level with a rock ledge and another catwalk, more bridges and more stairs. Then another and another, each smaller than the last, until at the *very* bottom there's something still shrouded in darkness.

In the vast empty space so defined is a...thing. It looks a bit like a chemistry model from high school, the kind where atoms are colored balls and the bonds connecting them are little plastic tubes. I have no idea what molecule is being depicted here, but we're well beyond the high school level, this is out past Organic

Chem and rapidly accelerating. The spherical "atoms" are glass globes a couple of feet across full of orbiting points of colored light, and the tubes connecting them strobe at irregular intervals with crackling magical energy. The bridges and stairways thread their way through this complex structure in a way that suggest they were built *around* it, perhaps to allow access to its various parts.

I've never seen anything like it. Never seen anything even *close*, not in two hundred lifetimes. Just the *glasswork* would be too much for the Kingdom, never mind whatever unfathomably complex magic is going on inside. This thing, in some deeply fundamental way, does not belong here.

I'm gawping. We're all gawping. I think I express our collective opinion well.

"Holy *fuck*."

Then about five more seconds of gawping before the monster comes climbing over the catwalk rail.

* * *

My first impression is of an octopus wearing plate mail. Two tentacles like articulated steel cables wrap around the railing, which looks too thin to support much weight but somehow does.[3] The body of the creature that pulls itself over the side is a squashed sphere covered in overlapping scales of armor, each the size of a knight's breastplate. Six more tentacles writhe around it. It slides across the floor, every movement accompanied by a horrible clang and clatter of metal so loud it's hard to hear anything else.

The tentacles reach for us. Maybe it's a *friendly* armoctopus,[4]

---

3 At least there *is* a railing. Darth Vader should take notes.
4 Wrong name. Now I'm picturing an octopus with human arms instead of tentacles, yuck.

but, you know, if you're a monster the size of a barn and you jump out at a party of dungeon-crawlers, then you've got to expect a certain response, right? In other words, I've got a fireball coming online, and I'm gesturing frantically while waving the others back. As the armorpus[5] pulls its body over the rail, I shout a Word, and the thing is engulfed in sweet cleansing fire.

"Is it dead?" Matthias shouts before the blast clears. And I groan out loud because everyone knows you *never say that*. If you ask "Is it dead?" or "Did we get him?" or, worse, confidently proclaim "No one could survive that," then the object of your attentions is about to emerge from the billowing smoke and absolutely *wreck your shit*.

The octopanzer[6] rushes out of the flames, apparently unharmed and much faster than I expected. Tentacles slam down on either side of me with a steel screech. I dance away and try a smaller, more focused firebolt, but it blooms against the armor without even leaving a scorch mark.

So, uh, not good? Not good.

Johann has his sword out, though God knows what he thinks he's going to do with it. Matthias and Tsav have him by the arms and they haul him backward toward the door we came in by, which is conveniently too small to let the octopanzer through. They need a few more seconds. I backpedal, one hand still on my red thaumite, and weave the fastest enhancement spell I've ever tried. There's a pop from one of my fingers as I try to bend it in two directions at once, but I can feel my strength swell.

The next time a tentacle sweeps down at me, I catch it with

---

5 Nope. Sounds like a stripper in a chain mail bikini.

6 I'm sure this is not grammatical in German but I like it, it sounds like a one of those bands whose logo looks like a snake orgy. Did you get down to GoreFest last weekend? Yeah, man, Octopanzer rules! ^m^

both hands, magically enhanced muscles straining. My boots slide across the grating, but I'm holding it, the tentacle tip squirming above my head. I *squeeze* and the armor creaks. There's give there, I *swear*, like there's some inner softness under all that metal—all I have to do is break through—

"Davi!" Tsav's voice is barely audible over the racket of steel on steel. "*Run!*"

I should. Obviously. But the answer is *right there*, I know it is, I've searched for a *thousand years* and whatever the fuck this place is, it *has* to be something to do with Tserigern and Cyrus and the time loop and *everything*. Fuck if some sashimi with delusions of grandeur and an aftermarket upgrade is going to stop me, right? If it bleeds, I can kill it, and technically it *hasn't* bled yet but I'm sure we can make that happen—

A second tentacle slams into my midsection and *wow* fuck, that hurts. I go flying back against the stone wall and hit it rather hard. I had time to buff my strength but not so much my toughness, and my vast experience having my body dismantled tells me I just broke half a dozen ribs and possibly popped a shoulder out of joint. I try to get right up to show this joker that a few busted ribs are no big D but instead I just slump forward and wheeze a little.

And then it hits me. Not literally, it already did that, but *reality* hits me. I could just *die* here and lose everything, *everything*. You'd think that would be a hard thing to forget, but the habits of two hundred lifetimes are equally hard to break, especially when a big sack of mega-thaumite is making you feel invincible. The sudden rush of terror is like nothing I've ever experienced. I want to scream but I don't have the breath. I want to curl into a ball but bending hurts too bad.

Something grabs my shoulders and hoists me up. This *also* hurts, but all I can do about it is flap my arms a little. For a moment, I think the monster has me, but then I can smell her, the rough-edged sweat of sexy bald orc lady, who has thrown my arms around her neck and cradles me against her boobs with both arms. I'd cop a feel but: pain.

Also, imminent danger. Tsav dodges right, then left, as tentacles slam down and the catwalk rings like a bell. She staggers through the doorway, where Johann and Matthias help pull her along. Tentacles snake after us, but the thing's main body can't follow. We stumble—well, they stumble and I'm carried like a toddler—out into the sun, and the metal slabs swing closed with a very emphatic bang.

This is something to worry about later, however. I've started coughing, which sends ice-cold stabs of agony through me and also sprays a worrying amount of blood into Tsav's face. She lays me down with Johann and Matthias on either side.

"Can you heal her?" Tsav says, opening my thaumite sack. Matthias does a comical double take at the mass of brilliant color within, while Johann is focused on me.

"I . . ." He takes one of the green stones, looks at me, and shakes his head. "I can't. I only know the theory."

"She's *dying*," Tsav says. "Help her."

"I don't know how!" Matthias is close to tears.

I cough and cough. In between agonizing spasms, I manage to grate out a couple of words.

"Give. It. To me." Cough cough ow. "Green."

"You can't heal *yourself*," Matthias says. "That's—"

Tsav has already put the chunk of thaumite in my hand.

Conventional wisdom does indeed hold that you can't heal yourself. But you know me, I'm always experimenting, especially since I get stabbed a lot. It turns out you *can* heal yourself, with approximately the same level of difficulty you'd face doing surgery on yourself—it's easy to get a bit distracted and make things worse. In short, it's only the sort of thing you should attempt if you're some kind of Rambo-level badass with a high tolerance for pain and no other options, a description for which I check all the boxes.

Fortunately, it's not *quite* the jury-rig I had to do on Matthias. All my parts are still inside, for one thing. It's just a matter of teasing them back into their correct orientations and patching the holes. And indescribable pain, yadda yadda yadda, you know the drill. Fuck my life.

(But I'm not dead yet.)

* * *

I enjoy a well-deserved absence of consciousness until evening, when I return to the waking world and find myself back in the wooded campsite we left that morning. Johann and Matthias are already snug in their tent, but Tsav is sitting up reading by the dying fire when I emerge.

"Hey," she says with studied nonchalance.

"Hey."

"Do I need to give you the lecture on not getting yourself killed again?"

"No." I sigh. "Thank you for saving my life at great personal risk. Again."

"If you die and the world resets, present-me ceases to exist, right? So arguably it's pure self-interest. My life literally depends on you."

I settle down beside her with a groan. "Have you been reading philosophy?"

"A bit."

"Don't bother. None of it was written with time loops in mind. This shit doesn't *begin* to make sense."

Tsav gives an amused grunt and closes her book with a snap. "You going to be okay?"

"Yeah." I'm still in quite a bit of pain. When we get back,

I'll have to have one of the palace healers smooth out my self-inflicted hack job. "Eventually."

"So now what?"

"Now we look for a can opener that works on giant octopuses,[7] I guess."

She shoots me a look. "You still want to get in there?"

"Of course I do. I've never seen anything like that place. It *has* to be related."

"I figured." She sighs. "It's not going to be easy, though. We can't exactly recruit help."

That gives me pause, but of course she's right. Johann could requisition soldiers or Guildblades, obviously, but that would mean exposing the secret to whoever we brought along. That would probably be bad, if only because the place clearly contains enough thaumite to ransom a dynasty's worth of kings.

"I'll think of something," I mutter, not thinking of anything.

The next morning, Matthias seems particularly eager to get back to the palace, and Johann is happy to accommodate him. I sense a change in attitude from the Prince's husband, and I can guess the reason. Our brief encounter with the octopanzer has reminded him that this is not simply an exercise in academic curiosity; hunting through old texts is one thing, nearly getting smushed by monsters quite another. In fairness to him, he's had some painful experiences with that lately. On the way home, he's polite but a little frosty.

We're back by midafternoon and I make my visit to the healers, then check up on a few of my plots and schemes vis-à-vis Johann assuming his rightful place on the throne. Everything still seems to be ticking over nicely, and there's been no more news of the Duke. So far, so good. I decide to have an early night.

---

7 Octopi? Octopodes? Octopoda? Have at it, internet.

Everyone has a little bedtime ritual, right? Bathroom, brush teeth, poke at red spot in the mirror and wonder if it's becoming a zit, change for bed, fetch a glass of water, that sort of thing. It's a time when the mind tends to wander while the body operates on autopilot, slipping smoothly down the railroad tracks of ingrained habit. This is the state of mind I'm in when I pick up the piece of purple thaumite I keep at my bedside and cast my mind out into the void to look for Mari.

Kind of awful of me, I know. But you can do a thing for only so long with no results before it fades into the background. I'm thinking about weighty matters like whether octopuses have balls and how you'd go about kicking them when they're wearing steel plate. Thus, it takes me a few seconds to regain my mental equilibrium when I finally, *finally* get a response.

[Davi? *Davi!*] Mari's voice is tiny, like someone on the other end of a bad phone connection. She sounds frantic. [Old Ones, Davi, if that's you, *say something, please* please please—]

[It's me!] Not the most original dialogue, I admit, but I'm thinking fast. I still can't feel the beacon. Mari's mind is difficult to focus on, like it's at the farthest edge of my range. That puts her somewhere close to the border of the Kingdom, which is both a long way off and much closer than I expected. [Where are you? What's happening?]

[Davi.] Her mental voice is choked up. [I don't have long. I'm sorry, I'm so sorry, I tried to stop them—]

My stomach lurches. [What do you mean you don't have long?]

[Doesn't matter, listen. Sibarae and Artaxes have betrayed you, the horde is *coming*, and—]

There's a mental lurch and the feeling of pain. The connection flickers and dies.

* * *

"Davi!" Tsav trails me as I storm out of our suite. "Davi, what's happening?"

I explain as I jog down the corridor, and Tsav is soon running grimly beside me. We pelt past alarmed servants doing the evening cleaning and a few drunken courtiers stumbling back from their revels.

"You lost the connection?" Tsav says as we round the last corner. "Does that mean—"

"Don't know. Gonna find out."

"How? If she's at the border, that's a couple of days' ride—"

I skid to a halt in front of a door and hammer my fist on it. There's a frustrating moment or two before it opens, revealing Gena in a nightgown. Behind her, Micah is already in bed, snoring loudly.

"The fuck do you want?" she says, before her eyes focus on me. "Davi? Fuck me, are we under attack again?"

"Not yet," I say grimly, pushing into the room. "You know the courier buffs?"

She blinks and follows me over to the dining table. "Yeah, course I do."

"I need to get to the eastern border in an hour."

Gena gives an incredulous snort. "I hope you've got a chunk of thaumite the size of my fuckin' tit, then, because—"

She cuts off as I empty my sack on the table. Gemstones worth fighting a major war over bounce and scatter. A chunk of red big enough to burn cities rolls behind a potted plant. Gena's jaw hangs open.

"Can you do it?"

"I . . . *fuck.*" She looks up from the hoard. "You're fuckin' serious?"

"Can you do it?"

"Yeah, probably." She grabs a brown stone, frowns at the cut, and picks up a green one. "Now?"

"Now. *Please*."

"All right." Gena glances at her still-snoring husband and shrugs. "Why not? Wasn't like I was gettin' any this evening."

"Tsav, stay here and make sure nobody interrupts her."

"You're really going to get there in an *hour*?" she says.

"If we can't do better." I lock eyes with Gena. "Hit me."

The Guildblade hefts the chunk of green, testing the weight. "Founders' fucking arseholes. Where did you— Never mind." She closes her eyes a moment. "Here goes nothing."

The collection of spells known as the courier buffs are meant to allow a person to run tirelessly and fast; as the name implies, they're handy for when you *really* need to tell Athens that Marathon turned out well but don't fancy dropping dead afterward. With a good caster and a few reasonable pieces of thaumite, someone so enchanted can beat a galloping horse in a dead sprint and keep up that pace for hours. The actual spell is a tricky combination of red (for the strength to run faster), green (for the energy to keep doing it), and brown (so your body can stand the strain). Like the combat buffs the Guildblades use, it needs to be maintained by the caster, so you can't use it on yourself.

I need to go much, much faster. I'm not sure if the spells will scale neatly—it's *possible* I'm about to rip myself to shreds, or at least break my legs and generally embarrass everyone. But Gena knows what she's about when it comes to this stuff, and I have to trust her. I fidget while she chants and gestures, layers of sparkling energy building up around me.

"Don't let her stop until I get back," I mutter to Tsav.

"What if you can't find her?" she says.

I grab a piece of purple. "I can home in on her with this." Then, considering, I fish the big piece of red from behind the plant. If Mari is in trouble, I need to be able to deal with it.

Gena finishes with a shout and a handclap. She shakes out her hands and grins at the big pieces of thaumite.

"Holy *fuck*," she says. "This stuff is the *tits*. Where did you get—"

But I'm already gone.

* * *

Specifically, I've taken a single step toward the door, rocketed through it, and impacted on the opposite wall of the corridor. Priceless gilt-painted wallpaper tears, plaster cracks and showers me with dust. I feel nothing but a dull thump, like my flesh is solid oak.

Another step, slow and careful, trying not to bounce off the ceiling. I careen down the hall. There's a set of glass doors leading to a garden, and I fumble for the knob. It comes off in my hand with a screech of metal. With an inward shrug, I step forward and the wooden frame cracks and splinters around me as shards of glass cascade away. They cut my clothes and shatter against my skin.

I feel a strange mania welling up inside me. I've been buffed up before, like Duke Aster at the battle, but never like *this*. It is, indeed, the tits. I have to remind myself of my purpose.

I'm outside now, but still surrounded by the palace buildings. I take a cautious step and it's more like a leap, crashing through a decorative hedgerow. Another, pushing off the ground like I'm in one of those gliding dreams, and the next hedgerow passes well beneath me. There's a wrought-iron gate coming up, leading out onto the palace lawns, and I exert a little more effort to sail over the top of it. Open space stretches ahead out to the palace fences, but beyond that is the city.

I take a broad turn south, stride opening up, leaving a dotted line of torn-up turf and flying grass behind me. The big road to the east runs in front of the palace; I avoid the main gates and instead leap the fence, landing on the roof of the first building beyond. Wooden shingles splinter and scatter beneath me, but at least the rafters hold. Another leap takes me down to the road beyond, and I remember to bend one knee and plant my fist to look like a proper superhero.

Then the road stretches out in front of me, more or less straight to the city gates and practically empty at this time of night. I start to run, carefully at first, strides lengthening as my confidence improves. A few late-night skulkers and wandering night watchmen look like statues frozen in my path, and I weave around them or jump over their heads. The east gate of the city is closed, but it's only ten feet high—a brief effort sends me soaring above it, landing in a skid and a spray of dust on the other side.

Now I can run. The road rolls on ahead of me, all the way to Shithole. My steps are more like leaps, each one propelling me yards down the road in long, floating bounds. The hard impacts are popping the seams on my boots, but my thaumite-infused muscles barely notice the strain. I feel like I could run forever and leap to the moon.

You know, I've always assumed the Guildblades were mostly just a collection of psychopaths. But if Duke Aster and his lot feel even a fraction like *this* when they're powered up, maybe they're more like drug addicts, chasing after their next magical high.

Focus, Davi. Mari's in trouble. I left her in charge of the horde, and something horrible happened. Sibarae, that fucking snake. I should have killed her while I had the chance. Would have, too, if I hadn't been high on my whole the-world-is-real revelation. *Fuck.* If she hurt Mari or the others—

I always figured that, in the worst case, Artaxes and his "hail the Dark Lord" attitude would keep the bad guys in line. Evidently his convictions are more flexible than he lets on. Fuck fuck *fuck*.

I'm pretty sure nobody's run half the length of the Kingdom in an hour before, but nobody's had a thaumite stash quite this large before. As long as the energy holds out, I feel unstoppable. Peasants all along the route are going to wake up tomorrow and gawk at my cratered footprints or the battered path cut through their crops where I had to detour. Birds explode from sleeping into shrieking panic as I pass through forests at a speed more suited for an F1 racer than a human being.

I put off getting out the purple thaumite until I'm halfway there. I tell myself it's because I don't need it yet, but I'm not buying my own story. I don't want to search for her, because what if she doesn't answer? What if smart, brave, prickly Mari and God knows how many others are dead now and it's *my fault*—

The gem digs into my fingers. I spit the simple Words of the spell between breaths, twist the fingers of my off hand. The darkened world ahead of me is overlaid with another sense, the sleeping minds of the peasants and townsfolk like darkened lanterns or distant fireflies. Running while casting my mind ahead is no simple trick, but I manage.

Please be there, Mari, please—

There. My triumphant whoop dies in my throat as I lock on to her, and her pain and fear flood through me. She's running, too, with all her usual determination, but I can tell she doesn't expect to get far. I feel her touch the sheathed dagger at her side, trying to decide what the right moment would be to kill herself rather than face what's coming.

[Don't!] My mental voice makes her stumble. [Please. I'm coming, I'm almost there.]

[Davi?]

[Just . . . stay alive. A little bit longer. *Please.*]

[I can't run any farther.] Pain, pain.

[You *can*. That's an order. Crawl, hide, do *something*.]

[I'm sorry. You left me in charge, and I failed. I'm sorry.]

[*No.*] My breath is coming faster and faster. [No apologies until I get there. Tell me where you are.]

[In the woods.] Pain. [There's a barn. Might slow them down.]

[Try it.] I can't tell from the link exactly how close I am, but the distance is shrinking fast. I veer off the road, blasting through stubbly fields toward a far-off tree line. [I'm almost there.]

For a second, there's nothing but panting from both sides of the line.

[They're coming in. Old Ones, they've got torches. I'm in the hayloft, if they see me, I'm going to *burn*, fuck fuck fuck please no—]

I have to slow as the trees whip around me. Branches snap and crack against my face, spinning away. Up ahead, I see a dark shape against the patchy stars, a barn tucked under the trees at the end of a country lane. People are milling around the out- side, dozens of them, and Johann would probably appreciate the traditional flaming torches. A number of them are hauling the big barn doors open while others slip inside.

I like to imagine a sonic boom washing over them as I skid to a stop, but I'm not moving *quite* that fast. Still, I tear up a con- siderable strip of dirt, shredding the tree roots in my path and shedding the last scraps of my boots. It's loud enough that most of the torch-wielding crowd turns to face me with the bewil- dered look of people who can't quite credit what their eyes just told them.

I'd imagined bandits or soldiers. But these are just ordinary people in homespun and leather, with no weapons but a few hoes and pitchforks. They're clearly flummoxed by my appear- ance, and in the brief time before they can come to a collective decision as to whether I'm a threat, I raise my voice.

"Everyone away from there, in the name of the Queen!"

A moment of shocked silence.

"'Scuse me, ma'am," one of the crowd says eventually. She's a big woman, pushing past some of the others. "You a Guildblade?"

"There's a wilder in there," another man shouts. "We all saw it!"

"It stole my chickens!" a woman says.

"You're lucky it was only chickens," an older man says. "Those things will take children, for preference, and eat them raw and squirming."

"That's right!"

"We won't stand for it!"

"I'll handle the wilder," I shout. "But I need all of you to leave *now*."

Angry muttering.

"Thing is, ma'am," the big woman says. "We'd all feel better if we saw the thing killed. Sleep better at night, I would."

"Me too."

"My kids won't let me hear the end of it!"

"So, if you could fetch it out and have its head off in front of everyone," she goes on, "we'd be much obliged—"

Liquid fire blasts upward in two columns on either side of the barn with a report like an artillery shell. The ground shakes and dust cascades from the building's rattled walls. One or two peasants fall on their arses. The rest are frozen, too stunned to flee. I speak into the ringing silence that follows.

"Go. Away."

They go. Which is good, because I'm starting to have thoughts about how I could incinerate them and be miles away before anyone noticed. No jury would convict me.[8]

---

8 Because if they did, I'd incinerate them too.

When the last of the torch-wielding mob has vanished into the trees, I approach the barn. Walking at a normal pace takes iron control, and my breath is tight in my chest. When I pull the door open, the wood crumbles in my hand. Oops.

"Mari?" I say. "Are you there?"

It takes a moment for her head to emerge from the hayloft. Bits of straw cling to her hair and the fur of her twitching fox ears. Her face is a mask of misery, streaked with blood and grime.

"Davi?" She looks like she can't quite believe her eyes.

"I told you I was coming. Can you get down?"

She glances at the ladder, shifts a little, and hisses in pain. "I don't think so."

I jump up instead, one easy stride to land among the scattered straw. Mari sits in a slick of blood, her clothes little more than rags, her white hair and tail stained gray. An arrow is stuck through the meat of her calf, drooling a steady trickle of gore. I can scarcely imagine how she got up here, propelled by desperate terror.

"I'm sorry, Davi," she says, ears flat with shame. "I failed you."

"Forget it. No more apologies."

"But..."

I gather her up, and she throws her arms around my neck like she's drowning.

* * *

Mari passes out a little ways into the return journey, exhaustion and blood loss overwhelming her as the forests and villages blur past. I kick myself for not bringing a chunk of green—even with Gena using the biggest one, I could have had enough to heal Mari's wounds. Instead, all I can do is jostle her as little as possible while I run at several hundred miles per hour.

When I get close to the city, I use the purple stone to contact Tsav, whose thoughts are frantic with worry. She and Micah, who finally consented to wake up, secure a cart from the palace stables and bring Gena to meet me at the gate with the rest of the thaumite. At my instruction, Tsav brings a big blanket and throws it around me and Mari before the two Guildblades can get a look at us. My clothes are in tatters anyway, so hopefully they chalk it up to modesty.

Gena lets go of the courier spells with a groan of exhaustion, her voice reduced to a croak. Weariness slams down on me immediately, along with a *heavy* feeling like someone's turned up the gravity a hundred times.[9] I force myself not to settle into unconsciousness just yet, taking the bag of thaumite and using some green to address Mari's wound. Thankfully, it's straightforward, and she barely twitches while I draw the arrow through and close the rent.

"I owe you an explanation," I tell Gena as the cart passes through the palace gates.

"Too fucking right you do," she says. Micah, sitting beside her, gives a wordless nod.

"And you'll have one. Just not right now, because I'm going to pass out any second."

Gena makes a face, but gives a reluctant nod. "I'm a bit fucking blitzed myself."

"Tomorrow, then." I still haven't figured out how much I can tell her. "But, thank you. I owe you . . ." I glance back at the blanket-bundled Mari. What's the value of a life *not* weighing down my conscience? "Quite a lot."

"Eh." Gena's tone softens. "Lot of good folks are alive thanks to your healing after the battle. Glad I could fucking balance it."

---

9 But I am going to be *so buff* when I finally get to Namek.

"Agreed," Micah rumbles.

Then, finally, we put everyone to bed. Tsav and Mari take the bed, at any rate, and I collapse on the floor in a bundled sheet. First order of business is sleeping for about twelve hours, which takes the edge off my weariness but still leaves me with the weird feeling of walking around with weights strapped to my limbs. Second order of business is a bath, because I am *filthy*. The soles of my feet are solid black with superheated dirt, and what's left of my clothes is fit only for burning.[10]

Third order of business is seeing to Mari, but she's still asleep, so I move on to fourth order of business, which is eating half the palace larder.[11] Even with magic supplying most of the energy, running halfway across the country and back in one night leaves you *famished*. The first round the servants provide barely makes a dent, and I send them back for more sausages and bacon. Just start carving pigs, basically, and I'll tell you when to stop.

Mari finally wakes up about halfway through this porcine serial killing. I hurriedly cram a few more strips into my mouth and shuffle the latest servant out, then lock the outer door. Discovering that I've got a fox-girl in my bed is not going to go over any better with the palace staff than it did with the peasants.

In the bedroom, Mari is in bed with the covers pulled up to her chin, eyes wide and hair matted, ears flat, basically the very picture of the sad kitten you rescue on Christmas Eve and end up keeping because *of course you do*. She relaxes fractionally at the sight of me, and a bit more when Tsav comes in.[12]

---

10 And bugs. Are you fucking kidding me with the bugs. I can skip breakfast because I got so much protein flying down my throat. How come Superman never has these problems?

11 Yeah, I was lying about skipping breakfast.

12 Thoughtfully while not wearing her disguise gem, since her human form would probably freak Mari out even more.

"Hey," I say, sitting on the bed beside her. "How do you feel?"

"I'm, um, okay." Her brow creases, and she tests her leg. "It doesn't hurt. Why doesn't it hurt?"

"I healed you," I say, and then remember that she knows nothing about human-style magic. Yikes. We're going to have a lot of explaining to do. Fortunately, she seems to accept this mystery among all the others and only shakes her head.

"The horde—" she begins.

"Will wait for a couple of hours," Tsav says.

I nod agreement. "Bath first, or food?"

Her face lights up. "Bath. Or . . . no, bath."

Bath it is. Her clothes are almost as bad as mine, so they also go into the burn pile. After changing out the water several times, I spend a while rubbing scented palace soap into her tail while Tsav helps her with her hair. When we finally sit down with the half-demolished breakfast, she's dressed in a spare bathrobe and looking almost like herself again. I give her a few minutes to gorge—she looks as famished as I was—before gently clearing my throat.

"If you're up for it, I'd like to know what happened."

"Oh." Mari pauses with a roll halfway to her mouth. Her ears droop. "I'm—"

"Please don't apologize again," I tell her.

"Okay." She takes a deep breath. "At first, everything was fine. Sibarae wasn't happy to just sit around, but everyone had your orders, and there was plenty of food and thaumite for everybody. Hufferth and Leifa backed me up, but there really wasn't that much for me to do.

"Then Artaxes came back. He'd been away for a while, nobody knew where. When he returned, he said something terrible had happened—that you'd disappeared on your expedition to the Kingdom, maybe captured by the humans. I didn't believe it, and I said so to the others, but when I went to use the communicator stone, it was gone. Somebody stole it from my room." Her ears sagged even flatter. "I think it was one of Sibarae's snakes."

"We lost contact with you," I mutter. "I figured I'd just fucked up making the thing."

Mari shakes her head. "After that, everything went wrong. At the next Council meeting, I tried to ask Artaxes how he knew about you and what else he could tell us, but all he would say was that someone needed to lead the horde to find you. Then he announced that the Old Ones had chosen *Sibarae* to do it. I said that was against the instructions you'd left, but she said that didn't matter anymore. Her snakes grabbed me and locked me up."

"Oh, Mari," Tsav says, putting an arm around her shoulders.

"That *fucking* iron-plated asshole." I take a moment to calm my breathing. Mari seems reasonably intact—nobody has *eaten her fingers*, for example—so at least Sibarae didn't get to indulge her darkest tendencies. "Did she hurt you?"

"Not . . . much," Mari says. "Just a little rough handling. Not long afterward, Jeffrey and Lucky snuck in, Leifa had sent them to make sure I was all right. They said she didn't believe it, about you being captured, and that she and the pyrvir were ready to grab me and fight their way out. But . . . I didn't think you'd want that. Sibarae would go after them, and most of the horde would be with her. Everyone would die. So I told them to play along."

"And leave you locked up?"

She gives a weak nod.

"That's . . ." I'm a little lost for words. "Exactly right."

Her ears perk up a bit, and I hear her tail wag under the table. Fox-wilders have a hard time concealing their emotional state. She gives a little cough into her hand.

"Anyway. The horde got moving. We crossed the mountains and followed the route you'd planned, staying away from the pyrvir. Sibarae kept me locked up, but I think Leifa warned her not to hurt me. It wasn't so bad. But the closer we got to the Kingdom, the more Sibarae talked about destroying the humans instead of rescuing you. And that *wasn't* what you wanted, right? So I, um, escaped."

"Just like that?" Tsav says.

She looks down, tapping her forefingers together. "It wasn't that hard. They weren't taking me seriously. And Jeffrey helped. He had supplies and a route all ready for me. If I stayed with the others, that'd just mean fighting, so I headed for the Kingdom as fast as I could. I thought maybe I could find you, if you weren't really captured, and warn you about the horde. I figured I'd just hide from everyone. It worked all right until I ran out of food." She makes a face. "There's nothing to *hunt* here."

I wince. Living off the land, as wilders are accustomed to doing, would indeed be a difficult prospect inside the Kingdom's borders.

"I had to steal food instead," Mari goes on. "I got away with it a couple of times, but some human spotted me grabbing a chicken, and I think he saw my tail. He just screamed and I ran for it, but he got his whole village to come and chase me. I was running away when you first contacted me." She shudders slightly. "Not long after that, one of them shot me. Then I was running through the woods, and—"

"I can guess the rest," I say as gently as I can.

Guilt eats at me, rising in waves. I did this. I wanted to be a Dark Lord, just for shits and giggles, and when everything went tits-up, I left Mari to try to ride herd on a boiling kettle full of snakes[13] with only a tin-plated religious nutcase for

---

13 Metaphor gone rogue alert!

backup. Sibarae could have taken her apart piece by piece and I would have had no idea until angry wilders came boiling over the border.

But this time I had some luck, praise be to Satan and every dark power in the universe. Mari's *Mari* and so in her diffident, determined way, she did the impossible and made it here. Now not only is she not dead but I've got a little bit of time before the mother of all bad days comes crashing down on my head.

Technically on Johann's mostly empty head, I guess. But it amounts to the same thing.

"Okay," I say aloud. "Okay."

There's a moment of silence.

"Okay what?" Tsav says.

"Okay I'm trying to think of what," I say. "But we're here. We're alive. We can do this."

"Where exactly is here?" Mari says. "Other than somewhere with nice baths and good food."

"We have a *lot* to catch you up on," I tell her. "First—"

"Actually." She's cringing a little. At first, I think she just doesn't like interrupting me, but I soon recognize the misery of someone delivering unwelcome tidings. "There's one more thing."

I set my jaw. "Go ahead."

"Amitsugu." Mari scowls. "Sibarae let him out and they're working together. She's made him captain of your original horde."

Amitsugu. Another big mistake, although in fairness, *most* people's drunken booty calls don't lead to, like, thousands of corpses. He'd been in indefinite imprisonment when I left, mostly because I couldn't bear the thought of either forgiving him or killing him and couldn't think of any other options. Under the circumstances, it's hard to fault him for signing up with the snakes. He's always been a realist, except when it came to our relationship.

"Okay," I say once again. "So that's . . . a thing." Deep breaths. "Sorry."

"It's not your fault," I say. "It's mine. Do you have any idea when they'll arrive?" It can't be long, not with rumors already reaching groups like the Canceri.

"At one point I was maybe a week's march ahead of them," Mari says. "But I moved slower once I crossed into human lands. My guess is they're only a few days from the border."

"So, what are we going to do?" Tsav says.

"The only thing we can." Deep breaths. "Go and meet them."

Chapter Eight

In order to reach the border around the same time as the wilders, we have to leave almost immediately. I explain the situation to the Prince; in spite of Matthias's evident disapproval, there's no way this will work if he doesn't come along. We bring Gena and Micah as well, for backup and because they're the only Guild members I halfway trust. Gena's not exactly thrilled, but she's willing to take Johann's word that it's important. Traveling light on fast horses gets us quite a ways by nightfall.

The failing light doesn't mean I'm out of things to do, unfortunately. First up is evacuating Shithole. Mari said the horde was following the route I outlined, the same one Tsav and I used. That means Shithole is the first border town they'll run into. The townspeople will undoubtedly close the gates and start shooting at the sight of wilders, and that's going to end with a pile of corpses and the chances of a peaceful settlement substantially diminished. So I grab my trusty chunk of purple thaumite and use it to create a mental channel between Johann and the mayor of Shithole, who is astonished at being contacted by his Crown Prince and diligently takes down his instructions.

Once that's done, we have to deal with Mari.

Mari has come with us, obviously. I can hardly leave her in the palace; quite aside from the fact that I need her help, it'd be asking to get caught by some indiscreet maid. Crafting Tsav's disguise took a sizable chunk of purple thaumite and several weeks' time, and I have neither to spare. For the first day, I supplied her with a long hooded cloak to wear while she rode behind me, but this attracted a lot of attention from the others. Nothing like a hooded cloak to announce that you are Mysterious and probably Up to No Good.

So, that first night, I decide it's time to rip the Band-Aid off. With the fire started and dinner cooking, Gena and Matthias have questions they've been sitting on all day and I can't put off answering them any longer. After a little coaching, I bring the debutante forward; with my arm around her shoulders, I can feel her shaking.

"Everyone, this is Mari." I pull her hood back, revealing her rapidly twitching ears. "She's a wilder."

"She's a *fucking*—" Gena stares. Her hand goes to her thaumite. I pull Mari closer and glare at her, and she relaxes a little. "She's . . . a wilder."

"So am I," Tsav says. She sits beside us, having removed her disguise stone.

"So are you," Gena says in a monotone.

"Another one?" Johann says. The back of Mari's cloak moves, and his face lights up. "Is that a *tail*?"

"Yes?" Mari squeaks.

"Can I touch it—"

"Johann!" Matthias lightly smacks the Prince. "Look at the poor thing. She's terrified."

"Mari has come a very long way," I tell them. "She's a messenger from the Dark Lord."

"The Dark Lord?" Gena bursts out. "There's a Dark fucking Lord now?"

"I thought Tsav spoke for the Dark Lord," Matthias says.

"Apparently matters have changed in the horde," Tsav says.

"The Dark Lord wants to confer with Tsav and Davi," Mari says with only a little hesitation.

This is the bit I coached her on. But the whole story is getting creaky, it's not going to hold up much longer. If I can kick Sibarae and Artaxes back into line, then it'll be time to tell Johann the truth. It's not how I *wanted* to start this negotiation, with the horde on the Kingdom's doorstep, but there's no avoiding that now. If, if, if, trying to thread a narrow bit of hope through this mess . . .

"Let me get my fucking head around this," Gena says after a little more explanation. "These two are fucking wilders, and fucking ambassadors from the Dark Lord, whose *whole fucking army* is here?"

"That's about the shape of it," Matthias says.

"And you're going to fucking try to make *peace* with them?" This is directed at Johann, and she belatedly adds, "Um. Your Highness."

"What?" Johann stops staring at Mari. "Oh yes. Peace. Obviously! I mean, it beats the alternative, right?"

"This is fucking crazy." Gena looks at her husband. "Back me up here, Micah."

The big man considers briefly.

"I think her ears are cute," he rumbles.

* * *

The path to the horde is marked by columns of smoke.

"Doesn't look like they're fucking interested in peace," Gena mutters as we pass another farmstead burned to blackened timbers.

"The Dark Lord is," I say. "Not all her followers agree." Which is why I'm going to have to remind them.

I'm desperately hoping the evacuation order reached these farms in time. This close to the border, people have to be accustomed to the occasional need to run for the woods, right?

Fucking Sibarae. I'm going to choke that snake until her eyes pop, and then peel the metal off Artaxes to see what's underneath. I was *so close* to getting this right.

Calm. I glance at Tsav, who takes in the smoky landscape with a slight frown. We're not done yet. I can do this.

Shithole, as we predicted, was directly in the horde's path. It has not fared well. Several fires are still burning, sending ugly black columns into the sky. Other buildings have been pulled down, apparently just for the hell of it.

We're spotted before we can get close to the town, and I grip my thaumite in case things get ugly. Thankfully, the squat, bulky shapes of the incoming wilder patrol are recognizable as pyrvir rather than Sibarae's snakes. A party of five of them trots up, weapons ready, but they stop in confusion at the sight of me.

"Sergeant!" I say. "What's your name?"

"Um. Helga, lord!" She straightens up, the rest of the patrol following suit.

"Helga." I take a deep breath. "What the *fuck* is my horde doing here?"

The pyrvir quails. "We're . . . coming to rescue you? I think." Her throat works desperately. "My captain says—"

"Never mind your captain. Where's Sibarae?"

"In the castle, lord!" She somehow contrives to stand even straighter. "She'll want to see you at once! I'll bring you and your . . . companions."

"Good. And send one of your people to summon Droff, Leifa, and Fryndi, if they're not there already."

"Yes, lord!" she snaps, hugely relieved to have clear instructions. "As you wish!"

One of the patrol hurries off, while the others form an escort. The humans in our party, who understood none of our conversation in Wilder, look at them apprehensively.

"These guys are okay," I tell them in Common. "If anything goes down, just remember shark-toothed dwarves and rock-monsters good, snake-people bad."

"What about minotaurs?" Matthias says a bit shakily. We're inside the town now, and members of the horde are starting to gather and gawk.

"Minotaurs are a bit of a question mark."

"And foxes?" Johann says.

I wish I knew. I see a fair number of white ears and tails in the crowd, but I have no idea what Amitsugu's been saying to them since his release. Most of the fox-wilders seemed disgusted by his betrayal at the time, but he's had weeks to work on their loyalties.

I drop back a little to talk to Gena, who is looking around a bit wild-eyed and has a white-knuckled hand on the hilt of a dagger. Micah, I'm glad to see, has one hand on her shoulder.

"Nothing's going to go wrong," I tell her.

"Uh-huh."

"But if it does, stick close to Johann and Tsav."

"If it does, we're all going to fucking die."

Maybe. But Gena's picturing a straight-up massacre of us by the wilders, while I'd like to hope that we'll at least have some of my old guard on my side. Droff and the stone-eaters wouldn't betray me. Would they?

They betrayed Amitsugu, in their painfully honest way. Hmmm.[1]

---

1 The military strategists among you are probably shrieking, "Why did you bring your *king* into the *enemy camp*, you absolute cretin?!" This is not an unfair question, but while it might be best for the Kingdom to have

I have to suppress a laugh when Helga, puffed up with self-importance, directs me to the "castle." It's a stone house with a protruding tower, belonging to some merchant now fled. More wilders are camped in the yard, including a whole squadron of snakes. I'm grateful for the crowd following us, who are a much broader cross section of the membership of the horde. I'm even more grateful to see Droff shouldering toward us with Leifa and Fryndi sheltering in his wake. Behind him, I spot Hufferth and a gaggle of other wilders I vaguely recognize as the heads of smaller contingents, which I'm less sure how I feel about. More high-ranking witnesses means less chance for quiet violence, I guess?

I greet the members of my original Dark Council in front of the "castle." Leifa immediately embraces Mari, and I get a weird moment of walking both worlds—from my time among the wilders, I can't help but parse the scene as a kindly old grandmother embracing a brave young woman in whom she has a vaguely maternal interest. But I can also see everything from Johann's perspective, or Gena's, where a girl with fox ears is being grabbed by a squat, broad person with coal-black skin, a wild bright-red mohawk, and shark teeth, while a muscular man with a bull's head and a humanoid pile of rocks look on.

The front door opens before we get to do any catching up. Sibarae was doubtless warned of my coming, so she had plenty of time to arrange her snaky features in their usual unpleasant sneer. Matthias shrinks under her gaze, and even Johann starts a little, unfamiliar with the sense of being sized up as potential prey. When she gets to me, she forces a smile so false it has to be a deliberate insult.

Johann tucked safely in the palace, if we're going to come to some kind of agreement, I really need him on hand to agree. More importantly, if *he* gets killed, *I* almost certainly do, too, and if I die, all bets are off.

Which tells me something. Even with my return, the snake thinks she holds a winning hand.

"Lord Davi," she says. "We're so glad to see you've escaped your imprisonment. And returned with prisoners in hand, no less."

I give a mental snort. As opening gambits go, it's not bad.

"Now that you're here, I look forward to truly beginning the destruction of the Kingdom," she goes on. "So far, the humans haven't been willing to stand and fight."

Thank goodness for that. I clear my throat.

"Yeah, we'll talk about it." I look over my shoulder at the crowd. "But not here on the doorstep."

"Shall we restrain your prisoners?"

"They're not prisoners." I raise my voice to make sure everyone gets it. "These people came here in peace, and are not to be harmed. Find somewhere for them to wait."

"But—"

"Inside," I snap, losing patience. "Now. Hufferth and the rest too."

This produces a burst of activity, to which Sibarae ungraciously accedes. We leave Johann, Matthias, Gena, and Micah in the merchant's old sitting room, with whispered assurances and instructions to sit tight. I get the sense they'd be more reassured if the wilders hadn't already ransacked the place and taken an axe to the bookshelves and the liquor cabinet.

The rest of us proceed upstairs, where the main dining room has been repurposed as a Dark Council chamber. Even shorn of most of the hangers-on, it's quite crowded, with Sibarae, Hufferth, and a variety of other horde leaders in addition to Leifa, Fryndi, and my own party. Droff pokes his head through the doorway, floorboards creaking ominously under his weight.

And, speaking of creaking, Artaxes is already standing at the other end of the table. As ever, he's clad head to toe in rusty iron armor with unnecessary spikes. I'd been hoping I could have a few minutes with the others before he turned up, but the fucker can move fast when he wants to.[2]

Everyone starts talking at once, making conversation impossible. I raise my hands for silence and wait until I get it.

"So, I'm back." I give them all a grin. "Like a bad penny. You're not going to get rid of me that easily." A bigger smile, ha ha it's a joke, but I stare at Sibarae for a moment too long. "But I'm surprised to find *you* all here. We seem to have had some misunderstanding concerning my orders."

I expect Sibarae to answer, but instead, it's bluff, honest Hufferth[3] who speaks.

"We learned that you'd been captured on your mission to the human lands," he says. "Of course we had to come."

Murmurs of agreement from all around.

"I see. And where does this information come from?"

Hufferth blinks, a little confused. "I'm not sure. Artaxes brought it to the Dark Council."

"Artaxes." I turn in his direction. "Where did you learn about my capture?"

"I receive reports," he grates, his voice as metallic as his visored helm. "They are usually correct, but there are exceptions."

"Kind of you to put this *unparalleled* spy network at our disposal." I look around the table. "Well. As you can see, I am *not* captured. Fortunately, Mari was able to find me, so I could get here before you made too much of a mess of things. Good thinking on Sibarae's part to send her ahead to find me."

---

2 Somehow. While I'm looking at him, he never manages more than a slow walk.

3 He and Johann have a lot in common in some ways. If not for Matthias, I might ponder trying to solve this whole issue by a state marriage between them.

I fix Sibarae with a look that means "I'll play along if you will," and her eyes narrow.

"However, I regret to inform you all that there's been something of a change of plans." I put my hands flat on the table and lean forward. "We're not destroying the humans after all."

* * *

Once again, many people are talking at once. But Artaxes's voice cuts through, effortlessly loud in that strange way of his.

"The Dark Lord *must* destroy the Kingdom," he booms. "That is the will of the Old Ones."

The babble quiets slowly so that I can answer.

"You say that," I tell them, "but have you heard it from them in so many words?"

Artaxes is implacable. "I am the conduit for their will."

"Your trials chose me, didn't they?" *I* know the trials were bullshit, *he* knows the trials were bullshit, but he's spent decades building them up for the other leaders in this room. "And I *am* Dark Lord, am I not?"

"You are," he grates. "But—"

"And if the Old Ones made me Dark Lord, and I say we *don't* destroy the humans, maybe *that* is the Old Ones' will? Maybe they're tired of Dark Lords not getting the job done and want to embrace another approach."

"There is no other approach," Artaxes says. But after that he falls silent, which I take as a tacit concession of my point.

"It's not that I don't *want* to destroy the humans," I lie with an approximately straight face. "*Obviously.* Fuck those guys. But having done my little bit of recon, I think we've underestimated them. They're not actually ten feet tall, but we've seen what they can do. Tsav was there."

"I was," Tsav says gravely. "And unfortunately, I have to agree."

Mutters of disagreement. But uncertain disagreement. This lot, the leaders of the horde, have mostly never seen an actual human. A few Guildblades might get as far as the Firelands, but to wilders from over the mountain like Hufferth and the others from the Convocation, the Kingdom is an entirely abstract notion. Only Tsav and Mari (and Droff, if he ever says anything) are from the raiding bands on the border, and they're both on my side.

That thought brings me up short for a moment, because there's one other raider who ought to be here: Amitsugu. Mari said that Sibarae had let him out and made him a captain, so where is he? Maybe he's ashamed to show his face, or he figured that I might try to kill him on the spot. Either way I don't like it, it's a complication I don't need.

Tsav goes on. "We infiltrated a Guildblade force"—this gets a few hushed whistles at our daring—"and accompanied them to meet a raiding band on the northern border. We were expecting to see a battle, but what we found was a slaughter."

She gives a more or less accurate account of the fight at the occupied village, ending with the augmented Duke Aster ripping the thaumite out of the poor fox-wilder with his gauntleted hand. I spot a number of clenched jaws and sympathetic winces. Tsav omits, of course, the ambush of the following night and the massacre of those same Guildblades by the Canceri.

Sibarae ventures into the silence that follows. "The humans are powerful, yes. But so are we. Not in living memory have so many wilders been assembled under one banner. This is our *chance* to fulfill the Old Ones' wishes and wipe this stain from the land forever."

Is that a glance between her and Artaxes? Sibarae certainly wasn't so hot on the Old Ones back in the ruined city. I got the sense she was in this for power, pure and simple, not from any zealotry. But she's certainly playing the part.

"And if we fail," I cut in, "what then? Yes, we've got a big horde. But because of that we represent the strength of the wild. If we fall, then the humans will go on a rampage, pressing the border outward and slaughtering even more wilders."

"It's a risk," Hufferth says to approving mutters from some of the others. "But what else can we do? If we pack up and go home, that certainly won't keep the humans from doing as they please. Either we fight or we show them that we're weak."

"There's a third option," I say. "We negotiate."

Artaxes slams his rusty gauntlet on the dining table. "There is no negotiating with humans."

"I disagree," I snap. "I've been in contact with Prince Johann, the human leader, and I think he would be willing to deal." Best not tell them he's downstairs just yet. "He can stop the Guildblades from crossing the border and keep the Kingdom from expanding."

"In exchange for what?" Sibarae hisses. "Tribute in thaumite?"

"Nothing like that. Just a promise from *us* not to cross the border either. An end to the raiding on both sides."

"They cannot be trusted," Artaxes says.

"They can be trusted as long as they're *afraid*," I counter. "And they're afraid of the Dark Lord. As long as a Dark Lord rules, we have the leverage to keep them in line. But not if we throw it away on an all-or-nothing gamble."

There's a pause.

"We don't represent all of the Wilds," Hufferth says. "There are raiders all over who won't listen."

I grin. "Then we *make* them listen. Johann understands it may take time to enforce the Dark Lord's authority, but we *will* make it stick."

They're wavering, I can tell. Even Sibarae looks thoughtful, tongue flicking in and out between her teeth. There's no reading Artaxes, of course, but he's not saying anything.

One more push. I spread my hands.

"After all, even if we conquer the Kingdom, then what? I've seen it, there's nothing there we want. There are no beasts[4] within the borders, the humans have wiped them out. That means no thaumite other than what they've hoarded. The land is worthless as territory.[5] Why spill our blood for it?"

"I support the Dark Lord in this," Tsav says. "We should make this bargain and leave the humans to rot in their barren country."

More muttering, along the lines of "She's got a point there."

"I know it's not what you assembled for," I say. "But the ways of the Old Ones can be subtle, and I believe this is the best path. If this is to work, we must present a united front, with no wavering and no more destruction or slaughter. Will you follow me?"

So close. I can taste it. It tastes like chicken.

Hufferth gives a bovine snort. "You are the Dark Lord. My axe is yours to command."

Yesssssss. I want to pump my fist but restrain myself to a Dark Lord-ly nod of acknowledgment. Hufferth has a lot of sway with the other over-the-Fangs leaders, and there's a small chorus of follow-ups along the same lines. That leaves Sibarae and her allies, plus old Clanky Boots pouting behind his rusty mask. I watch the snake-wilder's face, the flick of her tongue. If she's going to push to overthrow me, now's the time.

But it's not, and she knows it. The time was an hour ago, before I started talking. Hesitate and you've missed your shot.

---

4 Note the distinction in Wilder between *beasts* like stone-boars, which have thaumite and a wilder-style life cycle, and ordinary *animals* like deer or squirrels, which do not.

5 Odd way to think of such a fertile country, but true from a wilder perspective. A place with no beasts to hunt for thaumite might as well be a desert.

"I have no confidence in the humans, nor any fear of them," she says. "But if the Dark Lord wishes to negotiate, then I will support her." Another tongue-flick between sharp fangs. "In the event of treachery, my people will keep their blades sharp."

Oh *ho*. I see what you did there. Unlike the others, Sibarae has to be worried that I'm pissed at her for seizing control. But she knows I want the horde to stay together—come after me, she says, and there'll be war. Fair enough. There is going to be a *reckoning* for what she put Mari through, but I can wait.

Now the only question is what Artaxes will do. Protest, and be sidelined? Or agree with the Dark Lord and concede her authority? In the end, he goes with neither—he simply clanks out of the room without saying another word, leaving the assembled leaders muttering behind his back.

Peace with the humans! Time to give the humans the good news.

* * *

Tsav and I retrieve Johann, Matthias, and the two Guildblades and ride out with them through the gates of Shithole, while Leifa quietly but insistently takes charge of Mari. Wilders line the street to watch us go, mostly in silence, as though unsure whether they should be cheering or jeering. They'll get the news soon enough, nothing stays secret very long in the horde, but for now it all feels finely balanced.

Nobody says anything until we're well outside the town, when Gena lets out a long breath and slumps in her saddle.

"That was the scariest fucking shit I've ever been through, and I've eaten this lump's cooking." She thumbs a finger at her husband, then slides off her horse. "Founders' *nuts*, I have to fucking piss."

"My cooking isn't as bad as it used to be," Micah says mildly. "I took a class."

"I've never heard of so many wilders working together," Matthias says. "What did you *say* to them, Davi?"

"What we talked about, basically. Peace. The Guildblades stop raiding one way, the wilders stop coming the other way. The border stays where it is."

"The Guildblades aren't going to like that," Matthias says. "Neither is the Duke."

That's putting things mildly, but hopefully some of the preparations we've been making are starting to bear fruit.

"The Dark Lord has the same problem. The raiding bands on the borders don't want to stop. But she'll stop them if you do the same. It'll just take some time, I think."

"I thought I'd get to meet her," Johann says. "Isn't that why we came here? So I could talk to the Dark Lord. Did you meet her?" He glances at Tsav. "Does she have tusks? Or a tail?"

"Neither," I say.

And then, deep breath. Because he's got to know at some point, right? If this plan is going to move forward, then we need the money shot of Johann and the Dark Lord shaking hands in front of everyone. All that good peace conference stuff. He can hardly negotiate with someone who doesn't show up, and fuck if I'm putting Johann across the table from Sibarae.

That means it's go time, but my throat is inexplicably tight. This is *Johann*. I'm not going to say he and I were soulmates, but I've spent a lot of time in his company over the last thousand years. His presence—a bit goofy, a little slow, always good-hearted, bearer of the perfect ass[6]—has been a constant through life after life. Being honest with him will—well, I don't

---

6 I've been trying not to harp on that, since he's a married man now. But just for the record: daaaaamn.

know quite how he'll respond, but things will be *different*. And there's no going back.

"So," I say. "Here's the thing."

"Does she have wings?" Johann says. "That'd be cool. How come wilders don't have wings?"

"Power-to-weight ratio," I say. "You'd need something the size of a hang glider to get off the ground. Listen—"

"Ooh, or maybe she has, like, an extra set of—"

"*Johann*," Matthias says, taking his husband's arm. "Davi's trying to say something."

"Sorry." Johann gives me his guileless smile. "What is it?"

Another deep breath.

"The thing is," I begin.

Silence, except for the sound of Gena's relieved moaning by the side of the road. Tsav puts a hand on my shoulder, and I put on a shaky smile of my own.

"I am the Dark Lord."[7]

Further silence.

"Sorry," Matthias says. "What? You're…"

He trails off, watching my expression. Johann is still blinking uncertainly.

"But you're Tserigern's apprentice," the Prince says. "Right?"

"From a…certain point of view," I say. "But more… *recently*, let's say, I'm the Dark Lord."

"Does that mean you're a *wilder*?" Matthias says. He glances at Tsav. "Like her?"

"I'm not wearing a disguise, if that's what you mean," I say. "I look human. But there's this."

I pull my collar down, showing the collection of thaumite embedded above my breastbone. Johann leans forward, goggling, and reaches for me; Matthias grabs his arm.

---

7 You have no idea how hard it is not to say IRON MAN.

"Go ahead," I tell him. Touching someone's thaumite is a major taboo among wilders, but he can't know that. He hesitantly taps the red gemstone and it feels like someone flicking my funny bone. I give a little shiver and let my collar back up.

"But…" Matthias's mind is clearly churning through the implications. "You can do magic, I've seen you. You *healed* me. That's not possible, wilders can't—"

"They can't," I agree. "I'm apparently a special case."

"But then…" He trails off, muttering.

More silence. Gena trudges back to the group and looks around, then up at her husband.

"What'd I miss?"

"Davi's the Dark Lord," Micah says.

She barks a laugh, then narrows her eyes. "Fucking for *real*?"

"Apparently."

After a second, she laughs again. "Sure! Why the *fuck* not? This has been such a fucking weird day, I swear to all the Founders." She looks at Matthias. "One of 'em's a wilder, the other's the fucking Dark Lord. I suppose you're a wish-granting dragon that lives on the fucking moon?"

"If you're the Dark Lord…" Matthias swallows. "You were in the *palace*."

I nod.

"You could have killed us. Or the Duke. Everyone. Crippled the Kingdom."

"Davi wouldn't do that," Johann says. Then he looks at me in a way that makes my stomach knot. "Right?"

"Of course not," I snap. "Look. I lied about who I am because it was the only way to get *here*, to this moment. Everything I said about the Dark Lord wanting peace is true. But if I'd just turned up with a horde and spiky helmet, would anyone have listened to me?"

Matthias gives a shaky laugh. "My cousin certainly wouldn't have."

"Exactly." My chest loosens a little. "I have . . . visions, sometimes. Things that might happen. I know that's a little hard to accept."

"Maybe not *as* hard," Gena deadpans, "under the fucking circumstances."

I grin a little. "Whether you believe it or not, I've *seen* what happens if the wilders invade the Kingdom. It means ruin for everyone, and I think that I was meant to stop it. Everything I've done has been to try to avoid that future."

Which is true, in a roundabout way. I've been trying to save the Kingdom for a thousand years. For most of that time, I'd have been happy to feed all the wilders into a wood chipper, but maybe it's not an accident that the first time I tried treating them like people I've gotten this far.

Fuck me. What if there *is* someone watching me and tweaking the time loop, but they were right all along? That prick will be absolutely *insufferable*.

"You're the Dark Lord," Johann says as though still trying the idea on for size. "The *Dark Lord*."

"You don't sound upset by the idea," I venture.

"I . . ." He shakes his head. "I might have been a little worried about meeting the Dark Lord, actually. I don't want to screw things up." Matthias take his arm again, and they lean together. "Now I feel better. It's just Davi, right? She's cool."

"Yeah." I breathe out. "She is."

Another silence, but of a considerably more comfortable kind.

"So, what the fuck happens now?" says Gena.

Chapter Nine

Tsav comes with a series of small grunts at the back of her throat, one hand gripping my bicep hard enough to bruise, her rigid body slowly going soft and limp with a long exhaled breath. I collapse atop her, sweaty and sticky and satisfied, the pounding of her heart loud against my cheek. She cups my head with her free hand, thick fingers running through my matted hair.

"You're nervous," she says.

"Is it that obvious?"

"Only to me. You fuck better when you're nervous."

"What?" I push myself up on both hands to look her in the eye. "I do *not*."

"You do." Tsav is grinning. "There's an intensity. You're like, well, I don't know what is going to happen, but I can do *this*."

"So, what you're saying is it would be better if more things in my life were terrifying, from the standpoint of your sexual gratification?"

"Mmm." She puts a finger to her chin. "When you put it *that* way . . ."

I collapse back onto her, head pillowed on her breasts. "I'm doomed."

She drapes her arms around me and weaves her legs through mine. "Honesty compels me to admit," she murmurs, "that the baseline is pretty good."

"*Thank* you," I snort. "I think."

"But you are nervous."

"Of course I am. No takebacks, remember? And I don't know if tomorrow is going to end with a sing-along or a pile of corpses."

At this point, dear readers, you may be asking: Why did you skip to the climax, so to speak? We crave prurient details! To which I can only say, first, I've got to leave *something* for AO3[1] to sink its teeth into, and second, a lot of things happened during that chapter break and I can't be expected to recount *every* twist and turn.

The aforementioned fucking is happening in a tent along the shore of Lake Refta, several days after the events of the previous chapter. This is a few miles from Shithole and somewhat off the main roads, where there's an expanse of woodland large enough to accommodate the sprawling bulk of the horde. Getting everyone there, naturally, has been a trial.

The pre-peace-conference negotiations have necessarily included a lot of give-and-take about where to *put* all these wilders, how to feed them, and could they pretty please not destroy anything more than they already have? The inhabitants of Shithole, thank God, listened to the Prince's orders and fled just ahead of the horde's first scouts, so actual violence has so far been limited to cattle and chickens. As usual, I lean on Droff's

---

1 Fun fact for readers from the future: Before AO3 was a benevolent government ushering in world peace and prosperity for all, it was a fan-fiction archive! 🦒 THE MORE YOU KNOW 🦒

incorruptible stone-eaters to police the horde, preventing anyone from going joyriding in search of unguarded pigs.

In return, the logistical apparatus of the Kingdom has thrown itself into providing a steady supply of nonstolen pigs, along with everything else the horde needs for the duration. I had wondered if this was going to be hard to swing, but the very presence of the horde has concentrated everyone's mind wonderfully and Johann is benefitting from the human tendency to rally round the king in uncertain times. He may not be the Duke, but he's *here* and the Duke's not, and that makes all the difference.

Speaking of the Duke, I'm sure news has gotten to him by now and he's probably marching back at full tilt, which is why we've been in such a hurry to get this event together. We need a fait accompli before Aster sticks his idiot nose in.

In any case, while the palace event-planning staff has never had an occasion *quite* like this one, they're used to the vagaries of royal whim and can manage a last-minute feast or two. A pavilion has risen beside the lake with shocking speed, with two huge dining tents alongside it and an open grassy space for merriment. Strategic reserves of wine have been tapped and musicians press-ganged from the streets of Vroken to serve their Kingdom in its hour of need. That one guy who inexplicably makes sculptures out of butter is doing his thing, in spite of repeated efforts to get him to stop.

A Good Time Will Be Had by All, even if it's at swordpoint. No expense has been spared.

But, yeah. I'm nervous.

* * *

Even the stalwarts of the royal catering corps can't be expected to host the *entire* horde, so Leifa and I have culled the guest list to a mere couple of hundred. All the leaders are invited, of course, and a good mix from the rest, not obviously stacked with loyalists but not a bunch of frothing maniacs either. On the human side, Johann and Matthias—mostly Matthias, if we're being honest—have produced a roster of important Kingdom nobles and dignitaries who can be trusted not to start laying about with a greatsword at the sight of someone with a tail. A few of the more hotheaded have been scheduled for an avuncular talk with their Prince, who will explain the need to pull together and put a good face on humanity at this crucial juncture.

This is just the introductory feast, obviously. Tomorrow there's a working lunch with cocktails, and the day after that a celebratory barbecue. But one thing at a time.

Servants in royal livery are everywhere, hurrying to and fro over the grassy lawn, carrying platters, glasses, stacks of napkins, bales of tiny useless forks. Butter guy is wheeling out his latest creation, which is ostensibly the Queen but seems oddly heavy on the tentacles. Tsav is at my side, disguised, but none of the other wilders have arrived yet—we agreed it was better to bring them in once the humans were settled. Let everyone get a good look at one another and decide whether they were going to freak out.

The human procession is naturally led by Johann. He's up on a white charger and in his element, which is to say smiling and looking hot. The wind picks up at just the right moment to blow his hair and cloak dramatically behind him, because the world just works like that for some people, and when he shows his teeth, you can practically hear the light go *ting*. Matthias is behind him, and I have to say, the kid cleans up pretty good when he trades his slightly shabby scholar's robes for formalwear. If this is how Johann first saw him, I understand why he'd take an interest.

A squad of trumpeters tootles the Prince's arrival, and all

the servants stand to attention. He waves graciously, another Johann specialty, and slides smoothly off his horse with a flutter of his cape. A frown crosses his face, and for a second, I'm sure he's forgotten his lines, but the brilliant smile quickly returns.

"I just want to say thanks to all of you," he says, clear voice reaching across the grounds. "Today is important, and you are a vital part of it. Our guests will be unusual, but they are our *guests*, and you all understand what that means."

The staff, used to being ignored like part of the furniture by the people they serve, stare at him in awe. A chef standing near me has tears in his eyes. On the one hand, someone needs to tell these people that royals burp and fart like anyone else; on the other hand, without that reverence, it might be a *little* hard to get waiters to serve soup to walking snakes, so we'll call it a win for now.

Behind the Prince and his husband come the rest of the guests, counts and barons and the better sort of merchants, all decked out in their most ostentatious finery and looking uniformly a bit jumpy. They stare around, searching for heavily armed wilders screaming for blood, and don't find any. One well-dressed lady gives a start at the sight of the butter statue.

One thing distinguishes this gathering from court: no thaumite. Johann put the word out that arriving with visible gems to a meeting with wilders would be a bit like turning up to a formal dinner with baby-skull jewelry and finger-bone cuff links. I'm glad to see the nobles have taken it to heart. No doubt many of them have some stones in their pockets, just in case, but at least they're not on display.

I give the humans some time to sit down and get comfortable—and crucially to get through a couple of glasses of wine—before giving Mari the mental signal to bring in the wilders. They're as hesitant as their human counterparts if you know how to look for it. The humans don't, of course, so all they see is a savage horde rolling down on them. If things are going to get fucked, this seems like the moment, and I've got my hand on my thaumite in preparation.

Someone gives an involuntary shriek. A well-dressed man faints, his head bonking on the table since nobody is paying enough attention to catch him. Quite a few people take a firm grip on the flatware, as though they're going to fend off an eight-foot rock-monster with a salad fork.

"Mari!" Johann says. He's standing at the edge of the pavilion, equidistant between the feast tents. "So good to see you again."

"L-likewise." Mari's voice trembles only a little. Leifa's sewing brigade did a fantastic job on her costume, which has a high gray fur collar that offsets the brilliant white of her ears and tail. It's sort of a cross between an opera gown and a special forces dress uniform, capturing that "I will fuck you up, but *fabulously*" essence that's so important to formal clothing in a feudal society. "Thank you for arranging such a reception."

"Think nothing of it." Johann gives a formal bow, which Mari matches inexpertly. "Be welcome."

The little ritual seems to calm the humans, placing the newcomers in the familiar context of courtly etiquette. I see a few of them wondering at how this wilder girl speaks such perfect Common, and I allow myself a smile of satisfaction at a job well done. At the apex of the pavilion is a purple stone—I'm out of large ones, so Johann borrowed it from the royal treasury—imbued with a complex spell I spent most of the last two days crafting. It provides mental translation services in a wide radius, subtly enough that it's hard to even notice it's happening. The energy expended is considerable and it'll only last the night, but since the only available bilingual interpreters are Tsav and myself, it's worth the effort. I'm already aching at the thought of cranking it up again for tomorrow, though.

Mari stands with Johann in front of the high table as the rest of the horde representatives troop in, their formal costumes as varied as their bodies. Sibarae and the other snake-wilders wear only short leggings, as usual, but drape their upper torsos in complicated webs of gold and silver chain accented with colorful feathers. Leifa, Fryndi, and the other pyrvir didn't have the time or material to re-create the fantastic outfits I saw at the Jarl's court, but the low-rent versions are impressive enough when combined with bright red hair teased into towering, elaborate braids. Hufferth is bare-chested in a sort of barbarian chic, but he's oiled his horns and possibly his pecs as well. Euria, one of our small cadre of deer-wilders, has tiny bells hanging from each of her antlers like she's ready to be harnessed to Santa's sleigh.

Droff, of course, is just Droff. I proposed gluing rhinestones all over him to make a walking disco ball, but he wasn't a fan. Still, half a ton of walking rocks is impressive regardless of what it's wearing.

Once again, I find myself imagining what the mishmash of styles must look like to someone from Johann's court, and what the velvet and lace and long skirts of the humans seem like in return. Cultural exchange is never easy, and people on both sides are staring and whispering to one another.

Fair enough. Time for my grand entrance.

My Dark Lord outfit has been evolving over time, depending on our resources and the audience. Leifa's been working on it longer than any of the others, so it's correspondingly more elaborate, and I have to say, she's outdone herself. The cloak is the crowning glory, big and swishy, dark as night, occupying a comfortable midpoint between Dracula and Vader. Beneath it, the clothes have a somewhat martial cut, echoing Mari's uniform. Polished boots and tight-creased trousers, dark grays with silver and gold accents. My hair is tied back and businesslike, enclosed with a slim silver circlet. There's no sword-belt—we didn't want anybody armed—but a discreet pocket holds some of my thaumite in case of trouble.

It's not spiky armor and a great big helmet, obviously, there's nothing that *screams* Dark Lord, but at least if someone pointed to me and said "That's the Dark Lord," you might be surprised but not necessarily disappointed. The only thing I regret, as I become the cynosure of all eyes, is that I'm not about six inches taller.

Johann is staring along with all the rest. I can see something in his brain go *click*, the realization that I really *am* who I say I am sinking in, now that I'm wearing an appropriate costume. It's like the scene where the Nerdy Girl gets a makeover into the Hot Cheerleader and the guy finally notices her,[2] only with the Evil Queen instead.

"Prince Johann," I intone.[3] I give a half bow at the precisely correct angle to greet a peer, a detail that at least the human side can appreciate.

"Dark Lord Davi," he intones back,[4] and gives the same bow. "It is good to meet you, definitely for the first time."

Matthias jabs him surreptitiously in the ribs, for which I am grateful.

"Likewise. Thank you for your hospitality."

Johann waves a hand at the work of several hundred people over the course of days. "A trifle. Shall we begin the refreshments?"

"By all means."

We link arms and proceed to the high table, with Mari, Tsav, and Matthias following. This is the signal for the waiters to start directing people to their seats, which they do with

---

2 Which is dumb, obviously, I'd take the Nerdy Girl any day.

3 I've been practicing.

4 Damn it, how is he still better at it?!

surprising aplomb. Johann put Jeeves in charge of the staff on the wilder side, and clearly he's worked hard to instill them with his imperturbable ethos. Also, the sight of black-coated footmen gravely pulling back a chair for, say, a mouse in a cowboy hat makes me giggle.

"So far, so good," Tsav says in my ear.

"They're not actually killing each other, at least." I pick up my silverware, realizing I'm actually famished. I can't remember if I've eaten anything else today. Thankfully, waiters are beginning to circulate with the first courses. "Let's see if we can keep that going and make it to stage two."

* * *

Stage two would be "talking to one another," and it proves more difficult than I had hoped.

After soup and salad, I convinced the palace caterers to do the cheese-and-crackers thing buffet style, with large tables set up in between the tents spread with tempting treats. Everyone having had a few courses to settle their stomachs, it seemed like a good way to get the opposing sides to spend a little time at arm's length to one another.

Unfortunately, our guests aren't going with the program. Instead, they behave like awkward teens at a middle school dance, venturing from the safety of their own table only in groups, making quick raids on the snacks and then retiring quickly with the ill-gotten gains. Very uncooperative. If we finish the night with no humans and wilders having exchanged words, this whole event is not going to be very productive.

Time to lead by example. I grab Johann and venture out into no-man's-land. Parking him beneath the butter sculpture, I go over to the wilder side and enlist Droff, Hufferth, and Euria, who obediently follow me back to the center.

"Talk," I command them.

Silence.

"Droff is uncertain what to say," says Droff.

"You must have questions!" I tell them. "Aren't you curious at all?"

Hufferth shuffles awkwardly, then manages, "So ... how is it being a human?"

"Not bad, not bad," Johann says gamely. He clears his throat. "Er. How is it being a giant pile of rocks?"

"Droff cannot express an opinion. Droff has never been anything else."

"Right, right," Johann says. "Obviously."

"Do you feel privileged," Euria says, "that the Dark Lord has granted you the honor of her presence?"

"Davi?" Johann perks up. "She's a lot of fun, yeah. Did she tell you about the first time we met? She broke into my bedroom."

"In*deed*?" Hufferth says, raising his bovine eyebrows. "To what end?"

"To tell me about prophecy, oddly enough!"

"She is a generous Dark Lord," Euria says piously.

Better than nothing. I go in search of more compliant wilders. Matthias, who gets the idea, ventures into human territory to retrieve Gena[5] and Micah. I bring Jeffrey the mouse cowboy and Lucky the Lizard, whose eyes roll wildly as though I'm dragging him to his demise. But Jeffrey says something about the journey to get to human lands, and Micah says something about his adventures in the Wilds, and that's *something* to talk about so long as everyone avoids the subject of what they were *doing* in the other side's territory.

---

5 Who, incidentally, also cleans up nicely, in some velvety dark green fabric that emphasizes her generous curves. Micah, on the other hand, looks like a redwood in a tuxedo; he ought to have gone for Hufferth's approach.

Dinner parties, man. I'll never underestimate cucumber-sandwich-nibbling diplomats again.

In a few minutes, by dint of much effort, something approximating mingling is occurring. A lot of the conversations peter out after a few rounds of "What nice ears you have," and I must circulate constantly to get them started again lest people grab their cheese and head for the hills. When someone takes my arm, I'm halfway through babbling something about the weather before I realize who I'm talking to.

Amitsugu looks better than the last time I saw him, shattered and bound, but there's a new gauntness in his face.[6] His white hair, formerly hanging below his shoulders, has been cropped to the nape of his neck, which has the unsettling-for-humans effect of exposing the weird blank spots where his ears should be. His actual ears, flattened on the top of his head, have bald patches in their fur.

"Hello, Davi," he says. His teeth are small and pointed. "Can we talk?"

I swallow, surprised at the depth of my own feelings. Not attraction—dude's handsome, but at this point, I wouldn't touch him with a ten-foot pole—but *anger*. Lots of people have tried to kill me,[7] you'd think I'd be used to it by now. Usually I'm not one to hold a grudge. But if I'm being honest, some of the anger is at myself; not to let him off the hook, of course, but I should have seen it coming.

Gah. I have to say something.

"I'm not sure I'm ready to have a conversation with you."

His head falls a little and his ears flatten even further. "I'm sorry."

"Is that it? You want to apologize?" I can't keep the angry

---

6 It looks good on him, damn it. Those cheekbones are unfair.

7 Lots of people have succeeded at killing me, actually.

snap out of my words. "You were quick enough to join up with Sibarae when she took over."

"I had no choice, Davi."

"Funny. Mari had the same 'no choice,' and she walked until her feet bled and risked her life rather than choose the wrong way. You could learn a lot from her."

"I..." He stares at me, eyes luminous and golden. I can't stand looking at them any longer, so I turn away.

* * *

"Davi!" Tsav says when I stalk back to the pavilion. "I think everyone's running out of small talk."

I take a few moments to breathe while surveying the scene. The mixed groups have indeed mostly broken up, humans and wilders clumping together with their own kind and whispering amongst themselves. Johann is still giving it a valiant effort at the center table with Droff, but everyone else has exhausted their social reserves.

Fortunately, I was prepared for this eventuality. I have a secret weapon, something that has been bringing people together and crossing boundaries since the days of *Electric Boogaloo*.

That's right. It's time for a dance-off.

I give Matthias the signal and he runs to Johann. The Prince seems relieved to be liberated from his conversation with the stone-eater, and he launches right into the explanation of the evening's entertainment. Several groups of dancers have been recruited from both sides of the aisle, and the one deemed best (as measured by volume of applause) will be rewarded with the Prince's fulsome congratulations and, perhaps more important, a chunk of brown thaumite the size of a hen's egg. This gets people talking, since a gem of that size would be a significant catch even for most nobility. The whispering gets louder when Johann indicates that, in addition to our prearranged contestants, anyone present may try their luck.

The cheese trays are cleared away to make an open space, and the first rather nervous contender emerges. He's a bard of Johann's acquaintance who plays at court sometimes in between sojourns with the Guild.[8] His lute is a battered old thing, edged in steel plates to give it some durability as an impromptu club for when cutting insults aren't enough. The peacock feather in his broad purple hat bobs and wobbles whenever he moves his head.

Accompanying him are two young people, a man and a woman, both lithe and handsome but somewhat awkwardly dressed in layers of heavy, shapeless peasant's woolens. They take their places by the bard's side, looking quite a bit more confident than he does.

"Welcome," Johann says, for all the world like an announcer on a game show. I work a little bit of magic to give his voice some extra oomph. "Who are you, and what do you have for us?"

"Um. My name is Flambert the Magnificent," the bard says. "These are my friends Charity and Virtue. And we're going to do . . ." He trails off and leans a little closer to Johann. "Are you *sure* about this?"

"Quite," Johann says. He's grinning broadly.

The bard straightens up and grits his teeth in the manner of someone preparing to carry on, come what may.

"We're going to do 'When the Shepherd Girl Came Calling,' " he says.

---

8 For some reason, some parties of Guildblades insist that musicians are as important an element of a combat squad as swordsmen, wizards, and healers. Personally, I've always found it hard to hear even the most stirring martial melodies over the sound of clashing steel and breaking bone. I guess the real appeal is having someone to sing about your mighty deeds once you've done them.

If I'd been recording the scene for posterity, it would have been very interesting to go to the tape and see who among the nobles gasped and who stared in quiet incomprehension. This particular act is famous, or more accurately infamous, but only in limited circles. The sort of thing your friends tell you about while giggling, but only if you have cool friends.

In a world without internet, the Kingdom's progress down the Pornography branch of the tech tree has obviously been pretty limited. But "When the Shepherd Girl Came Calling" represents the apex of their efforts, the pinnacle of erotic expression, the Sistine Chapel of performative filth. It's normally performed in private drawing rooms or hidden theaters for a very limited audience, but given the circumstances, Johann and I agreed that it was best to go straight to the nuclear option.

Flambert the Magnificent takes a deep breath and starts to sing.

A full recounting of the events detailed across several dozen verses would relocate this chronicle to a very different section of the bookstore,[9] so an executive summary will have to suffice. A young man is at home on his farm when the titular shepherd girl comes calling. She offers to help with his daily chores, and he accepts. Together they sow crops, dig wells, mend buckets, harvest wheat, milk cows, wash pigs, and inspect sheep for parasites. Eventually the young man proposes marriage, and the shepherd girl accepts, but says the ceremony will have to be later because first she has to help the neighbor with *her* chores.

You can probably see where this is going.

I'm pleased to see that Charity and Virtue are as virtuosic, in their way, as Flambert the bard is with lute and voice. They wear the traditional costumes, which is to say that beneath Charity's ratty shirt and trousers he's in a sort of jock strap with a three-foot

---

9 Possibly the weird, slightly sticky section in the back, behind a curtain.

stuffed felt phallus stitched to the front. Virtue, for her part, carries some equally impressive artificial anatomy plus a variety of props to represent household tools, crops, and livestock. The dance—and it *is* a dance, these people are professionals—is graceful, funny, and mind-scorchingly filthy.

I like the bit with the sheep and the cucumber best. Judging by the shrieks and shocked laughter from both sides of the aisle, I'm not alone. The wilders are probably less appreciative of the nuances of the puns, but the sight of a giant dick getting stuck between boobs the size of watermelons requires no translation magic.[10]

The ending, where the shepherd girl flounces off in the nude and leaves her crestfallen fiancé speechless, draws gales of laughter. Afterward Johann starts the applause and the assembled nobles join in, hesitantly at first but gradually reassured this isn't a spectacular prank. The wilder side produces hoots, drumming, and shouted suggestions of various additional chores that need to be attended to.

All in all, a rousing success. The energy in the air means that the following acts, which are more ordinary, still get raucous cheers. I canvassed the horde for anyone with a particular aptitude for boogie and got a surprising number of takers. Next up is a trio of minotaurs who do a stomping, tumbling number to a fast, heavy beat, followed by some humans who go round in a circle with bells on. A turtle-wilder I'm not sure I've even *seen* before breakdances, and a pair of half-drunk lords try to do something involving kicks and fall down a lot, which may or may not have been part of the plan.

My own contribution comes at the end. The orcs who've

---

10 At least for the majority of wilders whose anatomy is sufficiently humanoid. Sibarae and the snakes are probably mystified by the boob gags, and I'd be very curious to know what Droff makes of any of it.

been with me longest remember our trek across the Firelands and the repertoire of marching songs I taught them along the way, martial classics like "Fat Bottomed Girls" and "Thriller," I collected some volunteers for a chorus and backup dancers, put in a bit of hasty practice, and proclaimed them ready to march out and tell the crowd that *Young man, there's no need to feel down.* Trying to spell out letters with their limbs just resulted in the orcs falling over a lot, so instead they pull off their shirts to reveal *Y, M, C,* and *A* daubed in bright red paint on big green bellies. The crowd, who have never heard of a Young Men's Christian Association or even (I belatedly realize) English orthography, are nonetheless swept up in the enthusiastic beat of the Village People's ode to gay cruising.

Once we're done, the band starts up and the dancing becomes general. Lubricated by alcohol and a feeling of transcendent strangeness, both sides seem to be throwing caution to the wind and venturing into arm's reach of one another. A few holdouts remain—fuddy-duddy nobles glaring with their arms crossed at these uncouth shenanigans on one side, Sibarae and a few followers grouped into a miserable knot on the other—but overall, Operation Get Down and Funky seems to be a success. Amitsugu is gently swaying opposite an elderly countess, Leifa is doing what looks like the twist to the delight of a party of young nobles, and a variety of orcs are twerking. Even Droff is vibrating in time to the music to show willing.

It is at this point, half-drunk and swathed in good vibes, that I commit the worst possible sin. Looking out at the multispecies jamboree, I allow myself, just for a moment, to hope.

Maybe this is it. Finally. Hundreds of lives, thousands of painful deaths, ten centuries, but maybe this is *it*. The golden route, the Jedi path, the true ending. Humans and wilders go on living with nobody slaughtering anybody.

Maybe this is what I was meant to do from the beginning.

Whatever mysterious force brought me here and kept me trying, maybe *this* is what it wanted. I might *almost* forgive the centuries of pain and suffering if the goal were really just to make sure everyone gets along. And if that's really true, maybe this time there'll be an after. Tsav and I can just . . . go live somewhere. Do a bit of Dark Lording on the side. Relax by a lake. Fuck like bunnies.[11]

Big mistake, thinking like that. Everybody knows that the guy who starts talking about his sweetheart and the farm he wants to retire to after the war is the next to get splattered. And if the *protagonist* starts doing it, watch out. I don't know if I believe in God and hubris, but I *definitely* believe in the inevitability of dramatic irony.

It should not have been a great surprise, then, that—just as I'm looking across the sea of dancing figures at the pavilion and thinking I should ask Tsav for a quick tango—something goes *BOOM*.

* * *

This is a big boom, even by my inflated standards. Orange-white fire blossoms in front of the pavilion, tossing dancers and chunks of flaming turf in all directions. The ground shudders. A wave of choking smoke rolls outward, drawing a noisome curtain over the scene. I hear screams.

Through the murk, new figures are visible, armored shapes moving with the long parabolic leaps of the hugely augmented, wreathed in skeins of crackling magic. They descend into the sudden confusion like destroying angels, kicking up sprays of dirt as they land, glowing swords drawn.

The murder-hoboes have arrived, kicking in the door and

---

11 Is that what I want? I think it might be. When did that happen?

rolling for initiative. One voice, magically loud enough to be heard over the din, is horribly familiar.

"For the Kingdom!" Duke Aster screams.

Fuck fuck fuckity flaming *fucking goddamn motherfucker*, are my first thoughts, my brain still trying to comprehend how quickly things have gone sour. In those few seconds, the swords start to rise and fall and the screams redouble. Another explosion *booms*, Guildblade wizards contributing their indiscriminate incendiaries to the general mayhem. Arrows whistle by, even though nobody can possibly see what they're shooting at.

Move, Davi, have your fucking breakdown later. Triage, retreat, salvage what you can.

Fuck fuck *fuck fuck fuck*—

But I'm moving, one hand jammed in my pocket to grab for my hidden thaumite. People emerge from the smoke and reel away, nobles in smoldering clothes and smudged makeup, screaming wilders. A Guildblade stalks past, a steel-and-magic shadow like a Technicolor terminator, intent on some prey I can't see. An orc with an *M* painted on his belly, partially engulfed in flames, runs in circles, while a fish-faced wilder shouts "It's a trap!" over and over, belaboring the obvious.

I need Tsav. Mari. Johann. Somebody. Too many people here I don't want to die, what was I thinking, what the *fuck* do I do if—

A figure emerges from the smoke, red hair scorched and bent at an off-kilter angle. Pyrvir. It's Leifa, her eyes locked on me. Thank the fucking gods.

"We've got to get people away!" I shout at her. "Clear the—"

She drops to her knees. The hilt of a sword is sticking out of her back. In the next moment, a taller figure emerges, a Guildblade woman in full armor. She grabs the weapon and yanks it free with a wet sound, and Leifa topples ungently to the smoking turf.

The Guildblade isn't wearing her helmet. She has long purple hair and striking features. I *know* her. Victaria of Nyle, a stalwart, good sense of humor and always up for a game of dice. She has a weakness for sugarcakes she hides from her companions, though they all know about it and giggle behind her back. Secretly hopes to get married one day and raise a gaggle of kids—

I close my fist around my red thaumite and incinerate her where she stands.

Fuck.

Leifa's dead. Everyone's fucking dead.

"Davi!"

Another huge figure approaches, and I clutch my thaumite tighter. But it's Droff, his massive stones scorched but apparently unharmed. Mari rides on his shoulder like a child, clutching his stony head. She's the one shouting at me.

"Droff was not aware of this part of the plans," Droff says, depositing the fox-wilder beside me.

"Davi, are you hurt?" Mari says. When I shake my head and point to Leifa, she gasps and covers her mouth.

"Droff would like to know what course of action to pursue," Droff says. Another explosion cuts through the smoke, bathing him in orange light and throwing weird shadows.

Die, I think. What else can we do?

But eventually, my voice emerges as a croak. "Get them away. The wilders, anyone who's left. Back to the horde. Defend... defend the camp, but *stay there.*"

"Good idea." Mari grabs my arm. "Come on—"

I pull away. "I've got to get to Tsav and Johann."

"But—"

"Go." I'm breathing hard. "Now."

The feasting ground seems transformed, alien, but I spot a flapping flag that I'm sure was part of the pavilion. I head in that direction, dodging around Guildblades hunting for prey, stumbling over bodies both human and wilder. No friendly fireballs in real life, and there are plenty of Kingdom nobility among the dead.

The pavilion has partly collapsed. A group of people huddle like prisoners in the still-standing end with a half dozen Guildblades around them. It takes me a moment to realize that these are most of the surviving human nobles, and that the Guildblades are facing outward, nominally protecting then. From the looks on their faces, they don't feel very protected. But I'm deeply relieved to spot Tsav among them, disguise stone glittering at her throat. *Smart* sexy orc lady.

Matthias is there as well, and I look around for Johann. I finally spot him out in front of the line of guards, shouting at yet another armored figure crackling with magic. I can't make out the words, but the Guildblade clanks away and Johann paces back toward the cordon. I hurry over.

"Davi!" He grabs my arm. "Thank the Founders. Duke Aster has attacked the party!"

"Yeah. It was hard to miss."

"People are dying, Davi!" His eyes are wide. "We have to do something!"

"I'm *trying*."

"Your Highness." The Duke's unnaturally loud voice is painful at close range. He appears out of the smoke, moving with the caution of someone trying not to launch himself into the air at every step. "I'm pleased to report that the immediate situation is in hand. We've established a perimeter and the wilders are dead or fled. My comrades are cleaning up the last resistance."

"*Stop!*" Johann yells at him. "Tell them to stop! What in the Founders' name do you think you're doing?"

Aster's helmet tips at a quizzical angle. "Blunting the threat to your person and the Kingdom," he says. "I was unfortunately in the far north when I received word of the invasion, but I gathered all the strength I could and marched day and night. We were fortunate to arrive in time."

"In *time*?" Johann throws up his arms. "We were having a *dance party* when you started blowing things up!"

"A dance party." The Duke leans forward. "With wilders."

"Yes! There was a . . . a peace agreement, and the Dark Lord said—"

"Was the Dark Lord at this dance party?"

"She's right here!" He points to me. "Davi, tell him!"

I'm trying to force my shock-addled brain into gear, and Aster's gaze hits me like a bucket of cold water. I clear my throat.

"I think the Prince may be confused," I tell the Duke. "It's possible he sustained a blow to the head."

"The hedge-wizard's apprentice," Aster booms. "Are you the one who encouraged him on this lunatic adventure?"

"Davi?" Johann says, crestfallen.

Fortunately for me, another fireball blooms and attracts the Duke's attention. While he looks away, I lean close to the Prince's ear and whisper, "If he believes you, he'd have to kill me. Tell him we need to get out of here and back to Vroken as soon as possible. *Command* him."

"I—" Johann nods and swallows as Aster's attention returns to us.

"The wilders seem to be in disarray," the Duke says. "Some of my comrades have pursued as far as the forest and encountered only light resistance. If we press on, we may be able to inflict significant damage before—"

"No," Johann snaps. "We have to get out of here. Everyone back to Vroken as soon as possible."

"Your Highness—"

"I *command* you," Johann says.

I hope I'm the only one who can hear the note of uncertainty in his voice. My himbo ex-boyfriend is not used to commanding anything more than a dinner menu. Aster is silent for a second, and it speaks volumes. I suspect he would dearly love to tell the spoiled Prince where to shove his commands. But inconveniently, there's a knot of nobility watching every move, certain to spread the word of whatever happens at this confrontation.

"You may be right," the Duke allows without acknowledging the C-word. "My comrades are brave, but even they are nearing the limits of exhaustion. Better to retreat while we can. I hope that we've at least dealt the leadership of the wilder horde a significant blow."

I think of Leifa, dead on the field, and wonder how many others died with her. My hand grips the red thaumite so tight that it aches. A twitch of my fingers, and white fire would engulf Aster, and I'm sorely tempted. But the other Guildblades are watching me closely, and in his current augmented state, I'm not sure even my power would be enough to kill him outright.

He turns away, and the moment passes. If only I'd incinerated him when we first met. Him, Sibarae, Amitsugu, Artaxes. I'd be better off if I'd burned them all.

Chapter Ten

It's déjà vu all over again.

The palace is buzzing with activity. Soldiers rush back and forth, heavy boots wreaking havoc on delicate rugs and clattering across flagstones. The Kingdom's martial apparatus, creaky after decades of relative peace, swings into operation with a rusty screech and a cloud of dust. The throne has called, and the lords have answered, marching to the muster with their levies and, perhaps more importantly, their thaumite. Soon the full might of the Kingdom will be assembled, from the doughty common soldiers to the magic-wielding nobles, and the army will issue forth to give battle against the fury of the Wilds.

And be slaughtered. Because I've seen this one before. I've *starred* in this one before.

I have to imagine the clatter and bustle, but it plays out in my mind like it has a hundred times before. In the dark of my bedroom, covers pulled around me in a tight ball, I can hear it all happening again. The inevitable fuckups and confusion. The confidence of the Kingdom's commanders, everybody assuring one another that no wilders can stand against them. The back-slapping and parties before the battle. And then, finally, the big day, and the brief conviction that everything is going well before I have to explain to Johann what "flanks" and "envelopment" mean . . .

Because the truth is, formidable as the Kingdom nobility are when fully buff-stacked, they've spent the last century or so adapting to fighting one another. The Guildblades are similarly specialized in short, sharp conflicts over limited areas. Faced by opponents with the numbers and the will to fade away, circle round . . .

Same as before. Same as always. They die. I die. The Kingdom falls.

Maybe it's time to bite the bullet and admit that this life is a failure just like all the others. I've got a dagger. Ten seconds and it can all be over. If there's one thing I'm *very* good at, it's killing myself. Giving up and trying again. It's what I do, right?

Sure, this time I don't know what comes next. But how bad could it be? Maybe I'll start a few days back and I can fix everything. Maybe I'll be back at the pool, and I'll hug Tserigern and this will all be a bad dream. Maybe I'll be back at the Convocation with Tsav.

Or maybe I'll finally be done. One quick stab, and then nothing. It would be a relief, wouldn't it?

Fuck. No no no. I don't *want* to die for real. But of those scenarios, it's starting over at the Convocation that really scares the piss out of me. I'd be back with Tsav, but a Tsav who'd lose everything she and I have shared over the past few months, everything she's taught me and everything she's learned. A lobotomized version of the woman I'm maybe-kinda-thinking I'm in love with. The thought makes me want to throw up.

She was right about me treating people like disposable objects. But I think, under my particular circumstances, that was the only way to stay sane. *Things* don't need to remember, they just go through their little pre-programmed responses depending on how you tweak the input. It's okay not to give a fuck about them, to slaughter them or use them as fuck toys or whatever else you need.

I don't *want* that. I don't want to turn *Tsav* into that. But I don't know if I'll be able to stop.

So, do something about it.

* * *

I slam the door to my bedroom open, badly denting the plaster on the other side. Tsav is sitting at the table, staring at the remains of a meal—I have no idea whether it's time for breakfast or dinner—as though she's not sure how it got there. When she looks up, I can see she's been crying.

"Davi . . ." She swallows and wipes her face.

"It's not going to happen," I tell her. I'm fizzing with manic energy, the power of deep exhaustion. "I'm not going to *let* it happen."

Tsav blinks. "Let what happen?"

"Any of it." I slash my hand in an imperious gesture. "Where's Johann?"

"Trying to talk some sense into Duke Aster, I think," Tsav says, still looking a little mystified.

"Then let's give him a hand."

I stride for the door, halting only when Tsav catches my wrist.

"Davi," she says, "are you all right?"

She's annoyingly perceptive sometimes. "No," I tell her honestly. "But what the fuck does that matter? I'm not going to let Duke Aster ruin everything." More than he already has, anyway.

"I understand that," she says. "But you should probably wear pants."

I look down at myself. Apparently, I'd gotten halfway through undressing before being overwhelmed by despair.

"I should probably wear pants," I agree, and allow myself to be escorted back to the bedroom.

* * *

A few minutes later, still energized but better attired, Tsav and I arrive at the council chamber. The guards outside look to bar our path, but Matthias, who's waiting just within, waves them aside. To my surprise, he hugs me, spectacles askew. I didn't know we had done enough grinding on our relationship to unlock hugging.

"You're okay?" I ask him.

He gives a sniffling nod. "It was horrible. I was *talking* to Baroness Gidjay and this nice sort of badger person, and then everything was on fire. *People* were on fire." He swallows hard. "I can't get the smell off me, no matter how many times I wash."

"I know." I squeeze him one more time, then pull back. "How's Johann?"

"I've never seen him like this," Matthias says. "He hates arguing with anyone, but he's been at it with Pallas for hours."

That's a surprise to me, too, but maybe it shouldn't be. Johann is a good person, deep down, and he *does* have a backbone; it just usually takes a lot of digging through the psychic detritus of years of carefree partying to find it. Apparently, Duke Aster has managed to blast a hole in record time.

"Is it working?" I say.

Matthias shakes his head. "The Duke isn't listening. And nobody else can see past the fact that there's a wilder army in the Kingdom. We've been getting reports . . ." He looks stricken. "It's not good."

I can imagine exactly how not good. Armies are destructive things, even in friendly territory. Keeping the horde from marauding was hard enough with the Kingdom providing food. As we speak, I have no doubt wilder bands are ripping up the countryside for miles around. Many people would have fled when the horde got close, but not all. Every burned village and slaughtered family puts peace further out of reach.

"I assume the Duke wants to march out and put them to the sword," I guess.

"As soon as he feels strong enough," Matthias says. "It won't be long. There are thousands of soldiers here already, and at least half the Guild, Gena says."

Another mistake the Kingdom forces tend to make if I'm not around to correct them. The nobles may be able to get here quickly, but the full muster of foot soldiers takes weeks. But why bother to wait if you expect your superpowered vanguard to crush all before it? And every day's delay means more of the Kingdom put to the torch.

"Have the wilders sent any envoys?" I ask.

"Not that we've heard from," Matthias says. He frowns. "I wouldn't trust many humans to let a wilder pass, though, flag of truce or not."

Fair. And I'm not sure anyone over there knows what a flag of truce even looks like. I need to contact Mari and get some information. My first attempt brought only the knowledge that she's alive but too busy to talk. For now, though, Duke Aster is the foe before us, and cracking heads in the horde can wait.

The council room has the traditional high-backed armchairs around an oval table, its wooden top stained almost black with the lacquer of centuries. For the moment, the venerable chairs have been shoved aside to allow the Duke to stand by the table in full armor, while a variety of maps have been unrolled and set with tiny figurines that Aster has apparently brought for the purpose.[1]

---

1 The little burning villages complete with cottonball smoke plumes are a classy touch.

Say one thing for the man, he knows how to throw himself into a role, and "leading the Kingdom to war" is one he's well prepared for.

Johann, standing beside him, is much less in his element. He looks beleaguered, in fact, with the same hollow eyes I saw in the mirror. Duke Aster is attended by several noble henchmen, the kind of people whose function is to follow the great man around and provide a sort of traveling consensus. Johann has only Jeeves, who shows considerably more aplomb than his master.

The Prince's expression on spotting me approaching is so pathetically grateful it makes me wince. Duke Aster follows his gaze and frowns at me, eyes narrowed.

"The apprentice," he mutters, and glances up at the door guards to rebuke them for letting me in. "With her servant, no less. I don't recall inviting you to any war councils."

"I invited her," Johann says. "Or I'm inviting her now. She should be here, is what I'm saying."

"Why? Have her so-called prophecies proved useful in battle?"

"I did save the Prince's life from the Canceri," I say offhandedly. "His husband—your cousin—as well. With Tsav's help, of course." I raise my eyebrows. "I'm not sure exactly where you were at that point? Occupied elsewhere, I expect."

Couldn't resist the dig, but it may not have been wise. The Duke's face grows thunderous. He eventually decides I'm not worthy of his time and rounds on the Prince again.

"*As I was saying*, Your Highness," he growls, "we're evacuating the palace as soon as possible. All nonessential noncombatants are being sent southwest to Marav, near where your mother resides. You and your household should join them." He glances briefly over his shoulder. "Take your pet soothsayer, by all means."

"I'm not going anywhere," Johann says. I meet his eyes and

give an enthusiastic nod, and some energy returns to him. "The people of the Kingdom need me."

"They need you to remain alive," the Duke says. "Which I cannot guarantee if you insist on joining us on campaign."

"Assuming there *is* a campaign," I put in mildly. "The party you crashed was a peace conference, wasn't it?"

"That's right!" Johann leaps to the offensive. "The Dark Lord wants peace. She told me herself." He gives me an exaggerated wink that the Duke is fortunately too angry to notice.

"Do you hear yourself?" he shouts. "The *Dark Lord* told you?! Why would you believe anyone who calls themselves a *Dark* Lord?"

"That's only the Common translation of the title," I put in. "The Wilder phrase actually means—"

"*Shut. Up*," Aster snarls. "Your Highness, if I *must* suffer this wizardling's presence, I will not be lectured like a schoolboy. She will speak when her opinion is requested."

"She's—" Johann begins, but I wave the matter aside over the Duke's shoulder. Johann pauses, train of thought visibly shifting tracks, and says, "Why *not* peace, if we can get it?"

"Because it's a trick," the Duke says, leaving off the "you fucking idiot" his tone clearly implies. "The 'peace conference' was doubtless a ruse to seize the Kingdom's leadership, thwarted by my own arrival. Any further overtures can only be similar plots. In any case, I doubt they will be forthcoming—having failed to win the day by guile, the Dark Lord will certainly now resort to force. Our only hope is to oppose her directly."

"You intend to offer battle, then?" I say.

"Of course. We will meet the wilders before they reach the capital."

"And what if we lose?" the Prince says.

The Duke snorts. "The assembled might of the Kingdom has never been defeated by the Wilds. These ignorant monsters have no idea what they're up against. Burning defenseless villages is a very different matter from facing the flower of the nobility and the fury of the Guild in open battle."

"I remember how well the flower of the Guild did against the Canceri," I put in.

He whirls, one gauntleted hand raised. I grit my teeth against the blow, but it doesn't land; Johann grabs the Duke's shoulder, and the touch is apparently enough to momentarily restore his senses. He glares at me, breathing hard.

"Good people died that night," he says. "Men and women who devoted themselves to the safety of the Kingdom instead of consorting with its enemies. I suggest, *apprentice*, you think harder about whose side you're on, or the rest of us might be forced to draw the appropriate conclusions."

"Oh, my loyalty has never wavered," I tell him.

He snorts in derision and shoves me roughly out of his way. "This is pointless. I have a war to plan. Your Highness, the Kingdom will know that I had no part in bringing you to the battlefield. If you insist on bringing yourself, then I will take no responsibility for your fate."

Duke Aster stalks away, boots clanking. His guards and yes-men go with him. Once he's gone, Johann sags against the table with a sigh, and Matthias hurries to his side.

"He won't listen," the Prince says. "I tried, Davi, I really tried to get through to him. But he won't listen."

"You did everything you could," I tell him.

Tsav speaks up. "What about the work we were doing before the Duke returned? Getting the nobles on the Prince's side. Can he just go to them directly?"

I shake my head reluctantly. "In better times, we might have been able to turn them against Aster, but not while there's a horde of wilders burning things down."

"You might have some support if you came with a peace deal

in hand," Matthias says. "I've been hearing some talk. Pallas may be confident, but not everyone is so certain we'll just swat the wilders aside. If there were an alternative to battle, they might be willing to take it."

"They won't listen to us unless we have a peace deal, but unless they listen to us, we can't *make* a peace deal, because the Duke will just ruin it." It's hard to keep the bitterness out of my voice. "Joseph Heller would be proud."

Everyone is used to letting my incomprehensible references slide by now. Johann clears his throat.

"If . . . if it does come to a battle, what then?"

I look down at the map and finger one of the figurines, a big armored one with a spiky helmet.

"Then we're screwed," I mutter.

"But Aster will win," Johann presses. "Right?"

I don't have the heart to answer.

* * *

What I really need is to find out what's happening in the horde. Exhaustion is tugging at my eyeballs, but I retire to my room for a bit of alone time with my purple thaumite. Reaching out to find Mari is easier now, since she's closer to Vroken.

[Got time to talk?] I send.

[Yes, sorry,] she says. [I was hiding.]

My eyes narrow. [Hiding from what?]

[Snakes. Davi, things have gone *really* bad here.] I can feel worry and grief pulsing in Mari's mind, but her mental voice is steady, as though she'd carefully prepared for this conversation. [Sibarae declared herself the new Dark Lord, and Artaxes is backing her.]

Not *entirely* unexpected, but I still feel a stab of rage. [Of course she did. That *fucking* snake and her iron asshole.]

[They're saying that you've betrayed us to the humans and forfeited the will of the Old Ones. After what happened at the party, some people are buying it. Everyone's hurting.] She pauses. [Leifa's dead, Davi.]

[I know.] I swallow hard. [I saw her die. I killed the Guild-blade who did it.] That doesn't help, and we both know it.

[What're we going to tell Odlen?]

I'd nearly forgotten about the pint-sized pyrvir princess. She'd been left behind with a camp of noncombatants before the horde entered Kingdom territory, and she was presumably still there, biting everything in sight. Leifa had practically adopted her.

The silence stretches a moment longer.

[Fuck,] I manage, and try to breathe. [Anyone else]—I want to say *important*, but it's too cruel—[that I should know about?]

[Lots of injuries, but it's not as bad as it could have been,] Mari says. [The humans retreated quickly, and we recovered all the wounded.]

[Okay.] Another breath. [Are you safe?]

[For now. Droff and his people are keeping me hidden.]

[Droff can't *lie*.]

[He says that doesn't mean he has to answer,] Mari says. [Besides, Sibarae's mostly just ignored the stone-eaters. Fryndi still meets with me sometimes, but I think he's wavering. Amitsugu's in charge of the fox-wilders again. The sveayir are really hurting, but I don't think any other leader has stepped forward to fill Leifa's place.]

[What about Hufferth?]

[He's playing along with the snakes, but I don't think his heart's in it. Sibarae's building a new force out of her own followers and anyone who hates humans enough, and that's the core of the horde now. I think Artaxes is encouraging her. Lots of little bands have split off, looking for loot.]

[Is Sibarae going to march on Vroken?]

[She's not telling anyone her plans,] Mari says. [But she has to, I think. What else is she going to do, this deep in human lands?]

[Okay.] I keep repeating it because I can't think of anything else to calm my racing heart. [Okay okay okay.]

[Davi, what are we going to *do*?] Mari's been keeping it together, but now her voice sounds small, desperate for reassurance. [Even if you come back here, I don't know if people would listen. The horde might tear itself apart, and then the humans would kill us all. But if we attack the city, then we'll have to fight them anyway, and Sibarae won't even think about retreating to the Wilds . . .]

The bloodthirsty idiots on both sides are certain they'll win the battle, and thus eager to have it. Naturally. Based on past experience, I strongly suspect Sibarae is right and Aster is wrong, but either way, it'll be a disaster. If only those two and their friends would fuck off together and leave the rest of us alone.

[I'm working on it,] I tell her. [I promise. Just stay safe for now, and I'll check in as often as I can.]

She gives her assent, and I release the connection. Before I let go of the purple thaumite, however, I sense something else—a mind brighter than everything in the vicinity, practically throbbing with the urge to communicate. I realize that it's the beacon I originally made for Mari, now in someone else's hands. Discovering the identity of the holder isn't difficult, but I hesitate a few long moments before making the connection.

[Hello, Amitsugu.]

[Davi.] The mélange of emotions that comes across is difficult to describe—relief, guilt, fear, anticipation. [Thank the Old Ones.]

[Don't thank anybody yet. Why do you have the communicator I left with Mari?]

[Sibarae took it when she captured Mari the first time, but she didn't know what it was for.]

[And you did?]

[I had an inkling. Mari talked a little too much around the fox-wilders, and there are a few of them eager to . . . keep a foot in both camps.]

[Lovely. So you're spying on my friends.]

[I spy on everyone. Once upon a time, that was why you made me, what was it? Captain of Shenanigans?]

[Which worked out so well for everyone.] I suppress a sigh. [What do you *want*? Is this just so you can gloat?]

[Gloat?] I feel genuine surprise over the link. [Davi, I want to *help*.]

[Help.] I can't hide my scoff. [Help *me*, the one you tried to kill, the one who threw you in prison. As opposed to Sibarae, who let you out and gave you your old job back.]

[Yes. Exactly.]

[Why?]

[Because you're right and she's wrong. Or, more precisely, she's crazy and you're not.] A brief pause. [Well. She's *crazier*, anyway.]

[Thank you. I think.]

[I've been working under Sibarae since we started the march, and she's getting worse every day. She's fallen hard for the "Death to the Humans" line. I don't know if she even has any plans beyond destroying the Kingdom anymore.]

[And you don't think that's a good idea?]

[I think a lot of us will get killed, even if we win,] he says. [And the humans aren't all bad.]

[You and the Redtooths used to raid them.]

[We did, and not just for food and thaumite. There were tools, wine, all kinds of useful things. Imagine if we could actually trade instead of killing each other in turns.]

I take a moment to consider this change of heart. It's *hard* to lie over a mental link like this, but it's not impossible. He could be working for Sibarae and trying to take me for a ride.

Somehow, though, I doubt it. The sincerity I feel in his mind borders on desperation. Sibarae doesn't seem the type for that sort of game, either; she's not without cunning, but she lacks the patience for extended subterfuge. And Amitsugu has obviously turned his coat a time or two before, so it's hardly out of character for him to do it again.

[All right,] I say slowly. [Let's pretend I believe you. What now?]

[I can tell you what Sibarae is planning. I sit on her war council.]

[Let me guess. She's marching on Vroken to kill us all.]

[Obviously, but I know the route.]

[Helpful if I wanted to set an ambush, I guess,] I say. [But we're trying to *keep* everyone from slaughtering each other.]

[I know.] There's heaviness in his mental tone. [But there has to be something we can do. You and the Prince seemed friendly, can you convince him to help?]

[The Prince is on board, but he's not in charge here. Duke Aster is, the one who crashed the party. He's intent on climbing to the throne on a pile of corpses.]

Amitsugu snorts. [Humans.]

[Says the guy who I helped assassinate his chief.] And for that matter, who tried to assassinate *me*. But there's an idea. [Can you get to Sibarae?]

[You mean...] He pauses for thought. [Unfortunately, I don't think I can. Too many loyal guards, and no one I trust to help. Besides, it wouldn't be good enough. There's a whole cadre of them gathered around her, snakes and otherwise. One of them would just take over, especially if Artaxes puts his thumb on the scales.]

[He does seem to be the éminence grise. Only rust-colored.] Something is prickling at the edge of my mind. [It's the same here. I could probably knock off Duke Aster if I had to, but then they'd chase me out and some other asshole from the Guild would pick up the mantle.] I give a weary chuckle. [The trick would be—]

And then I've got it.

* * *

The army of the Kingdom marches early in the morning, while the sun is only a dim suggestion at the horizon and the world is cloaked in mist. People line the streets as the palace gates open and the flower of humanity rides out four abreast. On a sunny day, light would have gleamed on polished steel and winked off countless facets of thaumite, the war gear the nobility has hoarded for generations dusted off and fitted to the latest crop of brave young sons and daughters. As it is, the knights look somewhat less than heroic, mist condensing on their plate and dripping off in tiny rivulets as though every man were sweating bullets. Heavy cloaks hang sodden and fail to billow.

The crowds, in turn, are somber and vigilant rather than enthusiastic. The capital's streets are thronged with refugees, heavy with the stink of their burning homes and full of fantastic rumors about the cruelty of the villainous wilders. Those who've turned out to watch their betters parade off to war have the attitude of nervous fans watching a hit-or-miss team head to the big game. "Don't fuck this up, guys" is written across every face.

Most of the army is bypassing the city, or we'd be here all day. The parade is only a few hundred nobles, drinking in the notional adulation of their subjects before riding out the eastern gate to meet up with the footsore infantry. The Guild contingent joins up at that point, too, hundreds of colorful murder-hoboes off to meet the climax of their personal campaigns.[2]

Tsav and I take the quiet route out the back, joining the army via the baggage train. It's not quite the traveling kegger Duke Aster's earlier expedition was, nobody doubts we're in for a serious scrap this time, but there are still nobles who wouldn't *dream* of getting out of bed without their favorite vintage of wine and a gold-enameled bathtub. Always important to look your best when getting slaughtered by monsters.

We march east, scouts riding ahead to search for the horde. Thanks to Amitsugu, I know exactly where we're going, but Duke Aster isn't exactly listening to my advice. Fortunately, the course I want him to take is also obviously the right move—there's only one significant river line between the horde and Vroken, a narrow but still formidable tributary of the Hedsine called the Gehr. We reach it while the main body of the horde is still a few days off, and mounted nobles and Guildblades gleefully chase down the scattered bands of raiders who've ventured across the fords. Not long after, though, Sibarae's main force arrives and makes camp on the other side.

That leaves us with one of the oldest military problems in the book: two armies on opposite sides of a big river. Proactive townsfolk have burned all the bridges for miles in either direction, so there's no chance of a dry crossing. The Gehr is fordable in several places, but crossing a ford with the enemy on the other side *suuuucks*; picture slogging through waist-deep water with arrows raining down on you and the best troops your opponent has got waiting when you stumble up the far bank, out of breath and out of formation. So there's a brief pause while both sides think about this for a minute.

---

2 Probably not one set of un-fridged family between them.

Not for too long, though. Neither Duke Aster nor Sibarae is the contemplative sort, and somebody is going to make a move. I just need to make sure it's the right one.

An hour before Duke Aster is scheduled to convene his war council and go over his options, Tsav, Johann, Matthias, Gena, and I are pre-gaming in Johann's tent. Gena is the newest addition to our little cabal, and she gives a start when she comes in and sees me and Tsav.

"Fucking hell," she says. "Sorry. I didn't realize you were back. And you're..."

"You haven't talked to anyone about that, have you?" I say. I've been trying to stay out of sight, lest someone who was at the party shout "Hey, aren't you the Dark Lord?" Most of the surviving guests are not with the army, fortunately.

She shakes her head. "Kept my mouth shut about all of it. Not like anyone's eager to hear. But..." She trails off, staring at me in fascination. "You're *really* the fucking Dark Lord?"

"Once and future Dark Lord, anyway," I say modestly.

"I thought you'd be taller," Gena says. "And shouldn't you have a big spiky fuck-off helmet?"

"I tried one, but you wouldn't believe the crick it put in my neck."

She snorts. "Never thought I'd be chatting with the Dark fucking Lord. Unless maybe I was tied up and about to be dipped in lava or some shit."

"I *am* about to tell you my evil plan," I point out. "Traditional villain monologue stuff."

"Right, but I'm on your side," Gena says. "Turns the whole fucking thing on its head, doesn't it?"

"Are you? On our side, I mean."

"Yeah." Gena scratches her neck, looking uncomfortable. "I got a close-up look at your fucking wilders and this isn't going to be a romp, whatever Duke Shiny-arse says. It's not like we're crawling some dungeon in the Wilds, where we can just fuck off home if it goes bad. If we lose here, we're *fucked.*"

"What about the rest of the Guildblades?" Matthias says. He and Johann, who had been talking quietly, come over to join the group. "How many of them would agree with you?"

"More than you'd think," Gena says. "Not a lot are fucking keen on peace if it puts us out of a job, obviously. But if the alternative is"—she waves a hand in the direction of the river—"then they're not happy about that either. A lot of us are pissed at Aster, too, for fucking off on his own after the Canceri attack. He'd have saved lives if he showed some fucking ball sack."

I've always figured the Guild would be the biggest obstacle to peace. And maybe they will be, once the wilders are back over the border. But even psycho killers can count noses, apparently, and the size of the horde is provoking some unaccustomed contemplation.

"Mind you," Gena goes on, "there's still plenty who are ready to fucking go. Aster's cronies and a bunch of the border types who didn't turn up for the last expedition. I don't think it's going to be as simple as the Prince giving a speech. Uh, no offense, Your Highness."

"None taken," Johann says cheerfully. "Speeches have never been my strong suit."

"There's no avoiding *some* kind of battle at this point," I say. "Too many people want to fight."

"So, what's the fucking move?"

"We let them."

I explain. Gena's face is stony. Johann, even though he already knows the plan, cheers and winces as I go through it again.

"Might work," the Guildblade says when we're done. "Might fucking work. The trouble is getting Duke Aster to go for it. If you suggest it to him, that prick will tell you to go fuck yourself out of spite."

"That's where you come in," I tell her. "Listen..."

* * *

Duke Aster presumably had to borrow a campaigning tent, since his own was trampled into the mud by angry crabs. I imagine one of his noble buddies obliged, since the thing is just as enormous and gaudy as you'd expect. The Duke is wearing his armor again to make himself feel martial, and he looks out of place among the rugs and hanging silks. Hopefully he's not turning into Artaxes.[3]

Gena's already there, along with Aster's usual cronies and several Guildblades I recognize as big shots in their murder-based hierarchy. Tsav and I follow Johann and Matthias in, and the Duke acknowledges us with a bare grunt and, in my case, a spiteful glare.

"—the majority of the wilders are encamped between here and here," the oldest Guildblade is saying. He's a grizzled guy with a salt-and-pepper beard, the kind of dude who first trains the protagonist and then dies to inspire him. I've forgotten his name, so I'll just call him Bob. He's pointing at a map draped carelessly across a camp table. "We haven't managed to scout far across the river. Every crossing point appears to be well guarded."

"*They* haven't been able to scout *our* side either," a younger Guildblade says eagerly. "A few have tried, and we've got their heads on spikes at the fords to discourage the rest."

---

3 Although having worn human-style armor, I do know how he poops—there's sort of a hatch. You need your squire's help, though. Related: never be a squire.

I suppress a wince, not that anyone is paying attention to me.

"So, what now?" the Duke snaps. He glares at the map like it's a recalcitrant subordinate.

"That is the question," Bob says ponderously. "We find ourselves at a tactical impasse, but strategically, the prevailing circumstances put us at a disadvantage—"

"In Common, please," Aster growls.

"Both sides are stuck here, and the longer we stay, the more villages get burned," I translate.

Bob gives me a sour look, but nods. "Also, the greater numbers of the enemy give them more options. They could leave a force here to mask the fords, for example, while taking the bulk of their horde up- or downriver to look for an unguarded crossing."

"So, *what now?*" Aster looks at Bob, then around at the rest of us. "Someone talk to me."

"Our chief advantage is logistical," I say, ignoring the Duke's obvious irritation. "The horde needs to eat. They're living off the land, stealing food from the villages and farms they raid, while we can draw on the entire west and south of the Kingdom for supplies."

"True," Bob says, stroking his beard. "If we wait, watching them closely and prepared to counter any move, it won't be long before they must either retreat or do something that exposes them to destruction."

"Wait how long?" Aster says.

Bob looks uncertain. "A few months, perhaps?"

"I agree with this plan," Johann says, as though reading lines from a script. "It seems sensible and likely to succeed. Ow." This last, quietly, because I kick him in the ankle. He drops his voice to a whisper. "What? I practiced for an hour!"

"Try not to *sound* like you practiced for an hour," I hiss back.

"We can't let those savages brutalize the Kingdom for *months*," the Duke says, and there are murmurs of agreement from both his noble friends and the younger Guildblades. "I've told the people I will destroy the wilders, and I *will* destroy them." His glance at Johann is contemptuous. "Not wait for them to get hungry."

"I understand, Your Grace," Bob says. "But the question remains, how?"

A silence falls. I catch Gena's eye and give a nod. She clears her throat.

"I had a thought, Your Grace. If I may?"

He grunts assent. She pushes to the fore and lays a finger on the map.

"Here, where the river winds toward us. The channel there is deep but narrow."

"Still too wide to jump, even with war augments," Bob says.

"Too wide to jump, but not to bridge," Gena says. Unlike Johann, she's a fine actor, and I can hear the excitement in her voice. She's even managing not to swear. "They don't think we can cross there, so they don't have more than a few sentries. We can easily drive them back with arrows at night, and then use brown thaumite to make an arch that spans the river."

The Duke frowns. "Is that possible? I've never heard of a wizard bridging a river in one night."

"One wizard? Never." Bob taps his chin thoughtfully. "But we have a great many wizards here."

"And more thaumite than has ever been gathered under one commander," Gena says. "All we need to do is use it."

Aster obviously likes the sound of that. "Once we have the bridge, what then?"

"Feint at the fords during the night to draw off their forces," Gena says promptly. "Then storm through the center at first light with the best we have. With any luck, we'll be torching their camp before they know what's happening."

"Giving us a good chance to take this Dark Lord's head

before she even gets dressed!" the Duke says, excitement growing. Staring at the map, though, he hesitates. "But . . ."

"The risks are grave," Bob says. "The force that crosses the
river could be cut off or outflanked once it breaks out of the
river bend."

The Duke, it must be said, isn't *completely* stupid. He may
not be a strategist, but the potential problems with this plan are
easy to see. I have a trump card to play, though, and I push in
front of Johann.

"You cannot do this," I tell him, selling it as hard as I can.
"Prophecy is clear—crossing the river like this will lead to
nothing but disaster. Please, Your Grace, find another way."

"Prophecy," the Duke snorts. "What has prophecy ever gotten right?"

"I think Davi's right," Johann says, still a bit wooden. "It's
too dangerous. Try to sound cowardly."

"What?" the Duke says as Matthias berates the Prince sotto
voce for reading his stage directions aloud. "Are you calling *me*
cowardly?"

"What?" Johann says. "No. I mean, uh, yes! Sure."

"But *you* oppose this plan. You favor extending this nightmare for *months* to avoid an open battle!" Aster raises his finger
triumphantly. "Which of us is the coward, hmm?"

I back up and whisper urgently in Johann's ear. He blinks,
then puts one hand across his forehead and says, "Alas, your
logic has undone me! I am in shambles."

"*Ha!*" The Duke slams his fist on the table, blood pump-
ing. "You hear that? The Prince doesn't want to fight. Well, *I'll*
bloody fight!" He pounds the table again. "Take the best we
have over the bridge and straight down their throats."

"There's some in the Guild who'll agree with the Prince,"
Gena says, making her disgust for such shirkers clear. "We
can't order them to cross."

"I'm sure there are enough good men to balance out the cowards," Duke Aster says. "Put the word out for volunteers. Anyone who wants to truly prove their mettle is welcome."

"Doom will befall you!" I feel a cackle coming on. "Dooooooom!"

"Someone get that madwoman out of here," one of the Duke's cronies says.

Two guards take me by the arms and drag me unceremoniously from the tent. They don't notice how broadly I'm smiling.

But *really*? Reverse psychology. Works on five-year-olds, Elmer Fudd, and idiot nobility. With Duke Aster's side of the blind date taken care of, all I need to do is contact Amitsugu again to confirm the reservation and then wait for the fireworks to start.

Chapter Eleven

I'm having my traditional pre-battle freakout. People are going to die, lots of people, and I'm not going to be able to take it back. *Aaaaaaaaah* existential crisis et cetera. It's becoming kind of a ritual, and as ritual requires, I cling to Tsav and wail for a little bit.

"Davi," she says with the patience of a saint. "Yes, it's going to be bad. But is it better than anything else you could think of?"

I give a teary nod.

"Better than what would happen if you did nothing?"

Another nod. I sniff.

"Then you're doing the best you can. Not everything is your fault."

"In fairness, a lot of things are my fault."

She gives me a squeeze. "Not this time."

She's probably right. But lots of people *are* about to die because of things I told them to do. Most of them are people I don't like, but still. A little existential crisis seems like basic respect.

I wipe my eyes with my sleeve and hug Tsav a little tighter, then look up at her.

"Are you doing okay? You've been quiet lately."

"That's my role," she says. "I loom silently behind you and provide moral support."

"You're very good at it." I lean my head against her chest with a sigh. "You know how much I appreciate you, right? I never would have gotten this far if not for you. Hell, I'd probably still be screaming my lungs out if it weren't for you. I feel like I don't say thank you enough."

"You don't." Tsav kisses my forehead. "But the sentiment is usually obvious."

"I think I love you, actually," I say. But I kind of mumble it into the soft space between her breasts, so I'm not sure she hears.

Probably better that way. Don't want to raise any death flags.

Once again, the morning is cold and misty, with only the first hints of dawn showing in the east. The sounds of an army shaking itself and preparing for battle are all around—clanking armor, shuffling feet, the shouts of sergeants and the chanting of wizards—but the actual people are invisible or vague shapes in the gloom, as though we've woken among an army of ghosts. Even fires and torches seem diminished, tiny points of light in an ocean of gray.

The plan was arranged more or less as I wanted, though of course, Duke Aster had to stick his oar in and make a few changes. I'd suggested (through Gena) diversions at the fords east and west of the actual crossing, a demonstration rather than an actual attack, but the Duke had thought it would sell the illusion better if we actually tried to cross the river. So hundreds of soldiers are going to thrash through the water and be cut down by arrows in the name of realism. The best I can do is have Gena leak rumors to the common soldiers that these attacks aren't expected to succeed, which will hopefully encourage them to give up as soon as they can.

Meanwhile, Duke Aster's volunteers, a hard core of his noble allies and Guildblade supporters, have gathered on the high, steep bank opposite the bend in the river. The Gehr loops toward us here, the other side forming a peninsula of mostly flat ground, cropland broken by occasional fences and farmhouses. Archers with augmented eyesight and strength have picked off the wilder scouts on the far side, leaving Sibarae blind (or so they assume) to what's going on.

The riverbank, a rocky cliff a dozen feet above the water, is thick with wizards. All of them hold brown thaumite of various sizes and cuts, chanting and gesturing in shifts, then backing off to gasp for air. There's a reason we don't build castles with magic; doing it the old-fashioned way is easier and less likely to fall over because somebody mispronounced a phrase. But if you've got the wizards and the thaumite on hand, you can't beat magic for *speed*.

Layer by layer, a bridge has risen from the depths of the Gehr where there was no bridge before. A single span turned out to be impractical, so two support pillars had to be built up first, rough stone columns that might have been natural formations. Now, under the wizards' supernatural encouragement, the arches of the bridge are slowly growing out from both banks of the river toward a junction in the center. Rocks flow and shudder like molasses, creeping closer and closer. Finally, with a collective shout from the builders, the arch joins, shivers for a moment, then stands firm.

It is, honestly, an incredible accomplishment. If humanity were more willing to work together and contribute massive amounts of thaumite to a common cause, the Kingdom would probably have a space program by now. I feel a little bad at the dishonest use this particular achievement is going to be put to, but at least the wizards who worked so hard to make it will be out of danger. Having done their part and exhausted themselves, they retire to the rear. There are still plenty of fresh spellcasters about, the squishies at the rear of various Guild-blade parties and the retainers of the nobles, more thaumite of all colors ready at hand.

The sun peeks over the rim of the world, turning the clouds a flaming orange and lighting up the mist. The Duke swaggers into position at the foot of the bridge and draws his sword, holding it aloft. His voice is already augmented with that stentorian ring he's so fond of.

"Friends," he intones.[1] "Countrymen. Brothers!"

Someone was up late writing a speech, which the Duke delivers with a good deal of pompous overacting and dramatic pauses. It goes on too long, and his arm gets tired of holding the sword overhead, so he plants it in the ground instead and pretends that was the plan all along. Basic stirring-paean-before-battle stuff: crush the enemy, defend the homeland, glory will be ours, the sort of thing naked apes have been telling one another to motivate the in-group to smite the out-group since the last ice age.

The pompous bloviating plays well with the nobles, for whom this sort of thing is bread and butter, and they wave their weapons and cheer. It's less successful with the Guild-blades, who are more used to fighting as a business proposition. But Bob, at their head, draws his own sword and gives a much shorter and more honest speech about how much thaumite there is on the other side of the river and how all they have to do is go and get it; this provokes cheers, hoots, licking of blades, and general bloodlust among the murder-hoboes.

"Augment!" the Duke shouts, and the wizards go to work. Layers of enchantment settle over the doughty warriors, a collective expression of magic that takes even my breath away. The

---

1 Nah, he's just shouting.

nobles may have less experience than the Guildblades, but they have more thaumite, massive war-hoards of carefully cut gems hidden away in castle vaults, deterring enemies by their mere existence like WMDs. Now, finally, they're put to use against a common enemy.

It would be inspiring if I hadn't seen this moment before, at various levels of desperation, several hundred times. Along with what comes after.

The fighters don't have my long-jaded perspective, of course, and I know how superhuman strength and toughness can make you feel invincible. They cheer louder with every spell until I start to worry the noise will carry clear to the other side of the river. It wouldn't do to start the fight too soon.

Speaking of. I step away a little bit and clutch my purple thaumite, reaching out to Amitsugu.

[Everything's going to plan here,] I tell him. [Is Sibarae playing along?]

[Perfectly,] Amitsugu says. [She's even pulled back the rest of our scouts to avoid spoiling the trap.]

It's a wonderful thing to command both sides of a battle. But once combat actually starts, my control is going to vanish as quickly as the mist. I tell Amitsugu to move ahead and switch my contact to Mari, who's being sheltered from Sibarae by Droff and the others from the OG horde.

[So far, so good,] I say. [But I'm waiting for something to go wrong. You gave everyone my message?]

[I did,] she says. [We're formed up on Sibarae's right, watching the ford.]

I wince. [Duke Aster insisted on a real attack instead of a feint. Try to, you know, fight gently.]

[Fight *gently*?] Mari's mental voice is alarmed. [Davi—]

[I know.] I try to exude calm. [Whatever happens, just keep our people together and ready to move.]

[I'll do my best,] she says. [Fryndi's getting unhappy, and not all of the sveayir are listening.]

[You'll manage.] The Duke is shouting again. [Here we go. Good luck.]

I cut the connection. Duke Aster is giving orders, sweeping his sword in grand gestures that seem likely to decapitate someone. He and the leading squad—a heavily armored wrecking crew of the toughest tanks the Kingdom can produce—head onto the freshly built bridge. I can see nervousness in their enhanced strides, but the magically shaped stone holds firm, and before long, they're running full tilt. The next group follows, then the next, each with a hoarse cheer. Armored warriors, archers in lighter kit, wizards, and healers following behind. All, I remind myself, volunteers. It's still hard to watch.

What follows is hard to see from my perspective, but I use my purple thaumite to roam mentally around the battlefield and keep an eye on things through other people's eyes. When they reach the other side of the river, the nobles and Guild-blades spread out, each adventuring party giving itself room to work. It's not a conventional battle line, but these aren't conventional troops, each fighter dripping with thaumaturgical potency. Once they fill the space in the riverbend, they start to advance, the last of the vanguard stepping off the bridge.

Back in my own head for a moment, I clutch my brown thaumite and start to mutter to myself.

On the other side, Sibarae has gathered her elites, her most dedicated and vicious followers. Snake-wilders, minotaurs, even a few sveayir, plus a wide coalition of the wilders from across the Fangs. They're coming the other way, intent on bottling up the human assault force and crushing them against the river. The diversionary attacks have already started, but thanks to Amitsugu's timely intelligence, Sibarae isn't fooled. The soft spot Duke Aster hopes to exploit isn't there.

But equally, my snaky rival has underestimated her foe. For all her guile, Sibarae hasn't fought humans before. She's heard descriptions from raiders, but even they only have experience with the Guildblade parties that cross the border or come to its defense. The really heavy artillery of the Kingdom is reserved for human-on-human violence.[2]

Being literally cold-blooded, Sibarae has arranged for a sacrificial front line, an advance party of eager fools drooling for a chance at first blood. The plan is that the Guildblades will smack these idiots aside, getting worn out and bogged down in the process, and then the heavies will roll in and finish them off. I get a glimpse through the eyes of a nervous Guildblade as they boil forward, snakes and lizards and lion-men and horned, bestial things out of a nightmare, a whole Halloween store brought to life and gone berserk. The humans keep advancing, wizards starting to chant, and the lines get closer and closer—

You'd expect them to collide like two trucks running into each other, a sudden stop and parts flying everywhere, but in fact it's more like a tank running into a soapbox derby car. Duke Aster and his buffed-to-hell vanguard barely even notice the lightly augmented wilders, leaping through them in long, floating arcs with their blades leaving trails of blood hanging in the air behind them. There's a moment of stunned surprise on the wilder side before they realize what's happening, and in that fraction of a second, arrows fly and fireballs blossom like crimson flowers ahead of the advancing tide of steel. All the idiots who thought this would be an easy victory come apart like an overripe banana in a blender.

I wondered if Sibarae would panic. Her mind is closed to me,

---

2 Which obviously makes no sense, when you think about it, but humans gonna human.

of course, but I can see from the way the wilders respond that she keeps her cool. Some of the front line breaks into flight, but more hunker down, letting the armored tanks pass by and then pressing forward to attack the ranged support behind them. The Guildblades and nobles aren't used to fighting in company, and the looseness of their line means plenty of the enemies slip through. Chaos erupts farther back as archers start shooting at point-blank range and wizards ring themselves with fire to ward off their foes.[3] Some of the frontline warriors turn around at shouts from their party members, and the forward momentum of the human forces slows.

At the same time, a new kind of enemy confronts them. Most wilders don't accumulate great stores of thaumite, either from lack of opportunity or because they use it to have children. But some chiefs and notable warriors can build up a stock, like the Redtooth leader Gevalkin or the pyrvir assassin I called Wonder Woman. While only a true Old One could match the strength and stamina of the Kingdom's finest, there are a lot of these augmented wilders in the horde, and Sibarae has gathered all she could as the hard core of her forces. They're a nasty surprise to the humans, who are just getting used to laying waste to everything before them. In the same way that no wilders have experience with the full might of the Kingdom's army, only the most experienced of Guildblades have any idea of the true heights of strength wilders can reach.

A few minutes more and it's pure chaos. A minotaur warrior lifts an armored knight overhead and slams him into the dirt, only to be peppered with a dozen arrows. A fast-moving snake guts a wizard and then bursts into flames as her companion screams for vengeance. Two axe-wielding fighters come together, one human and one pyrvir, exchanging ringing

---

3 "WTF DPS drew aggro LOLOLOL newbs"

roundhouse blows that threaten their own side on the back-swing.

A bloody fucking mess, in other words, with no lines and no prospect of victory except by being the last person standing. Perfect.

"Message from the Duke!" a nearby wizard shouts, clutching a pearl of purple thaumite. "He orders all reserves committed to the fight immediately!"

There's some grim looks going around. Anyone with an ounce of military experience can see that no good will come of pushing the attack. Feeding more meat into the grinder will only mean more hamburger coming out the other end. But with the army commander over in the thick of the fighting, there doesn't seem to be much alternative. Unless—

At this point, the bridge collapses. Oh noes, how could *that* have happened?

* * *

After a great deal of finger-pointing, the wizards conclude that the lower part of the bridge, rather than being shaped out of rock, was instead made from compressed earth that quickly started eroding in the spray from the river. They're eager to point out that nothing like this had ever been attempted before, and they *certainly* couldn't be blamed. Oh, hubris, hubris, and man is ever wont to fly too close to the sun and also I definitely helped a little.

Only once the remaining leaders on this side have established the crucial fact that no one here could possibly bear any responsibility for the disaster can we turn to addressing the disaster. By that point, things across the river are going quite badly indeed. Sensing weakness, and with no river preventing *her* from throwing in more reinforcements, Sibarae pushes as hard as she can. The Kingdom fighters give ground stubbornly, reestablishing a perimeter as they're pushed back toward the tip of the peninsula. Driven by fury and zeal, the wilders attack again and again, only to be driven back in a welter of blood each time.

I watch nervously, waiting for my moment while everyone around me panics and dithers. Even Sibarae's loyalists have to be nearing their limit by now, and I have no doubt she's calling in fresh troops from the rest of the horde. These are perhaps less eager to charge mounds of corpses to reach a gang of exhausted but heavily armed humans. There'll be a point where they hesitate, while the snake tries to whip them on, and—

There. The mist has cleared, and for the first time since the crossing, there's no sign of movement on the field. A line of armored warriors backed by the remaining archers and wizards holds the very tip of the peninsula, while a mass of wilders waits just out of bowshot. But the mass isn't pressing close, it's holding back. Given time, I have no doubt Sibarae could motivate them; or, just possibly, someone would stick a knife in her back and the horde would tear itself apart. I don't plan to let either scenario play out.

"Now," I say aloud. My jaw aches; I realize I've been clenching my teeth the whole time. I rub it, wincing, and speak louder. "Now!"

The others look up. We've retreated a little way, out of the main circle of advisors and hangers-on who are now attempting to figure out what to do. Johann is staring across the river, where little is visible from this vantage except smoke and occasional bursts of fire. Matthias clutches his arm, looking lost. Tsav hovers over me protectively, but her eyes, too, are drawn to the ongoing conflagration. None of them knows as much as I do about what's happening, but they can all guess.

"Now what?" Johann says.

Matthias pokes him. "The rest of the plan."

"Right." He blinks and shakes his head as though waking from a dream. "The plan."

This is, I admit, a little hard on poor Himbo Ex-boyfriend. Sending people to their deaths is not something he has a lot of experience with. A pedant might argue that we *didn't* send them, that in fact he and I were the loudest voices *against* sending them; that's the sort of technically correct argument that you can make to strangers on Twitter but not to yourself. There's blood on my hands, but *fuck*, what else is new?

He and I move toward the committee of not-our-fault. The furious argument ceases as the various seconds-in-command abruptly realize that not only is there someone with a claim to being in charge, but he's in an *excellent* position to say *I told you so*.

"Your Highness," somebody says. "The situation is—"

"I can see the situation," Johann snaps, doing a credible impression of decisiveness. "This has gone on long enough. Stop all attacks and stand by. We will speak to both armies."

"Speak to both armies, Your Highness? But how—"

"Allow me," I say, stepping up beside the Prince. I crack my neck, extend my hands, and produce my biggest chunk of purple thaumite.

Communicating with one particular mind is relatively easy. Doing a broadcast, leaving the mental energy out there marked with a *To whom it may concern*, is a lot harder. It's essentially the same spell I use to disguise Tsav, but on a much larger scale and over a much shorter duration. Various wizards are staring at me goggle-eyed as I chant, the committee is shouting more questions, but I ignore them. Bit by bit, as though assembling themselves from the remaining shreds of mist, two vast figures take shape above the river. Their feet fade into invisibility and their heads are far above the ground. Johann and me, mirroring our motions exactly.

The huge forms are obviously insubstantial, partially transparent and flickery. But they're visible all across the battlefield, and they come complete with audio that would make a Dolby engineer turn in his BWAM. Johann, staring up at himself, whispers, "Whoa," and the word rolls across the fields like a tidal wave, scaring up flocks of shrieking birds from the trees. I hastily dial the volume down a notch.

"You're on," I mutter, only to have it transmitted to uncounted thousands.

"Right." Johann straightens up into his best heroic pose, which to his credit is really quite good. "I am Johann, heir to the throne of the Kingdom. All human forces are to stop fighting at once."

He glances at me, and I clear my throat. This isn't a dinner party's worth of nobility watching. No going back after this one.

"And I am Dark Lord Davi," I say. "The same goes for the wilders. We're calling a halt to the battle."

I can see confusion around us, the various nobles and Guildblades staring at me in alarm. Tsav, Gena, and Micah have arrived, however, positioning themselves around me and Johann to discourage any intemperate intervention. Matthias, meanwhile, is giving a frantic explanation.

"Sibarae assumed leadership of the wilders against my wishes," I say, trying to picture what her face must look like right now. It makes me smile to imagine her shouting back at me; there are a lot of advantages to being the one with the hundred-foot amplifier. "It was never my intent to destroy the Kingdom. We have come to make *peace*, to stop the raids across the border in both directions."

"My intention is the same," Johann booms. "Guildblade attacks on the wilders will end, and so will wilder assaults on our people. This has gone on long enough."

"Minions of my horde, return to your camp." I stretch out

a pointing finger like I'm issuing their manifest destiny. "The human army will do likewise." My finger sweeps down at the corpse-choked field across the river. "In recognition of the suffering of both sides, the thaumite of the fallen will be distributed to all."

That's going to provoke some howls of protest from the nobility, since they don't want the booty to go to the more common sorts of humans. But it's time to spread the wealth around, not least because it will make humanity in general a lot better off if the stuff isn't locked away in doomsday vaults. And breaking up the biggest hoards on both sides will make it a lot harder to start another war. It is, I feel, a neat solution.

An hour ago, none of this would have worked. But quite a lot has changed in that crowded period; for starters, a large majority of the most bloodthirsty on both sides are now lying dead. I don't know if Duke Aster is among them—is it wrong of me to sincerely hope so?—but even if he survived, much of his power base has just been slaughtered. The same goes for Sibarae, who is certainly not foolish enough to lead from the front lines. By concentrating her loyalists at the point of impact, as Amitsugu so helpfully suggested, she ensured that casualties on the wilder side have been concentrated among the most warlike.

Those still on their feet have been given a lot to think about. And the balance of both armies are understandably reluctant to join in. Add to that the chance for a sudden bounty of thaumite courtesy of all those dead heroes, and peace starts to look like a very attractive option. Sibarae won't agree, of course, but I strongly suspect no one is listening to her anymore.

On this side of the river, the committee is subsiding, slack-jawed, as Matthias explains these details. The smarter ones among them are already calculating the new structures of power and noticing that all roads now lead to the Prince, which goes a long way toward muting their protests. I reach my mind out to Mari—two purple spells at once, tricky!—and I'm re-assured by her sense of elation.

[They're cheering,] she reports. [The old horde and the sveayir both. And we just got a messenger from Hufferth assuring us of his loyalty.] Her mental voice is a squeal of excitement. [You did it, Davi!]

[We're not done yet,] I tell her, muting the giant speaker-phone for a moment. I switch focus to Amitsugu. [Where's Sibarae?]

[Already heading back toward camp with a party of snakes,] he says. [Some of my people are trailing her, but I wouldn't be surprised if she doesn't stop until she gets to the border.]

[Let's not let her get that far,] I tell him. Leaving her at large was a mistake I don't intend to repeat. [Get some troops from Mari and take her into custody. Gently, if you can. More importantly, though, you have to find Artaxes. Same deal, let him come along quietly if you can, but keep him under lock and key.]

[I had eyes on him not long ago,] Amitsugu says. I can feel his irritation as he speaks to someone else. [There seems to be some confusion. I'll track him down myself.]

That throws a spike of anxiety into my elation. Artaxes has a way of turning up unexpectedly. If anyone has the power to still fuck this up, it's the old rust bucket. He has too much credibility with the wilders. Even so, I can't imagine he'd find a lot of buyers for his death-to-the-humans shtick *now*. Everyone who got excited about it the first time is dead.

First step done, anyway. Our impromptu cease-fire seems to be holding. On the peninsula, the remnants of the Duke's forces are too weak to charge, and the wilders are still holding off. On the flanks, the pointless attacks have stopped. The next step is to extricate the two armies, which will be like separating two fighters with knives at each other's throats; lots of moving very slowly while smiling and speaking softly. We'll have to rebuild the bridge, to begin with—

I'm about to shut down the giant projection spell when hair starts to prickle on the back of my neck. Something's *wrong*. The armies are quiescent, the nobles have stopped shouting at me, Amitsugu is in pursuit of Sibarae, but I can feel deep in my gut the tide turning once again.

I've been trying so hard not to hope, not to jinx it like last time. Isn't this *enough*? Leifa's dead. So are hundreds more, on both sides. You can't call this *too easy*, not by a long stretch. So please, dark lords of narrative and irony, can't I just *win* this time? One *fucking* time?

The wind is rising, blowing in our faces from across the river. It ought to be cool and clammy with dew, but it feels hot against my cheeks. It smells of ash.

"Run." My amplified voice echoes across the battlefield. "Everybody *run!*"

The spell catches its own output, my shout twisting upward into a feedback squeal that slides up the octaves like a demented jazz player until I pull the plug. The huge images vanish. I've already got Johann by the arm, dragging him toward the nearest cover while shouting at the others to follow. Tsav, Gena, and Micah respond quickly, and the big Guildblade grabs the still-gawking Matthias and hoists him into the air.

Clouds are billowing above the bend in the river like an alien mother ship descending, lit from within by a deep orange light. The shape that emerges from their base is incomprehensibly vast, the size of a castle tower, far too big to be a living thing. But it *moves*, huge wings flapping, streamers of smoke clinging to it like contrails. The orange glow emerges from its mouth, like its throat is a portal to the Infernal Regions.

I've always wondered where all the dragons were at. It seems like there should be dragons, dragons go with the whole post-Tolkien/Arthuriana/D&D fantasy zeitgeist like orcs and Dark Lords and knights in shining armor. The Kingdom has legends about dragons, but they always take place in Olden Times, and in the modern days, giant flying reptiles are nowhere to be found. In the thousand years I've been kicking around, I've never seen a dragon. I might have even, from time to time, expressed the sentiment that I *wanted* to see one, or that getting eaten by a dragon would be a good death to add to my extensive catalog.

Right about now, I profoundly wish I could take those thoughts back.

This dragon is particularly distressing. It's bigger than a 747, and your brain keeps insisting that something that size shouldn't *exist*, much less be able to fly by flapping its wings. It's just obviously *wrong*, like a building made out of feathers. On top of that, this isn't your classic streamlined fantasy dragon with sleek lines and smooth scales, built for elegance and speed. *This* dragon is some kind of horrible mutant monstrosity, scales spiraling into fantastic spikes, horns so long they twist around and dig in behind its eyes. And the *eyes*. They glow yellow orange, and on the left side of the skull there's one in roughly the conventional place, but on the right, there are half a dozen scattered across its brow and cheek, slit pupils staring in different directions.

One wing forks halfway to the tip, creating two vertically stacked membranes. The thing's thrashing tail splits and splits again, each branch crooked and asymmetrical. It sidesteps the raging controversy between four- and six-limbed dragons by having *five*, two back legs, two wings, and a crooked front claw amidships that trails two long tentacles like whiskers.

In short, it looks like the offspring of an ill-conceived one-night stand between Smaug and Cthulhu. Figures that I can't even have a *nice* dragon, I have to get the fucked-up nightmare version. I'm still processing this when a new amplified voice booms across the battlefield, metallic and ringing and horribly familiar.

"*No.*" The bass in Artaxes's speech makes my teeth buzz. "*Do not be fooled, children of the Wilds. There can be no peace with vermin. Victory is yours. You have but to reach out your hand and take it.*"

If I look close, there's a tiny figure perched on the dragon's back. Hard to see details, but you can make out the spiky armor just fine.

That *rusted*, non-pooping *motherfucker*.

The dragon opens its jaws and roars, weird and dissonant, like vast nails scraping across glass. Color gleams on the inside of its mouth. Thaumite, *lots* of thaumite, a hoard beyond the wet dreams of any murder-hobo, pieces so big I can see them easily even at this distance. More of them are plated down the thing's throat, glittering until they vanish behind the brilliant glow of its innards.

I realize two things in that moment.

The first is a bit of humble pie. Artaxes and the wilders talk about the Old Ones, wilders or beasts that have lived for centuries and built up unfathomable amounts of thaumite. They're the closest thing they have to gods. I, personally, never put much store in it. I'd met a couple of what I *thought* were Old Ones, beasts substantially bigger and more terrifying than their fellows. There was the ass-face worm under the ruined city, of course, and the ape-thing at the edge of the Firelands, the one they called—pause while I look up the name from the previous volume—Vexiatl the Border-Keeper, apparently. I killed both of them, so they couldn't have been all *that* big a deal, right?

Now I realize that those two, though they were "ones" that were "old," probably didn't count as Old Ones in the true sense of the phrase. Because *this* is an Old One, a creature from the depths of time, so incomprehensibly powerful that the idea of trying to fight it is like balling your fists and squaring off with a mountain or, like, the concept of impermanence; it's a category error. My sack of thaumite looks about as impressive as a Bic lighter next to a volcano.

So, you know, mea culpa, I probably should have taken the whole Old Ones thing more seriously. My bad. Apologies to any Old Ones reading who might have been offended.

The second realization is Artaxes has been playing me for a fool. And that, even as I run for my life like an ant fleeing a sadistic child with a magnifying glass, makes me *angry*. I thought I was pissed off at Amitsugu after he got me assassinated, or Sibarae after she ate my fingers, but those were mere flickers beside the white-hot incandescence of my current rage. I haven't even had the chance to think through all the implications, but already I'm contemplating doing things to that tin-plated gaping asshole that would make a cenobite blush.

Which, you know, all well and good, but in order to channel these emotions to a useful purpose, I need to *not die*. So run run run run run.

The dragon breathes fire. But *breathes* is too gentle a word, implying a gentle exhalation of billowing clouds of merry flames. The dragon *emits* fire in a beam whose sheer weight blows the ground apart, smashing people to bits before they even have a chance to burn. The lance of white-hot plasma slashes across the base of the peninsula where the survivors of the doomed assault had gathered. If Duke Aster wasn't dead *before* then, he certainly is *now*, blown into his component molecules along with everyone else in a hundred-yard radius. The dragon tilts its head, and the beam slews toward us, crossing the river in a massive cloud of superheated steam and scything through the field where I and the other VIPs have been gathering. Soil blows into dust, and rock detonates.

Having made the extremely good choice not to be standing there, I'm still bowled over by the shock wave, the trees of the little copse thrashing like they were in a hurricane while chunks of jagged-edged stone bounce past. All I can do is curl into a fetal position and hope nothing heavy lands on me while a scorching hot wind shrieks by.

Chapter Twelve

I didn't die! Fucking amazing. And neither did any of my immediate companions.

Unfortunately, that's the extent of the good news.

Skipping over a lot of the business of picking ourselves up, hugging and sobbing and changing piss-soaked undergarments, our little party joins a general exodus of humanity, a mob that used to be an army now united by the single overriding purpose of being somewhere else at maximum possible speed. At first, various nobles, raised on too many sagas of heroic last stands, try to rally the fleeing soldiers to fight back; I get to witness what happens to one of these brave rear guards from the relative safety of the road. No sooner has Lord So-and-so finished giving his inspiring speech and assembling a cheering mass of humanity around him than white-hot fire scythes down through the clouds like an orbital ion cannon, sterilizing the whole area down to the bedrock. Two or three demonstrations of this kind are enough to make the point to even the most dim-witted of aristocrats.

Once the human army has shattered into a thousand little groups too small to be worth incinerating, the horrible light disappears from the sky. Artaxes has a horde of wilders to handle the detail work, after all. They're a little demoralized and now somewhat startled by this turn of fortune, but it's hard to imagine that he and Sibarae are going to have any trouble convincing everybody they hold the Old Ones' favor after such a spectacular demonstration. They'll be after us, and all we can do is run back to Vroken, whose neglected city walls suddenly seem very important indeed.

Until a giant dragon blows them into dust, of course.

* * *

[Mari?] I'm almost reluctant to contact her, but I have to know. She's alive, at least, but I brace myself for the news that Sibarae's forces have slaughtered everyone I ever called friend. The way things are going, that would be about par for the course.[1]

[Oh, thank the Old Ones,] Mari erupts as soon as the contact solidifies. She sounds as desperate as I feel. [I *knew* you couldn't be dead, I knew it, Fryndi was saying he thought the dragon had gotten you but...] She trails off into incoherence, and my heart unclenches a little. If she's worrying about me, she's probably not about to die herself, right?

[Very nearly, but not quite,] I tell her. [Tsav and the others are with me.]

[Good,] Mari says, gulping air. [That thing—I had no idea dragons were *real*. Was Artaxes riding it?]

[As best I can tell. Mari, are you and everyone all right?]

[Those who stayed with us are, anyway.] She makes an effort to calm herself. [Hufferth's here, but some of the minotaurs have gone over to Sibarae. Some of the pyrvir too. The orcs and fox-wilders and stone-eaters stayed put.]

---

1 Ha ha! I make insouciant jokes to distract from the fact my stomach is in knots and I can barely breathe!

[Sibarae's back in charge, then?]

[There have been messengers running around announcing it. They're trying to gather up all the little bands that broke off from the horde. We told them no thank you and started marching in the other direction.]

Thank God for Mari. [Are you in danger?]

[Not unless they send the dragon after us. The horde is still getting itself together, and we haven't seen any humans who weren't running away.] Her brave voice cracks a little. [Davi, what are we going to do?]

[I'm working on it. For now, head west and south. Stay away from the city, I won't be able to keep the humans there from attacking you. There's some hilly wooded country to the west that should hide you and provide decent forage, I'll try to meet you there.]

[Okay.] I feel her fluttering anxiety.

[You can do this,] I say. [You've been amazing so far.]

[So far, it's all been obvious.]

[You'd be amazed at how hard seeing the obvious becomes when everything's going to shit.] I take a deep breath. [I'll check in when I can.]

So. Everyone's not dead. Good, in that there's something worth saving in this increasingly fucked-up life. Bad, in that now I have to figure out a way to do it. Save the Kingdom (what's left of it) and the horde (what's left of it) and somehow kick the living fuck out of Artaxes and Sibarae.

No problem. We got this.

Amitsugu is alive, but not taking my calls at the moment. Maybe he's hanging on a wall somewhere with Sibarae eating his fingers, maybe he's turned his coat yet again and he's licking her snaky slit. I'd give about even odds. Regardless, no help from that quarter for now. I update Tsav on what I heard from Mari, and she gives me a teary hug. Apparently, the fates of our companions were much on her mind; she's known some of those orcs a lot longer than she's known me, after all. Once we've both cried a little bit, I go to check on our other companions.

Johan and Matthias are engaged in a similar bit of coping with trauma when I first look in. Gena and Micah are calmer, but they've been in this business a long time. You don't become an expert Guildblade by going to pieces in the middle of a dungeon crawl. Still, there's a distant look to Gena's eyes that I don't like, as if she's going through the motions but can't actually see the way forward. Micah and I exchange a glance; he's worried about her too.

Johann and Matthias join the rest of us around the campfire soon after. All we have to eat is a rabbit Tsav spotted and I zapped with a firebolt, which is a bit thin for six people. But nobody complains as the greasy portions are handed round.

"So," Johann says after a while. "I thought that went well. What's the next step in the plan?"

The rest of us stare at him goggle-eyed, until the corner of his mouth finally twitches.

"All right, that was a joke," he says. "I'm not *that* dense."

"You—" Matthias starts. He runs out of words and settles for kissing the Prince, which goes on for quite some time.

"The plan," I say, over the sound of them making out, "is obviously fucked. We need a new plan."

"It had better be a fucking good one," Gena says, looking a little reanimated by the respite. "Because from where I'm sitting it looks like we're well and truly fucked."

"That is a distinct possibility," I agree. "But we have to try *something*."

"Or we fuck off into the hills and hide out until things settle down," Gena says. "We don't actually *have* to go down with the fucking ship, right?"

She stops, eyes shining, when her husband puts a large hand

on her arm. Gena looks up at him as he slowly shakes his head. She swears under her breath, longer and more vituperative than usual, then wipes her eyes on her sleeve and slaps her cheeks.

"Whoo! Okay. Kidding, obviously. New plan! What are we doing now?"

They're all looking at me. Plans are my department.

"I don't know," I tell them. "But I have an idea where I can find out."

* * *

That place, naturally, is the secret archive under the disused tower, back in the palace. It takes us a few days to get there. The gates are jammed with refugees fleeing to the presumed safety of the city, and only Johann revealing himself gets us through. The sight of the heir to the throne nearly causes a riot, but Johann says a few words about staying calm and working together, and it works wonders. The relieved guards hold their salutes as we ride fresh horses up toward the palace.

Vroken, naturally, is in an uproar. Rumors of what happened arrived almost instantly, and they've had days to fester by the time anyone with an authoritative account returns. On the east side of the city, the roads are jammed with people from the countryside wanting in; at the west gates, an equally long but substantially better-dressed queue of people are itching to get *out* to hide from the chaos in the country. I can hardly blame them.

At the palace, Johann takes charge of the headless bureaucracy, confirming the tragic death of the Duke and stepping smoothly into the place of The Guy Who Gives Orders. Some of those instructions come from me, of course, but increasingly Matthias does the work of filling Johann's somewhat empty head with useful ideas. Soldiers trickle in from the chaotic retreat, those who didn't take the opportunity to leg it to some place of imagined safety, and Johann puts them to work manning the walls and generally maintaining order. All well and good, until the giant dragon comes and annihilates us.

There are no windows in the secret archive, and I'm not sure how long it's been since I slept. Tsav keeps bringing me sandwiches and coffee from the palace kitchens, bless her. I have no doubt that I'm damaging precious historical documents with my rapid flipping around, but needs must when the dragon drives.

Eventually I call them in, Johann and Matthias and Gena. Micah's busy out on the ramparts, trying to keep up morale—the surviving Guildblades are spread thin. I haven't had time to assemble a proper crazy wall with torn-out pages and bits of string, but I do have a table covered in sketches and diagrams. It's nothing that would make sense to anyone else since I've been inventing my own notation as I go.

"You look like a fucking mess," Gena says as she comes down the stairs.

"I know." I rub my eyes, which are coated in sticky grit. My hair is so permeated with the dust of the archive it feels like papier-mâché. "We're in a bit of a hurry."

"I'd say so," she mutters. "Last from the scouts had the leading wilders only a few days out."

That's more time than I thought we had, actually. It must have taken longer than expected for Sibarae to round up the horde.

Johann is also showing the strain, his handsome face a shade paler than usual and bags starting to show under his eyes. Matthias is worse, clinging to the Prince's arm as though he needs the support. They settle at the table across from me and Tsav, looking down at the diagrams with mute incomprehension.

"Please tell me I'm not supposed to be able to understand this," Matthias says, pushing his spectacles up his nose.

"You're not," I say.

"What is it?" Johann says.

"A partial reconstruction of the spell in Cyrus's laboratory." I scratch my head, dust flaking away. "What I saw of it, anyway, before the octopanzer chased us off."

"That place?" Matthias's tired eyes narrow. "Is it important?"

"Yes! Probably."

"I'm fucking lost," Gena says.

I give a brief, rambling explanation of our discovery of the laboratory and aborted expedition to find it. Gena doesn't look like she's following much, but at the end she frowns.

"So, if this is the spell"—she taps the diagrams—"are you thinking it's something Cyrus left behind?"

"Maybe something that could help us against the dragon!" Johann says.

"No! I mean, yes. Both." I take a deep breath, which is a mistake, since the air is full of dust. It tickles my lungs into coughing. Tsav pats my back and hands me a glass of water. Finally, tears streaming from my eyes, I recover enough to croak. "Definitely something Cyrus left behind. Not going to help us against the dragon."

"Oh." Johann looks disappointed.

"So, what exactly is the point of any of this?" Matthias said.

I close my eyes for a moment. It's different for them, obviously. All they can see is the immediate threat—the horde, the dragon—and they want a solution. But the problem is bigger than that.

"Artaxes is Cyrus," I tell them.

Silence.

"Either that or he works for Cyrus. Or he's Cyrus's successor or something. But my money's on him being Cyrus under that armor."

"Cyrus is dead," Gena says. "He died a fucking long time ago."

"No!" I point at Matthias. "What happened to Cyrus?"

"He and Founder Satorel died defeating an Old One that threatened the Kingdom. An enormous dragon—"

The penny drops.

"*That* fucking dragon?" Gena says.

"I don't see a lot of other dragons around," I say.

"But they killed the dragon," Matthias says.

I point at him again. "*You* told me that nobody ever found the thaumite, no matter how hard the Guild searched."

"So, what, he made friends with it instead?" Johann says.

"More liked enslaved it, I suspect," I tell him. "He's got some spell that lets him control beasts, even Old Ones."

"That's not fucking possible," Gena says. "The Guild has been trying to figure that out for centuries."

"The Founders," Matthias says thoughtfully, "did a lot of things that seem impossible today."

"Exactly. Look—" I go to take another deep breath, then stop myself. "I told you that I have ... visions. I sometimes see the future, different versions of it, depending on what I do."

"It's true," Tsav says defensively when this garners skeptical looks from everyone but Johann. "I didn't believe her either, but she's predicted things she had no way of knowing."

"Do you know who's going to win the Founders' Day horse race?" Johann says excitedly. "Because I could make a *lot* of money."

"Hey." Matthias snaps his fingers. "Impending doom. Focus."

"Lots of people think they have visions of the future," Gena says. "Generally, it means fuck all. Or they're so fucking vague, they can claim to be right no matter what happens."

"You have a sister in Statsport," I tell her. "You two used to be close, but you haven't talked to her in years. You and Micah met when he was being chased by a frog-troll and you tripped it up with magic to save him."

"What the *fuck*?" Gena says.

"In one of the futures, we were friends," I explain.

"Do me! Do me!" Johann says.

"You have a sexual fantasy that involves being pegged by a woman in leather while she strangles you with a whip," I say. "Don't try to make it happen, by the way, it ends badly."[2]

Johann's eyes go very wide. I clear my throat.

"The point is, I see things. *Possibilities.* In most of them, Tserigern comes to me and tells me I'm the savior of the Kingdom. Then the Dark Lord attacks and I try to stop him and lose. I *always* lose." My anger flares again. "And the Dark Lord always has Artaxes with him. At first, I thought he was just sort of the high priest of Dark Lord-ing. But *he's* the one pushing the destroy-all-humans angle."

"And you think he's Cyrus." Tsav has been quietly putting the pieces together. "But Tserigern's prophecy came from Cyrus, telling you to *save* the humans. So . . ."

"So, Cyrus has been *fucking with me the whole time.*" It comes out as a growl. "I don't know what his actual game is, but whatever's in that laboratory is the center of it. The spell has something to do with *time.* It must be the cause of the"—I catch Tsav's eye—"the *visions* and everything else."

Another silence.

"I'm fucking lost again," Gena mutters.

"I don't understand where the whip comes into it," says Johann.

"I think I get it," Matthias says. "Assuming we believe what you're saying. But what can we actually *do*?"

"Get back in there," I say immediately. "Get rid of that octo-panzer thing and study the spell up close."

"And then what?" Matthias still looks doubtful. "Is that going to stop him from bringing the dragon down on us? Keep the wilders away from the walls?"

---

2   And the leather thong chafes something awful.

"It might," I say, a little desperation creeping into my voice. I've never been this close to the answer before. "There might be something there, some hint about how we can stop him."

"*Might* be." Matthias shakes his head. "It seems like a pretty thin reed—"

"*It's the only chance we've fucking got.*" I'm abruptly on my feet, and I don't realize I've thumped the table until I feel my hand stinging. Tsav touches my arm, and I shake her off. "Because Gena's right. We're well and truly fucked. In all those visions of me defending the Kingdom, you know how often we survived? *Never.* Not fucking once. The Dark Lord always comes out on top, and that's *without* a fucking dragon the size of a football stadium. So, yeah, it's a thin reed, but we can either grab it and hope or we can *fucking* drown. Because that *fucker* Cyrus is never, ever going to let me win."

"Hey." Tsav leans in from behind and speaks softly into my ear. "They're on our side."

They are. I come back to myself and look at the shocked faces across the table. *People, not recalcitrant tools.* I close my eyes.

"I have to do this," I tell them. "I'm sorry if you don't believe me. I would welcome your help, but I'm going with or without you."

Silence again.

"I mean," Gena says. "When you put it like that, what the fuck do we have to lose?"

"The city needs us," Matthias says. "There's so much still to do—"

Johann puts an arm around his shoulders and draws him close, touching their foreheads together.

"Be honest," he says. "Is any of it going to be the thing that saves us?"

"It's—" Matthias swallows. "Probably not."

"Then Gena's right. What do we have to lose?"

"Apart from our lives?" Matthias says weakly. "Last time, that thing nearly killed us."

"Last time," I say, "we weren't prepared."

* * *

"You left out a few things," Tsav says.

We're riding side by side. She's still not comfortable on horseback, but the palace stable master found her an old gelding whose placid gait wouldn't falter if a bomb went off. We don't have far to go.

"I know." I run my fingers through my hair. A night's sleep and a bath have done wonders for my appearance but barely touched the bone-deep weariness inside. "The whole time loop thing seemed like too much to pile on top of the rest."

"Probably," Tsav says contemplatively. "Easier to handle someone having visions of the future than the idea that you've already died hundreds of times."

"I know I've been slipping. Sending the Duke over the river, that was a very . . . old Davi thing to do. I'm *trying*, but—"

"Hey." She grabs my trembling free hand. "It's okay."

"Is it?"

"Fuck if I know, I'm not the high king of morality. All I can tell you is how I feel."

That helps, a little.

"But the others don't understand what this is like for you," she goes on. "You have to make some allowances for that. I'm not sure I do either, but at least I can try."

"A thousand years." My other hand goes tight on the reins. "That bastard has been screwing with me for a *thousand years*."

"You really think he's behind everything?"

"I'm sure of it. Nothing else makes sense."

"Why would he do it? It can't just be to torture you."

"I'll be sure to ask him. Right after I feed him his toes."

Never mind that Cyrus is a Founder, one of the most potent wizards who ever lived, with unspecified extra superpowers on the side, and evidently at least semi-immortal. The anger that has built up over two hundred lives finally has a target. Whatever it takes, Cyrus is going to *suffer*.

Deep breaths. We're getting there.

We make better time than on our last trip and reach our former campsite by midafternoon. As I hoped, it's occupied; I spend a little time with the purple stone before we get there, to make sure nobody is surprised.

"Davi!" Mari rushes over to help me off my mount. She clears her throat at the sight of the rest of my party and straightens up a little. "Dark Lord Davi, I mean. Welcome back to the horde."

Back to the horde. Ah, for simpler days, when it was just me, a gang of hapless orcs, and the firm belief that nothing mattered. I swallow a lump of undeserved nostalgia and look around the clearing. Most of the horde—this small sub-horde, not the larger part still commanded by Sibarae—is camped farther off in the woods, but as requested, Mari has gathered a few of my nearest and dearest to assist with this project. There's Jeffrey the mouse-wilder, Euria and a couple of her deer-people, Droff with several more stone-eaters, and Maeve with a contingent of orcs. A few fox-wilders under Mari's command complete the entourage.

My human companions stand behind me, and for a moment, it feels uncomfortably like we're the Jets and the Sharks about to *throw down*. But Johann steps forward and embraces Mari, who gives a startled squeak but doesn't otherwise panic, and that breaks the ice. Gena, Micah, and Matthias step forward as well, exchanging greetings with wilders they met during our dinner/dance-off. Tsav removes her disguise stone, drawing a delighted shout from Maeve.

I let them chatter for a few minutes, basking in the feeling that maybe we all *can* just get along. Then I clear my throat. Euria hears me and raises her voice.

"Quiet! The Dark Lord wishes to speak!"

"Um. Thanks." Everyone turns to me and I cough again. "Okay. I'm going to keep this short, the details aren't important. Basically, Artaxes is the bad guy here, he's behind everything, and it's his fault we can't stop the war."

"I guessed as much," Jeffrey drawls. "Since he was the one on top of the giant dragon an' all."

A few dark chuckles. I point up at the looming hill.

"In *there* is his base of operations, laboratory, that sort of thing. We're hoping there's something inside that can help us. Unfortunately, he didn't leave it unguarded, so we're going to have to get past the octopanzer—"

Maeve raises her hand. "The what?"

Kids these days, no classical education. "Big armored monster with tentacles."

Various nods. Everyone takes that in stride.

"So, we're going to go in there and we're going to kill it." I put on a stern look. "After that, and I can't stress this enough, *don't touch anything.* There's thaumite everywhere, but it's part of an active spell, and if you fuck it up, you could blow us all to kingdom come. Everyone got that? Other Vaclav, I am looking in your direction."

Maeve grabs one of the other orcs by the hair and forces him to nod. "We've got it."

"Droff must touch *something,*" Droff says, looking at his feet. "Droff cannot leave the ground."

"Don't touch anything *other than the floor,*" I clarify. "And the monster."

"Droff understands."

"Okay." Deep breath. The downside of gathering all your

friends to fight a monster is, however welcome the camaraderie, someone might die. Focus, Davi. We got this. "Let's go."

* * *

The door is obvious now, and it looks like no one has used it since last time. That bodes well—if Artaxes had found a moment to pop home, there's no guarantee he wouldn't have arranged some new surprises for us. I trigger the spell and the door opens, revealing the same corridor, complete with our footprints in the dust. Everyone raises their weapons, but the octopanzer doesn't show itself yet.

Gena starts casting buffs on me, which draws a lot of curious stares from the wilders. It's not the full stack, since I need my big chunks of red for offense, but hopefully it'll mean fewer broken bones this time. Micah and Johann get a similar treatment, which leaves Gena straining to keep everything going at once. Matthias stays beside her, well to the rear, with instructions to yank her out of danger if necessary—that much casting tends to occupy one's attention.

Preparations made, we advance to the inner doorway. The vast space of the upside-down-wedding-cake cavern stretches before us, crisscrossed with walkways and studded with glass balls like enormous Christmas ornaments. I can practically hear jaws drop among the wilders, and no wonder: Inside those balls is enough thaumite to set up your own empire. Arcs of crackling magical power flicker through the tubes between them, and even at this distance, the ambient charge makes my hair stand on end.

"Droff does not see a monster," Droff says, the only one unimpressed enough to make that observation.

"Wait for it." Last time, the octopanzer came to us. I'd rather fight it here, on the fairly open top tier, than venture down into the glasswork and possibly wreck something by accident. As if the octopanzer agrees, I quickly hear the clank of armor under the snap and growl of magic. "Here we go."

Tentacles come up over the edge, wrapping around the railing to haul the steel-plated body of the thing up and over the side. Watching with a bit more clarity, I note the smooth overlap of the scales, allowing movement without exposing gaps. Down at the bottom, where there's presumably some kind of mouth and/or ass,[3] a complicated visor-like arrangement allows access. Breaking through that is one possibility, it might be a weak spot, but getting at it is going to be hard.

Sticking with plan A, then. The others spread out in a semicircle while I stand in front and draw aggro.

"Hey! Come and get me, tinfoil takoyaki!" I doubt it understands, but the noise seems to draw its attention. Tentacles wind through the air in my direction, armor scraping and clicking. "I talked to all the lady and/or dude giant octopuses and they agreed that none of them would lay a tentacle on you, even *with* armor. What do you say to that—*oof*—"

This last because, naturally, my brutal roast of the creature had the desired effect. A tentacle smacks me in the midriff and I feel my feet leave the ground. Ribs creak but, thanks to the brown thaumite juju that Gena is pouring into me, don't break. Before the thing can fling me against the wall, I grab hold, wrapping my arms and legs around the tentacle like it's a greased-up supermodel.

"Droff!" I shout.

The stone-eaters rush forward. Droff grabs me by the shoulders and pulls, dragging the tentacle within reach of the others, and they all find handholds along the armor. Other tentacles snake toward us, but at my signal, the rest of the crew lets fly

---

3 Do octopuses have an ass? Sometimes I wish I could Google.

with arrows, spears, and sling stones, creating a terrific racket as they ricochet off the armor and diverting the monster's attention. It lasts long enough for the three stone-eaters to wrestle the tentacle to the floor. Droff sits on it, and not even the octopanzer is strong enough to shift his weight.

One down, therefore, and seven to go. We're not going to be able to immobilize all eight limbs, but we don't have to. I run around to the opposite side of the thing, yelling insults the whole time. That no longer attracts its notice amid the missile storm, so I up the ante with a firebolt, and that makes it rear up in annoyance. This time I've got one arm locked around the railing, so when the tentacle hits me, I can hold it in place myself.

The two remaining stone-eaters grab it, and now the octopanzer is, to put it bluntly, fucked. Droff has one tentacle stretched out full length on his side, and we've got another one on *this* side, meaning the thing's main body is immobilized between them like we're stretching it on a rack. It has six more tentacles, of course, and they flail mercilessly at the stone-eaters, rocking them and sending chips flying. Droff grits his teeth[4] and bears it, but I need to hurry.

I retreat out of tentacle range, grab my biggest red thaumite, and concentrate. This is going to take more work than the bronze door under the ruined city, but it's the same concept. To speed things up, I focus on a smaller area, a single armor plate on the creature's side, nicely immobile so I can concentrate my invisible death ray.

Steel doesn't *melt* until it reaches something like twenty-five hundred degrees, which is well into "oh *fuck* that's hot" territory and probably beyond my powers even with this much thaumite. However, *something* with a bit of flex is holding the

---

4 Not that he has teeth.

scales of the octopanzer's armor together, probably leather straps or some kind of fabric. My bet is that it will give out before Droff does.

Wham, wham, wham. I'm seriously starting to worry as the steel begins to glow cherry red. I can smell the ozone stink of hot metal, along with a delicious seafood-frying odor that rapidly sours into charred meat. The creature writhes in agony as I turn a chunk of its defenses into a branding iron. Then, finally, there's the explosive *bang* of something under pressure giving way. The orange-red scale drops free, revealing burnt and oozing flesh beneath.

"Now!"

The others need no encouragement. Arrows zip past from the orcs and the fox-wilders, shafts sinking to the fletching in the rubbery flesh. Moments later, Micah and Johann rush in with spears in hand, ducking past the spasming tentacles to plant their weapons amid the pincushion. There doesn't seem to be a skeleton in there to stop the points, so Micah slams on the spears' butts with his vast fist to drive them deeper and deeper like he's hammering giant nails with his bare hands.

Something in this assault finally strikes something vital. The octopanzer's thrashing turns spasmodic and starts to lose steam until it subsides into a weak twitching. The stone-eaters cautiously let up on the tentacles, and the rest of us gather around, though not *too* close.

"Is it dead?" Johann says, because of course he does.

"I told you not to say that," I say. "Never say that. It'll suddenly come back to life and rip your head off, because of irony."

"I think it really is dead, though," Matthias says.

The octopanzer is deflating a bit, clear liquid gushing from the ragged hole in its side. I have to admit it does look pretty deceased.

"Just . . . be careful of irony. Fucker will sneak up on you." I let out a breath and wince. Even with magic, the force in the thing's blows was no joke. "Everyone okay?"

"Droff will survive," Droff says. He's limping, I notice, a network of cracks spreading through one leg. "But Droff requests no more such plans for some time."

"Granted. And thank you."

The final tally on our side turns out to be one broken arm among the fox-wilders and one concussed orc, along with innumerable scrapes and bruises. Gena, muttering about overwork, comes up to tend to the injured. The wilders stare at her with wide eyes as she chants over them and their wounds vanish.

Mari, looking a bit shaky but triumphant, joins me at the railing, staring down into the depths of a laboratory. It's hard to see from here what occupies the very bottom layer, but I keep getting glimpses of movement from down there, a liquid churning unlike the flashes and arcs and magic throughout the structure.

"Good work," I tell her.

"You told me what to expect, but I didn't quite believe it." She puts her chin on the rail. "If Artaxes has something like *that* watching his doorstep—"

"Then he must ride around on a fuck-off big dragon?"

"Yeah." She looks over the edge. "Are you sure there aren't more of them?"

There's a thought I hadn't even considered. "God, I hope not."

"And all this—" She waves at the intricate collection of thaumite. "Do you have any idea what it's for?"

"Some. It's a spell, something Artaxes keeps running."

"Shouldn't we smash it, then? Maybe it's how he keeps the dragon under control."

"Would you rather the dragon be *out* of control?"

"Point," she admits.

"I can figure this out," I tell her, willing myself to sound more confident. "I just need to get a good look at it."

"Then you'd better get started," Gena says, straightening up from the last of the wounded. "It won't be much use after the wilders sack Vroken."

"I know." I blow out a breath. "Okay. I'm going down. The rest of you stay here and stay together. See if you can get the armor off that monster and find its thaumite, it must have quite a bit."

"I'll come with you," Tsav says, materializing at my shoulder. "Just in case."

I think about objecting. But there *might* be something else down there for all I know, some other guardian or trap. Tsav already knows everything anyway. I hold up the purple gem and nod to Mari.

"I'll check in regularly."

She gives a tired nod of her own. Tsav and I find a metal staircase from the top layer to one of the catwalks below and begin our descent.

The place is ... weird. Not just in its trappings—the crackling, snarling spell we find ourselves crawling through the middle of—but in its design. It has the feel of something built piece by piece, in whatever way was expedient at the moment, an accumulation of small decisions over a long period leading to a space shaped around its creator like a boot molded to a particular foot. Artaxes/Cyrus—I decide to think of him as Cyrus—has clearly been using it for a very long time.

And yet, in spite of that history, it contains nothing that would give us a hint as to his character. There are no family photos on the fridge, no nudie magazines tucked under the bed, no forgotten meals moldering in a dark corner. Just the glass-and-thaumite contraption, a few smaller assemblies of uncertain function, and racks of tools I don't understand.

It speaks of an intensity of purpose bordering on mono-mania. If Cyrus worked in an office, he would be the guy whose cubicle walls were bare gray, with a neat stack of paper and a single sharpened pencil on his desk arranged perfectly square to the corners. He'd eat plain rice by himself in the break room, never join a Friday night bar crawl, and win the award for Most Likely to Snap and Shoot Up the Place three years running.

Okay, maybe I'm speculating. But the amount of careful labor on display here is staggering, even with magic to help the work along. We're definitely in "building a replica of the Hagia Sophia out of toothpicks" territory here.

Nothing jumps out to eat us as we descend level after level. Some paths are dead ends, forcing us to backtrack. The buzz and crackle of the spell grows more intense the farther down we go, which only adds to my conviction that the secrets of this place are to be found at the very bottom. When we pass the final X-shaped catwalk on the second-to-last level, however, I pause.

The thing that's been *churning* down here is now revealed. It's a whirlpool set into a basin perhaps ten feet in diameter, a thrashing standing wave like the funnel that forms when the bathtub is draining. But the stuff in the pool isn't water; it looks more like liquid silver, or maybe mercury, as though you'd dropped the T-1000 into the world's most aggressive Jacuzzi. Bits of foam and spray fill the air but never hit the stone floor, evaporating into bright sparkles before they get there.

"Please tell me you know what that is," Tsav says.

"Not a fucking clue," I tell her. "Don't touch it."

"Do I look like an idiot?"

We take the final ladder slowly. The pool occupies the center of a flat space about twenty feet across, the lowest and smallest layer of the inverted cake. The vitrine contraption ends here, too, with one final glass sphere hanging only a few feet above the twisting surface of the pool. Thaumite shines brightly inside, red and green and brown and purple alongside colors of crystal I've only read about. The whole thing is humming with potential, like a bear trap armed and straining at its catch.

Alongside all this thaumaturgical heavy artillery, the presence of a simple writing desk is somewhat disconcerting. There's a thick leather-bound volume on it, exactly square to the desk's corners,[5] with a pen and ink laid neatly nearby. At the foot of the worn desk chair is a leather trunk, closed but not latched, with a complicated pattern of thaumite inlaid in the top.

And that's all. I would feel vastly more comfortable if there were, for example, a Chewbacca bobblehead as well. Too much cleanliness is a sure sign of a twisted mind.

"Well?" Tsav says after a moment.

"Well what?"

"You wanted a closer look."

"I'm still looking."

I stare at the pool for a while, then draw a wooden-handled knife from my belt.

"What are you doing?" Tsav says, guessing my intent. "You said not to touch it."

"I'm not *touching* it. I'm just curious what would happen if I did."

I toss the knife into the silver maelstrom, ready to dive for cover if it splashes or explodes. What actually happens is, if anything, stranger. The blade flips end over end as it falls toward the swirling surface, but it slows down the closer it gets until it's hardly moving at all. At the same time, though, there's a frantic sense of movement *around* it, a flicker in the air as though we were watching video on super-ultra-fast-forward. The wooden handle shrinks and deforms around the tang,

---

5 I knew it!

warping and splitting, then eroding away one splinter at a time. The blade itself is quickly covered by rust that creeps across it like mold, tiny pieces dropping away to crumble into dust. In what feels like seconds, the knife is gone, dissolving into red particles lost in the silver churn.

"Uh," I say. "Hmm. Definitely don't touch it."

"You don't say." Tsav looks upward. "Is it part of the magic?"

"I think so. Some kind of . . . power source, maybe? Reactor?"

I purse my lips in frustration. The prospect of parsing the massive spell hanging above us is already making my head hurt. The book is more promising—the kind of person who built this place is the kind of person who writes everything down in excruciating detail. I pull the chair out and flip the book open. The first page is written from edge to edge in a dense, practiced hand, like the author was mad about overpaying for paper.

And—

"Tsav." My voice is flat. "You can go back up if you want. This may take a while."

"Can I help? If we divide them up—"

"No." I grip the edge of the desk to keep my hand from shaking. "Not this time."

* * *

"Davi!" Tsav says when I reemerge with a huge grin on my face. "What happened?"

"I found a big button under the desk labeled KILL CYRUS," I tell her. "I pushed it and now he's dead. The dragon flew away and everything's fine now!"

"Awesome!" She blushes a little. "Listen, we've been talking, and even though you and I are soulmates and will stay together forever, I think we should also have threesomes with Johann sometimes. That *ass*, my gods."

"That ass," I agree solemnly. "How about right now?"

"That's what I was thinking," Johann says, taking off his shirt.

"I'm totally cool with this!" Matthias shouts from the background.

And then we all live happily ever after.

Okay, *fine*, obviously there's like a hundred pages left in the book.[6] But a girl can dream, right?

Tsav didn't go back to rejoin the others, but she retreated to the ladder to give me space, reading a battered book from her pack. When I push the chair back and possibly scream a little, she gets up and hesitantly comes over. I hug her and continue screaming into her cleavage.

"Hey." Her arms close around my shoulders. "It's okay."

It's really not. The scale on which it's not okay is hard to even communicate. It's bad enough when everything you thought you knew about the universe turns out to be wrong; it seems rude for it to be *so much worse* than you imagined.

"It's okay." She keeps saying it, quietly. "It's okay, Davi."

And eventually I stop screaming and just breathe for a while. My eyes are scratchy and red from tears. I tip my head back and look up at her.

"I think your boobs have magic calming powers."

"They do seem to have that effect on you," she says. "I'm glad I could be of service."

"Sorry to lose my fucking mind at you. Again."

"I'm getting used to it."

I give a shaky laugh. She squeezes me once more and cautiously lets go. I wobble a little but stay on my feet.

"That bad?" she says.

---

6 Wouldn't it be hilarious, though, if those hundred pages were just a blow-by-blow of days of hardcore fuckin'?

"Yeah. Maybe. I don't know." Honestly, I'm still sorting out how to feel. "I think I know what we have to do."

"But?" she says.

"You're *really* not going to like it." Fuck, *I* don't like any part of it.

"Shit." Tsav's lips purse. "This is one of those plans where you put yourself in horrible danger, isn't it?"

"Something like that."

We sit down with our backs to the stone, and I start to explain. I've already decided the others don't need to hear the whole thing, they'll only raise objections, but I owe Tsav this much and more. Because she's, deep breath, a *person* whose feelings I care about, rather than an object I make noises at to get it to behave how I want. See? I'm fucking learning, right? Only—

"No. Davi, *no.*"

"It's the only way."

"It's suicide!" Her face is more exasperated than angry, like I'm failing to understand something obvious. "It is *literally* suicide."

"Nothing I haven't done before, right?"

"Yeah, except you're about to *break the thing that makes you come back from the dead.*"

"I know what I'm doing."

Tsav rolls her eyes. "What in the course of our relationship could *possibly* give me that impression?"

I snort. "You know what, fair."

"Don't laugh this off, Davi. You are going to die, *for real.* No going back or trying again. You'll just be dead and the rest of us will have to fucking live with that."

My throat is thick. "It's not the worst thing I can imagine—"

"*No.*" There are tears in her eyes now too. "You do not get to *give up* at this point."

"Let me finish." I swallow hard. "If the world resets again, if I go back to the beginning, then you—*this* you, the person I fell in love with—cease to exist. Everything you and I have had will be erased. The same goes for Mari and Droff and everyone else. Johann and Matthias's marriage would disappear. Everything we've done . . ."

I shake my head. "*That* is the worst thing I can imagine. I don't want to die, Tsav. Fuck, I want to live forever, have a house by a lake with you and contemplate the universe and achieve enlightenment by multiple orgasms, all the good stuff. But I would rather *end* than let everything be wiped out. Can you understand that?" I sniff and wipe snot from my nose. "Please?"

There's a long silence. The two of us stare at each other, both faces wet with tears. Tsav snuffles and clears her throat.

"Why a lake?" she says in a small voice.

"What?"

"I understand us staying together forever, but what does the lake have to do with anything?"

"Fuck, I don't know. Why *not* a lake?"

"It's usually pretty boggy around lakes. And there are mosquitoes."

"There's always a lake in the boner-pill ads. I figured it was a requirement of the live-out-your-days-in-peace fantasy."

"I'm just saying, if the house is by a lake, we might need to worry about flooding—"

"*Fine*, we can build the house on the top of a mountain and literally freeze our asses off when we try to fuck outdoors—"

"Maybe a *river*, like one in a deep gorge, flowing water doesn't get stagnant—"

Giggles overcome us both simultaneously. It's a good thing we're sitting down, because my legs are shaking. I lean my head against Tsav's shoulder.

"Promise me," she says quietly.

"Promise you what?"

"That you won't give up. Not if there's the smallest chance."

"I swear it."

"Blood of the Old Ones." She heaves a sigh. "You're crazy, you know that? Only a crazy person would have thought of this."

"I am aware that my connection with sanity is a little tenuous." Maybe a little more than even I thought, if the notebooks are to be believed. "But it's not all bad. The thing about being crazy is nobody expects it. Least of all Cyrus."

"I thought you didn't know him."

"I know the type."

She snorts. "Well. Have you thought about how you're going to tell the others?"

"I'm thinking I had another vision of the future."

"Again?" Tsav laughs. "Those things are a menace, you know."

Chapter Thirteen

A great deal has to happen in a small amount of time.

Tsav and I convince the others. As I predicted, there's a lot of argument even with the abridged version of the plan, but in the end, Tsav's calm insistence that there's no other way carries a lot of weight. We game it out, keeping things simple, and make sure everyone knows what they need to do.

Johann writes a letter, seals it with his signet ring, then gives me the ring itself for extra authority. He actually looks relieved. Matthias seems nervous, and Mari is nearly inconsolable. I start to tell her what to do if I don't come back, but Tsav cuts me off with a meaningful glare.

If it comes to that, she'll take care of them.

Last but very much not least, it's time to break the time loop. I don't understand the intricacies of Cyrus's spell—I'm not sure I'd understand it if I studied for years—but taking something apart is always easier than building it in the first place. As of yet, I just want to disable the thing, not destroy it entirely, so I go to one of the upper nodes and remove a couple of pieces of orbiting thaumite through a hatch in the glass sphere. The structure shudders a little, but doesn't explode, and the hot-metal smell in the air abruptly redoubles. Other than that, the world seems unchanged.

But everything is different. I'm half convinced I can *feel* it, deep in my gut, but it's probably just stomach acid. The magical mechanism that has had me repeating my life for so many years is disabled, like a clock brought to a halt by the removal of a single gear. Cyrus, I'm sure, can fix it with ease, but if I were to die right now, then that really would be it. Not *maybe*, not *when will I wake up*, but for sure just *death* the same as everyone else. It's a strange feeling, like getting to the last boss of a game and suddenly realizing you haven't saved in days. Nothing's *changed*, but everything's different.

If I were really as world-weary and tormented as I sometimes pretend, this would be a perfect time to jump off the bridge and do a headfirst swan dive onto the rocks fifty yards down. See you later, suckers, Davi out! I watch myself carefully for any such impulses, and I'm mildly surprised not to find any. Hell, my feet tingle with a faint fear of heights as I make my way back to the others. In spite of all the *my life is pain* emo posturing, I'm not ready to be done here. There are things I want to do and people I want to do them to / have them do to me. I want to have a fucking *future* instead of the back-and-forth of the endless present. I have my found family and I'm keeping them, God damn it, and we're going to have tender moments and inside jokes and shared wonder and all that sappy heartwarming shit.

I *also* have a list of things I want to do to Cyrus/Artaxes that is decidedly less family friendly.[1] All I can say is that he'd better hope I don't figure out how to get the time loop going again, because if I do, he's going to spend ten thousand lifetimes suffocating in a steaming pile of his own *shit*, and that's just for starters.

---

1 Although I guess the things I want to do to Tsav aren't exactly PG.

What? I contain multitudes.

Unfortunately, another thing I'm certain of is that Cyrus now knows we're here. It was clear in the notebooks that he has a deep connection to the time loop spell and can tell when it's even slightly out of whack; wholesale tampering has to be setting off all the alarm bells. He can figure out where *I* am, too, although that may take longer. Either way, it's high time I was no longer here. With Johann's note in my pocket, I take our fastest horse and ride like hell for Vroken.

* * *

Dark clouds are gathering in the western sky by the time I arrive, and the first drops of rain begin to fall as I canter through the nearly empty streets of the capital. It's two in the morning or thereabouts, and the guards on the palace gates aren't happy to be roused. Their objections disappear when I show them the Prince's seal and signet ring. I leave the suffering horse to the care of the stable boys and demand to see the captain of the palace guard.

This turns out to be a tall and imperious woman named Sienna, who even roused in the middle of the night and wearing a fluffy pink nightgown gives me dominatrix vibes.[2] She gives me the kind of look you'd give to a cockroach that not only scuttled around your kitchen in the middle of the night but also had the temerity to knock on your bedroom door and ask if there was any more sugar.

"You're Davi," she says. "The magician's apprentice."

"Something like that." I thrust the sealed note in her face. "Read this."

---

2   I should introduce her to Johann in case he ever does want to do the whip-and-strap-on thing. As long as I get to watch.

"I—" Her eyes focus on the seal and she frowns and snatches the paper. "What is this foolishness?"

I wait while she reads. Her shoulders sag visibly.

"Where did you get this?"

"From the Prince, obviously." I flash the signet ring as well. "His instructions are clear, I think."

"To treat your orders as though they were his." Her teeth clench. "And what would those orders be, exactly?"

"To evacuate the palace. Everybody out within the hour."

"*Evacuate?*" she sputters. "There are hundreds of staff, not to mention the residents! Do you have any idea—"

"No," I say cheerfully. "That's why I'm telling *you* to do it."

"It's impossible. We'd never be able to arrange enough transport so quickly."

"Everyone has legs, last I checked. If anyone doesn't, carry them."

"I can't ask the noblewomen of the Kingdom to get up at two in the morning and *walk* in the rain!"

"I think you'll find that you can, if you consider the alternative."

She sucks in a breath and regains some of her poise. "What is the alternative?"

"At some point in the near future, a fucking enormous dragon is going to turn up. So the alternative is being here when it arrives."

Sienna pales. The stories from the battle have clearly made the rounds.

"The dragon's coming here?"

"Mmm-hmm." I leave out the part where I'm sort of causing that to happen. If I wander somewhere conspicuously uninhabited, Cyrus might get suspicious.

"I . . ." Something has clicked in her head, and I can see planning and logistics wheels start to turn in her mind. "Perhaps some kind of canopy to keep the rain off, and the footmen can carry lamps—"

"Sounds perfect. I leave it entirely in your hands. But sooner is better, understand?"

"Yes." She blinks. "I'll begin at once."

So, there's that taken care of. I don't need more corpses on my conscience if the dragon gets frisky. I make a brief stop in the kitchens and then head up to the Prince's Tower, which is tall and adjacent to the gardens. Then comes the hardest part: waiting.[3]

People bustle and shout and protest below. The sky continues to darken, black clouds sweeping toward us like grim cavalry. Spattering rain turns to a full-on downpour, hammering at the roof and thrashing the trees in the garden. I stand at the window and stare into the misty dark, lit only by the chiaroscuro flicker of thunderbolts.

Very moody. I do have to run to the toilet three or four times, because fear has sent my bladder into overdrive.

When a brilliant flash outlines the hulking shape against the clouds, it's almost a relief. The dragon glides over the city, impossibly big, a chorus of ringing bells and panic following in its wake. It ignores the furor, heading straight for my tower like a homing pigeon dead set on spending the night in a warm coop. As it approaches, it spreads its enormous wings to land, the blast of air sharp enough to sting my eyes and raise clouds of swirling leaves from the garden. The thing settles, claws gripping the earth, tearing up rows of ornamental shrubbery and crushing wrought-iron benches underfoot.

I step back from the window. A moment later, the dragon's weird single arm reaches up toward me. Foot-long claws dig into the masonry with a noise like a giant chewing Cap'n

---

3 Earwormed instantly. Thanks, Tom.

Crunch, and with no apparent effort the thing rips a huge chunk of the facade away and tosses it aside, leaving a hole in Johann's bedroom big enough to drive a truck through. Lashing rain immediately invades, soaking me to the skin.

Another flash of lightning reflects from the dragon's eyes, just at my level—one on the left, six on the right, all focused on me. However many times I went to the bathroom, it wasn't enough.

Then the dragon dips its head. A familiar figure in rusty armor stalks up the long curve of his mount's neck and over the top of its head, stepping neatly off its snout onto the floorboards. Artaxes's iron boots squish on the ruined carpets as he comes to stand across from me.

"Dark Lord Davi," he says, in that voice as creaky as his armor.

"Artaxes." I cock my head. "Or do you prefer Cyrus?"

The silence is broken by a roll of thunder.

"I wondered how much you had worked out," he says.

"Everything."

"Oh, I very much doubt that."

His tone has changed, an archness replacing Artaxes's blunt imperturbability. He gestures briefly with one hand, and the rusted iron falls away, pieces clattering to the floor like the world's worst striptease. He pulls the helmet off and tosses it aside, revealing a long, thin face with a mop of brown hair and sunken cheeks,[4] recognizably the man from a hundred statues throughout Vroken.

He's wearing a simple sleeveless vest and trousers, and his chest has a *lumpy* quality, like he has some horrible case of boils. In the next flash of lightning, though, the gleam of color shows the truth. It's thaumite, *lots* of thaumite, embedded in

---

4 Picture H. P. Lovecraft after a month on a starvation diet.

his flesh starting at the center of his chest and dappled outward across his pectorals and up his shoulders. The gems are bigger and brighter than anything I've ever seen, making the hoard I took from the ass-mouth worm look paltry in comparison. *More* thaumite hangs from chains around his neck and arms, like a sort of silver harness dripping with gems. They clatter as he moves, always within easy reach of his hands.[5]

"You're like me," I say, perhaps unnecessarily. "You can use thaumite like a wilder *and* like a human. All the Founders were the same, weren't they?"

Cyrus gives a grunt and an amused nod.

"And you're from Earth too."

Another nod, this one slower.

"Here's what's going to happen," I tell him. "You're going to take your dragon and go back to the horde. You're going to tell them to turn back and return to the Wilds. Then you're going to fly off yourself and never bother me again."

He smiles. It's sharp and cruel. His voice is sharper, too, without the helmet's muffling. "And why would I do that?"

"Because I know you need me for something." I take the long, thin knife from my pocket and press it to my chest. "And *you* know your time loop spell is broken. So if I push a little harder"—the point of the blade dimples my skin—"then whatever you're planning is ruined. Forever."

He stares at me. I try to watch his fingers. However good a wizard he is, he'll have to at least touch his thaumite before doing anything with it. The point of the knife digs its way through my thin shirt and pricks the underside of my breast. My hands are shaking.

"You're bluffing," he says eventually.

---

5 Honestly that's a great idea for keeping your spellcasting stones handy, I may have to steal it. Assuming I, you know, survive.

"I'm not."

"You believe you understand." He smiles like a lizard. "You think this is the first time you've made this threat?"

I'm shaking quite badly now.

"It's been a *thousand years*," I tell him. "You think I'm not ready to die?"

I'm not, I'm *not* fucking *shit* why did I think this was a good plan—

He gives a little shrug. "You never have been before."

And he flips his hand in a practiced motion. The thaumite chained to his arm leaps into the air, he stretches out to catch it without looking—

I jerk the dagger home.

* * *

There is some technique to stabbing yourself in the heart.

For starters, your heart isn't as far to the left as you probably think. Most of it is under your breastbone, which is a nice protected place for it to be. If you stick the knife in somewhere around your nipple, you're going to puncture your lung, which will hurt like hell and probably kill you but, and this is important, not *quickly*. You want[6] to be just far enough left that you feel the gaps between your ribs, with a blade thin enough to slip between and long enough to get the job done. If you're a person with boobs, come in from underneath and angle upward rather than trying to poke through all that fatty tissue.

Anyway. Suffice to say that this is another one of those skills at which no one anywhere can possibly have as much training as I do. In spite of my current condition—scared shitless and

---

6 *Want* may be the wrong word here. Strive never to end up in a situation where this knowledge is important unless you're, like, a heart surgeon.

shaking badly—I make a pretty good job of it. I can feel the tug of tough, thrashing muscle on the end of the blade, and my legs crumple almost instantly as my blood pressure plummets. It starts to hurt like a *motherfucker*, but my vision is already going gray; my knees hit the floor, then my head (ow) as I topple sideways. One last blink through a closing tunnel of vision, and then—

—*oh God and then* nothing *I'm dying I'm dying I don't* fucking want to die—

—the pain, which was starting to drift away, suddenly gets a whole lot worse.

Another blink.

Cyrus is standing in front of me, holding a chunk of green thaumite the size of a softball. His other hand is pressed to my forehead, and I can feel the absolutely colossal flow of pure life energy flooding through it and into my body. It fills me completely, sustaining me on raw magical power, which sounds sort of nice and wholesome but actually feels like electric fire surging through every blood vessel. My body doesn't *want* magic, it wants oxygenated blood, and pronto. But Cyrus is working on that, too, and I feel flesh knitting with horrible, unnatural speed. The knife slides out of the wound, *pushed* out by muscle and skin impatient with this foreign intrusion.

I feel my heart start up again with a wild double-thump, which is a new sensation even for me. A few beats later, Cyrus withdraws his power. All I can do is lie there twitching, my poor dumb body understanding that *something* horrible has happened to it but not too clear on the specifics.

"You're right," he says, his lip twisting bitterly. "I do need you. But please believe me when I say there is absolutely nothing you can do about it."

He reaches down and takes my wrist, lifting me with no effort whatsoever, as though I were an inflatable doll. A twitch of his finger, and the iron armor leaps into the air and spirals out the hole in the wall. We follow, Cyrus dragging me by one arm, my feet scraping limply across the sodden rug. He hoists me completely off the ground to step onto the dragon's snout, and I'm lashed by rain as the huge beast bends its neck to deliver us gently to its broad back. Then it spreads its wings and leaps into the air, demolishing more of the palace gardens.

Cyrus deposits me facedown on the rain-slick scales. I feel the slow working of the dragon's titanic flight muscles against my cheek as we climb. I get a glimpse of the city from above, but I can't find the energy to raise my head. In fact, the world is going gray again.

Well, I tell myself as I pass out, *that all went pretty much according to plan.*

* * *

I have broken the first rule of time loops[7]—"Never get captured"—and so it's hardly a surprise when I wake up strapped to a board. My arms are stretched above me, my ankles gathered together with a leather loop, and there's another band around my midsection, which leaves me pretty thoroughly immobilized. I'm still fully dressed and in possession of all my bits, though, so I'm tentatively counting it as a win.

First step—spend a little while freaking out about what happened. Being within seconds of final-and-for-real death for the first time in a thousand years earns me a little bit of justified gibbering; just thinking about it sets my heart to racing frantically. Perhaps it's afraid I'm going to abuse it further. I'm sorry, heart! I promise not to stab you again.

Okay. Freakout complete. Deep breaths. Where am I?

---

7 Though not, in this case, for lack of trying!

I'm in a tent. It's too dark to see much, but there's a table and some camp chairs. There's noises in the distance, people talking and doing camp things. I can't make out the words, but the language is definitely Wilder and not Common. Conclusion: I'm in the horde camp. A bit of a surprise, but I guess Artaxes stopped off to take care of some things.

So . . . I just wait, I guess. *Hang around*, as it were.

Doop dee doo.

This sucks. We're supposed to be getting to the exciting climax, damn it.

At least leave me one hand free so I can jerk off.

Good thing I spent all that time pissing.

The tent flap rustles, thank *God*. A slim figure enters; my eyes have adjusted by now, and it's not who I was expecting. Amitsugu. He looks at me with a sharp intake of breath.

"It is you," he says. "I was hoping I was wrong."

"Good to see you too," I tell him. "So happy you've managed to land on your feet. This is, what, your fifth time switching sides?"

A smile plays across his gaunt features. "Can you blame me in this instance? You certainly didn't anticipate the dragon."

"I didn't." Honestly, I don't have much anger left for Amitsugu. It's nice to think that he would have stayed loyal and died heroically standing up to Artaxes, but that would be radically out of character. "So, are you changing teams again? Here to let me loose and plot a dramatic escape?"

He shakes his head delicately. "The dragon, as it happens, is curled up behind this tent. For all I know, it's listening to everything we say."

Probably. Artaxes wouldn't risk any of my loyalists getting in here to finish me off. "Well. I didn't really want to escape anyway. Not my style."

"No." His tail swishes gently under his robe.

"Where's Artaxes?"

"Giving orders. We're changing our line of march, apparently. Heading west of the city."

Toward the laboratory. I suppress a gleeful grin. Still on track.

"No one understands why," Amitsugu says. "You don't happen to know, do you?"

I give as much of a shrug as I can in my restrained state. He sighs.

"If you're not intending to rescue me, why *are* you here?" I ask him.

"I...don't know." He licks his lips. "I'm not sure what Artaxes intends to do with you, but it seems unlikely that we'll meet again. I thought..."

"You want me to forgive you?"

His head jerks up. "Forgive me?"

"You know. For trying to have me killed. Then working for Sibarae, then working for Artaxes. All the betraying, generally."

"I don't need your forgiveness." But his ears are drooping.

"That's too bad. I'm giving it to you anyway."

A moment of silence.

"I admit," he says, "I'm surprised."

"Me too." This wasn't part of the plan, but it feels right. "You're a lot like me, I think. You act like a coldhearted bastard sometimes, but you do have feelings, and they come out to bite you at the worst times." I shake my head. "I used you start to finish to get what I wanted, whether it was control of the Redtooths or a self-pity fuck, and I expected you to just go along with it."

"You..." His smile returns, just for a second, showing pointed teeth. "I suppose you did."

"I'm trying to be a better person."

He raises his eyebrows. "Some might call it a little late for that."

"We'll see, won't we?"

He shakes his head.

"So, what are you going to do now?"

"Whatever the Dark Lord tells me to, I suppose," he says. "Whoever that turns out to be."

"Seems like the wisest choice."

Another silence. He stares past me, lost in his thoughts.

"If you've got nothing on your immediate schedule, you could eat me out for old times' sake," I suggest. "It's really boring being strapped to this board."

He comes back to himself with a snort. "I doubt our scaled friend would approve."

"Maybe it's into the voyeur thing."

Amitsugu clears his throat and draws himself up. "Goodbye, Davi. It has certainly been . . . interesting."

"I endeavor to provide satisfaction."

He turns to leave, then pauses. His tail swishes again.

"Mari," he says quietly. "Is she . . . all right?"

I hesitate. But there's no point in being cruel. "She was fine, last I saw her."

"Good. That's . . . good."

He slips out through the tent flap, and I'm left alone in silence.

* * *

"—utterly ridiculous!"

The voice is Sibarae's, rising in anger from her ordinary sibilance to a teakettle shriek. The tent flap opens and Cyrus enters, once again wearing the dark armor of his Artaxes guise. Sibarae is right behind him, also armed and armored, with a circlet on her head clearly intended to ape the one I wore as Dark Lord.[8]

"We have them *at our mercy*," Sibarae says. She's so focused on Artaxes that she doesn't even notice me hanging in the corner. "The defenders of the human city are weak and terrified. If they don't flee at our approach, they will break at the first assault. Everything inside—food, weapons, thaumite—is as good as *ours*."

"The city is not going anywhere," Cyrus says. His voice is barely recognizable. "This is merely a brief diversion."

"And if the humans regroup? Or evacuate their stores and leave us with nothing?"

"If necessary, I will deal with them." As if on cue, there's a deep rumble that can only come from the dragon outside.

"Then deal with them *now!*" Sibarae screeches. "What is in those woods that's worth the risk?"

"My own business."

His tone is dead, emotionless, but I fancy I can detect a hint of frustration. If I liked Sibarae, I might tell her to tread carefully. Obviously, I remain silent.

"Your business." She draws herself up. "*I* am the Dark Lord."

"Because I proclaimed you so."

"You proclaimed me because you needed my strength." Her tongue zips angrily in and out. "Don't think you intimidate *me*. We both know your piety is a convenient fiction. If not for my standing among the bands, the horde would have broken apart long ago."

Artaxes straightens a little, as though coming to some kind of decision.

"And yet," he says quietly, "we have suffered many casualties."

---

8 It's not enough that she turned on me, now she's biting my style!

"We would have had fewer if your pet had shown itself earlier!"

"Your own people have been particularly reduced since the battle. Along with those most ardent in your support."

Her lip twists in a snarl. "What is that supposed to mean?"

"It means that my need for you is much reduced."

Sibarae's eyes go wide and she opens her mouth to offer a retort. It never emerges, because something red and ropy slams in through the tent flap and wraps around her midsection, crushing the air from her lungs. I catch a glimpse of blank surprise on her features as she's yanked backward and lifted into the air. The red rope, as thick around as my thigh, is the dragon's tongue; the tent flap falls mercifully back into place as my snaky would-be rival is drawn past rows of jagged, serrated teeth and into the monster's thaumite-encrusted throat without even a scream.

Artaxes and I share a look, which I like to think encompasses our shared relief that neither of us will have to deal with *her* anymore.

"So, what happens now?" I ask him.

The armor drops away from him with a series of clanks and thuds. Cyrus pulls the helmet off and tosses it carelessly away, shaking out his shoulder-length hair. His thaumite chains click and rattle.

"We return to my laboratory," he says. "I repair the spell. I kill you. We try again."

"But everything's different now." I want to get him talking; there's a few more pieces of information I need to make sure the plan will work. But also, he has the *answers*, and I have a need to know so powerful my head is pounding. "I'm certainly not going to listen to Tserigern, now that I know he's your puppet, and you're not going to trick me as Artaxes. Whatever your goal is, I'm not going along with it. So why bother?"

"Poor Davi." He shakes his head and walks over to me. "Still trying to understand. You think this is the first time you've found me out?" His lips curl and he turns away. "With the right application of magic and torture, memory can be reduced to so much mush. I can make you a blank slate again. Believe me, I've had *plenty* of practice."

Chapter Fourteen

I'm too stunned by this revelation to even scream when the dragon's tongue comes back into the tent, winding around me and the board I'm strapped to and lifting us into the air.

Honestly, why scream? If the thing were to devour me, it would be, frankly, a relief. Instead, it just carries me gently to its broad back and sets me down among the twisted spikes and scales there. The tongue, wet and rubbery, lets me go, and the dragon bows its head to let Cyrus step up on its nose and board in this more dignified fashion.

He leaves the armor behind, I notice. I guess he doesn't think he'll need it again.

Or, rather, not in *this* life. Cyrus, obviously, keeps his memory between time loops as well. Whenever I die, he must reset to wherever he was at the beginning, armor and all; unlike everyone else in the world, though, he knows what's happening. He *did* this to me, to us, on purpose.

And he's taken my memory. More than once, by the sound of it. No wonder everything gets hazy when I try to think too far back. I'd guessed there must be *something* like that going on from what I found in his lab—numbered lists of experiments and trials that seemed to go too far back, far past the thousand years I've been counting. But hearing him say it . . .

Fuck. *Fuck.* At a certain point, the enormity of it rolls off you. When you've been trapped for a thousand years already, learning that it was somehow *much longer than that* is . . . a little hard to process.

What I mainly feel, apart from gut-churning terror, is the need to *know*. To get an answer to the one overriding question that has consumed my life.

"Cyrus," I say.

"Hmm?"

The dragon has risen away from the horde camp, spiraling up into the early morning sky. The thing is so large that here on its back the beat of massive wings feels like only a gentle rocking. It's been more than a day since I've slept, but whatever blast of concentrated healing he hit me with has me feeling wired, like I'm juiced up on Starbucks and amphetamines. I hang from my board, balanced against one of the dragon's spines, while Cyrus stands with his arms crossed and watches the landscape unfold beneath us. At this rate, we'll be back at the hidden laboratory in an hour at most.

"There's something I have to ask you. And I'd appreciate an honest answer. You owe me that much."

"I owe you nothing." He looks over his shoulder at me and sighs. "Go ahead."

Deep breath.

"When you're wearing the rusty armor, how do you poop?"

Silence.

"It seems like you never take it off when people are around. Do you have to, like, sneak away sometimes? Or is it magic, like you can go right in the armor and it gets teleported to some extradimensional outhouse? Or can you just concentrate superhard and not poop for weeks, and then when you finally have to, it's a shitpocalypse—"

"Have you ever wondered what it must be like to share the world with one other person?" he interrupts. "Everyone else you meet is nothing, a fleeting shadow, but that *one person* is a constant. This other axis on which the closed universe goes around. And around, and around, forever and ever. Just you and them, as lifetimes flit by."

I swallow. "It seems like—"

"Now try to imagine if that single person was *extremely fucking annoying*," he snarls.

"I like to think of myself as witty and urbane."

"Annoying."

"So why keep me around?" I try to gesture for emphasis, but my hands are still tied tight. "Why do *any* of this? You're immortal with godlike powers and your own enormous dragon, what do you need me for?"

He regards me stonily. "There's no point in explaining things to you."

"But you *want* to, don't you?" I raise my eyebrows. "Come on, you're going to erase my memory anyway. Give us a proper villain monologue. What's the harm?"

More staring.

"Is it something I did?" I ask. "Should I say I'm sorry? Whatever it was, I obviously don't remember it. Maybe we were roommates, and I used the last of the peanut butter without telling you?" I snap my fingers, or try to. "Ooh, did I steal your girlfriend? That happens a lot. I can't help it, I mean, *look* at me. Women see me and they just *know* that here's someone who would absolutely—"

"Davi."

"—I mean it wouldn't *hurt* if you'd experiment a little more, nothing crazy, but maybe think about—"

"*Davi.*"

"It *barely* hurts, is all I'm saying. You just have to relax."

"You are trying to bait me," he says wearily. "You won't succeed."

"But I might as well keep trying, right? We're going to be flying for a while and it's not like I've got anything else to do, tied to this board."

"I could take your tongue."

"Sounds messy. You could also just answer my questions."

He turns away with a sigh and waves one hand. I consider elaborating on my scatological theme, but decide not to push it.

"For starters, who *are* you? You said you're from Earth. Where? When?"

"My true name is Cyrus, as it happens. I was born . . ." He lets out a breath, as if winching the words up from a deep well of memory. "In London. In 1851."

"Thanks to *somebody*, I don't remember when I was born," I say. "But I feel like that was a long time ago."

"Dates are not something which greatly concern me any longer. Time is . . . subjective."

"I've noticed," I say dryly. "So how did you get *here*?"

"A mystery that I suspect will remain forever unsolved." At my expression, he sighs. "Did you think I was all-knowing? I was barely more than a boy. My family was visiting the country, some little town. I remember finding something in the gutter, a toy soldier all covered in mud. I bent to pick it up and the sky flickered. When I looked up, the town was in the middle of the forest, and beyond that, there were mountains like I'd never seen."

"The whole *town*?" I'm genuinely surprised. "Not just you?"

"The whole town. More than a thousand souls." He waves a hand. "Most of us died quickly. We had a few guns, but ammunition soon ran out. You can't make gunpowder here, did you know that? The chemistry works differently somehow.[1] A thousand humans, none of whom are what you would call warriors, surrounded by beasts and wilders."

"You weren't near any other humans? Was this over the mountains?"

For some reason this makes him smile. "You've been there. Or near there, at any rate."

"The ruined city?"

Cyrus nods. "At first, we stayed in the town itself, but one night it was overrun by a wilder band. The survivors fled toward the mountains. Other wilders were more curious, less hostile. We were an oddity, intelligent creatures without thaumite, animals that could talk. We knew a few things they didn't about metalworking, so we traded those skills for land and protection. On the spot where the Convocation was held, we built a new settlement. We prospered far more than we'd dared hope."

He's getting into the swing of it. No supervillain can resist the opportunity for a good lecture to a captive audience. Makes sense, really—villaining is a lonely business, and the temptation to unspool all those arguments you've been having with yourself in the shower is nearly unbearable. I'd guessed that Cyrus didn't have much in the way of friends and confidants, and I'd been right. Now he only needed occasional prompts from me to keep rolling downhill.

"Humans *breed*," he goes on with a sneer of contempt. "Like rabbits. Like rats. We didn't think it was anything out of the ordinary for decades. But a century on, our few hundred

---

1 I have, in fact, tried this, but I always assumed it was a deficiency in my memory that prevented me from introducing this world to the full horrors of modern warfare.

became a few thousand, then a few tens of thousands. We spread out, farmed more land. If the wilders didn't like it, their bands were now too small to dare trouble us."

"'We'?" I interject. "Normal humans don't live for centuries."

"Indeed. It wasn't long after we allied with the wilders that we discovered the existence of magic, but learning to harness it—what you call *human* magic—took generations. But ingesting thaumite, as the wilders do, that was simple. The only thing lacking was courage. Only a few of us dared."

"Especially after the first person exploded?"

"No one exploded in the beginning. Fear of the unknown was enough. Those of us who experimented kept it secret, or else were shunned.[2] It wasn't until later, when we saw what good it could do, that we tried to encourage the more adaptable in the new generation. And *they* exploded."

"Wait. Wait a minute. *None* of you had any problems eating thaumite? Not so much as a tummyache?" I frown in thought. "And then the kids exploded..."

I've always figured my ability to use both kinds of magic was either a fluke, some bizarre quirk of my genetics, or else a consequence of whatever weirdness caused the time loop. Cyrus's similarity could have been more of the same. But if *everyone* in the first generation had been fine...

"Experiments are impossible, of course," Cyrus says. "But I imagine you've reached the same conclusion I did. A human's ability to consume thaumite is somehow a consequence of journeying here from Earth. Perhaps an adaptation to this world made in transit. But it is one not inherited by any offspring, who revert to being mere animals." His

---

2   Three guesses which of those applied to Cyrus. He *reeks* of someone who's been shunned.

face hardens. "As though this world *tried* to embrace us, and failed.

"Not that the others saw it that way. They believed there was something special about those of us who'd used it. That we'd become more, or less, than human." He shrugs. "I'm not sure I disagree. In any event, there were schisms, coups and counter-coups, alliances and betrayals. The usual run of human stupidity. We who bore thaumite dwindled, failing to secure enough to stave off old age or perishing by accident or violence. The city, meanwhile, grew and grew. From ten thousand to a hundred thousand, and more. Wilder allies became subjects. Jungle was cleared for farms.

"I was flying when I had my epiphany." He gestures around at the misty air whipping past us, the patchwork landscape visible far below. "Not on this beast, of course, that came later, but using another that I'd broken to my will. I soared far above the city, a black mass of buildings spreading ever outward, sending out tendrils of farmland along the river veins to cut into the verdant, healthy jungle. I saw it for what it was.

"A cancer."

* * *

"Isn't that, you know, a *little* bit harsh?" I ask after he spends a few seconds in silent reverie. "Humans gonna human, as I like to say."

"That is exactly my point," he says, biting the words off in the manner of an irritable professor. "Humans have no alternative. No other way to behave. On our world, we are unextraordinary. All life seeks to grow endlessly, to dominate, until it reaches the limits imposed by space or food. You are familiar with the work of Malthus?"

"Vaguely. Probably I'd remember better if you hadn't, like, mucked about in my brain."[3]

"On Earth the land already groans under the weight of humanity. The sky is black with coal smoke and the water is poisoned by industry. And it will certainly grow worse—"

"—bad news about that, actually—"

"—until humanity destroys itself. But *here*, things are different!" He turns to face me, eyes shining. "The wilders are *better* than we are. Their ability to grow is limited by the thaumite they harvest from beasts, ensuring that their numbers cannot outstrip the ability of the land to sustain them. Beasts and wilders, in turn, prevent the animals from growing without limit. It is a perfect system, with intelligent creatures that are part of their world rather than above it.

"In that moment, I felt like I could see the future. Our kind would spread and spread, using the curse of unlimited reproduction to overrun the wilders and tear their world apart. I knew it had to be stopped, the cancer excised. I knew—"

"Wait. Hold on a minute." I shake my head. "I get that you guys brought some new technology over, but it's not like you were the *only* humans in the world. There's humans all over, right?" I've always figured there had to be other humans out there *somewhere*. It can't just be the Kingdom, can it?

But Cyrus is shaking his head. "Of course not. Don't you understand? This world, this planet—*we are not native to it*. That is why we sweep through it like a fresh plague through a virgin city. *We do not belong here*."

I have vague memories of Earth examples. Rabbits in Australia, species of birds on Pacific islands wiped out by shipboard rats. For a little while, I don't know what to say.

---

3 Probably not. Original-me doesn't strike me as the type who knew the details of eighteenth-century economic treatises.

"So, I became Artaxes," Cyrus goes on. "I went among the wilders and built a following. I turned their vague reverence for the Old Ones into a cult with purpose, and I learned to break Old Ones to my will with magic." He indicates the dragon on which we stand. "That gave me authority, and I used it to anoint the first Dark Lord, the Chosen One.[4] He raised an army the likes of which the Wilds had never seen and marched on the city.

"But the humans were more tenacious than I anticipated. They fought hard, with magic and those thaumite-bearers who remained. When it became clear they would lose, they sent an expedition over the mountains into unknown territory, hoping to outrun the Dark Lord and start again. I urged the wilders to pursue, but the destruction of the city and the bounty it provided meant they were less interested in completing their purpose and more in dividing the spoils. They didn't understand, as I did, that chasing the enemy away was not enough. That if any humans escaped, the cancer would spread. They were content to be left to themselves.

"Frustrated, I abandoned them and rejoined humanity for a time. There were only eight of us thaumite-bearers remaining by then, the final remnant of the first generation who'd been born on Earth. The other seven, by virtue of their power, had become the leaders of the exodus. No one knew the role I'd played in the war, and they accepted me among their number."

"The Founders," I supply.

"Obviously." Cyrus waves a hand. "Their presence forced me to move cautiously. I bided my time as we established the Kingdom and subdued the initial threats. Before long, humanity was again prospering and filling the land with its cursed

---

4 Like I said, that's the problem with Chosen Ones. It implies someone doing the choosing.

offspring, and the eight had divided to pursue their own interests and feuds. One by one I killed them, or encouraged them to kill one another. Satorel was the last. In truth I suspect she knew my intentions and planned to kill me in turn. But she didn't know that the dragon we sought together was already under my control.

"Once they were all gone, I kept myself hidden and allowed memory to fade into myth. The humans of the Kingdom forgot almost everything, as humans do, and busied themselves with the mundanities of power and profit. While they did, I studied magic as no one ever had, and eventually I came to a solution."

"Burn all the humans with your giant fucking dragon kinda seems like the obvious choice."

"Tempting, but no. I could have destroyed the cities and towns, but humans would simply flee into the countryside and burrow into the world like ticks. I had tried to excise the tumor once and failed. I knew that whatever happened, I could not risk failing again. Humanity was still largely contained, but an incomplete destruction would backfire, sending humans fleeing in so many directions they would be impossible to fully root out. The cancer would metastasize and this perfect world would be lost. I *had* to get it right, but the certainty I needed was impossible."

Having figured out the next bit of the plot, I can't resist speaking up. "So, your solution was to *trap the entire world in a time loop*? That doesn't seem a *little bit* deranged?"

He shrugs. "Why should it matter? No one but you and I knows that it's happening. When I finally get things right, all the excised loops will vanish and history will continue as it should. There will be no evidence apart from my own memories."

"And mine," I sputter. "I'm still waiting to hear where *I* come into this fucking story."

"As a result of my foolishness." His lips twitch. "I built the time loop spell, but there were certain constraints that no amount of study could eliminate. The spell needs an anchor, a person whose death is the catalyst to begin again. And I discovered that this person *could not be from this world*. The extra element of alienness, of being *outside*, allowed the loop to function.

"But, of course, I was the only one left from Earth. I could not be the anchor, since I was needed to complete the spell. If I had known, I could have imprisoned one of my fellow Founders, but it was too late for that. I admit that I briefly despaired."

"Boo-hoo, my plan for temporally assisted genocide didn't work out, sad panda emoji."

He sighs. "In time, of course, I realized my mistake. Whatever had brought our town here could not be a singular phenomenon. Anything that happens once can happen again. I dedicated myself to research once more, and eventually I discovered a way to pierce the veil between worlds. It was lucky I'd waited so long; there is an . . . energy pool, you might say, that allows such things, and it rebuilds itself exceedingly slowly. Centuries must elapse between each event. There was only enough to bring a single person through this time, instead of a whole town."

At this point, I can hardly breathe. Some of this history I'd guessed at, some was new to me. But *this* is personal. *This* fills me with a choking rage that makes my hands flex against my bonds to the point of pain. Cyrus watches me, amused.

"You . . . *did* this to me?" I say when I'm halfway calm. "You brought me here *on purpose*? Just to be a component in your *fucking spell*?"

"I did," he says mildly.

"You absolute—"

The string of profanity that follows is not expressible in any known font, not even Wingdings. I can't swear I'm not making the words up on the fly, having achieved through sheer rage a connection to some kind of primal, universal ur-profanity of which all other swearwords are merely dim reflections. Through me, new curses were entering the world, dripping with vile meanings that scholars of blasphemy and sexual perversion would take decades to fully comprehend.

Cyrus only raises an eyebrow. Maybe he's heard it all before.

* * *

It's a few minutes before I regain the power of speech, or at least speech that isn't detailing the disgusting sexual exploits of all branches of Cyrus's extended family. Finally, panting and dripping spittle I can't wipe from my mouth, I run down.

"Why . . ." I have to pause for breath. "Why *me*? What the fuck did I ever do to you?"

Cyrus unexpectedly barks out a laugh, sharp as a gunshot.

"You think I *chose* you?" he says. "If I'd had a *choice*—well, suffice to say we'd have finished long ago. No, the magic that reaches across the veil is blind. It latches on to the first target it can find. I have nothing against you, any more than the fisherman has a grudge against the trout he happens to hook for dinner. At least," he adds reflectively, "I had nothing against you at the time. That was before I got to know you."

"Fuck. So you just yanked me from Earth and turned me loose?" That's not right, there has to be more to it. "What's all the business with Tserigern and being the savior of the Kingdom and that shit for, then? If all you needed was an anchor for the spell, why not just keep me in a cell and kill me whenever you need to try again?"

"Since I am not an *utter* fool, that was naturally the first thing I tried." Cyrus sighs. "The problem, as ever, is inadequate tools. I tried claiming the Dark Lord's mantle myself, but the wilders never responded with adequate fervor."

"Because, and offense absolutely intended, you have all the charisma of a dead fish."

He snorts. "Other Dark Lords proved similar failures. The wilders were capable of breaking the Kingdom, but none showed the ruthlessness I required, the drive to eradicate every last human and end the threat forever. I needed someone I could *mold*. But the time loop consumes resources at a prodigious rate; I couldn't spend decades recruiting and training someone without resetting it. But I realized there was one candidate available with whom I had all the time in the world.

"People are malleable, you see. Live long enough, watch the generations pass by, and you realize they are simply a product of their environment. Control the environment and you control the person. Achieving precisely the right combination of factors to get what I require takes a great deal of experimentation, naturally, but I have eternity. And so I began my greatest work."

"Your greatest work being *me*? Turning me into fantasy Mega-Hitler?"

"Into the tool that I require."

"You—" I try to stifle a laugh, but a few deranged giggles escape. "Okay. So why set me up as the *savior* of the Kingdom?"

"So you could understand the pointlessness of the endeavor!" Cyrus's voice rises. "You've seen their corruption, their foolishness. The leaders, the empty-headed Prince and that fool of a Duke. The monsters in the Guild. The way they take the gifts of a perfect world and squander them in excess and war. Fail often enough, I thought, and you would come to believe as I do."

"Yeah? And how's that going for you?"

"You made yourself Dark Lord, did you not? Avoiding every marker I set to push you the other way?"

"Yeah, but . . ." I work my jaw as though trying to chew that disturbing thought. "Only, like, *ironically*."

"It could have been a first step along the path." He sighs. "All useless now, of course. If there is one thing I have learned about you, it's that you are utterly contrary. Once you become aware of being pushed in one direction, you refuse to do anything but run the other way."

"Yeah, that sounds like me. I'm ornery."

"And so we must begin again." He turns away from me, looking out at the forest below us. "I will scrape you clean, like a palimpsest, and adjust my approach. Perhaps in another thousand years, we will be having a different conversation."

I have my own thoughts about that. But I keep them to myself, because I recognize the hill ahead of us. We've come to the laboratory, and it's nearly time to roll the dice.

Chapter Fifteen

The dragon lands atop the hill, causing a dozen small land-slides. Cyrus lifts me easily, board and all, as the dragon bends its head and deposits us in front of the hidden door. Fresh earth has covered it, but he parts it with a few muttered words and a wave. The metal portal swings smoothly inward.

"No doubt your friends have some tiresome rescue attempt planned." He looks over his shoulder and sighs. "Before long, the horde will arrive and secure the area, but for the moment I think a dragon will be sufficient to keep watch." He hauls me into the corridor and gestures the metal slab shut behind us.

The main landing is still occupied by the corpse of the octo-panzer, half-dissected and stripped of its thaumite. Cyrus clicks his tongue at the sight of it.

"If you knew the work that went into securing that crea-ture..." He sighs. "It's always been your way, I suppose. You break things rather than appreciating them."

"Only when they try to kill me first."

"No matter. The reset will restore it."

He stalks out along one of the metal bridges, dragging me behind him. Ahead is the glass sphere with an open hatch, where I removed a piece of the massive spell whose architecture fills the artificial cavern. Cyrus regards it with a pained expression, like a museum curator discovering that someone has snipped off a chunk of the Mona Lisa with dull scissors.

"I admit," he says, "I expected your sabotage to be a little more wanton. Not that you have any understanding of what you're doing regardless. I don't suppose you're willing to produce the stone you stole?"

"Sorry. Must have left it in my other pants." There's something moving behind him.

"Of course. And so I must cut another." He regards me with the sort of detached irritation one might give a lab monkey who refused to perform for its banana. "Your capacity for sheer perversity continues to astound me."

"Hey! There's no call to go around saying I'm a pervert just because I like having weird, borderline dangerous sex sometimes."

"Davi..."

"A girl has *needs*, come on. Like your sex life is above reproach. I bet there's a whole room somewhere filled with just the strangest shit—"

"You're trying to distract me." He glances around, first at the glass globe and then back to the door. "What are you planning?"

"Nothing! Obviously nothing. Whatever you do, don't look straight up."

Cyrus frowns, trying to decide whether following my advice or not following it is the way to go. During that half second of hesitation, Droff reaches down from the ceiling and hits him very hard.

* * *

I once asked Droff if, as a rock-monster, he could phase through earth; he responded by asking me if I could phase through meat. The latter remains a distant dream[1] but the former has at least partially become reality. Droff's stocky legs are half-sunken into the flat stone ceiling, enabling him to hang there like an oversized barnacle before stretching to his full height and clocking Cyrus on the temple with one massive fist.

The impact is enough to send the wizard pinwheeling through the air, toppling off the railing and descending through the web of catwalks. It's too much to hope that he'd fall all the way to the bottom, though, and he manages to get a hand on one of the railings, arresting his fall with a bone-snapping jerk. Unbothered, he hoists himself up, already grabbing for his chained thaumite.

With a merry chorus of bowstrings, a dozen arrows zip across the lab. A few miss the mark but most hit Cyrus, sticking into him from all angles. None sinks deeper than an inch into his flesh. He slaps them away with a roar and starts chanting.

I'd hoped things wouldn't be *quite* so lopsided, but I should have known better. Cyrus has more thaumite embedded in his flesh than Gevalkin did. If the pyrvir assassin was Wonder Woman, then he's more like Superman's big brother. Our only advantages are surprise, numbers, and the fact that he can't fit the fucking dragon in here.

My friends, as you've probably gathered, did not return to the palace with me as Cyrus assumed. Instead, they remained on the premises even as I closed the door behind me, spending the day preparing and hiding themselves. Now they've emerged, orcs and fox-wilder archers spread across the multiple levels of the laboratory. A second volley whips down toward Cyrus and draws bright pinpricks of blood.

---

1 Someday I'll perfect a spell to give myself meatwalk.

"*This* is your idea of a plan?" he bellows, grabbing a chunk of red thaumite so big it'd make Indiana Jones wet his pants with envy. "Lead your friends to their deaths?"

Fire lances out from his pointing finger, aimed at a fox-wilder woman halfway along a bridge. She sees it coming and dives aside, but the burst of white-hot flame tears the catwalk in two and chars a black streak into the ceiling. The severed halves of the bridge shudder, giving a horrible metallic screech and twisting slowly to one side as the metal grating folds in on itself. The fox-wilder takes a flying leap and makes it to another bridge below while the end of the damaged span sags downward and collides with one of the glass spell-globes. The sound it makes when it shatters is like a tray full of champagne flutes hitting the floor all at once.

Even from up here, I can see the "oh, *fuck*" expression on Cyrus's face. No blaming anyone else for that one, smart guy; tossing blasts around recklessly is going to set you back a few years each time. I was tempted to smash the whole thing to splinters before we left, but this way is much better. *We* don't have to worry about breaking stuff.

By this point, Droff has freed himself from the ceiling and tumbled inelegantly to the catwalk. From the other direction, Mari comes running, spear in hand.

"You're not dead!" She sounds like she doesn't quite believe it.

"Hurrah!" I agree. "Get me off this thing."

She yanks a knife from her belt and goes to work on the ropes. Droff, shaking his stony head, clambers to his feet with some difficulty.

"You okay?" I ask him.

"Droff does not wish to be upside down again, either."[2] He peers over the side. "The wizard survived."

---

2 Really curious about the physiology here, it's not like all the blood can rush to his head.

"He's a tough motherfucker." My hands come free, and I clutch them to my chest in an agony of pins and needles. Come on, body, no time for this. "We have to keep him busy."

Down below, an attempt is underway to do just that, more arrows whizzing past or sticking into Cyrus's skin. His robes are coming to pieces under the barrage. Instead of fireballs, he summons a flaming blade like mine, casting about for the closest opponent. Spotting Maeve two levels up, he *jumps* like an anime ninja, landing hard enough to dent the grating. She scrambles away, avoiding the blazing weapon, and before he can catch Maeve, Euria emerges from behind a stairway to charge him with lowered antlers. The impact sends the surprised Cyrus into a tumbling roll, and I glimpse something green and sparkly fly away.

The chained thaumite. Very convenient, but maybe a touch more vulnerable than a good old-fashioned sack. Mari gets my legs free and hands me a bow, a quiver, and my own thaumite stash, minus what I lent to Gena. I grab the knife from her as well, leaning against the railing while feeling returns to my feet. Painfully, I nock an arrow.

"The chains!" I shout loud enough to echo through the lab. "Hit the chains!"

Aim. Draw. Breathe. Loose. The arrows sing through the air, slipping under Cyrus's outstretched arm and hitting one of those dangling silver chains. Glittering links go flying and a big brown gem falls away, clattering to a catwalk floor.

This has the happy side effect of distracting Cyrus before he can skewer Euria. He looks up in my direction and leaps again, reaching a bridge halfway up. Sparks fly around him as more arrows hiss past, ricocheting off the metal.

It's *working*. I nock another arrow, shoot, and see another bit of the wizard's thaumite spin off into the void. Without his gems, he's just a heavily augmented wilder—tough, certainly, but we've killed tough things before. If we can take him down—

Cyrus drops to his knees. For a moment, I think he's going to *surrender*. I should know better.

"Enough," he says, doing that trick where his voice carries to every corner of the room. "That's *enough*."

Then he's on his feet again, brown thaumite in hand. His fingers twist in rapid-fire gestures.

"I expect a certain amount of *trouble* from you, Davi," he spits. "It seems to be your nature. But do you really think this is going to stop me? I am *done* playing with you fools."

I hear stone grinding on stone. Doors are opening on every level, hidden until now, revealing closet-like chambers.

"You are *children* and I am the parent, treating you with kid gloves because I do not want to make a mess. Congratulations, then. You have finally earned the belt."

Tentacles slither on stone.

* * *

The things that emerge are clearly related to the octopanzer, but now in a new fun size for added convenience. They have a rounded body held up by a mass of muscular tentacles, with plates of armor fastened to their sides. Their protection isn't as complete as their big brother's, but it's still formidable, and their tentacle tips sport vicious blades. Metal screams against stone all over the lab as they lumber forth.

Cyrus himself spins around and raises his red thaumite again. He spots an orc on a catwalk above and makes a quick gesture. Liquid fire stabs out, obliterating the wilder, the bridge, and a chunk of glassware behind it. Bits of shattered thaumite tumble out of the stream of fire.

Fuck me. That . . . escalated quickly.

I take another shot—I don't think he'll blow *me* into dust, however mad he is—but Cyrus sends streamers of fire whipping around himself, their hot winds knocking the arrow off course. He jumps again, landing only one bridge below me. His eyes are wild and bloodshot, his face twisted in an angry rictus.

Time to run! Run run run. I gesture frantically for Mari and Droff to head in the opposite direction while I sprint for the end of the bridge.

"Is this what you wanted, Davi?" Cyrus leaps again as I reach the stairs. "To make me mad? Congratulations. You're going to spend the next twenty years in a tiny cell while I put everything back together."

"I'll have time to work on my reading, then!" I call back, taking the stairs two at a time.

"That will be difficult without hands." Flame crackles around him. "Or arms. Or eyes."

Yikes. Okay.

Up ahead, a stone-eater is fighting one of the octo-things, two tentacles clutched in her rocky hands while the others batter her. I race in from behind with my red thaumite, and a blade of fire lances into the creature's exposed top side. It sags and the stone-eater tosses it aside with a grumbling grunt of thanks. I round the corner to the next staircase, descending, Cyrus stalking unhurriedly after me.

"Should I keep some of your friends alive?" he shouts. "Take them to pieces, bit by bit, for your amusement?" I hear a rumble, then duck as a shower of hot gravel lands all around me. "Perhaps not."

Fuck fuck *fuck*. There's fighting all over the laboratory, and I can't stop long enough to help. Droff holds one of the monsters in place while Mari spears it; below, a fox-wilder bleeds in torrents as he scrambles away from sharpened tentacles whirring like blender blades. Jeffrey the mouse, sling spinning, sends lead bullets caroming off an octo-thing's armored body. Somebody's screaming.

Down. I keep heading down. Last chance. Mari's knife is tucked into my belt.

"Perhaps," he says, "this cleansing was overdue. I may have been too lenient with you for the past thousand years. Results may improve if I take a more direct hand."

He leaps over the side of a bridge, pushing off the rail like he's doing fucking parkour and landing directly in front of me. His few remaining bits of thaumite jingle wildly on his chains, but he has the red one firmly in hand. I pull up short, glancing down and gauging the distance. Not yet not yet not yet *fuck*.

"Gonna incinerate me?" I say. "That'll make it a bit hard to finish out the plan, won't it?"

"There are so many things I'm going to do to you." He stalks forward, dropping the red gem to dangle from his arm. "You will *beg* to burn. You have before, you know."

Lovely fellow, this one. I back up, try to keep my eyes on his. I must give something away, though, because he turns wickedly fast, to throw up a hand and block Micah's descending axe.

Gena's husband is wreathed in magic. Somewhere— hopefully somewhere out of the way—Gena is concentrating on the rest of my thaumite, maintaining as many buffs as her concentration will allow. Half of those are applied to Micah; it's not quite Duke Aster's full war powers, but it's on top of him being a giant fucking monster of a person in the first place. He swings his axe with both hands in a blow that would have carved an elephant in two.

Cyrus tries to block it, but even his augmentations aren't up to the task. Two fingers from his left hand go spinning away in a splatter of red as the axe carves through and leaves a long gash in the metal walkway. The wizard screams and slams Micah in the chest with his other hand, a blow that looks as though it should be about as effective as a mosquito bite. The big man staggers away, grunting, and coughs blood. Cyrus sneers and grabs his red thaumite again, his half hand dripping.

I ought to be running full tilt, but I pause at the staircase and raise my bow. Nock, draw, *loose* a snap shot at practically point-blank range. If I missed this one, they'd throw me out of Legolas Academy. The arrow nails the big red gem dead-on, knocking it from Cyrus's grip and breaking it free of its chain. He grabs for it, misses, and nearly takes Micah's axe in the face as the warrior recovers. Cyrus is snake-fast, though, and ducks under the blade, grabbing Micah's arm as the weapon passes and sending him over the edge of the rail with some kind of aikido flip. Micah hits the floor of the next level down with a heavy *oof*.

I'm running again, off one stairway, across a bridge, down another, metal ringing under my boots. The catwalks aren't as long here, nearly to the bottom, the glass spheres and tubes of the spell clustered more tightly. I charge past the battered corpse of an octo-thing, heading for a ladder leading to the penultimate level.

Just as I get there, the stone *twists*. Metal screams as the ladder is torn away from its brackets, falling sideways with an enormous clatter. Another support gives out with a pop, and the whole bridge tilts, sending me stumbling against the railing. My bow slips from my hand and tumbles away. I reach for my thaumite, but Cyrus has a small red stone already in hand, and a pinpoint blast of fire scorches my fingers and sends the bag of gems to the floor. I back up, the catwalk wobbling beneath me, until my back is against the wall.

"There's nowhere left to go, you fool." He comes forward, thaumite raised. Not quite far enough. Almost, *almost*. But he stops, as though wary of any more tricks. "Come here like a good girl and I may allow your friends to live."

"Until you reset the universe, you mean."

"Until then, yes. But given the damage you've done, that may be decades. Is that worth nothing to you? The lives they might have?"

For a moment, I think about it. People are dying. There's no guarantee my last card is worth a damn.

And somewhere at the back of my brain, the seductive voice of fear. Cyrus will fix the *loop*, my tormentor, my prison, my personal hell. But while in the loop, *I can't die*. This existential terror that grips me, banished forever.

Maybe it's worth it. Maybe sometimes you just have to take the *L*, right?

Obviously not. *Never give up.* I promised Tsav.

Five more steps.

In a split second, I grab Mari's knife and press the blade against my chest. My free hand steadies me against the railing.

"This again?" Cyrus shuffles a step closer. Four. "Really?"

"I told you. I'm ornery."

He takes hold of his green thaumite, which is unfortunately not one we've managed to detach. "I would have thought you were smarter than that. You saw how this plays out."

"And yet you're hesitating." I give him my best grin. "Not sure you're fast enough?"

"Your hands are shaking. Not sure this is really what you want?"

"I told you. After a thousand years—"

He scoffs and waves at the destruction around us. "This isn't the plan of someone ready for the end. You had plenty of time for that."

"I won't say it's my first choice. But at least I'll die *me* and not let you muck around in my head."

"Die *you*?" Cyrus sighs. "There *is* no you! You're a vessel I scraped clean and rebuilt to serve my purposes."

"Please. You can't believe that." Something shakes the lab,

and we both sway. "You know what your problem is? You fundamentally don't understand that *not everyone is like you.* 'How hard could it be to make someone into a genocidal Dark Lord?' the clever wizard says. 'After all, that's what *I'd* be if I was given half a chance!' And it somehow has never crossed your mind, in however many thousands of years you've been trying it, that most people just *aren't fucking psychopaths*!

"Congratulations, Cyrus. You really are something special. Back on Earth, you'd probably have become a garden-variety serial killer or politician or something, but here on your perfect world, being a bastard is so much more rewarding, isn't it? But apparently that's not enough for you."

I lean back against the rail with a sigh, one hand still gripping the dagger.

"It doesn't matter how many times you break me down and build me up again. I'm not going to slaughter everybody, not even if I'm convinced it doesn't really matter. Your project is fucked, man."

"We," he says tightly, "shall see. Now, come here."

I fix my eyes on his and smile. His lips twists. Four more steps.

"I'm tired," I say.

And for the second time today, I stab myself.

Time slows down like Zack Snyder's directing. Cyrus grabs for his green thaumite, starts running forward. One step. Two. Up above, magic flashes and metal skirls. I fall to my knees, leaning against the rail. He keeps coming, already spitting words of power. Three.

Four.

The dead octo-thing twitches.

Then Tsav explodes from underneath it, wreathed in magic and drenched in monster gore like some horrible avatar of vengeance. She's powered up with all the rest of my thaumite, everything Gena could throw at her, and Snyder ramps the speed up as she surges across the catwalk toward Cyrus. The wizard may be stronger than any ordinary mortal, but he *weighs* the same, and Tsav's considerably greater bulk impacts him around the midsection. She tackles him like a linebacker finally getting a shot at the quarterback, arms out, lifting him off the ground and carrying him across the catwalk to the rail.

I fall forward, fingers loosening.

The rail hits Cyrus in the back of the knees and Tsav lets go. He topples over, green thaumite still in one hand, the other scrabbling for a hold and not quite getting it. But he's twisting in midair like a cat, getting ready to hit the ground and bounce upward, teeth bared in a snarl.

Except Tsav has chosen her spot with care. There are no more bridges underneath him. Not even the hard rock of the floor. Just two stories of empty air, and the vortex.

Cyrus seems to realize it halfway down. He turns his head and starts to scream, but there isn't time. He hits the swirling pool of silver droplets, the dark heart of the time spell, spraying glittering drops of raw temporal energy in an evanescent fountain. Like my knife, he slows down as he passes the surface, moments stretching like he's dropped through the event horizon of a black hole until he's barely moving at all.

Simultaneously, time seems to speed up around him. His clothes are the first to go, turning black and rotting off his body. His hair grows out like a stop-motion Nazi's, forming a wild mane streaming behind him. The chains holding his thaumite erode and break away.

But his body endures much longer than the knife did. It'd be fascinating to watch, if I weren't currently in the process of expiring myself. The thaumite embedded in his flesh *shrinks*, slowly but surely, consumed from within. There's immortal and there's *immortal*; even Old Ones don't live *forever* if they can't get new stones to keep themselves going. Cyrus has a *lot* of thaumite, so it takes a while, but at some point, the magic runs out. Then, in a relative eyeblink, he's gone, flesh rotting to nothing and even his skeleton falling to dust as eons stream past.

I don't know if he was aware of every second of all those millennia in the void. But I like to think so. It warms my heart.

Or would, anyway. I hit the catwalk face-first, and die.

Epilogue

That's it! I'm totally dead. End of story.

Really.

Bad guy defeated, world saved-ish, minus a few bits and pieces here and there. Heroine tragically sacrifices herself, too good for this fallen world, ascends to heaven on a cloud of white and starts corrupting some of those celestial virgins. The end.

Why are you still here?

Do you need a section break?

* * *

How about another one?

* * *

Okay, *fine*. We're not going to get *quite* that grimdark up in here. Leave that to Joe.

The thing is, there is some technique to stabbing yourself in the heart.

If you angle the knife the wrong way, you're going to

puncture your lung, which will hurt like hell and probably kill you, but, and this is important, not *quickly*.

It helps to have lots of practice.

I don't actually pass out, which kind of sucks, because a collapsed lung filling with blood is not my favorite sensation. It would have been nice if Tsav cradled me gently to her chest, because if you're dying painfully, at least you can be pressed against some A-grade titties; unfortunately for me, she's a practical sort, and ran off to fetch Gena rather than indulging in theatrics. The surviving octo-things are still at large, but Mari and the others seem to have gotten the hang of them. Gena, looking exhausted, stumbles down next to my almost-corpse with some green thaumite and does the thing, so we can all live happily ever after.

* * *

Except the ones who didn't, of course. We carry out with us the half dozen wilders killed fighting Cyrus and his octopuses. Droff and his remaining companion show no inclination to gather up the gravel remnants of their fallen comrade, so we leave them be. By the time we extract ourselves, injured and limping, the dragon—free at last of Cyrus's control—has thankfully fucked off.[1] We spend the next couple of days healing and burying the dead and, at least in my case, staring into space a lot. Tsav seems to sense that I need some time to cope, and she keeps the others from bothering me too much.

You've seen the cartoon about the dog who caught the car? Flapping like a kite with his jaws clamped on the bumper at

---

1 Not actually sure what I would have done if it hadn't. Kind of a flaw in the plan, if I'm being honest.

highway speeds, thinking, *Well, what the fuck do I do now?* That's me, trying to come to terms with the fact that I maybe, kind of, um, *won?* For once? For *ever?*

I should be dancing. I should be apocalyptically drunk and ready to make world historically bad decisions with a variety of partners. I should be screaming to the heavens and pissing on Cyrus's grave, not that he got one.

But all I can think about is what's *lost*. How many people died, here and all along the way, and how they're now just gone from the world as though they never existed. Some of them are my fault, some aren't. Does it matter?

Should I have let Cyrus reset things and tried again? Maybe if I had another shot, I could *really* get it right, find a way out that saves everybody. Perfect game, high score, 100 percent completion, platinum achievement. Is it *selfish* of me to want to escape while I have the chance?

And now ... what? I've lived a thousand years—or a lot more than that, apparently—but this is uncharted territory. A future that isn't calibrated or predicted, crafted or optimized. I'll be pushing through one day at a time, trying to figure out what's best, just like everyone else.

It's near dawn on the second day when this thought comes to me. Sleep has eluded me, and I'm sitting on a rock under the gray pre-morning sky. The revelation lands like a thunderbolt, so shocking that I literally bolt to my feet.

Just like everyone else.

For a thousand years, the world has revolved around me. Everything that happens, every stubbed toe and tragic death, has in some sense been *my fault*, because I *could* have reset the world and tried to prevent it. I always had a choice, a say, a veto. Power, but also responsibility, like Uncle Ben says.

And now it's gone. I'm free.

I'm not the protagonist anymore.

* * *

The sun comes up, brilliant pinks and oranges setting fire to the sky, and syrupy light turning the forest gold. Tsav emerges from our tent and finds me rolling back and forth on the ground, laughing my ass off. I try to explain my epiphany, but all she wants to know is why I'm not wearing pants.

* * *

You probably want to know what happened to everybody. Cue up "Don't You (Forget About Me)":

The remains of the horde accepted my authority as Dark Lord again. They didn't have many other choices with Hufferth and Amitsugu backing me up and Sibarae and Artaxes vanished. In any event, the most ardent death-to-the-humans types had died back at the river, and the enthusiasm of the survivors for further fighting was mostly spent. At this point, everybody was happy to go home.

Johann and Matthias took over as the undisputed rulers of the Kingdom, and we all agreed to give peace between humans and wilders a real shot. The Guild of Adventurers, similarly denuded of the most fanatic of its members and greatly reduced in political stature, could no longer make much of an objection.

Will it work, in the long term? Who knows. There are whole swaths of wilder bands, down on the southern border, who never even got the word about the Dark Lord, and there's going to be human nobles unhappy with the whole arrangement. It's going to take a whole lot of effort from the Crown and the, uh, spiky helmet to make it stick. But it's a chance, at least.

Cyrus was convinced humans would inevitably ruin this

world, but I'm more optimistic. If we start using magic more to improve people's lives and less to blow one another up, we might get somewhere. The notes he left, ironically, are a good start—there are tricks in there that even I didn't know. And of course, the haul of thaumite from the secret lab has made Johann's power considerably less dependent on noble approval. Maybe we can get to the leviathan state and the demographic transition and all that good stuff, right? Malthus can go fuck himself.

Or maybe not. I don't predict the future anymore.

As for my companions, Mari screamed bloody murder when I told her I was making her Dark Lord. But somebody needs to make sure the wilders live up to their half of the bargain, and I think she'll be good at it. She's got Droff to help her,[2] and Jeffrey and Euria and the others.

I extracted a promise from Amitsugu not to go within a hundred miles of her, but he says he's retiring to the mountains to become a hermit. Before long, I fully expect him to be on the floor of his hut betraying the spiders to the ants or something.

Johann, naturally, became king when his mother finally passed away. He and Matthias raised a whole passel of children, so the Kingdom's succession is in good hands. Last I heard, Matthias was dreaming up a scheme for a public university and magical research center, while Johann had so much fun posing for the official oil painting that he commissioned a royal art gallery.

As for me and Tsav—we compromised on a mountain *with* a lake. There's a little house and some woods to walk in and

---

2   And maybe those two will finally kiss omg the sexual tension is unbearable. Then they can get married and adopt Odlen, see, I have a whole plan. #FoxRock

nobody knows where to find us. Maybe someday we'll check back in with the rest of civilization, maybe not.

After a thousand years, I need a *long* vacation.

* * *

Okay, you can stop reading for real now.

Acknowledgments

I'll keep this short and sweet—for the origins of this project, see the first book!

Thanks to my wonderful wife, Casey Blair, as always, and to beta reader Rhiannon Held. Thanks to Seth Fishman and his team at the Gernert Company, and to everyone at Orbit: my editor Brit Hvide as well as Nick Burnham, Bryn A. McDonald, Natassja Haught, Stephanie A. Hess, Xian Lee, Blue Guess, and Angela Man.

And most of all, thanks to you!

extras

orbit-books.co.uk

about the author

Django Wexler graduated from Carnegie Mellon University in Pittsburgh with degrees in creative writing and computer science, and he worked for the university in artificial intelligence research. Eventually he migrated to Microsoft in Seattle, where he now lives with two cats and a teetering mountain of books. When not writing, he wrangles computers, paints tiny soldiers and plays games of all sorts.

Find out more about Django Wexler and other Orbit authors by registering for the free monthly newsletter at orbit-books.co.uk.

if you enjoyed

EVERYBODY WANTS TO RULE THE WORLD EXCEPT ME

look out for

THE BONE RAIDERS

The Rakada: Book One

by

Jackson Ford

You don't mess with the Rakada. The people living in the grasslands of the Tapestry call them the Bone Raiders, from their charming habit of displaying the bones of those they kill on their horses and armour.

But being a raider is tough these days. There's a new Great Khan in the Tapestry. He's had it with the raider clans, and plans to use his sizeable military to do something about it. And then there are the araatan: fire-breathing lizards the size of elephants, roaming the grasslands in search of dwindling food supplies.

Sayana is a Rakada scout, and she loves her job. But if she wants to keep it, she's going to have to do something drastic. Like convincing her clan to ride araatan, instead of horses. Sayana doesn't quite know how to get that done without being eaten and/or cooked alive, but she'd better figure it out fast — or she and her clan, along with every other raider in the Tapestry, will be wiped out.

One

Garrick

"I was out taking a piss, and I nearly stood on her!"

Garrick slowly opened one eye. Which was a huge mistake, because that was when his hangover chose to announce itself by whanging hard against the inside of his skull. He closed his eye with a pained grunt, rolled back over.

When it came to pissing on people, he didn't want to know. He really didn't.

"Nearly kicked her in the head." The speaker was old Batu, just beyond the flap of Garrick's tent. The man was addressing a crowd, it sounded like: a hubbub of excited voices. "She was down in the long grass, all sneaky. If I hadn't been keeping an eye out, no one would have found her. No one!"

Garrick rather doubted that. Batu couldn't find his arse if the directions were tattooed on the back of his wrinkled hands. None of the villagers could.

A burst of agonising light lanced through his cracked eyelids. Someone, some deeply evil fuck, had pushed open the flap of his tent. He held up a hand, but it did no good whatsoever.

"Garrick, you need to come!" a hazy shape shouted. "Batu caught a raider!"

The shape vanished as quickly as it had appeared. Garrick propped himself up on his elbow, blinking, tongue sour in his mouth.

Raiders.

Been a while since any had come this way. The new Khan and his army were exterminating them, wiping them off the face of the Tapestry. All part of the Khan's grand plan for this land.

A raider scout that allowed themselves to be caught was a very poor raider indeed. Chances are, old Batu didn't know what he was talking about. Still, Garrick didn't trust the villagers not to cock this up. Somehow.

With a sigh, he found his way to his feet, doing his best to ignore the horrid pounding in his brain. To his left, his anvil sat, dark and silent. Tools nearby, arranged neatly on a wooden bench.

He would have given anything to stay inside; the tent was unbearably hot, dust hanging in the still air. But it would be hotter out there, where the twin suns could cook you in your boots.

Garrick supposed he'd be needing his axe, for show if nothing else. It lay propped against the fabric wall. His fingers closed on the weapon's worn haft. He slotted it into the sheath on his back as he stepped out, squinting into the searing midday light.

The blacksmith stood a head taller than anyone in the village. He was tanned and lined, but the skin at the neck of his sleeveless, boiled leather jerkin was still pale pink. Unlike the men of this land, with their neat goatees, his beard ran to his chest in a black river, flecked with grey rapids.

He'd come to the village a year before, a traveller passing through. He spoke the language, and had bartered for a place to sleep and a cracked bowl of millet broth. He'd ended up liking the place, and had stayed, offering his skills at metalwork. There were rumours of what had driven him from the west, whispers of scandal and betrayal. Garrick would only smile when asked, and say that it was a long time ago.

There were plenty of settlements just like this one in the massive, rolling grasslands of the Tapestry. It stood on a hillside, which ended in a cliff high above a rushing river. The colourful felt tents – *gers*, they called them in these parts – ran all the way up the gentle slope to the cliff edge.

As Garrick ducked out of his own *ger*, another villager brushed past him. This one was laughing – at what, Garrick didn't know, only that they sounded nervous and they were way, way, *way* too fucking loud.

Garrick clutched his splitting skull; he'd once been told that the fermented mare's milk they drank in these parts – *airag*, they called it – wasn't that strong. He briefly fantasised about finding the man who'd told him that, and beating him to death. The basic stuff wasn't, to be sure, but the people of this land had a way of distilling it that did horrible things to your brain.

He took several deep breaths. As he did so, and without really meaning to, he glanced to his left.

At the damned banner.

He'd been trying not to think about it; honestly, it was part of the reason he'd got so drunk last night. Soldiers had planted it two days before, at the bottom of the hill. Two white suns and a moon, crowned with orange flame on blue fabric, rippling in the warm wind. The Khan's Will, it was called.

Raiders weren't the only thing the Khan seemed set on exterminating. Villages like this one weren't part of his grand plan. Ditto for the many groups of nomads wandering the Tapestry, with their horses and wagons.

The old Khan had been content to let all of them exist, as long as they paid him tribute. The new one? *That* evil little prick wanted everyone under his thumb. Which was bad news if you happened to like living out in the grasslands of the Tapestry.

The Khan wanted an army. He wanted manned borders, garrisons at areas of strategic importance. The official reason was to be ready if Dalai invaded, from the north, or Ngu, from the south. Garrick rather suspected it was because the man liked the idea of thousands of troops at his beck and call.

And instead of scattered villages and roving bands of nomads, he wanted a single shining city, with a giant wall and leagues of farmland. Karkorum. His capital. He wanted everyone in the Tapestry in one place, where he could keep an eye on them.

That was the point of the banner. *Hello, villagers: those of you who can hold a sabre, deliver yourself to military training post haste. Those who can't, deliver yourself to Karkorum, and report for work. Those city walls aren't going to build themselves, and that grassland won't become nice, ordered rows of crops unless you put your backs into it.*

Didn't like the idea? Didn't fancy starving in a crowded, diseased slum, or suffering forced marches for no good reason? No problem. You could run, or you could . . . no, actually that was about it. Run, and hope you escaped the Khan's notice, or that one of the battalions roaming the Tapestry didn't come across you. *Good luck.*

The whole thing pissed him off. Life in the Tapestry was hard, but it suited him. Living in a nation-sized military camp did not.

Since the soldiers planted that banner, the whole village had been in an uproar. Everyone knew what moving to Karkorum meant – nobody came back from there. So they'd argued and debated and fought, and wasted valuable time.

Later today, the soldiers would be back, asking pointed

questions about why the villagers were still here. The kind of questions that usually ended up with someone's heart on a wooden stake.

Hangover or not, Garrick intended to be long gone before things got to the hearts-on-stakes bit. He had no intention of fighting in the army, or slaving away in the city, and he couldn't stop the Khan on his own. This land was finished, but he wasn't. He'd go north, over the mountains perhaps. To a place where they made booze that didn't hollow out your skull from the inside.

Still, he'd deal with this raider situation first — if it was indeed a raider situation. Least he could do.

He frowned as he took in the crowd: an angry, noisy mess of people surrounding their captive. The crowd was moving, dragging their prisoner up the narrow street between the *gers*, stepping past the village's single wagon – an ancient contraption with three remaining wheels, the bare axle propped up with wood blocks. In all the time he'd been here, Garrick had never seen it move. No one even seemed to know who it belonged to.

When this village decamped, headed to Karkorum to begin their fabulous new lives in service to the Khan, it would be the only thing left behind. A monument to what the Tapestry used to be.

He trailed the crowd as they dragged their prey to the edge of the cliff. The river sat fifty feet below, gleaming in the suns, reflecting a midday sky filled with puffy, billowing clouds. Beyond the river, shimmering grass stalks stretched to the mountains on the horizon.

He was going to miss this place. What a waste, to empty it of people, force them to live behind walls or in military camps.

There was a dusty, ancient wooden pole sunk into the ground near the cliff – Garrick had never got around to asking what it was for. Chances were, no one would know anyway. They were tying someone to it as he arrived, shoving her to sit on the dirt, binding her wrists above her head with a strip of rough cloth.

For once, old Batu had been dead right. This was no traveller. Travellers didn't wear paint. Hers was a jagged red slash, running from right temple to left jawbone.

"Found her skulking in the reeds, I did!" Batu bleated, to anyone who would listen. "If I hadn't had the boys with me, she would've run me through. Nearly took off Nugai's ear before we got her pinned."

Nugai grinned as several others slapped him on the back. Blood trickled down the side of his head, staining his beaded blue healer's headband.

The scout wouldn't stop struggling. She was young, twenty perhaps, with a round face and a hard twist to her mouth. Tall — over six foot, easily, with a body like a reed. Skin covered in nicks and scars, mementos of past battles.

Her hair wasn't cut short, like so many other raiders. Instead, she had a single long, black braid running down to her waist.

One of the villagers grabbed it, laughing as he wrapped it around the pole and tied it to itself in a clumsy knot, pulling the scout's head back against the hard wood. They'd taken her sash, and her faded grey *deel* hung open, the robe showing tough leather underneath.

Some of the villagers were passing the girl's sabres around. The fact that she had two weapons was strange in itself: fighting with twin blades was stupid. It looked flashy, but you couldn't defend yourself, or grapple. You'd get skewered if you didn't move like lightning. It was exactly the kind of fighting that they liked in the palace in Karkorum, funnily enough, where all you had to do was entertain the Khan while he had his breakfast.

"She's Black Hands!" someone shouted. "Has to be!"

"Not a chance," said another voice. "We sent them running ages ago."

Garrick grunted at that. There wasn't much *we* about it, if he remembered right. Just him.

"Arkan's Eagles then. None of them even know the right way to hold a blade, no surprise one of them got herself caught."

"Down by Arsi's tent." Batu was still going. "Found her myself when I went to take a piss!"

Garrick crouched, studying the scout. She caught his eye and actually snarled at him. It sounded forced, theatrical, like a mummer in some play.

He found he pitied her, just a tiny bit. If you had to pick a career with no future in the Tapestry, being a raider was at the top of the list. Even the ones still out there, which apparently included this young pup, were on borrowed time.

Awfully hard to make a living as a raider if there were no settlements left to raid, after all. *Or if the army is taking special pleasure in wiping you out.*

You could give up, of course. Pretend to be a villager, or try to join the army yourself. Just another citizen obeying your Khan's orders. But if they caught you . . .

There was something about this raider, though, that made the skin on the back of his neck prickle.

"Who do you ride with?" he murmured, just loud enough for her to hear. "Speak."

She spat at him. The glob of spit didn't quite make it, splashing into the dirt. The raider lashed out with her unbound feet, catching nothing but dust. Twisting against the rope around her wrists.

There was a necklace at her throat, most of it hidden beneath her leather armour. The thing prickling the back of Garrick's neck started to move down his spine as he reached over, snagging the string, ignoring her bared teeth. Lifting it out.

Bones.

Polished white chips, threaded on the woven string.

Most raiders in the Tapestry weren't worth a damn. You could fight them off on a good day, stand your ground. But most didn't mean all. And there was one group in particular, a group who Garrick had only heard of, never actually seen . . .

Panic had a strange way of showing itself. For such a vicious emotion, it always came on gradually. The set of someone's shoulders. A tiny crack in another's voice.

It started to spread through the villagers behind Garrick the moment they saw the bones. The woman gave him a slow, twisted smile, and for the first time, she spoke. Above the trembling murmur of the crowd, her voice carried perfectly.

"You are so fucked."

And just like that, the villagers lost their minds.

They all started shouting, bumping into each other, scrambling in their haste to get away. One of them still held the scout's sabres, nearly impaling another villager as he spun in place. A word kept coming up, rising above the tumult again and again.

Rakada.

Garrick didn't believe in the gods of this land. Didn't believe that Father Sky and Mother Earth had woven the Tapestry, thousands of years before. But he couldn't help himself thinking, just for a second, that they were vindictive bastards nonetheless. First the Khan's Will, and now this? What else could possibly befall this village?

He forced himself to look away from the woman's triumphant smile. "Enough," he bellowed.

Amazingly, they listened.

He turned slowly, taking in the frozen villagers. His hangover was gone. *This* was why they needed him: to be a steady hand when others wavered.

He couldn't protect them from the Khan's Will, no one could ... but he could stand firm against raiders. Even these raiders.

"Bayar," he said, his lips barely moving. The man with the sabres gazed up at him, trembling. "Get everyone to safety. Take them to the river, and follow it east. Where it widens, the grass is tall enough to hide in."

There was the sound of wood on leather as his axe slipped free. "The rest of you: with me."

"Do you know what the Rakada are?" one of the women snarled. "Do you know what they *do*?"

"You want your bones hanging from their horses, pale man?"

"It's a trick! It has to be! We need to fight."

"No no no. We ransom her, yes? Back to those monsters."

"The Bone Raiders won't care. Cut her throat, and have done with it! One less raider to fight later ... "

Garrick tested the weight of his axe. How much time did they have? Minutes? How long before the Rakada missed their scout? He listened hard, forcing his way past the panicked voices of the villagers. Listened for the sound of howling, carried on the wind.

The sound of rattling bones.

They didn't come. Instead, there was a very peculiar, rumbling growl.

Garrick turned, thinking it was too late, that the Rakada had already arrived. But the thing coming along the edge of the cliff towards them, from the north, wasn't a raider. It wasn't a soldier, come to carry out the Khan's orders.

It wasn't even human.

Garrick had heard stories of war elephants, in the kingdoms

beyond the mountains. He'd seen huge crocodiles in the rivers of the southern deltas. The thing walking along the cliff looked as if a sorcerer had melded the two, brought them together to create the single biggest creature Garrick had ever seen.

The lizard – that's what it was, a fucking *lizard* – was twice his height at the shoulder, with a massive, muscular body swaying from side to side. Scales the colour of summer grass. The tail swished the air, the end a thick, bony club the size of a boulder.

Four powerful legs stuck out, thick as tree trunks, the knees bent at ninety degrees. Feet with splayed, hooked claws as long as sabres. Garrick stared, mouth slack, amazed at how quietly it walked. Something that big shouldn't be able to move that silently. It wasn't fair.

And the head . . .

A full half of its length was taken up by a long, tapering snout; the teeth reminded Garrick of the knives he'd made when he was still an apprentice smith. Jagged and uneven. Behind the teeth was a forked tongue the length of a man's arm, purple as mountain flowers. Two horns stuck up from the top of its head, little nubbins of grey bone.

The crowd froze, trying to understand what they were seeing. Because *araatan* – that was the name for them, wasn't it? – didn't come into the Tapestry. They didn't come anywhere *near* the Tapestry. They lived in the distant Baina Mountains: solitary, retiring animals that ate goats and wild horses, along with any tragically unlucky tigers who got a little too ambitious with their hunting grounds.

Garrick had certainly never seen one – and definitely not one casually marching into the village, a hundred miles from the nearest mountain. It didn't make sense.

For a strange moment, he wondered if the captive scout might have summoned it – that *this* was the Bone Raiders' real trick, that they could somehow command *araatan*. But no, the bound woman was staring at the animal too, eyes huge and horrified.

The lizard's eyes found Garrick, each as big as his head, yellow and feral. Before he could even suck in a breath, it started to move faster, feet pounding the earth. Coming right for him.

Move, Garrick thought. And he did.

Not even close to fast enough.

An enormous, clawed foot took him at the waist. His left leg bent the wrong way, snapped like a twig as he crashed to the ground. Axe gone. He couldn't cry out, couldn't even breathe.

Hot breath on his face, stinking of old meat. Jaws, teeth, tongue, open wide above him. If he could just find his axe . . .

The jaws didn't snap shut. A bright point glowed inside them, and a wave of hot air buffeted Garrick, thick and syrupy. The screams of the villagers rose around him.

No—!

And then there was nothing but fire.

Enter the monthly

Orbit sweepstakes at

www.orbitloot.com

With a different prize every month,
from advance copies of books by
your favourite authors to exclusive
merchandise packs,
**we think you'll find something
you love.**

facebook.com/OrbitBooksUK

@orbitbooks_uk

@OrbitBooks

orbit-books.co.uk